DEADLY DESIRES

RACHEL MCLEAN

READ ZOE'S PREQUEL STORY, DEADLY ORIGINS

It's 2003, and Zoe Finch is a new Detective Constable. When a body is found on her patch, she's grudgingly allowed to take a role on the case.

But when more bodies are found, and Zoe realises the case has links to her own family, the investigation becomes deeply personal.

Can Zoe find the killer before it's too late?

Find out by reading *Deadly Origins* for FREE at rachelmclean.com/origins.

Thanks,

Rachel McLean

CHAPTER ONE

THURSDAY

Amit Hussain stepped down from the bus and yawned. He had to be up early for work tomorrow and was looking forward to his bed.

He watched the bus pull away, lights receding into the December night, and brought his rucksack down from his shoulders. The three others who'd got off at his stop hurried away, no doubt eager to be out of the cold.

There was a thick hedge behind this stop, separating the road from a patch of scrubland the council never seemed to clean up. Amit knew where the thinnest part was, the least thorny. He pushed through, holding his rucksack to his chest for protection.

On the other side, he grabbed the plain white shirt he kept in his rucksack and flapped it out. Mum would be tired, but she had eyes like a hawk. This shirt had been ironed when he'd worn it to leave the house this morning. And his job processing insurance claims didn't justify creases.

He shrugged off his coat and tugged his t-shirt over his head. Yellow with black stripes, clinging. *Hot*, he'd been told.

He stuffed the t-shirt into his rucksack and pulled on the shirt.

"Alright?"

Amit looked round to see a figure pushing through the hedge he'd just come through. He froze, half expecting it to be his older brother.

He nodded in acknowledgement but said nothing.

"Good place to hide out, here."

"S'pose so." Maybe if he was polite, they'd go away.

The figure approached. It was a man, dark and slender. Amit couldn't make out his face in the darkness.

"I saw you on the bus. Liked your t-shirt."

Amit smoothed his shirt down. He'd been wearing his padded Superdry coat over the t-shirt. OK, so he hadn't zipped it up, but still. This guy would need to have been looking closely.

Amit straightened up and tried to make out the guy's face. Was he being picked up, here next to the bus stop?

It wouldn't have been the first time he'd met someone on the bus. But he didn't like doing this so close to home.

Get rid of him, he told himself. Mum would be watching the clock across from her chair. She knew which bus he was on, would have the window open so she could hear it making its way along the Alcester Road, even in December. It would have passed the house by now.

"Thanks, mate," he said, trying to sound confident. "I've got to get off."

A hand landed on his arm. "Stay a bit."

Amit wanted to shrug the hand off, but something told him not to.

"Sorry, mate. My mum's waiting. You know what it's like."

A laugh. "Women, eh?"

Amit didn't know much about women. He didn't hang out with girls much. Although he loved his sister, she lived in a different world, with her husband and her baby and the way she had of making him feel younger than he was. His dad didn't like him spending time with girls, and it suited him anyway. His mum was the only woman in his life and he wasn't naive enough to think she was a typical example of the species.

"She'll have my hide if I don't get back."

"Nah, she won't."

Amit tried to laugh. "You haven't met my mum."

"Five minutes. I like the look of you."

Amit felt his stomach clench. Fear battled arousal. He hadn't even seen the man's face. He could be his own age. He could be old enough to be his father.

He shivered. "Sorry, mate. Not worth it." He tried to sound confident, breezy, despite the goosebumps prickling the back of his neck.

"Bad move, pal." The hand tightened.

Amit pulled away, or tried to. But the man was stronger than him. He was held fast.

"Come on, mate," Amit said. "How about I give you my number, we can meet up?"

He wasn't about to give his mobile number to a stranger. For one thing, his dad checked his contacts every Friday night. For another...

But it might get rid of him. Stall him. He could use a fake number.

"Nah," the man said.

Amit pulled again. He eyed the hedge, wondering if he had the strength to drag the man through it and call for help.

But what would he say to anyone who came? *I just got home from the gay village and this guy's trying to hit on me.* People round here knew his parents.

"OK," he said. Maybe if he gave the guy a kiss that would get rid of him. Or at least, he might let go of Amit's arm while they were kissing.

He leaned towards the man, his eyes closed. The man smelled of dust and metal. Probably worked on a building site.

A hand landed on his cheek.

"Ouch." Amit brought his free hand up to his face, confused. His heart was racing. His mates had warned him about older men who liked it rough.

He couldn't do this. He couldn't even pretend.

"Just let me go, please?" He sounded like a kid now, not the twenty-year-old he was.

The man laughed then spat. Amit felt it pass his cheek. "No chance. You're coming with me."

Amit swallowed. "I need to get home. My dad's gonna kill me."

"Oh shut up about your fucking dad. Bloody poof."

Amit felt his knees weaken. This was no pick-up. He had to get away from this man, and fast.

He steeled himself, then pulled his arm down and sideways, managing to yank it out of the man's grasp. He turned back towards the hedge and threw himself through it, not caring what it would do to his face.

"Oi! Get back here."

There was movement behind him as the man crashed into the hedge. Amit could make out the lights of the houses opposite the bus stop. He was almost through. Almost safe.

He stumbled through thick brambles and out into the

evening, relief flooding through him. As he straightened up, he felt a hand on his ankle.

Amit yelled as the hand pulled. He fell forward, his forehead hitting the concrete. Pain surged through his face, making its way into his neck and down his body. Nausea and faintness followed. He blinked, dizzy.

"You're not going anywhere."

Amit felt something soft grasp his mouth. He grunted, shaking his head from side to side. The man was on top of him, his bulk pinning Amit to the ground.

Please, let a bus come along, he thought. *Let someone be out walking their dog*.

But there was no bus for another half hour. And it was dark here, quiet.

He yelled but all that came out was a muffled grunt.

"Shut up, fag." The man's breath was hot in his ear. He stuffed something into Amit's mouth. Amit felt the nausea turn to lightness and then heaviness. His head slumped forward, smacking into the pavement for a second time as he lost consciousness.

CHAPTER TWO

Zoe Finch forked a third helping of chicken chow mein into her bowl. This stuff was good. She'd never been to this restaurant before, had let Carl choose. He'd chosen well.

She topped it off with a helping of the crispy fried duck and lifted her bowl closer to her face, diving in with her chopsticks.

"You like your food, don't you?" Carl leaned back opposite her, smiling.

She chewed, shrugging. She waited a few moments to swallow, then wiped her mouth with a napkin – cloth, fancy – and nodded.

"There a problem with that?"

"God, no. It's refreshing to go out with a woman who doesn't eat like a sparrow."

Zoe raised an eyebrow. "You bring a lot of women here."

Carl rolled his eyes. "You know what I mean. And no, this is the first time I've been here. With anyone. It's good, isn't it?"

"Mmm." Zoe swallowed the noodles she'd shovelled into

her mouth while Carl was talking. Maybe she should try to be a bit more ladylike, a bit less herself. But she couldn't see the point of pretending to be someone she wasn't. If Carl was going to like her, it had to be the real Zoe Finch, not an avatar invented for the purposes of dating.

She wiped her mouth again. "How d'you find out about it?"

"Constable Good, at Kings Norton."

"You still working there?"

Carl's gaze shifted to his hands, resting in his lap. He'd long since finished eating and had been watching her for the last ten minutes. DI Carl Whaley was slender, but not skinny. Zoe guessed you couldn't stuff yourself full of Chinese food if you wanted to maintain a figure like that. She wondered if he worked out but hadn't found the right time to ask.

"What is it?" she said. She pushed her chair back and surveyed the food. It was tempting to finish it off – it really was good, even to someone who'd as happily eat a Big Mac as a Michelin starred meal – but she had to concede defeat. She'd ask if they did doggy bags.

"Nothing," Carl replied.

Zoe pushed her bowl to one side and leaned on the table, her hands pointing towards his. "I know when you're lying."

He met her gaze. "Alright."

"Good. So... what is it? I assume it's something to do with your anti-corruption investigation."

Carl's eyes darted from side to side. "Shush."

She smiled at him. "I don't think anyone's spying on us here."

His pupils were dilated, his breathing fast. He wasn't about to dump her, was he? This was only their third date, if she counted the clandestine meeting in a pub in Kingstanding a month ago, the one where she'd told him her suspicions about her old boss Detective Superintendent David Randle. Which, of course, she didn't.

No, she told herself. He wasn't about to dump her. His body language had been attentive all evening. He'd angled his legs towards hers in the cab, he'd walked close to her on the way to the restaurant, and he'd been relaxed with her as they'd eaten.

This had to be work.

"Spit it out," she said. "I'll find out through Lesley anyway. May as well hear it from you first."

"What makes you think Lesley knows?"

Zoe raised an eyebrow. Her boss, DCI Lesley Clarke, was one of those coppers who had an eye on everything, but didn't get too close unless she needed to. A source of support, but not of interference. Zoe liked working for her.

Carl sighed. "Alright."

"Thanks." Zoe took a sip of her Coke Zero.

"You've got a vacancy in your team," he said.

"Yes," she replied, hesitant. Her DS, Mo Uddin, had been moved across to another team. She missed him: the two of them had been friends for over eighteen years. "Lesley says she's been putting out feelers in local CID for someone who might be able to step in," she added.

"We've got someone for you."

"Professional Standards have picked out my new DS?"

"You know we like to place people where they can be of most use."

"Where they can spy on their fellow coppers, you mean."

Carl twisted his lips. "It's important work we do, Zo."

"Don't call me that. Only Mo gets to call me that."

"Sorry. Zoe. Look, Lesley's approved it. He's a good detective, experience in a variety of teams. And you've met him."

"I've worked with him?"

Carl's eyes left hers. "Not exactly."

Realisation stabbed her. "It's bloody Ian Osman, isn't it?"

"Zoe—"

"I wondered why you'd let him go back to his old nick without so much as a whimper. You're using him to spy on Randle, aren't you?"

DS Ian Osman had been the subject of her last case. His children had gone missing, and there had been suspicions that it was because he was bent. The link to the kidnapping had proven false, but he was still bent.

"You want me to babysit him? Keep an eye on what he's up to and pretend to have him working cases at the same time?"

"He's agreed to work with us," Carl said. "He'll carry on with his associations, report back to me. And he'll keep an eye on Randle for us."

"But Randle's not at Harborne any more. He's closer to your lot, in Lloyd House."

"Randle's too clever to do anything at Lloyd House. I believe he had contact with Ian, when you had him in custody."

Detective Superintendent David Randle had been Zoe's boss until a couple of months ago. Now he was Head of Force CID. She knew he was dodgy, but hadn't been able to prove it.

"Really?" she said. "If he's too smart to do anything at Lloyd House, he won't have been stupid enough to talk to Osman right under our noses."

Carl shrugged. "There's nothing concrete. But you know Randle. Both of them have been working for the same organised crime gang. But the difference is, Osman's turned. We can use him. And I trust you to keep an eye on him."

"Gee, thanks."

"Don't be like that. We were having a nice meal."

"You were buttering me up, more like."

Carl sighed. He dumped his napkin on the table. "Zoe. Please."

She shook her head. "I know you're doing your job, Carl. But this..." She waved her hand across the table. "You've spoiled it."

"I'm sorry. I didn't mean to. If you hadn't asked..."

She felt fire lick at her insides. "Don't blame me."

He raised his hands in surrender. "Sorry. Let's order some dessert. Maybe a coffee."

"No."

"Oh, come on." His eyes were sharp.

"I've lost my appetite," she said. "Let's just call a cab."

"One, or two?"

She eyed him. Insisting on going home alone would be petty, when he'd taken the trouble to pick her up. And he only lived a couple of miles from her.

"One," she said. "But just drop me off. I need an early night."

CHAPTER THREE

FRIDAY

AMIT WRAPPED his arms around his bunched-up knees, shivering.

He wore the yellow and black t-shirt and his jeans. His shirt had gone, along with his coat and rucksack. When he'd woken up he'd been bare-chested, the t-shirt on the dusty floor beside him. He'd grabbed it and put it on, his fingers trembling. He didn't like to think of the man removing his t-shirt. Of what else he might have done. But there was no sign of his jeans having been undone.

It was getting light. There was a high window in the wall opposite, dirty and crusted with cobwebs and moss. It was tiny, no more than a peephole. Amit had tried to open it but it was fixed glass, there for a scrap of light and nothing else.

The room was stuffy and dank at the same time. There was a smell of dust and metal that reminded him of the man looming in on him by the bus stop.

How far from home was he? Had the man dragged him all the way here, or carried him? He hadn't seen a car, and the man had said he'd seen him on the bus.

Amit tried to remember getting off the bus. There'd been three other people, all hurrying off into the night. No one had stopped to look at him. If the man had been on the bus, he must have walked away and come back again.

Either that, or he hadn't been on the bus at all. Maybe he'd been in a car, watching. Waiting for Amit to disappear behind the hedge.

He shuddered. Had the man been stalking him? Did he know his habits?

Stop it, he told himself. No point in getting himself worked up. He had to focus on getting out of here.

His hands were tied with blue garden twine. He tugged at it every few minutes but that only made the knots tighter. There was a door in the wall next to him. It was wooden, with peeling brown paint and rusting metal hinges. If Amit had been bigger, he might have been able to bust it open.

But Amit was skinny. A slip of a boy, his granny called him. Every time he went round she would put out bowls of daal and insist he ate. *Got to get your strength up*, she told him. *Build some muscle*. If the girls were going to notice him.

He knew his mum and granny were trying to fix him up with a girl from Manchester. A relative of his granny's friend Mrs Bangura. Amit had never met the girl, but he knew there were photos. He hadn't been given the opportunity to look at them, and he hadn't asked.

He heaved himself up, a struggle with his hands tied and his legs protesting, and hobbled to the door. He leaned against it, his ear to the wood. Motionless, alert.

Silence. No one outside. He wondered if he was in a building, or if this was some sort of shed or outhouse. Maybe he should call out. In this part of Kings Heath, the houses were close together, almost all terraced. If he was in an outhouse, someone would hear him.

But then, what if he wasn't in Kings Heath at all? And worse, what if the man heard him? What if he decided to shut him up?

Amit wished he could be more decisive. In the Manga comics he read, the heroes wouldn't be cowering behind a door, listening for their attacker. They would be kicking the door down. Overpowering the man and getting away. They would be yelling their noisy heads off till someone heard and let them out.

But this wasn't a comic. This was real life. His mum would have missed him. She'd know the bus had been and gone. Maybe she would have waited for the next one. But when that one passed her window with no sign of him, she'd have raised the alarm. She'd have woken his dad, roused the community. There would be men out looking for him.

He should shout. If they were looking for him, he needed to let them know where he was.

"Help!" he cried. His voice was thinner than he'd expected and he had to swallow a few times before calling out again. "Help! It's me, Amit! I'm here!"

He heard crashing beyond the door. *Shit.* He stumbled backwards, crashing into a wall.

The door flew open. A man stared at him. He was the same height as Amit but broader, with muscles taut under a tight blue shirt. He looked at Amit like he was a dog fit only to be put down.

"Shut the fuck up!" he hissed through gritted teeth. "Be quiet."

The man was tense. He exhaled slowly and deliberately

through his teeth, like he was calming himself down. He unclenched his fists and smoothed them on his dirty jeans.

"Be quiet." The man's voice was low. "Do as you're told, and you won't get hurt."

Amit nodded. He wondered if anyone had heard him. If people were banging on this man's door right now. If they'd been able to work out where he was calling from.

The man took a step towards Amit. He had a wary look in his eye, almost like he was scared of Amit. "I don't want to hurt you," he said. "But you have to shut up."

Amit nodded. He needed to pee. *Not here,* he told himself. *Hold on.*

"Good." The man turned and yanked the door open. Amit got a glimpse of a room beyond. It was grey and dusty too, even darker than this one. A chest of drawers sat in a corner.

So he wasn't in an outhouse. He was in a house somewhere. Maybe an abandoned one.

The door clattered shut and a key turned. Amit tried to remember any empty houses nearby. Were there any that were derelict?

He had no idea. He was a twenty-year-old man with a life to lead. He didn't watch what was going on in his neighbourhood.

He slumped to the floor, his limbs trembling.

CHAPTER FOUR

"Morning, DI Finch."

Zoe gave DCI Lesley Clarke a nod. "Morning, ma'am."

"We need to have a chat."

Zoe poured water from the kettle in the station kitchen into a mug. Coffee, instant but strong. It would have to do. Lesley was rummaging in the fridge.

"I think I might know what it's about, ma'am." Zoe leaned against the counter and sipped her coffee. She grimaced.

Lesley stood up, a limp-looking sandwich in her hand. "Oh yes?"

"You're allocating me a new DS."

"Word does indeed travel fast. Carl Whaley told you?"

"Yes, ma'am." Zoe felt heat rise up her neck.

Lesley tipped a finger to her nose. "Don't worry, Zoe. I've seen how the two of you are together, but I don't plan on blabbing it to the rest of the station." She peeled open the sandwich wrapper and curled her lip. "As long as it doesn't affect your ability to do your job."

"Not at all, ma'am." Zoe knew plenty of coppers who dated or were married to colleagues. She'd dated Inspector Jim McManus, many years ago. She'd steered away from men on the force since then, but could see the sense in it. Civilians didn't understand when you were dragged out of bed to answer a call at 3am. They didn't understand when your eyes glazed over because they'd said something at dinner that gave you a breakthrough on a case.

"Good," said Lesley. "Then I expect you'll give DS Osman a warm welcome."

Zoe cleared her throat. "We'll do our best, ma'am."

"Wouldn't expect any less of you."

Lesley left the kitchen, still sneering at her sandwich. Zoe poured two more drinks: white coffee with three sugars for DC Rhodri Hughes and chamomile tea for DC Connie Williams. Connie was on a health kick. It'd be over before the week was out, and she'd be back on her builder's tea.

Zoe almost poured a third drink for Mo, but then caught herself. She missed him. She knew he wasn't enjoying working for DI Frank Dawson. But Mo was professional. He wouldn't let that get in the way of his job.

In the team room, she placed a mug on each of the constables' desks. "Morning, both."

"Morning, boss," replied Connie. "Thanks." She sipped her tea, hesitant, as if it might bite her. Rhodri slurped his coffee and grunted. Zoe considered reminding him to thank her, but then remembered she wasn't his mum.

Zoe perched on the edge of her desk. "So, what we got?" She still hadn't moved into the inner office, the one reserved for the DI, but probably would when Ian joined them. She had a feeling she'd need to assert her authority over him.

Although staying out here to keep an eye on him and the rest of the team might be a better idea.

"I'm just finishing up the paperwork on the Corkhill case," said Connie. "CPS has asked for a summary of the documentary evidence."

"Good. You'll be finished today?" asked Zoe.

"This morning."

"Thanks. What about you, Rhod?"

"I've had a breakthrough with Trevor Hamm, boss."

Zoe perked up. Trevor Hamm was an organised crime boss. A man who'd crossed their radar many times, but to whom they'd never managed to make anything stick. "Go on."

Rhodri looked over his monitor. "I went for a pint with Cal last night, from Handsworth nick."

Zoe laughed. "Don't tell me. Four pints of Fosters and a pizza on the way home to soak it up."

Rhodri leaned back in his chair. "Five actually, boss. And a kebab."

"Close. So what's your social life got to do with Hamm?"

"Well, you know Stick Adams is in Winson Green Prison, boss?"

"I do."

Simon 'Stick' Adams was one of Hamm's thugs. He'd attacked two of Zoe's team and broken bail. They'd found him when searching for Ian Osman's kids.

"Hamm visited him," said Rhodri.

"Nothing illegal about that."

"No, boss. Not if you don't smuggle contraband in while you're at it."

"Hamm took something in for Adams?"

"Not himself, no. He took his new girlfriend with him. The drugs were in her bra."

"Not very original."

"No, boss. But Adams has had visitor privileges revoked and the girlfriend—"

"Who has a name, I imagine."

"Yes, boss. Sorry, I didn't get it."

"Right." They'd be able to track her down easy enough. "So what about Hamm? He walked away, I bet."

"What do you think?"

"Of course he did." Walking away while his associates took the fall was what Trevor Hamm did. His young Lithuanian wife had suffered a worse fate, drowned in the canal. Accidental death, the coroner had said.

"What's all this about Hamm?"

Zoe turned to see DI Frank Dawson standing in the open doorway. She tensed, feeling the hairs on the back of her neck stand up.

"DC Hughes is just telling me, Frank." Zoe made a point of using Frank's first name at every opportunity, to remind him he wasn't her boss any more. She knew he didn't like it.

"So you've got some rumours and tittle-tattle from your mate at another nick, DC Hughes, and you think that's worth bothering your DI with," said Frank.

"I think everything's worth bothering his DI with," replied Zoe.

Dawson laughed. "You would." He turned to her. "One of the things you're going to have to learn fast at this level, DI Finch, is to prioritise. You can't just listen to any old bullshit your team tell you. You have to filter. Learn to spot the juice."

He gave her a patronising smile and turned on his heel, letting the door slam behind him.

Zoe turned to Rhodri, determined not to let him and Connie see that Dawson had rattled her. "Carry on, Rhod."

"Yeah, so anyway, the girlfriend's been taken to Handsworth nick, right? Possession with intent."

"Of course."

"Yeah. And Hamm's insisting he's never met her before. That she was on Adams's visitor docket separately and she was Adams's girlfriend, not his."

"That's bullshit," said Zoe. "Have you *looked* at Simon Adams lately?"

Connie looked up from her screen. "Yeah, doesn't sound likely."

Rhodri looked at her. "Too right, Con." He turned to Zoe. "Hamm's lying. Can't we do him for it? Perverting the course of justice, or something?"

Zoe put a hand on the back of his chair. "I appreciate your enthusiasm, Rhodri. You want to be like the Untouchables."

"The who?"

"The Untouchables? American cops, prohibition. They took Al Capone down for tax evasion, not illegal supply of alcohol, money laundering, violent crime, all the rest of it. Got him sent down."

Rhodri's eyes were alight. "We can do the same, boss."

"No, Rhod. I'm sorry, but we can't." She raised a hand and started counting on her fingers. "First, we've got no evidence. Second, Adams will go along with it. He knows which side his bread's buttered." She pushed down the third finger, her eyes on Rhodri. "And third, I want to get him properly. I don't want to hide behind some perverting the course of justice bullshit."

Connie nodded, her eyes shining. Zoe gave her a smile.

Simon Adams had hit Connie over the head and locked her up on a building site. All on Hamm's orders. Zoe wanted him to pay.

"We'll get him, you two. Eventually, he'll slip up."

CHAPTER FIVE

Adam glanced sideways at Mitch, hardly believing his luck. This guy was seriously hot. A few years younger than he was, and ripped. The sort of guy you saw dancing at the Jackal but never got the nerve to approach.

Instead, Mitch had approached him. And they hadn't even been in a club. He'd just come up to him in Selfridges, while Adam was shopping for jeans.

"Hey."

Adam had turned to look at the cute young man talking to him, then looked around to see who he was really addressing.

"I've seen you, in the Jackal," Mitch had said.

The Jackal was a gay bar. By day it was a spot to drink coffee and people-watch. And by night it boasted drag acts and the best parties in Digbeth. It was where Adam went on Friday and Saturday nights. To drink, to dance, and sometimes to meet men.

"I go there," Adam had said, feeling his pulse pick up.

He'd slipped a finger into the cuff of his shirt surreptitiously. His heart rate was elevated.

"Saw you there last Saturday," Mitch said. "I meant to come over. Say hi."

"Ah. Well, hi."

Adam had never been chatted up in broad daylight before. Mitch, by contrast, had been at ease, comfortable making conversation with this stranger. Then he'd invited Adam for coffee. They'd gone to the Loft Lounge. A couple of lattes had turned into cocktails and before long they were kissing.

And now they were in a cab, heading back to Adam's house.

He always insisted on coming here when he met a guy. He felt safer that way, and it gave him control.

They rounded the corner to his street in Moseley and he leaned forward, telling the taxi driver to pull up. Mitch grabbed his hand and kissed it. Adam looked back at him, aware that his eyes were reflecting the same expectant sparkle that he could see in the other man's eyes.

He paid the fare and they climbed out of the cab. Mitch grabbed his hand as they walked and swung it playfully.

"Nice street," he said.

"Thanks. Mine's the second one on the right."

Mitch whistled. "Fancy."

"I didn't ask you where you live."

Mitch shrugged. "Nowhere like this."

"I'm sure it's not all that bad."

Another shrug. "A flat in Digbeth. Near to the scene. A bit grimy, next door neighbour's a drug dealer. But that can be handy, sometimes." He winked. Adam wondered why he hadn't told him he lived around the corner from where they'd been sitting when they'd decided to come back here.

Adam looked up at his semi-detached house as Mitch opened the gate. It seemed so dull compared to a flat in Digbeth. So vanilla. Adam the doctor, not Adam the man.

"Come on," he said. He shook off his irritation with himself and opened the front door. Next door, Amelia was arranging fairy lights around her porch. She turned to him, dropping the lights.

"Evening, Doctor Hart," she said.

"Adam," he told her. "I keep telling you..."

She chuckled. "I like having a doctor next door. Makes me feel safe. Anyway, you have a nice evening." She turned her gaze on Mitch. "Nice to meet you."

"You too," Mitch replied. So he was hot *and* polite. Adam couldn't believe his luck. Maybe he should slow things down. This one could be a keeper.

Mitch ran a finger up Adam's inner arm, making him wilt. *Maybe not.*

"Oh and there was another gentleman asking for you," Amelia said, "about an hour ago. I told him you were out, to come back later."

Mitch squeezed Adam's hand. "Boyfriend?"

"No," Adam muttered. He called over to Amelia. "What did he look like?"

"Tall, thin." She patted her shoulder. "Muscly."

"Sounds cute," muttered Mitch.

"Shush," said Adam. "Did he say what it was about?" he asked Amelia.

"Sorry, no. Should I have asked?"

Adam waved in dismissal. "No. It's fine. If it's important, he'll come back."

He opened the front door and dropped his keys on the hall table. He stood back to let Mitch go ahead, trying to remember what state the house was in. He'd been going out shopping, not clubbing. He'd never expected to bring anyone home.

Mitch went on ahead, peering through doorways. "Nice place. What d'you do?"

Adam let the front door slam. "I work in A&E, at the QE." The Queen Elizabeth Hospital was a couple of miles away, in Edgbaston. Adam didn't say that he was a senior consultant.

"Cool." Mitch nodded and turned back to Adam. He reached up to the back of his neck and wrapped his fingers round, pulling Adam in for a kiss. Adam felt his insides liquefy as their tongues wrapped around each other.

Finally, Mitch pulled away. "Can I have a glass of water?" he asked.

Adam smiled. Mitch was full of surprises. "Sure you don't want a beer?"

"Whatever you've got. Kitchen through here?"

Mitch had been standing with his back to the kitchen door while they'd been kissing. He pushed it open and stepped inside.

"Oh, hello," he said, sounding surprised but amused.

"What's up?" Adam asked.

Mitch turned back to him. "Your visitor. Your ex."

"It wasn't an ex."

"Whoever he was, he's back."

Adam pushed Mitch out of the way. A dark-haired man sat at his kitchen table. He placed his hands behind his neck, looking to all intents and purposes as if he owned the place.

Adam's breath caught in his throat. "Who are you? How did you get in?"

The man reached for an object on the kitchen table. A knife. Not one from Adam's kitchen, but a curved one. It looked sharp. The man jabbed it into the table. Adam gasped. Mitch's hand tightened on his arm.

"Were you snogging out there?" the stranger said.

Adam blanched. "What?"

Mitch took a step forward. "Look, mate. I don't know who you are or why you're here, but I think you should—"

The man stood up, his eyes on Adam. "Your kitchen window, it's almost all glass. Thought you'd never bloody stop."

He spat, leaving a blob of phlegm on the kitchen floor. It reflected the low sunlight from the window.

Adam's gaze flicked to the back door. Had he left it open when he'd taken the rubbish out earlier?

He clenched his fists at his sides. "Please, leave my house."

The man barked out a laugh. "No chance, not after how long I've been waiting."

He lifted the knife and ran his thumb across the blade. "Now do as I say, and you won't get hurt."

CHAPTER SIX

DS Mo Uddin sat across from Mr and Mrs Hussain in their dining room. The room was decorated with photos of the couple's children, framed photos from school days, one graduation and one wedding. The polished table held nothing but a vase of deep red flowers and smelled of Pledge.

"Tell me when you last saw your son."

Mrs Hussain dabbed her eyes. Her husband put a hand over hers on the table. He blinked back at Mo.

"Yesterday morning, Thursday. He left for work, got the number 50 bus like he always does. He was going to the cinema with a friend afterwards, told us he'd be on the bus at ten past eleven."

"I sat over there," Mrs Hussain whispered. She pointed to a chair in the living room, which had been knocked through into this room. The chair sat by the front window, angled for a view of the TV and the footpath leading up from the street. The window was covered by a net curtain with scalloped edges, but Mo could still see the traffic on the Alcester Road rumbling past.

"You often wait up for him?" Mo asked.

"Always. I like to be sure they're safe. Even Safiya." Her eyes went to the wedding photo. A handsome young couple, the man mid-height with cropped hair, the woman young and pretty with dark eyes that made Mo think of his own little sister.

"When did you start to think he might not have caught the bus?" Mo asked.

Mrs Hussain shrugged. Mr Hussain leaned across her.

"She woke me at twenty to twelve. When the next bus had gone, and he still wasn't home."

"It's not like Amit to miss a bus," his wife said. "But I didn't want to panic."

She looked at Mo, her eyes full of the very panic she was trying to avoid. Her husband's face darkened. He blamed her, Mo realised. It was tempting to throw blame at the nearest person in situations like this, even if there was nothing they could have done.

"But you didn't call the police until this evening."

"He's twenty years old," said Mr Hussain. "I knew you wouldn't take it seriously. We had a search party of our own, though. Men from the community. In the early hours of this morning."

"I assume that was fruitless."

"It was." Mr Hussain rubbed the dark circles under his eyes. "Nothing. And then he didn't turn up to work this morning."

"Did he say he might be staying at a friend's, anything like that?"

Mrs Hussain shuddered. "No. Of course not."

"We wouldn't have called you if we thought he was with a friend," her husband said. His wife leaned into him.

He sat motionless, supporting her weight like a pillar of stone.

Mo knew what his own dad would have been like if he'd disappeared at that age. Angry, more than anything. But times had changed. If one of his own daughters went missing, he would stop at nothing to get her back.

But Amit Hussain was an adult. At the age when young men made rash decisions.

"OK," he sighed. "I'm going to ask you for a list of his friends. Phone numbers and addresses, if you have them. And his employer."

"It's all here." Mr Hussain reached into the inside pocket of his jacket and brought out a neatly folded piece of paper. Mo surveyed it, the couple's eyes on him. It held over a dozen names, all with phone numbers and addresses. Plus the name of Amit's employer: Southfields Insurance. Their phone number and address.

"We've spoken to all the families on the list."

Mo looked up at the man. "The young men, or their parents?"

A shrug. "Parents, mainly. We know them all."

Mo eyed the list again. He had no doubt that Amit had friends who weren't on this list. They would probably be the best source of information. But the young men on this list – no women, he noted – were a starting point.

"Thank you, Mr Hussain. Mrs Hussain. Like I say, Amit is an adult. He's probably just decided to go away for a bit. There haven't been any arguments, in the family? He hasn't said anything about wanting to leave home?"

Mrs Hussain shook her head. She wiped her cheek.

"No," said her husband. "Amit's a good boy. He goes to work, he sees his friends, he always tells us where he is." He glanced at his wife. "His mother waits up for him, she's a light sleeper. He's on the bus he says he'll be on. Every time."

How many young men are that reliable? Mo thought. He wondered what the consequences might be for Amit, if he let his parents down.

"Thank you." he repeated, wondering if he was wasting his time. Amit would no doubt turn up in a few days, in trouble with his parents but unharmed. "I'll let you know if we get any useful information."

CHAPTER SEVEN

SATURDAY

"He's an adult, Zo. I'm not sure there's much we can do."

Zoe and Mo walked into Harborne police station. They'd met for breakfast at Café Face on the way in, their regular haunt, and compared notes on their current caseload, Mo's missing person and Rhodri's daft ideas about Trevor Hamm. They were still talking about Amit Hussain as they crossed the station car park.

"But his mum told you he's reliable," Zoe replied. "Always gets the bus he said he will, never comes home late."

"He's twenty. What were you doing when you were twenty?"

Trying to steer clear of my alcoholic mum, Zoe thought. "He's two years older than Nicholas," she said. "*He's* an adult too. D'you think I wouldn't move heaven and earth to track him down, if he went missing?"

"That's different."

Zoe stopped walking and raised an eyebrow. "Because his mum's in CID?"

"No." Mo ran a hand through his hair. "I don't know. I've

got Dawson breathing down my neck, telling me to drop it. He wants me working on some community outreach work he's got going on, partnership with local CID."

"Doesn't sound like Dawson's style."

"That's what I thought. But he's got a bee in his bonnet about crime prevention since he got back from London. He has a point."

"Yeah. Not very sexy, though."

Mo held the door to the station open for her. "Since when was working in Force CID sexy?"

"Since I started here." She winked.

"Get you." Mo laughed as they headed deeper into the building. "How's things with Carl?"

"What's that got to do with me being sexy?"

They passed a couple of uniformed constables who averted their eyes as if they'd been listening in. Zoe frowned and lowered her voice. "He told me he's sending Ian Osman to work in my team."

Mo stopped walking. "Blimey."

"Yeah."

"You told Connie and Rhodri? Does Lesley know?"

"Of course Lesley knows."

"But Connie and Rhodri..."

"That's my first job. Before he gets here later today."

"Good luck with that."

Zoe knew that her DCs would find it awkward working with a man they'd suspected of kidnapping his own children. They both knew he'd been under suspicion of connections to Trevor Hamm, the man responsible for Connie breaking a leg on a previous case. But Zoe knew she could count on Connie to be circumspect.

Rhodri, she wasn't so sure.

"Anyway, you get back to your misper. I think you should follow it up."

Mo sighed. "I will. It's better than community outreach."

"Indeed."

She gave Mo a light touch on the shoulder as he left and then turned towards her own office. First job, tell the team about Ian. Second job, move her stuff into the inner office.

She opened the door to find three officers inside. Connie sat at her desk, her eyes fixed on her screen. Rhodri was at his, eyes down on his phone.

Ian Osman sat at the third desk, the one that Mo had been using until two weeks earlier. He was unpacking the contents of a cardboard box, making himself at home.

Shit.

"Morning," said Zoe.

Connie turned, her face thunderous. Rhodri angled his head to look up at his boss, but didn't sit up straight. Ian continued unpacking.

"Right," Zoe muttered. She put on her best teacher voice. "Connie, Rhodri. In my office. We need to chat."

She left Ian watching in silence as Connie stood up and brushed her trousers down and Rhodri dropped his phone onto his desk. He cast a contemptuous look in Ian's direction as he made for the inner office. Ian gave Zoe a look of disdain. She returned it with a breezy smile.

"Close the door." Zoe sat behind her desk and gestured for the two DCs to take the seats opposite.

An object in the corner caught her eye. "Who put that there?"

Rhodri scratched his neck. "Er, it was me, boss. Thought it'd make the place festive, like."

The Christmas tree had seen better days and half the fairy lights didn't work. But it was the thought that counted.

"Thanks, Rhod," Zoe said. The constables exchanged a smile.

"Anyway," she said. "I owe you both an apology. I should have told you about this yesterday."

"What's going on, boss?" asked Rhodri. Connie clasped her hands in her lap, pinching her fingernails in a way that made Zoe wince.

"DS Osman has been assigned to our team. He'll be working with us now that Mo's with DI Dawson."

"But he's at Kings Norton," said Connie.

"And besides," said Rhodri, glancing round at Ian through the glass partition and lowering his voice, "you told us he was under investigation."

"He was," said Zoe. She wasn't about to tell her team what she knew, not if she wanted the three of them to work together. "He isn't anymore."

"How so?" said Rhodri. "You don't just bounce back from having Professional Standards investigating you."

Zoe flashed a look at Rhodri. "Constable, I suggest you rethink your tone. Sergeant Osman has been assigned to us. He was sent home after the investigation into his kids' disappearance and he's back at work." She licked her lips. "I think given everything he and his wife have been through, he deserves our sympathy. Not our vitriol." She sharpened her gaze on Rhodri. To his credit, he flushed.

"Yes, boss."

"Good." Zoe turned to Connie. "I know this isn't easy. I know it's a shock. And I know I should have given you more notice. But it's what we're stuck with. Can you work with Sergeant Osman?"

"Yes, boss." Connie would have spontaneously combusted if she'd looked any more uneasy.

"Good. So who's going to call him in?"

"I will." Rhodri lifted himself from his chair and opened the door. "Ian?"

"He's your senior officer, Rhodri."

"Sorry, ma'am. Sarge?"

Zoe rolled her eyes but let it drop. She didn't like being ma'amed by her team at the best of times.

Ian came in, looking between the three of them, smiling nervously. "Ma'am."

"Call me boss, not ma'am. And grab yourself a chair."

Ian retreated into the outer office and dragged in the chair from his own desk. Rhodri and Connie waited in silence, neither of them meeting Zoe's eye.

"Thanks, Ian. Now, I'm not sure you've been introduced to the team. DS Osman, this is DC Connie Williams and DC Rhodri Hughes. I'm sure they'll make you very welcome."

CHAPTER EIGHT

Amit was hungry. The man had thrown in a bag of crisps and a bottle of water on the first day. Amit had checked the crisp packet and left it at first, aware it wasn't Halal. But when his hunger had grown too great on the first night, he'd devoured its contents greedily, throwing up in the corner afterwards in disgust.

The smell had diminished a little now. It was dull and sweet instead of sickly and cloying.

This house, wherever it was, must be the man's home. Amit remembered the room he'd seen beyond the door: grey and dusty. Like this one, but darker. Where were they?

He sipped the dregs of the water. He'd managed to make it last. He'd been here two full days now, judging by the light coming and going in the window. He'd been taken on Thursday night and now it was Sunday morning. Assuming he hadn't been unconscious for longer than he thought.

He tipped his head back, holding the water bottle over his mouth. His throat felt dry and his stomach ached.

If the man didn't bring more water soon, he'd die of

thirst. He knew it took a few days to die of thirst, but much longer to starve. He had no idea which was worse.

The door creaked and rattled. Amit screwed the lid back onto the bottle and shoved it behind him, against the wall. It felt like something of his own, to be hidden. He tried to stand but his legs were numb.

He watched as the door opened and the man came through. He gazed at Amit, his eyes flat. Amit stared back, his heart pounding.

"Stay right there." The man pointed at him. Amit nodded. The door was still open. Could he make a run for it?

No. He was down on the floor, and his legs weren't obeying his instructions anyway. By the time he'd pushed himself up and made it to the door, the man would be on him.

Amit hated himself for rationalising everything like this, for inventing reasons not to be brave. His father had told him he was spineless, dropping out of his degree course after he'd been bullied. Maybe he was right.

The man left the room, not closing the door. Amit stared after him, trying to see into the darkness of the next room. His eyes had grown accustomed to the dimness in here, but it was like solid black through there.

The man returned with a trestle table. He pulled it open and set it up in front of Amit.

'Stand up," he barked.

Amit pushed his shoulders into the wall and heaved himself up. His ankles hurt. He should be walking around, keeping himself supple. But he'd been trying to conserve energy.

The man left again. Amit stood by the wall, staring at the table. What was happening?

The man returned with two folding chairs. He opened one and placed it at the table. He thrust the other one at Amit's hand.

"Go on then."

Amit stared back at him. He lifted his hands: *I'm tied up*. The man snorted and grabbed a knife from his pocket. Brusquely, he reached out and cut the twine, not once making contact with Amit's skin. There was a heavy smell on him: blood?

"Go on then."

His mind racing, Amit opened the chair and placed it at the table, facing its partner. The twine slid to the floor.

The man gestured for Amit to sit. His eyes not leaving the man's face, Amit did so.

The chair was hard and unstable, but it felt good to sit on something that wasn't the floor. He let himself relax into it, realising how tired he was.

The man sat in the other chair. He didn't look at Amit but instead fished in his pocket. He brought out a mobile phone and placed it on the table, sideways. The back of it faced Amit.

The man bent to the phone and fiddled with it. Amit watched.

"What are you doing?" he asked.

The man's head lifted. "I told you to shut up."

Amit swallowed. The man went back to the phone, muttering under his breath. He had a bald patch on the top of his head, just a small one. There was a mole in the centre of it.

At last the man seemed happy with whatever he was doing. A red light appeared on the back of the phone: he was filming. Amit stared at the red light.

He felt panic rise up. The man was going to kill him, and post it on YouTube.

"Please don't hurt me," he whispered.

The man leaned back, crossing his arms over his chest. "That's up to you."

Amit touched his chest. His t-shirt was grubby now, heavy with sweat. "I don't understand."

"You're an idiot as well as a pervert."

"Sorry. Please, explain." Amit stared at the man. Was it a mistake, engaging with him?

The man leaned across the table. "You're sick, pal. I'm the cure."

CHAPTER NINE

ZOE GOT out of her car and walked towards the crime scene. A uniformed constable stood to one side of the pub, in front of the tape. Zoe showed him her ID then made her way along the alleyway behind him. At the rear, a tent had been erected. White-suited forensic scene investigators moved around, and she could hear the low hum of people working. The courtyard was surrounded by industrial buildings on two sides, the pub on the other two.

One of the white suits turned to her. Adi Hanson, forensic scene manager. "Zoe, my favourite detective."

She shook her head, smiling. Adi flirted with her every time they met. He had done since before Nicholas was born. It meant nothing, or at least that was what she hoped.

"What have we got?" she asked.

"Two men, both white, twenties or thirties, difficult to tell. One taken away in an ambulance, the other still here I'm afraid."

Zoe rounded Adi to see the body. The pathologist crouched over it, making notes on an iPad. The victim was medium height and well-built, with broad shoulders and a face that would have been attractive. From the waist down he was drenched in blood.

Adi's techs were working methodically around the courtyard at the back of the pub, scanning the ground for anything the killer might have left behind.

"Any chance it was just the two of them?" Zoe asked. "A fight gone wrong?"

The pathologist stood up, her hands in the small of her back. "That's extremely unlikely. Unless they were involved in some kind of sick sex game."

Zoe raised an eyebrow.

"Both of them were castrated, Zoe. One of your PCs gave me a report on the man taken to hospital. And the other one, well..." The pathologist removed her face mask. Dr Adana Adebayo, the fiercest but most effective pathologist Zoe had worked with, shook her head. "Never seen anything like it."

Zoe knew Dr Adebayo had seen worse scenes than this. "How so?"

Adana grimaced. "It's not the crimes, Inspector. Don't get me wrong about that. It's the workmanship."

Zoe took a step closer to the body. "Workmanship?"

A sombre nod. "Neat incisions. Sharp instrument. The only thing missing was anaesthetic."

Zoe grimaced. "How can you tell?"

Adana pointed at the man's face. "If he'd been put under, he wouldn't have bled so much. Anaesthetics cause hypotension. Lowered blood pressure. And of course, you have other measures during surgery, such as transfusion. But if it hadn't been for the blood loss, this man would have lived. Castration should be a relatively straightforward procedure."

"Do you think the killer knew that?"

Adana shrugged. "Not for me to say. All I can tell you is that the killer had some knowledge of surgical procedure. He either didn't understand correct administration of anaesthetic, or he did, but decided to ignore it."

"He wanted his victims to bleed out."

Adana sighed. "Again, detective. You're encouraging me to put myself in the mind of this man. I can't do that. All I can do is tell you what I see from the corpse he created."

"Of course. I'm assuming the attack didn't happen here."

"Definitely not," said Adi. "There's a faint blood trail along the alleyway, but not anything like you'd expect if it happened here."

"And you couldn't perform surgery in a courtyard at the back of a pub," added Adana.

Zoe turned to Adi. "Did the killer leave any traces?"

"Nothing yet. Uniform are combing the area. We've closed off the inside of the pub and that'll be next."

"An ID on the victim?"

"His pockets were empty. Not even a few pennies in change. Someone emptied his pockets, and they wore gloves to do it."

Zoe nodded. Even the dumbest of criminals knew to wear gloves. She had a feeling they weren't dealing with the dumbest of criminals here.

"What about the knife? Surgical?"

"Not quite," said the pathologist. "It was thin and sharp, but there are nicks where it caught on sinew. Different from what you'd get with a scalpel. If I had to hazard a guess, I'd say a craft knife."

"Like a Stanley knife?"

"No. Stanley knives are shorter, broader. Craft knives,

when properly maintained, are as sharp as you can get outside an operating theatre."

"Right. Thanks, both of you."

Zoe walked back towards the cordon. She could hear raised voices.

At the front of the pub, a crowd was gathering. She turned to a uniformed sergeant.

"Get this cordon widened. We want access to this full stretch of pavement, and the roadway for the time being."

"How many bodies have you got back there, detective?"

Zoe looked round to see a middle-aged man advancing on her, pushing against the cordon. Erwin Norris, Birmingham Post.

"We have one body, Norris. There'll be a full statement when we're ready to release one. Now we need to widen this cordon, so I need you to move away."

"Is someone targeting gay men?"

Zoe dug her fingernail into her palm. "We have no reason to assume the killer's motive right now. Like I say, I'll let you know when we have more."

"Should Birmingham's gay community be scared?"

It was all Zoe could do to hold herself back. One man killed. No ID, let alone information on his sexuality, and suddenly the press had it as a hate crime.

She needed to nip this in the bud. She smiled at Norris.

"OK, Erwin. Tell you what, we can have a chat later. After I've done what I need to do, you can buy me a coffee. I'll give you what I can. But on one condition."

"Which is?"

"No speculation till you've spoken to me. Print the facts if you want, but stick to them."

"Print? You just get off the ark, Detective?"

"You know what I mean. Do we have a deal?"

"Alright then."

"Good. Now bugger off and let me do my job."

Norris slunk away, glancing back at her as he retreated to his car, his phone at his ear.

Zoe returned to the tent. Adana was packing up her kit, making notes. Zoe looked down at the body. The man wore a denim jacket over faded jeans and a tight white t-shirt. His jeans were turning brown, stiffening with the blood.

"What about the other victim?" Zoe asked. "The one that went off in the ambulance. Did you see him?"

The pathologist snapped off her gloves. "Left before Adi or I got here. You'll have to ask Uniform."

"I will. When's the postmortem?"

"Give me a minute to catch my breath, huh?"

"The sooner we know what happened to this man, the sooner..."

Adana waved a hand. "I know, I know. But it's Sunday. And I've got a backlog, two old ladies who died suddenly. Yes, I know that doesn't sound like a priority. But since Shipman we're more vigilant."

Zoe sighed. "Just tell me when."

"Tomorrow morning. That's the best I can do."

"This is a murder enquiry, Doctor. You know as well as I do that the first twenty-four hours—"

"Look. This is a sexually motivated crime. The only injury is to his genitals. It's normally women you see mutilated like this, but..." she gestured around the area. "Given where we are."

Zoe gritted her teeth. She didn't like people jumping to conclusions. "Send me your report as soon as you have it," she said, and turned away.

She found the PC who'd been first on the scene sitting on a bollard at the front of the pub, drinking tea from a polystyrene mug.

"Constable Burstow, is it?" she asked.

He looked up and placed his hand over his cup as if he'd been caught skiving. "Yes, ma'am."

"It's OK. You've had a shock, I imagine. You drink your tea."

"Thanks, ma'am." He took a noisy sip. His hands trembled.

"Tell me what happened."

"We got a call at seven fourteen am. Landlord, locking up. This place is open till six thirty in the morning on a weekend. He said he'd found two bodies."

"When did you get here?"

"Seven twenty-one. Me and my partner Bill, PC Jeffries, we came from Digbeth police station." He pointed in the direction of the police station, no more than half a mile away.

"Then what?"

"Sorry, ma'am." Burstow put his cup down and stood to face her. "PC Jeffries went to speak to the landlord while I came round here. Found the two of them back there, behind the Biffa bins." He pointed.

"One of them was alive," she said.

"I thought they were both dead at first, ma'am. But then PC Jeffries joined me and we checked them both. One of them had a pulse. Faint, but it was there. The other was gone." His face clouded.

Zoe nodded. "You called the ambulance."

"Called it in at seven thirty-seven, ma'am. Ambulance arrived three minutes later. They tried to stop the bleeding but weren't getting anywhere by the looks of it. They went off with him at seven fifty-two."

"Thanks, PC Jeffries. Did you manage to get a photo?"

He pulled himself up straight. "Took a photo of the man who went in the ambulance. I thought you might be wanting it."

He held out his phone. On it was a photo of a young blond man, his face pale and his eyes closed tight. It was in profile, blurry but better than nothing.

"Well done, Constable. Send that to the Force CID office. I'll be needing a full statement from you later on, plus a copy of your notes."

"No problem, ma'am. I don't suppose you know how he is?"

"Sorry, no," she said.

"Of course. I hope he made it. He was in a bad way."

Zoe took a deep breath. She looked up to see a Ford Focus pull in at the kerb. Ian Osman. She steeled herself.

"Ian. That was quick."

"I was on my way to the station, ma'am. They caught me on the Aston Expressway."

"Less of the ma'aming, please."

"Sorry, boss. What we got?"

"Two men, both genitally mutilated. One of them's back there, with the pathologist. The other was taken to—" She called out to PC Burstow. "Which hospital did they go to, Constable?"

"City Hospital, ma'am."

That made sense. City Hospital, on the Dudley Road, was the closest.

"Right," she said to Ian. "I'm getting over there. I want to see if I can talk to the second victim before there's a chance of him dying too. You talk to the pub landlord. See if we've got any potential witnesses, people leaving the pub late, anyone in overlooking properties. And keep in touch with the FSIs. Adi Hanson's in charge, he's the white suit over there with the hint of a new beard poking out."

"I've met Adi, boss."

"Good. Now, do I need to tell you what to ask him? What we're looking for?"

He clenched his jaw. "One, an identification. Two, a weapon that might have been dropped. Three, trace materials left behind by the attacker. Fibres, bodily fluids, that sort of thing."

"Good. If we can get DNA, we're home and dry."

"No problem, boss."

"Thanks. I'll see you later."

CHAPTER TEN

THE MAN WAS in surgery when Zoe arrived at City Hospital. Knowing she'd get no joy from anyone in the surgical unit, she made for A&E where she found the registrar who'd been the first to treat him.

Dr Batra looked as if he was on the wrong end of a very long shift. His scrubs were dishevelled and his face beaded with sweat. The bags under his eyes were big enough to carry one of Zoe's mum's off licence hauls.

"Come in here," he said, leading her into a small consulting room. He landed in his chair as much as sat in it, and wiped his brow.

"I was only with him for ten minutes, maybe fifteen," he said. "He was losing a lot of blood. We started the process of prepping him for surgery and he was taken up there twenty minutes after he arrived."

"Can you describe his injuries?"

Dr Batra wiped his brow again. He had a far-off look in his eyes. "Both of his testicles had been removed. To be honest, the cuts were neater than you'd expect from the state he was in. I'd almost have thought it was done right here."

"Is castration a procedure that happens here?"

"In testicular cancer or advanced prostate cancer cases, yes, sometimes. When I was a junior doctor I did a stint in Oncology and there was one patient who'd had the procedure. This didn't look all that different, to be honest."

"D'you think the person who did it was a surgeon?"

"Not one you'd ever want operating on you. There were no precautions taken, nothing to prevent blood loss. The poor bastard would have died if he hadn't been brought in when he was." He slumped back in his chair. "The paramedics said he was found round the back of a pub."

Zoe nodded. "Him, and another man. The other victim didn't make it."

Dr Batra's expression softened. "Poor bastard."

"When you admitted him, did he have any ID on him?"

"Nothing. The clothes he was wearing, and nothing else. Not even a set of house keys." He eyed her. "You'll be wanting to know who he is."

"I'm hoping he'll be able to tell us that, when he's conscious."

"Yeah." The doctor stared into space. He squeezed his eyes shut then open again and straightened his back. "I'm sorry, detective. I need to be getting back to work."

"How long have you been on shift?"

"Working a double today. Started yesterday afternoon."

Zoe checked the clock over the door: nine thirty am. Even she didn't work those sort of hours. She nodded. "Well, you take care," she said. "I'll give you my card, in case you think of anything that might be useful."

He shrugged. "Can't imagine what. Like I say, I was only with the poor sod for ten minutes." He took the card. "But yeah, of course."

Zoe left the room, wondering if the doctor would have remembered anything non-medical even if he had seen it.

CHAPTER ELEVEN

Zoe entered the team office. Rhodri was at his desk, Connie in the inner office, trying to manhandle the board.

Zoe went in. "D'you need a hand?"

"Thanks, boss. Just wanted to get this out of your way."

"No need."

"Well, now that you're using this as your office... the rest of us need access."

"You're right. Here, let's do it together."

Between them they lifted the board off the floor and hauled it into the main office. Rhodri watched them, bemused.

"I'd offer to help," he said.

"But you're too busy sitting on your bum," replied Connie.

"No. What I was going to say was that I didn't want to patronise you."

Zoe gestured for Connie to help her place the board on the floor, leaning against a wall. She dusted her hands off. "What you're forgetting, Rhodri, is that you're fifteen years younger than me. And stronger than Connie. We would have appreciated some help."

"Sorry, boss." He stood up. "Want me to put it on the wall?"

"That's facilities' job. You call them, get someone in here."

"Righto." Rhodri picked up his phone. He was probably mates with half the facilities team anyway, no doubt went drinking with them. Zoe had never been good at that sort of thing, making friends all over the station. And the rest of the stations in Birmingham, in Rhodri's case. She'd always assumed it was a privilege afforded to smokers, forming their unofficial networks while they huddled outside for a fag. But Rhodri had never smoked, and yet had networks across the force.

"How did you get it down in the first place?" she asked Connie.

Connie reached into her pocket. "My multitool, boss. Useful for taking computers apart, fixing my bike. I used it to release me and the sarge when we were locked up on Trevor Hamm's building site."

Zoe nodded. Connie could look back at that incident with pride now, especially with Stick Adams in jail.

"Where's Ian?" she asked. The two constables shrugged. "He not been back yet?"

"Sorry, boss."

"Right. We need to have a briefing, and I can't do it without him."

She caught the glance between Rhodri and Connie but decided to ignore it. She dialled Ian.

"Boss."

"I was expecting you back at the station by now."

"Sorry, boss. We managed to track down about twenty people who were in the pub till closing time. We're working through them all now."

"Uniform can do that. We just go back to the ones who've got something useful to tell us. What about the landlord?"

"He's being helpful. Didn't see anything, though. Wants to know if he'll be able to open his pub tonight. This time of year, he stands to lose a lot of trade."

One man had been killed and another seriously injured. But the landlord wanted to protect his profits.

"Tell him he can open when we're ready," she grunted. "Remind him it's a murder enquiry."

"Will do."

"And then, get yourself back here. I want to recap on where we are."

"Right, boss. Sorry, boss."

Zoe hung up. She didn't like Ian Osman sucking up to her. When he'd been under suspicion of involvement in his kids' abduction he'd been nothing like this. Shifty, untrustworthy, aggressive. Never slimy.

Carl, you owe me one, she thought.

Someone from facilities was already in the office, screwing the board to the wall. When it was done, Rhodri fist-bumped the man and Connie stepped in to work on it with him. They cleaned off notes from a previous case and started sticking up photos. Since they had no ID on either victim, and no suspect, there were no mugshots. Instead, all they had were crime scene photos. Zoe watched as Rhodri tacked them to the board, wondering what possessed someone to do a thing like that. Especially someone with surgical skills. Did she need to trawl the hospitals, speak to all the surgeons?

The door opened and Ian walked in. "Sorry, boss."

"Stop apologising. You were doing your job."

"But..." He looked at her, irritated, then stopped himself. "Right. So what's up then?"

"Gather round, everyone."

Connie stood back from the board. Rhodri perched on the edge of Connie's desk, which was closest to the board. Connie sat behind him, leaning sideways to peer round his gangly frame.

The board held two photographs of the dead man. In one, he lay on the ground, his legs bent to one side, his jeans soaked in his own blood. Another shot was a close-up of the face. For the other man, they had the photo PC Burstow had taken. There would be more photos coming in, she knew. Gruesome ones, of the men's injuries.

"We need to find out if the hospital took photos of the man after he was taken there," she said.

"I doubt they'll have been thinking about evidence, boss," said Ian.

"Still, worth a try."

She surveyed the board. The four of them stared at it, Connie occasionally looking round at her, expectant.

"I tell you what bothers me," said Rhodri.

"Mm?" said Zoe.

"He took the time to put their jeans on after he did it. They'd been zipped up and everything."

Zoe stepped in. "You're right."

"There can't have been that much blood when he did that," said Ian. "He'd never have managed to grip the zipper."

"Good point. He must have used something to stop the bleeding. Either that or he had something to help him zip the jeans up, some sort of attachment to the zipper. We need to ask Forensics if there's any evidence of swabs, towels, any fibres."

Ian made a note. "Got it."

Zoe leaned back. "So. There's forensics. A crime like this, he must have left something behind. Then there's the post-mortem, and the surgery on the other victim. Anything the doctors can tell us, once they deign to talk to us."

"Possible CCTV, boss," said Connie. "And eye witnesses. I can have a look if anyone was filming around there last night, anything on social media."

"Good. You look for any video. Rhodri, I want you to collate witness statements. See if there's anything at all, anything suspicious." She turned to Ian. "Are they talking to people living in the area too?"

"They are."

"Good. Rhodri, talk to your mates in Uniform. Get all the statements together and find anything interesting. Sergeant Osman will follow up."

Rhodri nodded. Ian said nothing.

"We need to work out who these two men were," she said. She peered at the photographs. "We'll have to do an appeal. I'll talk to the press."

"What about the killer?" asked Ian. "From the look of those wounds, he's a medic."

"This city has got a lot of medics. We need a link. Something to tie the victims to the killer. The only way to get that is to find out who they are."

"Surely there aren't that many gay medics?' asked Ian.

Zoe rolled her eyes. "Why d'you assume he's gay?"

"He cut their testicles off. He was trying to emasculate

them, to humiliate them. Maybe he tried to have sex with them, and they refused."

"Both of them?"

A shrug. "I dunno. A threesome, or something. Maybe he felt humiliated and decided to take it out on them. Given where the bodies were found..."

"It could just as easily be motivated by homophobia," Connie said. She picked at the skin on her forearm.

Ian shook his head. "It's too intimate."

"Since when were you the expert?" said Zoe.

"I worked on the Karlson case, boss."

"Ah." Peter Karlson had preyed on prostitutes eight years earlier, killing four of them before the fifth managed to escape and identify him. "This crime looks completely different," she said. "He mutilated those women. Caved their faces in."

"He amputated their breasts," said Ian. "Sexually humiliated them. Like this."

"I'm not sure. I think we need to keep our minds open."

Ian shrugged. Zoe grabbed a whiteboard marker and wrote question marks next to the facial photos.

"First priority is to find out who those men were. I'm on that, you all have your jobs."

CHAPTER TWELVE

Erwin Norris was waiting for Zoe in a greasy spoon inside the indoor market, not far from the crime scene. He was a fat, balding man with wispy hair combed over the top of his head and glasses that made his eyes bulge. He sipped a latte – surprising, Zoe would have had him as a tea drinker – as she approached.

She took the seat opposite him. "Mine's a black coffee, please."

He blinked at her, then remembered their earlier conversation. He took a gulp of his coffee and stood up, patting his pockets for change. He returned with another latte and a black coffee.

Zoe shuffled in the uncomfortable chair and sipped her coffee. It was surprisingly good.

"So," she said.

"So," he replied.

"I checked your newspaper's website. You held up your end of the deal."

"I'm a man of my word."

She pushed down a laugh. "Well, thank you. I guess I owe you that."

"We aren't here for small talk," he said. "Tell me about those bodies."

"One body. The other victim is still alive."

Norris opened a notepad. "Where did they take him?"

"City. I don't want to see you camped out there."

"So who are they?"

She took another sip of her coffee. A mother with a toddler and a baby sat down at the table next to them, casting a wary smile in their direction. Zoe lowered her voice. "We don't know."

"Neither of them?"

"Neither man had ID on him. We've got a witness who says he'd seen the dead man in the pub a few times before, but no names. That's where I need your help."

"You want to do an appeal."

"Not a full-blown appeal. But you can publish the photos, ask the public if they can identify the men."

"We'll be inundated with crank callers. Especially given where the bodies were found."

"Publish the police hotline. We're used to crank callers."

"Good. We'll still get crank calls at the paper, though."

"Nothing I imagine you can't handle." Zoe knew he wouldn't be on the end of the phone batting off the crazies and homophobes.

"S'pose so," he said. "So what you gonna give me, in return for my co-operation? You do know the Evening Mail are running with this as a hate crime already?"

"We've got no evidence it's a hate crime."

"I heard they'd had their balls cut off."

Zoe glanced at the next table. The woman shifted in her seat, retreating from them. She wore the look of someone pretending to be focusing on one thing but in reality concentrating very hard on something else.

"Finish your coffee, Norris. Let's move."

He downed his latte and followed her out of the market. They wove between stalls and shoppers. It was busy today, trade gearing up in time for Christmas. The stalls were festooned with fairy lights and tinsel, and a fair proportion of them were selling Christmas trinkets too.

Once they were outside, Zoe found a bench. Its surface was cold, but she didn't plan on staying long. "I don't want you speculating on motive yet. I'll give you these photos, and you'll publish the information number. Just report the facts."

"Since when did I do that?" He laughed.

She reached into her inside pocket. "These photos I'm about to give you. They're from the crime scene."

Norris's mouth formed an O. He stared at her hand, breathing shallow.

"We don't normally release crime scene photos, as you know. But these are clean. They're photos of our victims' faces."

She placed the two photographs in her lap. The first was of the dead man. He was pictured square on, from the neck upwards. His face was greying and his eyes closed. There was no sign of injury. The other was the blurry photo of the other man that PC Burstow had taken on his phone.

"Poor bastards," said Norris.

"Yes. One of these men is alive." She pointed. "And the other didn't make it. Be tactful in your report, please. There will be relatives out there who don't know their son, husband or father is dead yet."

Norris raised an eyebrow. "Husband?"

Zoe gritted her teeth. "Gay men marry too, you know. Or did we leave you behind in the dark ages?"

"Fair point." He took the photos from her and hurried away.

CHAPTER THIRTEEN

Amit's eyes sprang open. There'd been a noise, something new.

He sat up, trying to ignore the pain in his legs, and listened. He'd grown used to the smell of this room, the mustiness. And the dim light from the high window.

He put his ear to the door, expecting to hear footsteps. The man was coming back. He'd have his phone with him again. Yesterday he'd sat Amit down and interviewed him. That was the only word for it. He'd asked him to start at the beginning, go back as early as he could remember. Amit had done as he was told, bemused. Why did this man want to know his life story?

They'd reached Amit's teenage years at the end of the first session. The man had told Amit to go over his childhood again and again. He was obsessed with Amit's relationship with his parents, wanted to know how he felt about them, if he loved them. If he'd been neglected by his father, or mollycoddled by his mother.

Of course he had. Didn't all fathers ignore their kids?

Didn't all mothers love them? Amit had told the man about the speech day at school when his dad had turned up but ignored him, eager to talk to the head teacher. The time he'd cracked his head open in rugby practice and his mum had taken him to the hospital, crying all the way. His dad had told him to get right back there in the scrum.

So far, so normal. Why did this man want to know it all?

Then, in the afternoon, he'd moved on. Starting from when Amit was fourteen, and working up to his eighteenth birthday. He'd asked him about his friends, the girls he knew (barely any), his relationship with his sister and brother.

Amit had answered honestly. If all the man was doing was conducting a social sciences experiment, then maybe he'd let him go.

But the man had made no effort to cover his face. He'd sat right opposite Amit, staring him in the face. OK, so it was dim in here. But they both knew Amit would be able to identify him if he ever got out of here.

Amit felt a shiver run down his back. He was never getting out of here. Some weirdo had locked him up to ask him about his life story, and once they'd reached the present day, he would kill him. He had to string it out. Invent some stories.

He tensed. There it was, the new sound again. He leaned on the door. It was barking. A dog.

Amit hated dogs. His sister had been bitten by one as a toddler and his mum had never allowed them near any of them after that. He wondered if the man was deliberately bringing a dog in to test him. See if he could cope.

He'd cope. If all he had to do was put up with a dog being in the room, he could do it. It would fill time, postpone them reaching the present day. He could wax lyrical about Safiya being bitten by the dog, give the man more material.

The barking receded then stopped. Just someone walking past, taking their dog for a walk. Amit hadn't heard movement behind the door for hours now. He walked to the window, lifted his face to it.

"Help!" he called. "My name's Amit Hussain and I've been locked up. Get me out of here!"

The door flew open. Amit sank to the floor, staring at the man. The man's face was twisted in rage, his fists clenched.

"I told you once, you little fuck! Shut that trap of yours, or I'll shut it for you."

Amit nodded, shuffling away from the man. Had he been out there all along, listening? Waiting to catch Amit out?

"Eat," the man grunted. He threw a bag of crisps at Amit's feet. A bottle of water followed it. Amit had long since given up worrying about the crisps being Halal. He'd repent for it once this was over.

He opened the bag as the door slammed shut.

CHAPTER FOURTEEN

IAN PULLED up outside his house. He stretched his arms above his head, banging the roof of the car, and yawned. He eyed the house, his spirits low.

Since the kids had come back, Alison had moved into Ollie's room. He'd had trouble sleeping, and would wake in the night screaming. Alison preferred to be next to him, than to have to dash in from their room.

Ian's bed felt very cold, and very big.

He heaved himself out of the car and walked up the path to his front door. Something was different about the house. He paused, looking at the front door, the windows. He surveyed the garden. Had Alison been weeding?

Then he realised. The scaffolding was gone. They'd finished replacing the roof.

He opened the front door. "I'm home, Al!"

She was in the kitchen, just inside the front door. A pan rattled on the stove and the microwave was beeping. She didn't acknowledge him.

He slid an arm around her waist from behind, kissing her on the neck. She tensed.

"I said, I'm home."

Alison turned, her face creased with anxiety. "Ollie's worse."

Ian felt his shoulder slump. "How?"

"He was talking."

"To you." *Not to anyone else,* Ian thought. After their son had been dumped in their front garden by a kidnapper, he'd refused to speak until his sister had come home, tracked down by Ian's new DI. But in the last fortnight Ollie had started talking to his mum.

"He's stopped again," Alison said. "Won't even look at me." Her eyes welled. "Ian, what am I going to do?"

"What are *we* going to do, you mean. He's seeing a psychologist. She'll help."

"He won't talk to her."

'Look, love. These people are trained. They know how to get kids to open up. It takes time."

"I know." Alison's voice was subdued. It was hard on her, he knew. Her boss at the school had insisted she take time off to look after her children. Ollie hadn't returned to school since the abduction, and Maddy was on short days.

"Come here," he breathed. Alison let him pull her into his arms and kiss her on the cheek. He hesitated then kissed her lips. She kissed him back, lightly.

"I've got to finish dinner."

He smiled into her eyes. "What is it?"

"Shepherd's pie. Maddy's favourite."

Ian hid his irritation. They'd eaten shepherd's pie every other day for three weeks now. "Sounds lovely."

He was about to head into the living room to check on his

children when he remembered the scaffolding. "They finish the roof, then?"

Alison paled. "Sorry, Ian."

"What?" He heard his voice harden. "They buggered off in the middle of the job?"

"Stuart Reynolds came by. He said they'd need more funds."

Ian sucked in a breath. He wasn't about to tell his wife where the funds for his house renovations had come from. Or why they might have been cut off.

"I'll talk to him," he said.

"Please. It's watertight, but it's unsightly."

He kissed her. "Promise."

CHAPTER FIFTEEN

THE MAN WAS AWAKE NOW, sitting upright in his hospital bed. Zoe was ushered through a by a stern ward sister, who warned her not to put him under any strain.

"Don't worry," she reassured the woman. "I'll go easy on him."

She sat in the chair next to the bed and gave the man a smile. He looked shellshocked, dazed. She wondered how long he'd known about the castration.

"My name's Detective Inspector Zoe Finch," she said. "I'm in charge of the investigation to find the person who did this to you."

He stared at her. His eyes were bright with repressed tears. He had mousy blonde hair and large blue eyes in a tanned face.

"The first thing I need to know," she said, "is who you are. You didn't have any ID on you when we found you."

He shook his head. She clasped her hands on her lap.

"I know this is hard," she said. "You've been through a

terrible ordeal. But please just tell me your name. And anything you can remember."

His eyes widened. He looked scared.

"I'm a police officer," she said. "I can keep anything you tell me strictly confidential. Do you have any family I can contact?"

He shook his head. She put her notepad away. No pressure, the nurse had said.

"Do you remember anything?"

He shook his head, then closed his eyes. He leaned against the pillows, his face tilted upwards and his eyes closed as if in sleep.

"Anything you tell me, I don't need to pass on to anyone else. I can contact your family, but they don't need to know what happened until you're ready to tell them. Or where we found you."

His eyes darted open. So he knew that much, at least. Or did he?

"Please," she muttered.

"Adam," he whispered.

"Adam," she repeated. "Is that your name, or...?"

A nod.

"Your name?"

Another nod.

"Adam what?"

He shook his head, clenching his eyes shut.

"Can you remember where you live, Adam?"

He opened his eyes and turned to her. "Amelia."

"Is that your wife?"

"No. Amelia."

"I need to know who Amelia is."

He gestured towards a glass of water on the side table.

Zoe handed it to him. He drank slowly then gave it back to her.

"My neighbour," he croaked.

"Amelia is your neighbour."

He nodded.

"You live alone?"

Another nod.

"Can you remember your address, Adam?"

"That's enough now." A nurse was behind Zoe. "He needs to sleep."

"I'll just be a few more minutes."

"You can come back tomorrow, when he's had some rest."

With a murderer on the loose, tomorrow was too long to wait. Zoe leaned in towards Adam.

"Is there anything you can remember?"

"Mitch," he whispered. "Mitch."

"Who's Mitch?"

"Mitch."

"Come on, now. If he remembers his full name or address, we'll let you know straightaway."

Zoe stood up and turned to the nurse. "Whoever's on shift has to call me immediately. DI Finch, Force CID. Here's my card."

"Of course." The nurse's face was pinched. "Now let him sleep, please."

Zoe turned back to Adam, whose eyes were closed. She stared at him, clenching and unclenching her fists.

CHAPTER SIXTEEN

Mo SAT in the dingy flat, trying to blot out the smell of stale food and decay. The sofa he sat in was soft and covered in stains, threatening to swallow him if he didn't escape it soon. The room was dim, only one desk lamp against the December evening.

"You say you met Amit through a friend?"

Kai Whitaker nodded. He was short and slender with a tattoo of a robin on his wrist. He was a similar age to Amit, about twenty. But there the similarity ended. Amit lived wrapped in wool in his parents' house in Kings Heath. This man was living in a squat in Bordesley Green.

"He was cute. I like Asian guys." Kai leaned back and gave Mo a look like he was sizing him up. This kid was young enough to be Mo's son, but he had the look in his eyes of a man who'd lived more in his twenty years than Mo had in twice as long.

"So how long have you known him?"

"Two months. We see each other every weekend, I take him clubbing sometimes."

Mo nodded. "He's your boyfriend."

Kai spat out a laugh. "How old are you? Boyfriend? Nothing like that. He's cute. I wanted to see more of him. The whole boyfriend thing is way too old-school for me."

Mo wondered how Amit felt about 'the whole boyfriend thing'.

"When did you last see him?"

"Thursday night, the Jackal. A bunch of us got together. Drinks, dancing, you know the kind of thing."

It had been quite some time since Mo had indulged in drinks and dancing. Two young daughters kind of put paid to that. But he nodded, wanting the man to keep talking.

"Did he seem different at all, the last time you saw him? Did he talk about any problems at home?"

"His dad. Disciplinarian. Amit hates him. You could tell that just from talking to the guy for five minutes. It was like an aura, radiating off him. Dad-hate."

"What about his mum? His sister, his brother? Any problems there?"

"His mum's a fusser, she waits up for him when he goes out. He's like a prisoner. His brother sounds cool. Don't know much about his sister."

"Were you with him at the end of the night, when he left for home?"

"Yeah. He was grumbling about having to catch the bus. Always got the same one, his mum waits for him. His dad tears him a new one if he gets home late. So good little Amit went running home to mummy and daddy. Spoiled my evening, it did."

Spoiled Amit's evening considerably more, Mo thought. He'd had to work through three levels of acquaintance to find this kid: an old schoolfriend, then a colleague of the schoolfriend, then an ex-boyfriend of the colleague. Finally he'd got to this man who knew the real Amit. Not the one in the photos on his parents' dining room wall.

"Did you see him get on the bus?"

"Yeah. Waved him off an' all."

"Was he alone?"

"Yup." Kai stared off into space, no doubt remembering the last time he'd seen Amit.

"He didn't say anything about wanting to leave home, run away?" Mo asked.

Kai shook his head. "He hates his dad, yeah. But he'd never do that to his brother. He loves him. The sun shines out of his arse, far as Amit's concerned."

"Is there anywhere he might be staying, somewhere he might have gone for a while?"

"Amit never goes anywhere. He went on holiday with his folks last year. But that was the only time he's left Birmingham in his life." Kai shook his head. "Can you imagine that?"

"I'm not thinking of him staying away from Birmingham," said Mo. "I'm thinking of him staying away from home."

"Nah. He knows he'd have to go back in the end like, and what would he tell his dad?" Kyle shuddered. "Not worth the aggro."

"Have you got any photos of him?"

"Didn't his mum give you one?"

"I want one of him in the kind of clothes he'd have been wearing on Thursday. The same ones, if possible."

Kai pulled his phone from his back pocket. "Yeah, Dan took one and put it on Instagram." He scrolled through his feed, frowning. "Here you go." He held out the phone. Amit sat in the middle of a group of four men, in a bar. Kai had his arm around him and was breathing into his ear. Amit wore a striped black and yellow t-shirt.

"I like that t-shirt," Kai said. "Makes him look fit."

"Can I have a copy?"

"Course. Where d'you want me to send it?"

Mo gave him an email address and felt his own phone vibrate in his inside pocket. He pulled it out and checked the photo.

"Thanks." Mo pushed down on the sofa cushions and hauled himself up. He gave the man his card. "If you think of anywhere Amit might be, or of anyone he might have talked to, you call me straightaway. Please. If you hear from him, or from anyone who's heard from him."

"Course, man. This sucks." Kyle rubbed at his forehead with his fingertips. "I miss him."

"His mum and dad do too."

Kyle snorted. "Whatever. You find him, huh? Amit's a good guy."

Mo nodded. He'd been making that promise to too many people lately.

CHAPTER SEVENTEEN

Zoe pushed the front door closed with her foot. She dumped her bag on the coffee table in the living room and plonked herself down on the sofa.

Adam's face was in her head, the blankness behind his eyes. She hoped he'd remember something, and soon.

Who was Mitch? And Amelia? There was no way she could track down three people just from their first names. Even if two of them lived in the same street.

"Hey, Mum." Nicholas was in the kitchen. Zoe smelled garlic frying. Nicholas wiped his hands on a tea towel and stuffed it in his belt. "I'm making Bolognese. Zaf's coming over."

"You want me to get out of the way?"

Zoe's new kitten jumped onto the sofa next to her and rubbed its face against her hand. She stroked it absentmindedly. "Hey Yoda," she murmured to it, her attention on her son.

"Not if you don't want to," Nicholas said. "We're going out after we've eaten."

She stiffened. "Where to?"

He shrugged. "Not sure. Maybe the pub, maybe into town. Why?"

"You've got school tomorrow."

"Don't worry. I've done my homework and I won't stay out late." He grimaced and went back into the kitchen. Zoe heard him cursing under his breath, followed by the sound of the bin being opened.

Zoe followed him. "You OK?"

"Burnt the garlic. Shouldn't have come out while it was cooking." Nicholas reached up for the garlic pot on a shelf near the hob. "Start again, huh?"

"Sorry, love." She stepped in but he took a pace back.

"Let me focus, Mum."

"OK. But I want you to be careful."

He looked up. "What, with this garlic?"

She shook her head. "We found two men who'd been attacked this morning. Round the back of a pub in the gay village."

He stopped stirring. "Who?"

"We don't have their names yet."

Nicholas looked up. "Dead?"

"One of them, yes. The other one's in hospital."

"What happened to them?"

"You know I can't tell you that."

"All I have to do is a quick Google search."

Zoe sighed. She heard the front door slam: Zaf.

"They were castrated," she said.

Zaf came into the kitchen, Yoda on his shoulder licking his ear. He held onto the cat by the scruff of the neck and tickled it under the chin.

"You talking about the Digbeth Ripper?" he asked,

sidling up to Nicholas and giving him a peck on the cheek. Nicholas smiled then glanced at his mum and stiffened.

"Is that what they're calling him?" Zoe asked. "He's not a ripper, he's..."

"Ripped their balls off, according to the internet." Zaf grabbed his phone and showed Nicholas a photo. "They want to find out who this guy us."

Bloody Erwin Norris, thought Zoe.

"That the one who lived?" Nicholas asked.

Zoe peered over Zaf's shoulder. "No." Was this man Mitch? Had that been what Adam was telling her? Or was Mitch the killer?

"Someone chopped two guys' balls off and dumped them round the back of the Jackal pub," said Zaf.

"Eww," said Nicholas. He emptied a bag of mince into the pan.

"Yeah, right," said Zaf. He pulled the kitten down from his shoulder and cradled it in his arms like a baby. He made cooing sounds and tickled its tummy.

"It's not funny," Zoe said. "A man's dead."

Zaf looked up from the kitten, which was playing with his fingers. "Only one of them? Connie wouldn't tell me."

"Well, good for her." DC Williams was Zaf's big sister, and a very sensible one at that. Zoe reached out and took Yoda from him. The kitten mewed at her but let her scratch between its ears.

"She's so cute," said Zaf. He leaned in and rubbed the kitten's back. "I'm gonna miss her when I go to uni."

"Me too?" said Nicholas, pouting.

Zaf laughed. "We'll go to the same uni," he said. "You're not getting rid of me that easy."

"And you might both go to Birmingham," Zoe said. The two boys exchanged a look.

Don't push it, she told herself. Hold him close and she'd only push him farther away.

She handed Yoda to Zaf. "Anyway. I want you to be careful," she said. "We have no idea if someone's targeting the gay village, or gay men. I suggest you stick to the local pubs for a while."

"Mum, that's lame." Nicholas pushed the mince around the pan, more forcefully than he had been doing. "We're always together. We'll be fine."

"The two victims were probably together. And they were very much not fine."

Nicholas shook his head, his lips tight.

"Just take care is all I'm asking, Nicholas. Just until we catch him."

Nicholas carried on stirring, not meeting her eye. Zaf chatted to the kitten, trying to pretend he wasn't there.

CHAPTER EIGHTEEN

Charlie checked the patio doors were locked and turned off the light on the back of the house. He'd spent most of the evening out there, setting up the fairy lights that framed Yanis's shed at the bottom of the garden.

Yanis liked to call it his shed, but really it was a garden office. Wired in, with its own lighting and wifi, sometimes it was warmer in there than the house itself. And now it had its very own Christmas decorations.

Charlie padded into the kitchen, wishing he'd thought to bring his slippers downstairs. The side door was locked, too. He poured a glass of water from the tap and swallowed a couple of Ibuprofen. His head was hurting, and he had to be alert tomorrow for the monthly sales meeting. Hopefully it would be short, give them time for the Christmas lunch.

He rinsed the glass out and placed it on the draining board. He turned out the light and made for the living room.

Charlie did this every night. He'd grown up in a rough neighbourhood and had got used to keeping an eye on his stuff. Which involved spending money on good locks, when he could afford it. Now, despite living on the leafier side of Moseley, he was still security-conscious. Yanis said it was a drag, but Charlie insisted they should protect their belongings even more now they lived here. After all, if you were a thief looking to get your hands on some valuable stuff, would you try your luck in the inner city, or here in Moseley?

He checked the bay window at the front. They never opened the top windows at this time of year, but you couldn't be too sure. He took a moment to admire his handiwork in the front garden. The bushes flanking their drive were strewn with tasteful white fairy lights. The oak tree that probably wasn't theirs, given that its roots went under the pavement, was decorated too. It was Christmas, but not the kind of tacky Christmas his parents had gone for. No flashing lights and pop-up Santas here.

"Charlie?" Yanis's voice came down from the bedroom. He would be in bed with his laptop, checking email. Yanis was always checking email. The shed had been an attempt to separate Yanis's business from his home life, a vain attempt to get him to switch off at the end of the day. But as Yanis was always reminding him, when you ran your own business, you could never switch off. There was no one else to take the slack. So Charlie took it instead, in the time he wasn't able to spend with his husband.

He left the living room and went to the front door. He opened it to check there was no junk mail in the porch, taking in the scent of the tiny real tree he'd put in there, and reached out for the porch door. It was unlocked.

He frowned and yanked the handle, activating the deadbolt. They left the outer door open in the daytime for deliveries, but always closed it after dinner. Charlie would have preferred it to be left locked in the daytime too, what with

Yanis working at the bottom of the garden. But Yanis had insisted he didn't want to be running back and forth taking in deliveries. And Yanis's IT business involved a lot of deliveries.

Come to think of it, the inner door had been unlocked too. Charlie felt a chill grip his chest, then shrugged it off. He'd been out there testing the lights in the oak tree before dinner. He must have not closed it properly afterwards.

Stop worrying, he told himself.

Even so, he took a moment to peer out of the porch and onto the street. It was quiet and still, the only sound traffic from Wake Green Road behind the houses opposite. Charlie berated himself and shut the inner door, making sure it was dead-bolted.

At last he was satisfied. He considered checking the kitchen door one more time then told himself not to. Yanis was waiting. And he'd been in a playful mood tonight, sticking on a Christmas playlist and pouring out bubbly while Charlie did the decorations. Maybe he could be persuaded to put his laptop down...

Charlie mounted the stairs, his footsteps light, and went into the bathroom. He cleaned his teeth thoroughly, counting in his head for two minutes, and checked his face for spots. All clear. He admired himself in the mirror for a moment – only a couple of grey hairs, it didn't do to be ageing too fast when your husband was eleven years younger – and wiped his face with a flannel.

He pushed the door open, ready to tempt Yanis away from his laptop.

Yanis was sitting in bed, the laptop thrown to one side. He leaned forwards, pushed away from the pillows by the man kneeling behind him.

The man had a knife to Yanis's throat.

Charlie felt the breath leave his body. Yanis stared back at him, his eyes wide. His skin was pale and he was sweating. Charlie raised his hands, his gaze flicking to the man with the knife. He was young, Yanis's age, with dark hair and a strong jaw. He stared back at Charlie, his eyes cold.

"Don't hurt him," Charlie said. "Take me instead."

Yanis's mouth drooped. He let out a sob.

"Please," said Charlie. He looked at his handsome husband, wanting to leap over there and wrestle him from this monster's grasp.

"We have money," he said. "I can bring it to you."

The man smiled. "I don't want your money."

Charlie felt his chest dip. "The car?"

The man laughed, a harsh guttural laugh. "Fuck your car."

Yanis whimpered.

"Please," Charlie whispered. "Please don't hurt him."

The man shifted the blade against Yanis's neck. Yanis closed his eyes. He was trembling. Charlie looked at the knife. *Don't move,* he thought. *If you shake too much, it'll cut you.* He looked into his husband's eyes, which were narrow.

The man removed the knife from Yanis's neck and Yanis slumped in his grasp. The man still had an arm round Yanis's shoulders.

The man pointed the knife at Charlie. Charlie stared at him, rooted to the spot.

"Do as I tell you," the man said. "And neither of you will be hurt."

CHAPTER NINETEEN

SUNDAY

Ian left the house early. He had someone to see, and didn't want his new DI suspecting anything. He'd be in that office before anyone else, his nose clean and his reputation intact.

Stuart Reynolds's unit was in Selly Oak, a two-mile detour from the office. He pulled his car up outside and walked to the front door, determined not to skulk around.

He pushed the door open and rapped sharply on the front desk with his ring finger. The front office was empty as always, but he could hear power tools from beyond the door into Reynolds's workshop.

The door opened and Reynolds emerged, wiping his hands on a grubby cloth. He wore a navy hoody with the hood up.

"Might have known you'd come sniffing around."

"I'm not sniffing anywhere," Ian replied. "I want to know why you've left my roof half-finished."

"You know why. I told that lovely wife of yours."

"She said you needed more money."

Stuart dropped the cloth on the desk between them. "Intelligent woman, your wife. Knows how to take a message."

"I don't have more money."

Reynolds pushed his hood back and shrugged. A bruise spread across his nose and under both eyes.

"How d'you get that?" Ian asked.

Reynolds moved his fingers towards his face then dropped them again, his expression hardening. "None of your business. Now you find those funds, and I can start work on your roof again."

Ian surveyed the bruise. From the colour, a mix of yellow and dark purple, it was less than a week old. "Did Hamm's lot do that?"

Reynolds grabbed the cloth and twisted the ends around his fists. "I told you, none of your business."

Ian knew that Zoe had found Hamm in the Canalside Hotel, when they were looking for his daughter Maddy. Someone must have given her the location. He wondered if it was Reynolds.

"You finally saw sense," he said.

Reynolds chuckled. "Unlike you."

"Don't know what you're talking about."

"No? Oh come on, let's not beat around the bloody bush here. We both know who we work for, and what he does. That's how you get your roof done and your bathroom tarted up. It's how I make my business purr like a jaguar on speed."

"It doesn't have to be like that."

"Oh no?"

"No."

"Go on then." Reynolds tugged on the ends of the cloth. "How does it have to be?"

"You can stick to regular clients. Make money the normal way."

"I'm used to doin' it like this."

"I bet you are. And when my boss eventually takes Hamm down and you go down with him?"

"She's not going to do that." Reynolds leaned over the desk. His bruise looked painful from this angle. Ian wondered which of Hamm's sidekicks had done it. "Because if she does, you're in the shit too."

Ian took a step back. Did Zoe know about his deal with Professional Standards? DI Whaley hadn't given him much in the way of instruction, just told him to carry on what he was doing and pass on information.

Trying to turn Stuart Reynolds straight certainly didn't come under the description of carrying on what he was doing. And he needed that roof fixing.

"Alright," he said. "You carry on as you are. You'll be back at my place within the week, finishing what you started on that roof."

CHAPTER TWENTY

Ian and Connie were already in the office when Zoe arrived. Rhodri was right behind her, muttering apologies as he slid his coat onto his chair. It was less than four degrees outside and the two of them brought a rush of cold air into the office.

Connie had been working on the board. She'd written Adam's name, and the names *Mitch* and *Amelia*. She'd added question marks after both of them.

"So, where are we?" asked Zoe.

"Post mortem's this morning," said Connie. "I spoke to Doctor Adebayo, she wants you there."

"She does, does she?" Zoe considered asking one of the constables to accompany her, then decided against it. The experience would be useful for them, but they had work to do.

"What about forensics?" she asked.

"They were..." Rhodri paused, unsure of the best word to use, "attacked away from the scene, and brought there at least an hour after the unlucky one died."

"How do we know that?"

"The blood, boss. It's all on the victims. Hardly any at the scene. Just flakes of it, that fell off their clothing, or maybe off the killer. Nothing in the way of blood spatter."

"Anything with the killer's DNA? Blood, semen? Any fibres?"

"Nothing, boss."

"OK," she said. "That means there's another crime scene. One that might be covered in blood."

"He'll have long since cleaned up," said Ian.,

"It's not as easy to clean up that amount of blood as people think. We need to get an address for one or both of these men. The killer could have broken into their houses, attacked them there. There'll be traces of blood. Maybe DNA from their attacker."

"We've still got no idea who either of them are, boss," said Connie.

"No. All we have is three names." Zoe pointed at the board. "Adam, Amelia and Mitch. Adam's the man in City Hospital. Or at least that's who he says he is."

"Adam who, though?" said Rhodri.

"Rhod, if I knew that, I wouldn't be standing here. But the question is, who are Mitch and Amelia?"

"Mitch could be the killer," said Ian.

"Or he could be the other victim. No way of knowing. Amelia's a neighbour."

"Doesn't that narrow it down?" asked Connie. "Adam and Amelia, living next door to each other?

"If we had surnames, maybe we could check the electoral register," Zoe said. "But two first names... and they might not be next door to each other."

"Amelia's not a very common name." Connie sat at her

desk and tapped on her keyboard. "192.com gives me a hundred Amelias in Birmingham. That's the most it gives you. I'll need to check the online electoral register."

"You can do that?" Asked Zoe. "For first names?"

Connie nodded. "I can pull out all the Amelias, add them to a spreadsheet with addresses. Then do the same for Adams."

"There'll be a lot of those," said Rhodri.

Connie's tongue poked from between her lips.

"Not so many in the same street as an Amelia," said Zoe. "You're going to compare the street addresses, am I right?"

Connie nodded. She looked up from her screen. "Got it."

Rhodri whistled. Even Ian looked impressed.

"Go on then," said Zoe.

"Adam Hart, seventy-six Sandford Road. Amelia Dowd. Right next door at number seventy-eight."

"Nice work," said Zoe. "That has to be our first priority. Ian, you go to the post-mortem. Give my apologies to Adana."

"Lucky me."

"She'll be fine."

"Hmm."

Zoe liked Dr Adebayo: she was straight-talking and good at her job. But the men in the team were terrified of her.

"Connie, I want you with me in Moseley. Your reward for tracking him down."

"Shouldn't we go and visit him first?" Connie asked. "To check?"

"I don't want to plant any false memories in his mind. We'll talk to the neighbour first. If we get an ID, we can check it out with the hospital then check his house: it could be a second crime scene."

"Potential crime scene," said Ian.

Zoe refused to bite. "Ian, did you get anything from eyewitnesses?"

"Three people who might have seen something, according to Uniform. I'm following those up today."

"Not yesterday?"

Ian's expression soured. "It took a while to work through them all, boss."

"Hmm. OK. Post-mortem first, then report back when you've spoken to the witnesses. Take Rhodri. We need a description of the killer, if we can get one."

"I do know that," said Ian.

"Of course you do." Zoe turned to Rhodri. "Any more forensics? Anything left behind, prints, anything like that?"

"Nothing, boss. The guy knew what he was doing."

Zoe raked a hand through her long brown hair. This attack made no sense. It looked like a random attack, maybe on two men on their way home from a night out. But Adana had said the knife work showed expertise. And the killer had taken time to leave no traces.

"I checked social media, boss," said Connie.

"Of course. And?"

"We managed to get a couple of photos of the area from Facebook. People leaving the pub, earlier on. But it was dark. There are plenty of people milling around, but I'm not sure we could identify anyone."

"What about CCTV?"

"There's a building site up the road. It's got cameras, but they're all angled on the site. They capture some of the area beyond, but it's too dark."

Zoe nodded. "OK. Well, keep trawling. See if you can get any social media images from inside that pub, or any of the other pubs and bars nearby. We might be able to get a photo of the victims, before they were attacked. Maybe the killer's with them."

"On it," said Connie.

"Good." Zoe sighed. "OK, I'll go to the house on my own. Adi'll join me, if I need him."

The door opened behind her. Zoe looked round to see Mo sliding in, looking uneasy.

"Mo, how's things?"

"I think I have something we need to talk about, boss."

CHAPTER TWENTY-ONE

Charlie sat in the armchair by the back window. The doors to the garden were still locked and the key had been removed. Beyond the door to this room, in the hallway, the man prowled, occasionally coughing or treading on a loose floorboard.

Yanis sat opposite him, on the sofa. They had tried to hold onto each other when the man had brought them down here, clinging together on that sofa. But the man had jabbed Charlie in the gut with the handle of his knife and snapped at him to move across to this chair. The two of them had been here for hours now, with Yanis occasionally looking across at Charlie as if he knew what to do. With Charlie's upbringing, Yanis always expected him to know what to do. This time, he had no idea.

Charlie needed the toilet. He could smell urine and guessed that Yanis had been unable to hold it in. He resisted looking at his husband's stained jogging bottoms.

"What's he going to do to us?" Yanis whispered.

Charlie's gaze darted to the door and then back to his husband. He shook his head. "I don't know."

"It's him, isn't it?" Yanis's eyes were wide, his face blotchy. "The Ripper."

Charlie felt bile rise in his throat. The Digbeth Ripper. It had seemed so ridiculous when he'd read it in the local paper, so sensationalist. Surely it was just an isolated incident, two men who'd got unlucky.

But now here he was, in his comfortable suburban home, with his handsome husband, facing the man who might have killed one man and come close to killing another.

"It might not be," he whispered.

The door opened.

"Shut the fuck up," the man snapped. "I already told you." Charlie met his eye, refusing to be cowed. The man was medium height, with cropped dark hair and a face you wouldn't look at twice in the street. He had no birthmarks or moles, no scars, nothing to make him stand out. But he'd allowed them to see him.

The man looked between his two captives. "In fact, I'm sick of this." He jerked a thumb in Yanis's direction. "You. Back upstairs."

"I'm sorry," Yanis gulped. "I'll be quiet. Let me stay here."

Yanis would feel safer with Charlie here. Just like Charlie felt safer with Yanis sitting opposite him. With the man out of the room they could almost pretend this was a normal morning, sitting together in companionable silence.

Except Charlie should be at work and Yanis would normally be in his cabin by now. The man had brought them down here while it was still dark. He'd spat at them to keep quiet, waving the knife around. They'd sat through the dawn, staring at the door and wondering what was going to happen.

"No," the man barked. He made a beckoning gesture with his arm and grunted at Yanis. "Follow me."

Yanis looked at Charlie. Charlie stared back.

The man was at the door. He turned back to Yanis. "Now, you fucker!"

Yanis stood, the stain on his joggers unmistakeable. He held his hands in front of it, trying to hide his embarrassment. The man gave him a condescending look. "Animal," he muttered.

Yanis's eyes were on Charlie as he left the room. Charlie stood, desperate to hold onto him, to keep him here. But a sharp glance from the man sent him back to his seat. The man held the knife, sharp and serrated. Charlie didn't like to think what a knife like that might do to a person. And if the reports about the men they'd found in the gay village were true...

The door slammed as Yanis left with the man. *Don't hurt him*, Charlie thought. "Leave him alone," he muttered.

It was his fault. The man must have got in when he'd left the front door open, checking the Christmas lights. Had he been hiding in their bedroom all evening, waiting for one of them to go to bed? Charlie had been downstairs locking up for ten, maybe twenty minutes after Yanis had gone up. Had he been on the bed like that the whole time, a knife at his throat, waiting for Charlie to appear?

Charlie pushed out a shuddering breath. He turned to look out of the window. If he banged on it hard enough, would a neighbour hear? Jaya next door would be alone by now, the kids on their way to school and her husband at work. Sometimes she went into the garden to hang washing out, but

Charlie only ever saw her from the bedroom window. If she wasn't there, banging on the window would be pointless, reckless even. And even if she did hear, how would she know he was calling for help?

He stood slowly and slid to the windows. The doors were locked, Charlie had already checked three times. A cat slunk across the lawn, stalking something Charlie couldn't see.

He jumped at the sound of the door creaking open behind him.

"No point trying to get out," the man said.

Charlie held himself straight, not wanting the man to see how scared he was. "What have you done with him?"

"With who?"

He wasn't going to give this man their names. "With my husband."

The man spat on the carpet. "Don't call him that."

"My husband," Charlie said, defiant. The man took a step towards him.

Charlie shrank back, but he was already against the glass. "Don't hurt him."

"Why should you care? He doesn't care about you."

Charlie frowned. "He does."

A laugh. "You didn't hear what he said about you. Amazing the truth people will tell you, when you've got a knife."

Charlie mustn't let himself believe this man. Yanis had said nothing. Of course he hadn't.

"We've got money," he said. "I can tell you where it is. My car keys..."

The man put his hands on his hips. "You dumb shit," he said. "You haven't got a clue, have you?"

Charlie held his gaze. The man licked his lips, looking

Charlie up and down, then snorted. "Think you're something. With your fancy house and your *husband*." He dug a finger into his nose and pulled it out. He surveyed the snot on the tip of his finger then reached out and wiped it on the wallpaper. Charlie watched, his heart racing.

"No," the man said. "You'll learn."

"What will I learn?"

The man stopped towards him again. "That you're an abomination. That you're sick." He held a finger up. "Wait there."

The man turned and left the room. Charlie felt his muscles relax. He waited, suddenly thirsty.

The door opened again and the man returned with a canvas bag over his shoulder. He wrinkled his nose as he slung it onto the sofa and unzipped it.

"You want to fill it," Charlie said. "Take what you want. Then leave us. Please."

The man sighed. He gazed at Charlie for a moment then struck out with the back of his hand in one sharp movement. Charlie stumbled back into the windows. He put a hand up to his nose, which felt like it was on fire. Broken?

He let the glass take his weight, trying to block out the pain, as the man rummaged in his bag. He'd have done this to Yanis too, when they were out of the room. Is that why Charlie couldn't hear Yanis? Was he unconscious?

Charlie's skin prickled. He put a hand out to steady himself. Mustn't faint. Yanis needed him.

The man was setting something up in the centre of the room. A tripod, with a phone screwed to the top of it. He kept glancing from it to the armchair Charlie had been sitting in. It was aimed at the chair.

Was the man going to kill him, and film it?

"Sit down." The man jerked his head towards the chair. Charlie contemplated refusing, then thought of Yanis. He stumbled to the chair, his hand to his nose.

"Stop fucking around with your bloody nose."

Charlie withdrew his hand. His nose had been broken twice when he was a teenager, and healed twice. He knew how long it would take to heal again.

"Sit."

Charlie slumped onto the chair, fatigue hitting him. He'd been awake all night, adrenaline pumping through his veins.

The chair was soft and comfortable, cradling him. He wished he could curl up and go to sleep, make all this go away.

"Sit straight." The man fiddled with the tripod and checked his phone. The camera was pointing at Charlie.

The man nodded and stood back from the tripod, seemingly happy with his setup. He looked at Charlie.

"Now," he said. "We're going to have a nice chat."

CHAPTER TWENTY-TWO

"What's up?" Zoe asked. She and Mo were in her office. Outside, Connie leaned into her computer screen, looking through social media. Ian and Rhodri were on their way out.

"This might be nothing, boss, but then... it might be something."

"What? And please, I'm not your boss anymore."

"That missing person case I'm working on? Amit Hussain."

"He not turned up yet?"

"I tracked down his boyfriend."

"He's staying with him."

"No. But they were out together on Thursday night. Drinking in the Jackal. Where you found your two."

"So he was drinking in the same pub? I bet hundreds of people drink in there every night."

"It's a hell of a coincidence, Zo. One guy goes missing after spending an evening there, and two others are attacked and dumped round the back."

"But they weren't attacked there. I think I've got an address for one of them. I bet that's where it happened."

"What's your theory?" Mo asked.

"A sexual encounter gone wrong, maybe?"

"So you're not working the hate crime angle."

"Dr Adebayo thinks not. And Ian..."

"What's Ian know about it?"

"He worked the Karlson case. Reckons these are sexually motivated. Not hate crimes at all. And it's all too neat. Surely a homophobe would have hacked at his victims, not neatly castrated them."

"You think a sexually motivated attacker would have been any neater?"

Zoe shook her head. "I really don't know. I'm heading over to the address I've got now. I'm hoping we'll find some clues there."

"I still think we need to consider that Amit might have been taken by the same guy."

"Adam and his friend were attacked two nights before they were dumped, as far as we know. How long's Amit been missing?"

"Since Thursday."

"If it was the same man, he'd have turned up by now." She swallowed. "Be glad he hasn't."

"OK. But if things change..."

"If they do, tell me. Does Frank know you're here?"

"Frank doesn't want me working the case at all."

"Missing adult, probably not a crime at all."

"That's not it. If it was a twenty-year old woman, he'd be all over it."

"But young men just aren't interesting enough. Especially young gay men."

Mo pursed his lips. "That's DI Dawson's take. Not mine."

Zoe hesitated. "D'you want to come with me to interview the neighbour, check out the house?"

"I'm supposed to be doing paperwork for Dawson."

"Where is he right now?"

"Out at a liaison meeting."

"Well, then. What he doesn't know won't hurt him. Come on."

CHAPTER TWENTY-THREE

SANDFORD ROAD WAS a wide street with imposing terraced houses, nothing like the poky terrace in Kings Norton that Zoe had grown up in. Zoe parked her Mini a few doors down from number seventy-six.

"Quiet area," said Mo. "Do we know what Adam does for a living?"

"All I've got is a first name. A surname too, if Connie's hunch is right."

"Connie find this?"

"She checked the electoral register for the two names. Adam and Amelia. He said Amelia was his neighbour. Came up with this."

"She did all that, just with a couple of names?"

"She's going to go far, our DC Williams."

"Yeah."

They got out of the car and made for number seventy-eight. Amelia Dowd's house. Zoe looked at the house next door as she passed.

"Maybe we should knock on the door," said Mo.

Zoe walked up the path to number seventy-six. The windows were dark and there was no sign of movement inside.

She pressed the doorbell and waited. After a few moments she knocked, loudly.

The door to number seventy-eight, just across a low hedge, opened. An elderly woman wearing a pink sweater peered out at them.

"Can I help you?" she asked.

Zoe showed her ID. "We're looking for Adam Hart. Is this his house?"

"Yes. I haven't seen him since Saturday, though."

"Is your name Amelia Dowd?" asked Mo.

The woman put a hand to her chest. "It is. Why?"

"I'm Detective Inspector Finch," Zoe said. "This is Detective Sergeant Uddin. Do you mind if we have a chat?"

The woman took a step back. "Oh, dear Lord." She looked between the detectives. "Is Adam alright?"

"We'd rather talk inside, if you don't mind," Zoe said.

The woman's face was pale. "Of course." She turned into the house.

Zoe and Mo rounded the hedge and entered Amelia's house. The hallway was narrow and dark, but they were soon in a bright living room with photos of what must be children and grandchildren.

The woman still had her hand on her chest. She stared at them, her eyes full of worry.

"Please, tell me if something's happened to Adam. He's such a nice man. A good neighbour. It doesn't bother me that he's gay."

Zoe felt Mo stiffen next to her. She gestured for Amelia

to sit in a well-used armchair and lowered herself to the sofa opposite. Mo sat next to her.

Zoe wanted to reassure her, but she had to get a positive ID first. "Mrs Dowd, do you have any photographs of Adam?"

The woman frowned. "Please, call me Amelia. And no, I'm sorry I don't."

Zoe brought her phone out of her pocket. She'd had the nurses take a photo of Adam in bed, looking much better than in the one taken by PC Burstow. She held it out to Amelia.

"Oh," the woman grasped her necklace. "He's in hospital." She sank into her chair. "At least he's not..." She looked back at Zoe. "He's not, is he? Dead?"

Zoe gave her a reassuring smile. "He's recovering, I'm glad to say. Can you confirm that this is your neighbour, Adam Hart?"

"Yes. Of course it is. Can I visit him?"

"He's lost his memory. But yes, it might help him if you did. I have to warn you though, he was the victim of a violent attack."

Amelia bit her lip. She looked at the photo. "When?"

"We don't know that just yet. He was attacked and left behind a pub in the city centre."

Amelia's eyes widened. "Oh God. The Digbeth Ripper."

Zoe pushed back irritation. "That isn't an official name."

"I saw it in the paper. But the photo... he was unconscious, his eyes were closed. I thought it looked a bit like Adam. But then I thought no, he's a doctor. A surgeon. He'd never be involved in something like that." Amelia looked up. "Who was the other man?"

"Do you know if Adam had a friend or a boyfriend called Mitch?"

Amelia shook her head, her face blank. "Not that I know of. He knows a lot of people, through the hospital. Adam's wonderful with people. It's why he's so good at his job." Her smile turned to a frown. "Wait a minute. You asked if he had a friend called Mitch. Is that the other man, the one who was...?"

"We don't know. Adam has given us three names: his own, yours, and Mitch. That's all we have right now."

"He did have a friend with him on Saturday. Nice young man, very good looking." Amelia flushed.

"What time was this, exactly? Were they both at the house?"

"Yes. Adam came home with him, about five o'clock. I was putting up my lights, around the porch. But there was another man, knocking on the door earlier."

Zoe sat up straighter. "Did he give you his name?"

"No. I'm sorry. He told me he was looking for Adam. I told him to come back later."

"Can you describe this man?"

"He was wearing a hat, a black woolly one. He had a round face, and nice eyes. He was very polite, very friendly."

Zoe felt her stomach clench at the thought of the killer knocking on this woman's door, making small talk with her.

"Did he say why he was looking for Adam?" Mo asked.

"No. Just that he wanted to see him. Do you think that's the man who attacked him?"

"It's a possibility," said Zoe. "We'll need to ask you to help put together an e-fit. That's an image of the man. If you don't mind?"

"Of course not." Amelia stood up. "Which hospital is Adam in?"

"City Hospital," said Zoe. "I'm going to call a colleague. A car will take you to the station, where you can do the e-fit. And then I'll see if I can arrange for you to see Adam."

CHAPTER TWENTY-FOUR

IAN AND RHODRI entered the mortuary beneath City Hospital. Ian had done this plenty of times before, but he wasn't so sure about his colleague. He didn't much appreciate being asked to babysit.

"You wait there, while I get us signed in," he said. Rhodri hung back, rubbing his arms. *Wait till you get in there, son*, thought Ian. *You have no idea what cold is.*

Once he'd registered the two of them, they went through to the post-mortem suite. Dr Adebayo was already inside, working on the body.

Ian and Rhodri pulled on aprons and went through. The temperature dropped. Rhodri shifted from foot to foot and Ian gave him an irritated look.

The doctor looked up. Disappointment crossed her face.

"You." She eyed Ian.

"Dr Adebayo."

"Who's he?"

"DC Rhodri Hughes, Doctor," Rhodri said. "We met before, when you did the autopsy on Irina Hamm."

"Post-mortem. We're not in America. I remember you now. You looked like you were going to puke over the body."

"Sorry, ma'am."

"Do I look like a police officer to you?"

"No." Rhodri's eyes were wide. Ian resisted a snigger.

"Well, don't call me ma'am. Doctor Adebayo is my name." She glared at Ian. "And don't forget it."

"Right," muttered Rhodri, shifting between his feet. Ian was tired of dragging this pimply constable around with him already.

The pathologist paused to screw the top on a jar holding something Ian couldn't identify. "So where's Zoe?"

"She had to go to a second crime scene," he said. "A *potential* second crime scene."

"She going to be sending me more bodies?"

"No. But we will get more forensics. Hopefully."

"Good. Keep Mr Hanson on his toes. I'm nearly done here, but I can show you the pertinent elements."

The body was laid out on the metal table. Naked and pale. His chest had been sewn up, neat stitches in a Y shape. His wrists and ankles had red marks on them, rope burns maybe. The area around his testicles, which had been stained with blood at the crime scene, was pale, two dark wounds the only evidence of what he'd suffered. Ian shivered.

"Right," said Dr Adebayo. "Let's start with his injuries." She took hold of the man's penis and gently pushed it out of the way. "Both testicles have been removed. Incisions made at the base of the testis, with a sharp implement. I've already told you I think this was a craft knife." She pointed. "See how there's some light snagging right there?"

Ian nodded, his lips firmly shut. Rhodri grunted.

Bloody hell, thought Ian, wishing he hadn't brought the constable. *Don't throw up*.

"If he'd used a scalpel, that wouldn't have happened. At least, not at that angle. It's too fine for a Stanley knife, much too precise for a kitchen knife or anything like that. So I'm saying a craft knife. Well looked-after. Clean, sharp."

"Do you have more on the cause of death?"

"My analysis hasn't altered. He bled to death. Horrible way to go, and it shouldn't have happened. Castration is a routine procedure, they do it all the time up there." She jerked her head towards the hospital above their heads. "But this man wasn't able to form the clotting agents necessary to clot his blood at the site of the incision."

"He was a haemophiliac?"

"He had von Willebrand disease. Deficiency of von Willebrand factor in the blood, helps with clotting. It's more common than haemophilia, but less well known, because no Russian tsars had it."

"Can that help us identify him?" Ian asked.

"Like I say, it's not uncommon. But yes, you might want to check the relevant units in the local hospitals. He might have been registered with them. But equally, he might not have known he had it. I can't tell which type of the disease he had. Probably type two or three, given the effects. If it was type three, he'd definitely have been registered with a specialist. Type two, maybe not."

"Type three is the most severe?"

"It is. The blood of an individual with type three von Willebrand's doesn't clot at all. Given the fact that no measures were put in place to prevent blood loss from either of the men, type two might have been enough."

"So the other victim lived because he was able to clot his blood?"

"Not quite how I'd have put it, but yes. He shouldn't have bled so much, though. I've seen the photographs. You'll need to talk to his attending consultant. Find out what they have to say. But if this had been done with the proper anaesthesia, things might not have turned out the way they did."

Ian looked down at the body. "The marks on his wrists and ankles. Was he tied down?"

"It looks like it. The material used was tough and thin. Not rope, but garden twine maybe. Something without much elasticity. The location and angle of the marks would indicate that he was lying down at the time."

Poor guy, thought Ian. What sort of monster tied people down and forcibly castrated them?

"Have you found any distinguishing marks, any tattoos? Anything to help identify him."

Dr Adebayo lifted the man's left arm. On the underside, just below his armpit, was a small tattoo of a bird. "Just this," she said. "He doesn't have any unusual moles, any birthmarks. But someone will remember this tattoo."

"Why have a tattoo there?" Rhodri asked.

"No idea," said the pathologist. "It limits the number of people who will have seen it. But it'll help you." She returned the arm to its place on the slab, her movements gentle.

"Now leave me," she barked. "I'm a busy woman."

CHAPTER TWENTY-FIVE

Zoe and Mo approached Adam Hart's front door for the second time. This time they had a key, provided by the ever helpful Amelia.

"We should call Adi," she said. "Get his team down here as soon as they can."

"I'll do it." Mo took his phone from his pocket.

Zoe slipped on the protective overshoes she kept in her car and a pair of gloves. She turned the key in the lock and pushed the door open, gently.

She peered inside. The hallway was a mirror image of the one next door. In this one, a large mirror brightened the space and made it seem wider.

"Hello?" she called. "Is there anyone here?"

Silence.

"Adam?" It was ridiculous, she knew: Adam was the man in hospital, Amelia had confirmed it, and there were too many coincidences for it not to be the case. But she had to be sure.

She turned to Mo. "Let's wait for the Forensics team. How long?"

"Fifteen minutes."

"That's ages."

She looked back into the house. If the killer had attacked Adam and Mitch here, she'd be able to smell it. All she could smell was bleach. The forensics wouldn't be immediately visible. But they would be there.

It had started to rain. Light drizzle made the street seem bleaker than it had when they arrived.

"Let's wait in the car," said Mo. Zoe nodded.

Amelia's front door opened. "Everything alright out there?"

"Yes, thank you. You just wait inside. The squad car will be here very soon."

She turned to Mo. "I'll go with her. I want to be there when Adam sees her."

"I'll get a lift back with Adi."

"Or the squad car."

Mo nodded. She steered him back to her car and dialled.

After five minutes on hold and two transfers, she finally got through to the trauma ward.

"It's DI Finch, senior investigating officer in the Adam Hart case." She resisted saying *Digbeth Ripper*.

"The who case?"

"Have you had a call from my station? We've got a name for him."

"Hang on a minute."

Zoe rolled her eyes at Mo as she waited.

"Yes, a nurse is talking to him now. We're getting a psychologist down. Do you need to speak to him again?"

"I do," Zoe replied, "And I'm going to bring somebody

with me. Amelia Dowd, his neighbour. It seems they're friends. Talking to her might jog his memory."

"Visiting isn't for another two hours."

"This isn't a social call."

"Wait a moment."

The line went quiet again. Zoe tapped her fingers on the steering wheel. The rain had intensified, splashing off the windscreen.

"That's fine," said the nurse. "We'll let him know to expect the two of you."

"Thank you."

A car pulled up behind them: Adi. Zoe got out and walked to it.

Adi climbed out, smiling at her.

"Not now," she said.

Adi's face fell. "Just being friendly."

"I know. Sorry." She stepped into her protective suit. "But we've got a potential crime scene there and I just want to get it secured."

Adi gave her a mock salute. "No problem, Inspector."

She gritted her teeth and led him to Adam's front door. He pulled on his protective suit when they got there.

"Can't get it wet," he said, catching her questioning look.

Zoe shrugged and put the key in the lock.

"Go on," said Adi. Zoe opened the door, again faced with the narrow hallway.

"Right," said Adi. "Anywhere in particular I should be looking?"

"No idea. This is where one of our two Digbeth victims lives. Adam Hart, currently in City Hospital."

"You asked for his permission to come in?"

"It's a crime scene," she said. "And the neighbour gave me a key."

Adi's mouth twisted. "Very well. But if Lesley doesn't like it, I'm not taking the fall."

"Of course not."

She let him go ahead. He sniffed as he entered, glancing at her in recognition of the bleach smell. He worked his way through the hallway, checking surfaces methodically. Zoe looked on, checking her watch from time to time.

Adi turned back. "Someone's been cleaning up in here. Can you cordon off the end of the path?"

"No problem."

Mo stood outside, on the path. People were gathering behind him, neighbours wondering what was going on. "I've got it," he said, and went back to Zoe's car.

At the end of the hall was a glazed door leading into a long narrow kitchen. Adi beckoned and Zoe followed him through. Sliding doors filled the back wall and the kitchen worktops were made of granite. The floor was covered in smooth tiles, which gleamed. The chlorine smell intensified, pricking Zoe's nostrils.

"Nice place," said Adi. He stood on the threshold, scanning the space. "That table, by the window. The chairs have been pushed out. Three of them."

"The killer and the two victims?" asked Zoe.

"That would be a leap," said Adi. "But you might want to check if your Mr Hart lives alone.

"Right."

"If not, you'll be wanting to know who came visiting."

"His neighbour said he brought a friend home with him on Saturday. And another man was looking for him."

Ad sniffed. "The amount of bleach in this room, there's a

good chance it happened here and the killer cleaned up after. I'll check those chairs for fibres, blood. The table too. It's pine, so it'll have been difficult to clean."

"Thanks, Adi."

She heard a car pull up outside. Mo called through from the doorway.

"I have to go," she told Adi. "Visit the victim."

CHAPTER TWENTY-SIX

The door opened and Amit sat up. He felt weak, the four bags of crisps he'd been given nowhere near enough to fill his groaning stomach.

The man dragged in the table and then two chairs. He placed one of the chairs near Amit, facing the table. He put the other one opposite it.

The man left the room. Amit straightened, his pulse picking up pace. The door was open.

He pushed himself up, his eyes fixed on the door. The man came back through, carrying a shoebox.

"Thought you were going to escape, did you?" The man gave him a lopsided smile and placed the shoebox on the table. He turned and locked the door.

Amit slumped to the floor. He needed water.

"I need to drink," he whispered.

"You can drink after this."

"Now."

The man raised his head, his eyes blazing. There was blood on his t-shirt. "After."

Amit swallowed. His throat felt like it might close up.

"Sit down."

Amit stayed where he was.

The man rounded the table and glared at Amit. He brought an object out from behind his back. Amit stared at it.

A knife. Long, serrated, curved. Amit shrank back from it.

"Like I say, sit down."

Amit heaved himself up. He staggered to the chair and sat in it, his legs weak.

The man was pulling things out of the shoebox. Not a phone this time, or a camera. A green bag, with medical symbols on it. Amit shrank back.

The man rifled through the bag. Amit stared, his breathing shallow. What now?

At last the man brought out a packet. Inside was a syringe. Amit swallowed.

The man looked up at Amit. He smiled. "This is what you need."

Amit blinked back at him. He was going to anaesthetise him, then hurt him. Or he was going to give him something that would kill him.

Amit pushed the chair back and staggered to his feet.

"I've still got more stories to tell you. My sister, the time she got bitten by..."

"I don't give a fuck about your sister." The man lifted the knife. "Now pick that chair up and sit down."

"No."

The man barked out a laugh. "Not like you've got much choice. Just sit the fuck down, will you?" He came at Amit, the knife in his hand.

Amit's knees gave way and he crashed into the chair. The man laughed again.

"You really are a pansy, aren't you?" He grabbed Amit by the front of his t-shirt and heaved him into the chair.

Amit landed heavily on the chair, hitting his hip. His chest filled with heat.

He stood up. "No! You can't do this."

The man's hand landed on his shoulder. "Shut the fuck up!" He pushed him down to the floor.

Amit's feet moved beneath him, not fast enough. The man straddled his chest. He held the knife in one hand and the syringe in the other. It was full.

Amit stared at it.

"Now hold still."

The man plunged the syringe into Amit's shoulder. Amit gritted his teeth, his eyes on the man's face.

CHAPTER TWENTY-SEVEN

ZOE DROVE Amelia to City Hospital in silence. The woman fidgeted with her fingernails on the way, clearly nervous.

"Thank you for doing this," Zoe said. "I'm sure Adam will be pleased to see you."

Amelia nodded, her face tight. Zoe pulled into the car park and parked as close to the entrance as she could, which, it being a hospital car park, meant she was half a mile away.

"When will you need me to do the e-fit?" Amelia asked. "I thought that was first."

"I thought it better for Adam to see you first," Zoe said. "And I need to be with you when he sees you. I want to see if he remembers anything."

"Very well."

Amelia had been so helpful in her own front room, so welcoming. But coming here to sit beside her neighbour's hospital bed, accompanied by a police detective, wouldn't be easy. Zoe wished she knew how to calm the woman's nerves.

"Here we are." They reached the trauma ward and Zoe opened the door. Amelia hesitated.

"I read about what happened to him in the newspaper," she said. "Will he be in pain?" Her face was clouded.

"The doctors will have given him painkillers. If he's not well enough to speak to us, we don't have to stay."

Amelia nodded, her mouth a tight line. Zoe gave her the most reassuring smile she could muster then approached the nurses' desk.

"DI Finch and Amelia Dowd, to see Adam Hart," she said.

"Visiting isn't till..."

"I already agreed this with your colleague. I'm hoping Adam can help with our inquiries into who put him in here."

The nurse was young. Zoe hadn't seen her before. She glanced at Amelia. "Sorry. Yes, it's OK. You know the way?"

"Yes."

Zoe led Amelia to Adam's bed. Amelia followed slowly, her footsteps tight. Adam was sitting up in bed, reading.

Zoe felt herself relax. This wasn't the dazed, barely conscious man she'd seen last time.

She approached the bed, giving him a smile. "Adam, I'm Zoe Finch. We met yesterday."

He stared at her. "You're working on my case."

"That's right. And I've brought you a visitor."

Zoe stood to one side and let Amelia pass her. The woman shuffled towards the bed, blinking. Adam gave her a joyful smile.

"Amelia!"

Amelia's body language shifted. She leaned towards Adam and took his hands in her own. "Adam, I'm so sorry."

"It's not your fault. It's so good to see you."

Amelia nodded, her eyes welling. "Are you in pain? Tell me if you need me to leave."

He shook his head, his face bright. "No. Stay. I only found out my name a few hours ago and now here you are. You can't believe how good it is to see you. How's Archie?"

Amelia turned to Zoe. "Archie's his cat."

Zoe couldn't remember any sign of a cat in the house. But if he remembered his neighbour and his cat, then he might be able to recall who'd attacked him. She wanted to dive in with questions but hung back, watching the two of them.

Amelia's hands were still clasped around Adam's. "Is there anyone you want me to call? Your parents?"

Adam's eyes flickered. "My mum. She lives in Manchester."

"Yes, of course. Will I find her number in the house?"

"In the left hand drawer of the console in the hall. There's a book. Triona Hart."

"That's a nice Irish name."

"She was born there. Did I never tell you?"

Zoe cleared her throat. "I'm afraid no one will be allowed in the house for a while, Adam. My colleagues are there right now, examining it."

His expression dropped. "Of course." He pulled his hands out of Amelia's. "Yes." He tucked his hands beneath the sheets and looked away.

Zoe put a hand on Amelia's shoulder. "Could you go and fetch him a cup of tea, please? I'm sure the nurses will be able to help."

Amelia looked up at her. Realisation crossed her face. "Of course."

Zoe took the seat she'd vacated. "Adam."

"Detective."

"Call me Zoe. Please."

"You want to know if I remember."

"Yes. I hoped that having Amelia here might help."

He nodded. He glanced down at the bedsheets, which were raised by some sort of support, keeping them away from his wounds. "Does she know what happened to me?"

"I'm afraid it's in the local papers. So yes, she does."

He closed his eyes, leaning back. "God."

"How much do you remember?"

"All of it."

"All of it?"

He nodded. "From getting home with Mitch, right through to that man telling us he was going to perform surgery on us." He looked at Zoe. "He held us for over twenty-four hours. He... he tried to talk to us. To 'cure' us."

CHAPTER TWENTY-EIGHT

Zoe looked back at Adam. "What do you mean, cure you?"

"He filmed us. Both of us, at my kitchen table. He talked to us. At us. Some bollocks about wanting to convert us." He looked at Zoe. "To being straight."

"What?"

Adam nodded. "Mitch got angry with him. That's when he got nasty." His face clouded over.

"Mitch? Is that the man you were with?"

"I heard he didn't make it."

"Sorry. Were you close?"

"I just met him. Christ, if he hadn't..."

"Do you know Mitch's surname? Where he lived?"

"Sorry."

"Don't worry." Zoe wondered if Connie would be able to work her magic with the name Mitch.

"I'm sorry to make you relive this, Adam," she said. "But I need to understand what happened to you. We never know which detail can help us find the perpetrator. Can you describe him?"

"He was ordinary."

"In what way?'

"Average height, not fat, not thin. Quite good looking, nothing to make you cross the street. Short dark hair."

"Any scars, birthmarks? What accent did he have?'

"Local, I guess. No distinguishing features that I remember."

"I need you to tell me what happened. Can you start at the beginning?"

Adam's eyes flicked past Zoe. She turned to see Amelia standing behind her with a plastic cup of tea. Adam smiled as Amelia approached and set it on the table next to him.

"I'm interrupting," she said.

Zoe gave her a tight smile. "I'll call for someone to give you a lift home."

Disappointment showed on Amelia's face. "Oh."

"I don't want you hearing this, Amelia," said Adam.

"I do know," the woman said. "I read the papers. "I'm so sorry..."

Zoe stood up. "I need to interview Adam. I'll need to talk to you as well, after, to find out what I can about the man who was asking for him."

Adam frowned. "He was asking for me?"

"Don't you remember?" said Amelia. "I told you there'd been a man at your door. He wanted to know where you were."

"What did he look like?"

Zoe clenched her fist. Witnesses conferring like this made their evidence less reliable.

"He had a hat on. A black woolly hat."

Adam shook his head. "I don't remember a hat."

Zoe put a hand on Amelia's arm. "I'm sorry, but I can't talk to the two of you at once. One of you might think you saw something, when it's really what the other one saw."

"Oh. Yes, of course. I'll get the bus."

"I'll get that squad car to take you home."

"Riding in a police car, Amelia," said Adam. "I'm jealous."

Zoe looked back at him. What sort of man came round from a brutal attack and was able to reassure his elderly neighbour in the middle of giving evidence?

"I didn't ask what you do for a living," she said to him.

He frowned. "I'm an A&E consultant. At the QE. We're not there now."

"We're at City Hospital. It was closest to where we found you."

He nodded. She wasn't sure how much he knew about where, or how, they'd found him.

She looked at Amelia. "Come with me." She turned back to Adam. "Will you be alright for five minutes?"

"I'm not going anywhere." He gave her a half-hearted thumbs-up.

Amelia slid round Zoe and bent over Adam, giving him a kiss on the cheek. Zoe's neighbours were all students, the tenants changing every year. It would be nice to build this kind of relationship with the people you lived around.

"I'll be back soon," the woman whispered. Adam smiled at her.

Zoe led her back the way they'd come, to the main reception. "Do you mind waiting here?"

"No problem." Amelia took a seat and pulled a book from

her handbag. Zoe dialled the station and made the arrangements.

She touched Amelia's arm. "I'll be round to see you again. The car will be here in about twenty minutes. They'll take you to the station to do the e-fit with one of my colleagues, then drop you home."

"You've been very kind."

"And you've been very helpful."

Zoe walked back to the ward. Adam was sitting up in bed, sipping the tea Amelia had brought. Zoe pulled the chair up to his bed.

"I'm sorry about that," she said.

"Is she alright?"

"She's had a shock. But you need to worry about yourself."

He shrugged. "I'm here, aren't I? The lucky one."

"How much do you know about what happened to Mitch?"

"I asked the nurses. Eventually one of them told me he didn't make it."

"I'm sorry."

"I barely knew him. He was only there because of me. If I hadn't taken him home with me..."

"This isn't your fault."

"Still."

"I need you to tell me what you remember about your attacker."

"He was weird."

"Weird how?"

"One minute he was rough, swearing at us, throwing around every homophobic slur he could think of. Believe me, I've heard them all before."

"But then..."

"Then when he started filming, he changed. He was articulate, intelligent even."

"He was filming?"

"He set up a phone. Propped it up with some books."

Zoe would tell Adi to make sure his team dusted any books in the kitchen for fingerprints. "Why did he video you? Was it sexual?"

"Nothing like that. He interviewed us. Tried to influence us."

"To do what?"

"To convert."

"He thought he could convert you to being straight?"

"Yeah. There I am, sitting next to the hottest guy I've ever brought home, and some weirdo's trying to tell me to fancy women." His body dipped. "Oh God, poor Mitch."

"What kind of things did he say to you?"

"He asked us why we thought we were gay. What it was that 'turned' us. Had theories about our mothers, about our childhood. Mitch told him he'd never had a mum. The bastard loved that, thought it was proof of his theory. Then he tried to convince us that we would be better people, more use to society, if we slept with women instead of men. He was articulate, structured. He'd put some thought into it."

"I have to say, you're very calm given what you've been through."

"It's how I cope." He eyed her. "Compartmentalise. Surely you do it too, in your line of work?"

"Tell me everything you can remember about what he looked like. What he wore."

"A black t-shirt, black jeans. His face... it was normal. Sorry, I know I'm not being much help."

"What about his ethnicity?"

"White. British."

"You said he had dark hair?'

"Yes, cropped short."

"Was he wearing a jacket or coat?"

"I remember thinking he must be cold. But there was no sign of one."

"Have you been told where you were found?"

"Out the back of the Jackal. Ironic, as that's where I first saw Mitch." His expression sharpened. "Could he have been watching us? Followed us home?"

"It's a possibility."

Adam shivered.

"Can you remember how he got you from your house to the pub?"

"I can't remember any of that, sorry."

"You were unconscious."

"He'd already..." Adam sucked in a breath.

"I know this is hard."

"Sorry. It's just..."

"Can you describe it in medical terms?" *Compartmentalise*, she thought.

He nodded, closing his eyes. "He made me lie on the table. My own bloody kitchen table. It became an operating table."

Zoe swallowed. "He made you?"

"He told me that if I didn't, he'd do it to Mitch."

"So when your attacker told you to lie on the table, where was Mitch?"

"He was tied to the chair the man had 'interviewed' him in. He hadn't been happy with the answers to his questions."

"How did he restrain him? Mitch was well built."

A sad smile flickered on Adam's lips. "Yeah. Not big, but he clearly worked out. He tried to fight back, but the guy had a knife. Like a hunting knife or something. He threatened him with it, then tied him up. He used garden twine, at least that's what it looked like."

There was so much to unpick here. She'd have to come back to the knife. She'd get a drawing of its likeness along with the e-fit from Adam.

"Once you were on the table," she said. "What did he do?"

"He restrained me."

There had been marks on both men's wrists where they'd been tied up. Garden twine, Adam had said. Adam's fingers went to his own wrists, which he rubbed.

"And then what?" Zoe asked.

"I couldn't see what he was doing. He told me to keep my head down, to lie still. I don't perform that kind of surgery, but I know enough to understand that it was in my interests to do as he said."

Mitch wouldn't have had such knowledge, thought Zoe. Maybe he resisted, which was why he'd come out of it worse.

"But I felt it," Adam continued, his voice catching.

"You felt him cut you?"

A nod.

"Where?"

"My scrotal sac," he said, reverting to medical language. "He..."

"We can come back to this," Zoe said. They had the physical evidence, Adam didn't need to describe it. Not yet.

"No," Adam brought a fist up to his mouth. "You need to know. The pain... it was like nothing I've ever felt. My testicles. He started cutting, and then I passed out."

Zoe watched him for a moment, giving him time to recover his composure. He wiped his eyes then pulled himself up straighter.

"I'm sorry I can't tell you more. I assume he did the same to Mitch?"

"He did. But Mitch bled out."

"Where?"

"Sorry?"

"Did he die in my kitchen?"

"We don't know. That's what my colleagues are—"

Adam looked away. "Sorry. I need..."

Zoe stood up. "I will have to come back," she said. "I have more questions."

Adam nodded. "I know."

"Try to remember anything you can about your attacker."

"I've been thinking of little else." He slumped against the pillows. Zoe turned to see a nurse approach. They seemed to have a sixth sense for this.

"Thanks, Adam," she whispered as she left.

He was silent, his eyes closed and his shoulders trembling.

CHAPTER TWENTY-NINE

Zoe walked out of the hospital, the low sunlight attacking her vision. Images ran through her head of the killer laying Adam out on his kitchen table and attempting to perform surgery.

She looked up at the hospital building. Surgical skills, Adana had said. Was the killer in this building somewhere, carrying out surgery on patients?

He could be working in any of Birmingham's four surgical hospitals, or anywhere in the West Midlands. It was a wide pool, but she was determined to get her hands on a list of surgeons carrying out castrations in the area.

She walked back to her car. There was a parking ticket on it. She'd forgotten to pay. She snatched it off the windscreen and cursed herself.

She checked her watch: four thirty. If she hurried, she might catch Amelia at the station. She could run her home, get that interview out of the way.

She slid into the car and plugged in her phone. As she did so, it rang.

"DI Finch."

"Boss."

"Ian. How was the post-mortem?"

"Rhodri looked like he might pass out at any minute. And Mitch had a blood disorder, his blood didn't clot. That's how he died. But that's not why I'm calling you."

Zoe didn't like her newest team member badmouthing the others. "What can I do for you, Ian?"

"We've got two more victims."

She straightened in her seat. "Bodies?"

"Both alive this time. Both castrated. They're on their way to City Hospital."

Shit. She glanced around the car park. Where did the ambulances enter?

"Where were they found?" she snapped.

"Another bar. They were left inside this time, on the dance floor."

"Where are you?"

"I'm on my way there. The Lizard Bar."

"I know it." Nicholas and Zaf had been there a couple of times. She shuddered, wondering where her son was now.

She eyed the entrance to the car park, considering waiting for the ambulances. But the doctors would have a job to do.

"Ian?"

"Boss."

She swallowed. "Both castrated?"

"That's what I'm told."

She heard voices at the other end of the line.

"Does Adi know?"

"He's still at Adam Hart's house. There's another team coming."

"OK. I'm on my way."

CHAPTER THIRTY

A UNIFORMED CONSTABLE took Zoe's name at the door to the Lizard Bar. She shrugged on her protective suit as she entered, snapping on gloves as the door closed behind her.

The room was larger than she'd expected, brighter. The bar dominated the space, with light reflecting off the optics and the rows of multicoloured glasses above them. Exposed brick lined the walls, giving the bar an industrial feel.

Windows filled two sides of the space, looking out into the gloom of the December evening. A uniformed constable was sticking plastic sheeting up to keep people from looking in. It wouldn't be long before the press arrived.

Beyond the bar was a group of white-suited techs. Zoe approached them, her suit rustling. She knew the forensic scene investigator Adi had sent. "Yala," she said, holding out her hand.

Yala Cook turned and shook it. "I've only been here ten minutes. But it's already clear the injuries weren't sustained here."

"Oh?" Zoe gestured towards the smeared blood on the

floor between them. Markers had been placed at key points and one of Yala's team was kneeling down taking notes.

"There's nowhere near enough blood. What there is will be from when they were disturbed by the paramedics."

"Did you see them before they were taken away?"

"'Fraid not."

"What can you tell so far?"

"Not much. No sign of anything being left by the attacker, apart from the two victims themselves, that is." She pointed at the markers. "They'd been left top to tail."

"Top to tail?"

"Like sardines. One man's feet next to the other man's head."

"Any significance in that?"

"Not that I know of."

Yala's specialism was digital forensics. She'd helped them trace a hack that had been made when Ian Osman's children had been kidnapped. But Zoe knew she was an experienced crime scene tech as well.

"OK," she said. "Tell me if you find anything useful."

Ian was behind the bar, talking to a man in a denim jacket with a trim beard. Zoe approached them.

"Detective Inspector Finch," she said. "You are?"

"Hal Bigham," the man replied. "I run this place."

"Was it you who found them?"

He drew in a slow breath. "Yep. Not going to forget that in a hurry. Is it the Ripper?"

She ignored the question. "Was there any sign of a break-in?"

Hall nodded. "Lock on the back door was busted. I came in via the front, didn't discover it till after..."

Zoe turned to Ian. "Have we had a chance to check the lock?"

"Forensics are working on it."

"Good."

She turned to the bar manager. "Have you got CCTV cameras? Security?'

"We do." He looked proud of himself.

"Do they operate in the daytime?"

"Sure do."

"We'll need you to give us the recordings, please." Something for Connie. She hesitated. "In fact, no. Let's look at them now." She wanted to know if they were looking for the same man, the 'ordinary' looking man with cropped dark hair.

"Be my guest." Hal led Zoe and Ian through a door behind the bar. It was flush to the wall, painted black along with the wall surrounding it.

"You trying to camouflage this, or something?" Ian asked.

"Don't want the punters coming in the office. We try to lock it every time, but you can't be too careful."

"Hmm." Ian glanced at Zoe.

The manager stood aside to let Zoe and Ian pass into a tiny room barely two metres square. It was dominated by a desk and a large but battered office chair. Paperwork covered the surface of the desk but neatly, in a well-ordered grid.

He turned on a computer monitor and flicked through a few screens, then stood up and gestured at the chair. "Be my guest."

Zoe sat down, looking at the screen. It showed four simultaneous camera feeds, covering the four sides of the building.

"Can these be separated out?" she asked. "They aren't exactly high resolution."

"Course they can. But I thought you'd want to check them all first."

"Thanks. What am I looking at?"

He leaned over and rolled the mouse around. "Half an hour ago, when I got here." He stuck his tongue out and clicked the mouse. "I've set it to run backwards for you, so you don't miss anything."

"Thanks." This man was almost too helpful. Zoe clicked the mouse button and watched as the outdoor scene unfolded in reverse. The manager appeared, walking backwards towards the building in the upper right hand image, then went out of shot and appeared in the image below it.

"I park on Pershore Street," he said. "Means I come round the side of the building to get to the front."

She nodded. Ian had his hand on her chair, making her uncomfortable.

The four scenes unfolded in front of them. The bar was on a corner, meaning two cameras looked onto the street. The third gave out onto a courtyard garden and the fourth to an alleyway.

"Back door's below that camera." Hal pointed to the camera over the alleyway. Private, Zoe noted.

They watched the reversed scenes in silence. The picture darkened and lightened as clouds went overhead.

"Stop," Ian said. He pointed to the top left feed, the one over the back of the bar. Zoe leaned in. A man was walking backwards towards the camera, facing away. He wore a dark hat and a heavy coat.

After a few seconds the man disappeared.

"He's just come out of the back door," Hal said. "That's the only way you can go from there."

"Can you rewind fifteen minutes," she asked, "and put it on forwards. I don't like watching it backwards."

"Sure." He leaned over her and clicked the mouse button. The screen went black for a moment and then the same feeds reappeared. In the centre of the top left feed was the man, facing towards the camera but with his head down.

"Take it back a couple more minutes," she said. He did so. The alleyway was empty now. Zoe clutched the edge of the desk as they waited for him to appear.

Sure enough, after a few seconds the man appeared in another of the feeds, on the street side of the bar. He walked out of shot and into the one in the alleyway. The three of them watched as he approached the camera, his head lowered. He wore a dark hat, with no features and no brim. Just like Amelia had described.

He came in and out of shot a few times, moving around immediately below the camera.

"He's breaking in," Hal said. Zoe nodded.

After a couple of minutes he came back into shot, this time walking away from camera. He pushed a trolley.

"That's my keg trolley," Hal said. "Bastard nicked it."

Zoe raised an eyebrow. "You sure?" If it was still here, it might have prints. Although the man in the images was wearing gloves.

"Can't find it," Hal said, shrugging.

The man went round the side of the bar, disappeared for a few moments and then reappeared with the trolley. This time it was laden. He had it tipped backwards and was struggling with the weight of a large sack.

Zoe's mouth dropped open. "Shit."

"He brought them in here like that, cool as you like,"

breathed Ian. Zoe nodded. She eyed Hal; she didn't like having him here.

But it was his recording. And they'd need to release at least some of this to the public.

The man reappeared in the feed again. He still had the trolley, but it was empty. He repeated the exercise, disappearing with an empty trolley and returning with it full. The second victim.

"Have you got CCTV inside the bar?" she asked.

"Sorry. Just motion sensors."

She wondered if the attacker knew this. He'd certainly known when to keep his face obscured, but then it wouldn't be difficult to spot the cameras.

She turned in the chair. "Do you recognise him?" she asked. "Is he a regular here?'

"I can barely see him."

He was right. "We'll have an e-fit to show you in a short while. I'd be grateful if you could check that out."

"No problem." He checked his watch. "What do I do about tonight?"

"You won't be able to open tonight, I'm afraid." She turned back to the screen. The man was leaving now, pushing the trolley and the two empty sacks. He rounded the building and walked off towards the north, his gait confident. A woman passed him, her head down in her phone.

"We should appeal for witnesses," said Ian.

"I'll talk to Lesley," Zoe said. "We need to involve the press." She stood up. "We'll do our best to be out of your way by the morning. But we'll have to talk to your staff, and your neighbours."

"OK." Hal glanced towards the door, no doubt remembering what had been waiting for him when he entered the bar earlier.

"Can you describe what you saw when you came into the bar?" Zoe asked him.

"I already told the sergeant here." Hal nodded towards Ian.

Zoe turned to him. "You get a detailed statement?"

"Yes, boss." Ian pursed his lips.

"Right." She wanted to get out of this cramped office. "OK, I'll confer with Sergeant Osman. We may need to come back to you though, for more details."

"Of course."

She pushed the door open, relieved to be back out in the bar. Yala's team were over by the windows.

"You found something?" Zoe asked.

"It might be nothing."

Zoe approached Yala. One of the techs was on the floor, gathering something into an evidence bag. "What is it?"

"Hair, ma'am. There's skin attached."

"You think one of the victims had a go at their attacker?"

"Or the other way around. We'll run a DNA check, see what we find."

"Good." Zoe looked around the space. Hal was emerging from the office with Ian. "Were the men conscious when you found them?"

"One of them was. He groaned, that's how I found them. I heard him." Hal swallowed. "The other one was out cold. He's still alive, you say?"

"They're both in hospital."

"Let me know how they get on, will you? I feel... responsible."

"It's not your fault."

"I know. But still..."

"I know. I'll get that e-fit sent to Sergeant Osman for you to check over. And let us know if you remember anything else. Anything unusual happening here the last few days, any fights."

"We're not that kind of place."

"I wasn't..."

"We're not. I know people assume things about gay bars, but this place is safe, it's open. Look at all those windows, for God's sake."

"I'm not accusing you of anything," she told him. "My son comes here."

His mouth dropped open. "Really?"

"Really."

But he won't be coming here again in a hurry, she thought.

CHAPTER THIRTY-ONE

Nicholas turned his key in the front door.

"Hello!" he called out. It was just gone ten pm.

Yoda slunk down the stairs and wound herself round his feet. He bent to pick the cat up.

"Hey, Yoda," he muttered. "Where's Mum?"

He hung his coat on its peg and went into the living room. The coffee table held the remains of his mum's breakfast: two coffee mugs. The floor was a mess, tissues everywhere. He looked down at the kitten.

"Did you do this?"

Yoda meowed at him. She had a tiny, high-pitched meow, the cutest thing he'd ever heard. She liked to grab tissues out of the box with her teeth, and strew them around the place.

He raised the cat up in front of his face and frowned at her. "Bad cat." She replied with a silent meow, her mouth opening and closing. He grinned and ruffled the fur on the top of her head with his fingers. He couldn't get annoyed with her when she looked at him like that.

Nicholas dumped the tissues in a wastepaper basket and

carried the kitten into the kitchen. He opened the fridge and surveyed its contents, frowning. Eggs and mushrooms. "An omelette, Yoda." He placed the cat on the floor and grabbed a pan. Zaf had said his mum would cook for them but they'd ended up staying out all evening and all he'd had was a bag of peanuts.

As he broke the eggs into a bowl, he heard the front door open. He tensed as it closed again. Voices came from the hall, talking in low whispers.

He'd been expecting her to be here when he got home. It felt like she was never here. He was damned if he'd call out to her.

"Nicholas?" Zoe's voice got louder. He poked at the eggs in the pan, swishing them around to cover its base.

"There you are." She leaned on the doorframe, smiling at him.

"Here I am."

"Sorry I wasn't here earlier." She approached him, a hand extended. He ducked to avoid it. "You been OK?"

"Fine."

"Good. Carl's with me. He won't stay long."

Nicholas shrugged. He liked Carl. He had an air of trustworthiness, and talked to Nicholas like he was a grown-up and not a kid. But he wasn't in the mood for being nice tonight.

"What you been doing?" Zoe grabbed one of the slices of mushroom from the chopping board and popped it in her mouth, then pulled a face. She swallowed it and opened the cupboard to pull out a pack of Digestives.

"Homework."

"You been in all evening? I'm sorry."

He shrugged again.

She put the pack of biscuits down. He heard the TV go on in the living room: Carl.

"We need to talk," said Zoe.

"I'm tired."

"It's important."

He turned the heat down and faced her. "What?"

She screwed up her mouth and took another Digestive from the pack. "Have you seen the news tonight?"

He shrugged. He hadn't seen the news, but he'd walked past the Lizard less than an hour earlier. He'd seen the white-suited techs, wondered if his mum was in there. He knew what this was about.

Zoe stepped towards him. "There's been another attack, love."

He felt his muscles tense. "Has there?"

"We found them in the Lizard Bar."

He gripped the wooden spoon tighter. "Dead?"

"Not this time. Badly injured though. You know I can't talk about the details."

"How many?"

"Two men. Like last time."

He nodded and turned back to the hob. The eggs were burning.

"Nicholas."

"What?"

"I know you and Zaf went to the Lizard, last weekend."

"Not a crime, is it?"

"No. But I'm worried. I'd prefer it if the two of you stuck to each other's houses for the time being."

He wrinkled his nose.

"Please?'

"Maybe." He turned the heat off and reached up for a plate.

"Where were you tonight?"

"Here. I told you."

Her expression changed, her stance too. She was releasing tension he hadn't noticed she was holding in. "Good," she said.

He grabbed his plate and held it up between them. "I'll leave you two in peace."

"You don't have to."

"It's OK." He brushed past her and went up to his room. He needed to talk to Zaf.

CHAPTER THIRTY-TWO

Amit opened his eyes. His head felt like it was being crushed between two breeze blocks and every muscle in his body yelled at him.

He reached down to feel his legs. They were loose, weak. He'd been waking up dazed and disoriented in his prison, but never like this.

He squeezed his eyes shut again, struggling to focus. It was dark, and he could smell something unfamiliar. He wrinkled his nose. It was an outdoorsy smell, leaves mixed with dog shit.

He yelped and jumped up, stumbling and almost falling again.

He lowered himself to the ground, holding himself as steady as he could. This was all wrong.

He rubbed his eyes and tried to focus. He could see a light, blurry and indistinct. It kept coming and going. He could hear rustling. Trees?

His breathing was shallow, his chest tight. He felt like he

might pass out. *Hold it together*. He had to wake up. To focus.

He took a series of deep breaths, reaching inside himself for strength. His legs felt like blancmange. He'd barely moved for three, four days, he'd lost track. He'd tried pacing around his prison, but it felt so pointless.

He raised an arm and looked towards the light. The man was interviewing him again, filming him. He had a light pointed at his face. Amit thought of a film he'd watched with his brother, some Cold War thing with interrogations deep in a vast Russian building.

But the smell. And the sounds. He was outdoors.

Slowly this time, Amit stood up. He held his hand out in front of him and brushed something soft. He started. Expecting his captor to reveal himself at any time, he took a step forward. The leaves hit his face. He grimaced but carried on walking.

The air around him was cold, attacking his skin like ice. He shivered, pulling his t-shirt tight around him. He didn't have his coat.

He took a few more faltering steps forward, his vision returning. He felt dizzy and his fingers tingled, but his senses were coming back. He heard a screeching sound, a fox maybe. He thought of the dogs he'd heard.

He held himself very still, careful not to lose his balance, and turned his head to look back where he'd come from. There was a tangle of bushes, dark and squat in the gloom. Not a building, like he'd expected.

He turned to face forward. Up ahead was an open space, grass at his feet. He was in a park.

He made an involuntary sound, somewhere between a whimper and a moan.

Should he run? *Could* he run?

There was no sign of the man. The light that had been so blinding was a street light, over a path up ahead.

He stumbled towards it. The light wasn't so bright now, just the dim kind of lamp they used to illuminate parks. He stood beneath it and stared at his own hands. They trembled. His mind still felt woolly.

He had no idea where he was. He couldn't smell the leaves now, or the dog shit. Instead, he could smell grass, and the distant smell of cigarette smoke. He heard that screech again, sharp and guttural. A fox, definitely.

Beyond the grass was a street. Houses. His own street? Amit didn't live near a park. There was that patch of grass near the bus stop, where the man had grabbed him. But this was larger, more open.

He suddenly felt exposed. What if the man was watching him? What if this was some kind of game for him? Or a test?

Amit scanned the buildings opposite, then turned to check the park. It was empty. He fought to steady his breathing. *Don't lose it*. Not now.

He clenched his fists, drawing in all the strength he could. There was a gap in the fence up ahead, leading out of the park. He ran to it, his steps clumsy.

At the street, he stopped and looked up and down. There was a bus stop a hundred yards away. He lifted his wrist. Amazingly he still had his watch. Ten past eleven. What bus route was that stop on? Would there still be buses running?

He patted his pockets: empty.

But still, the bus stop might have a map. He'd be able to work out where he was. He jogged to it, unable to run.

He crashed into the bus stop, letting the metal take his

weight. He scanned the street again, looking for the man. Where was he? Why had he let Amit go?

His arm ached and his skin tingled. He rubbed his bicep, then felt a lump. The site where the man had injected him. What with?

He could deal with that when he got home. For now, he was out of that cell. He was alive. He'd seen the man's face, and yet he'd been allowed to go. To live.

He pulled himself upright and blinked at the sign on the bus stop. It wasn't his route, the number 50. But there was a map, and the roads were familiar. He was less than two miles from home.

He could walk.

Should he run? Was the man watching him? Would he grab him at the last moment?

Amit had no choice. He had to get home. Even though his parents were going to kill him.

He took one last look at the map, committing it to memory, and started to walk.

CHAPTER THIRTY-THREE

MONDAY

Zoe stood at the back of the press room in Lloyd House, Mo next to her.

"Dawson let you out?" she muttered.

"Dawson's right over there." He pointed. Sure enough, DI Dawson sat at the side of the room, an ankle crossed over a leg. As if aware they were talking about him, he looked round and squinted at them. Zoe gave him a nod which he returned.

"How's he treating you?" she asked.

"The usual. God knows what his stint at the Met was supposed to be for, but it hasn't changed him."

"No."

They straightened as Lesley came through a door at the front of the room. She was accompanied by Detective Superintendent David Randle. Zoe tensed at the sight of him. The two senior officers sat down, a press officer Zoe didn't recognise beside them. Facing them, in neat rows for the time being, were members of the press. Zoe spotted Erwin Norris near the front, his bald head reflecting the lights.

"Nationals are here," said Mo. He nodded in the direction of a Daily Mail reporter.

"God knows what they'll make of this."

"I dread to think."

Lesley cleared her throat and took a gulp from a glass of water. "Thank you for coming, everyone. I have a brief statement to read. I'm joined by my colleague Detective Superintendent Randle, Head of Force CID."

Randle straightened his tie, already straight enough, and surveyed the room. His gaze snagged on Zoe and she gave him a polite nod.

"He getting involved?" asked Mo from the corner of his mouth.

"No idea." The last thing they needed was David Randle sticking his nose in.

"Where's Ian?"

"In the office, with Rhodri and Connie. Working over the CCTV, trawling through witness statements."

"You missing out on that?'

Zoe hated being away from her team, away from working the case. But Lesley had insisted. Lesley was the official SIO on this one, but Zoe was the one leading the investigation on the ground.

Lesley picked up a sheet of paper. The press officer nodded and squared her shoulders, looking out at the room.

"Yesterday afternoon," said Lesley, "officers were called out to the Lizard Bar in Digbeth. We found two men with similar injuries to the men found at the Jackal on Sunday."

One of the journalists barked a question but Lesley ignored him.

"The two men are now being treated for their injuries at City Hospital. We're told they are both stable."

"You spoken to either of them yet, Zo?" Mo muttered.

Zoe shook her head. "One of them was in surgery till the early hours. The other's unconscious."

"Poor bastards."

She'd been hearing those words a lot lately.

"I'll be going over there later," she said. "We still don't know who they are."

"No ID."

"Not a scrap."

Lesley eyed Zoe across the heads of the journalists. Zoe clamped her lips shut.

"We are not speculating on a motive, but it is safe to assume that we are looking for the same perpetrator for both crimes. We've asked you here today because we need help identifying three of the victims as well as their attacker."

The press officer, a short Asian woman with long thick hair that almost obscured her face, picked up a remote control. A screen came to life, showing the e-fit that Connie had helped Amelia Dowd piece together the previous evening. Amelia had taken to Connie, commenting to Zoe that she was a lovely wee girl.

The image on the screen was of a man wearing a dark hat with no brim. His eyes were brown and his chin rounded. Otherwise his face was unremarkable.

"This is an e-fit of the attacker," Lesley said. "We've been told he's of medium build and height. But given the nature of the attacks, we can safely say he is muscular, perhaps someone who works out."

"Is he gay?" asked the Daily Mail reporter. Zoe dug her fingernails into her palm.

Lesley eyed the reporter, looked at the e-fit and then back

at the reporter. Zoe bit her lip, imagining what Lesley really wanted to say.

After a moment's hesitation, she replied. "We don't know."

"That was restrained," muttered Zoe. Mo nodded.

"Is this a spate of homophobic hate crimes?" asked another reporter. "Was it a sexual encounter gone wrong?" fired a third.

Lesley raised a hand. "If you don't mind. We also need help identifying these three men. They are three of the victims."

The image switched to photographs of the two men found in the Lizard, plus the mysterious Mitch and a close-up of his tattoo. Zoe had asked Connie if she could use the same technique to track him down as for Adam and Amelia. But with just one name, it was impossible.

"Somebody will know these men," the DCI said. She looked into one of the TV cameras. "Maybe one of them is your family member, or colleague. If you recognise any of them, please call this number."

A phone number came up onscreen below the photos.

"We'll be releasing copies of these images," Lesley said. "And they're already on the West Midlands Police website and Twitter account. Now if you don't mind, we want to get back to the investigation."

"Who's in charge?" called a voice. Zoe shifted in her shoes.

Lesley's eyes flicked across the crowd and held Zoe's gaze for a moment. It had been decided that with this case being sensitive, the identities of the investigating officers wouldn't be revealed.

But Erwin Norris knew Zoe was working the case.

"DCI Clarke and I will be leading the investigation," Randle said, giving his audience a cool look.

Another voice rang out. "Is it true that the lead officer on this has a gay son? Isn't that a bit rash?"

Zoe's eyes widened. Mo put a hand on her arm. She felt the blood rush to her head.

"Like I say," said Randle, "DCI Clarke is SIO on this investigation. She's the person you should be talking to."

Erwin Norris, sitting two rows back from the front table, turned to catch Zoe's eye. She glared back at him. It might not have been him. Any of them could have seen her at either of the crime scenes. But how did they know about Nicholas?

"I'll fucking kill him," she muttered. Mo's grip on her arm tightened.

"Don't," he said. "He's not worth it."

CHAPTER THIRTY-FOUR

Amit huddled against the back wall of the house, convinced he was getting frostbite.

Over the last few days he'd been scared, tired and dazed. That room he'd been kept in had been cold. But nothing like this.

Frost covered his parents' back lawn, plants draped in a layer of white. He could see his breath in front of his face. He was only wearing his jeans and t-shirt.

But he knew that his brother Ruhaan came out here in the mornings to put Sheba, their cat, out. Ruhaan would let him in, and he could avoid his dad.

The back door opened. Amit breathed a sigh of relief, steam rising in front of him. He stood up and jiggled his stiff legs.

He shuffled to the door and peered round. Ruhaan gazed into the garden, muttering to the cat.

"Ruhaan?" Amit whispered. Ruhaan turned to the sound of his voice and gasped.

"Shit, bro. What the hell are you doing out here?"

"I didn't want Dad to see me."

"You been out here the whole time?"

"Course not." Amit lowered his eyes. The wooziness had gone now, replaced by numbing fatigue and shivering limbs. His arm still ached where the man had injected him.

"What happened? How long you been skulking in the back garden?"

Ruhaan closed the door and came outside, glancing back into the utility room beyond. Their mum would be in the kitchen, making Dad's packed lunch.

Ruhaan hesitated a moment, then reached out and grabbed his little brother, clutching him in an awkward hug. Amit slumped into it, letting Ruhaan take his weight. They hadn't hugged since they were in primary school. It felt good.

"Shit man, you're freezing. We need to get you inside."

Amit shook his head. "Not till Dad's gone."

"You can't hide from him forever. Where have you been?"

"Some guy grabbed me."

Ruhaan looked him up and down. "Grabbed you?"

Amit shivered. "At the bus stop. Thursday night." He rubbed his arms. "What day is it?'

"It's Tuesday. You seriously don't remember what day it is?"

Amit looked down. "He drugged me."

"Who, man? Who was this guy?"

"A white guy. He shut me up in his house. He fed me crisps. They weren't Halal."

Ruhaan laughed. "That's the last of your worries, bro." He looked back through the glazed back door. The cat was weaving around their feet, miaowing to be let back in to the warmth of the house.

"I'll get you a coat," Ruhaan said. "Dad'll be gone soon. But you'll have to tell him. Mum too. She's been..." He shook his head.

Amit could imagine how his mum had been. A woman who sat by an open window in December to wait for her son to come home wasn't the sort of woman who would find it easy to deal with him disappearing.

"What you gonna tell them?" Ruhaan asked.

Amit shrugged. "Dunno."

"You got to tell them the truth."

"No way."

"Why not?"

"Cos of why he took me."

"Why? Cos you're Muslim?"

"No." Amit eyed his brother. "Cos I'm gay." The last word was a whisper.

"That's bullshit." Ruhaan's eyes widened. "Oh, fuck."

"What?"

"You don't think it was the Ripper, do you?"

"What? Who's the Ripper?'

"The Digbeth Ripper. Been attacking gay guys." Ruhaan's mouth dropped open. His gaze flicked downwards, to Amit's crotch. "Did he... hurt you?"

"Not really." Amit didn't want to tell him about the injection.

"You gotta go to the police."

"No."

"Did you see the man's face?"

Amit nodded.

Ruhaan put a hand on his shoulder. "Well, then. You gotta tell them."

"I'm not telling anyone."

"You gotta. You could help them catch him."

"I don't want to talk about it."

Ruhaan shook his head. "You always were an idiot." He put a hand on the door handle. The cat butted up against it, impatient. "I'll get you a coat or something. Stay hidden till Dad goes. Go in the shed or something."

"I slept round the back of it. It's locked."

"Shit, man. I'll come get you."

"Thanks, bro."

Ruhaan gave him another hug. He sniffed. "Good to have you back."

CHAPTER THIRTY-FIVE

The team were already waiting when Zoe arrived at the office. Ian sat to one side, Connie and Rhodri together a little way from him. Adi Hanson was there, with Yala and two other techs.

Sitting next to the board, picking at her fingernail, was a woman Zoe didn't recognise. She was short, with dark hair piled on top of her head. She wore the highest heels Zoe had seen outside the red light district.

Zoe frowned at the woman and perched against Rhodri's desk. Rhodri grunted and moved some paperwork out of her way. Lesley would be along shortly, after she'd finished with the press.

The woman gave Zoe a wide smile, her eyes narrow. "You must be DI Finch."

"I am. And you are?"

The woman held out a hand. "Petra McBride."

She had a broad Scottish accent and a firmer handshake than her diminutive stature would suggest. Zoe withdrew her aching hand, wishing she could wring it out. She was still none the wiser.

The door banged open and Lesley hurried in, muttering to herself. She slammed into the chair next to Petra, apparently not puzzled by the woman's presence.

"Those fuckers," she grumbled. "Sorry about that, Zoe."

Zoe shrugged. "Nicholas has never hidden his sexuality. Nor have I."

"Too right. But those bastards in the press think he'll be next."

Zoe recalled her conversations with Nicholas, her concern about him. "No reason he would be, ma'am."

"Even so. If you want extra protection, you tell me."

"Just because my son's gay, I don't think that makes me a target."

"You're SIO on a serial violent crime case. Don't be too blasé."

"I thought you were SIO, ma'am."

Lesley waved a hand. "We all know that's for show."

Zoe had only been SIO once since being promoted, on the case to track down Ian Osman's kids. It would be nice for her second outing to be official. But she understood the politics.

"Will the Super be joining us, ma'am?"

"David? Not on your nelly. He's scarpered off back to Lloyd House."

Good. The man made Zoe uneasy, with her knowledge that Carl and his colleagues in Professional Standards were investigating him.

"Anyway." Lesley looked between Zoe and the newcomer. "You two introduced yourselves?"

"I wouldn't..." began Zoe.

"We have," said the woman.

Zoe was about to disagree when the door opened again. DI Dawson breezed in and leaned against the wall by the door. "Don't mind me."

Zoe bristled. She turned to Lesley, expecting her to send him back to his own caseload.

Lesley sniffed. Clearly not, then.

There was a pause, then Lesley nodded at Zoe, indicating for her to take charge. So she meant what she said about being unofficial SIO.

"OK," said Zoe. She walked to the board. The team had added photos of the four victims, plus what names they had: Adam Hart, and 'Mitch'. The photographs of the latest two victims had question marks above them. They had been taken at the crime scene, before the ambulance had left.

One of the men was overweight, with thick dark hair and a port-wine birthmark on his left temple. In the photo his eyes were open, but only just. The other man was slimmer, with cropped hair and olive skin. His eyes were closed and his mouth hung open.

These were the same photographs they had released to the public. Another humiliation for the latest victims of the so-called Digbeth Ripper.

"We have four victims," Zoe said. She pointed to Adam's photo. "Adam Hart is an A&E constant at the QE."

The Scottish woman raised her hand, twirling a biro between her fingers. "Sorry."

"Yes?" said Zoe. She glanced at Lesley.

"What's the QE?"

"The Queen Elizabeth Hospital."

"Who are you?" Dawson called out from the back. He

had his arms folded across his chest and was giving the woman a surly look.

"Doctor Petra McBride."

"You from City?" asked Rhodri.

Petra smiled at the constable. "No, son. I'm from the University of Dundee."

"I'm sorry," said Zoe. "But what kind of doctor are you? And why are you here?"

"I thought you'd been introduced," said Lesley.

"Not properly," replied Zoe.

Lesley huffed out a laugh. "Then why the fuck didn't you say? This is Dr Petra McBride. She's an expert in criminal psychology. Especially violent and repeat criminals."

"A profiler," said Zoe.

Dr McBride shook her head exaggeratedly. "No, lassie."

"Like in *Mindhunter*?" asked Rhodri. Zoe wished she could start this briefing again, take control over what was supposed to be her meeting.

Petra gave Rhodri an exaggerated eye-roll. "I'm no' from the FBI, if that's what you're thinking, son."

Rhodri shrank back in his seat. Zoe leaned forward.

"Can you tell us what your role is in this case?" she asked.

"No problem." Petra stood up. "DCI Clarke here has invited me to help out, to give you a hand with getting under the skin of your perp."

"We don't say perp in the UK," said Ian.

"Hah! Well I'm not going to say UNSUB, am I?" Petra replied, raising her eyebrows at Rhodri. Zoe had no idea what she was talking about. She had no interest in watching crime on TV, whether true or fictional.

"Getting under his skin," Zoe said. "What does that mean?"

"I've worked with other forces around the country. A couple on the continent. Very nice work, that was." Petra had a far-off look in her eyes. "So my job is to look at the crimes and see what that tells us about the kind of bastard that might have done it." She cocked her head. "That make sense?"

Don't patronise me, thought Zoe. "Perfect sense. So what can you tell us about the *perp* in this crime?"

She heard a commotion at the back of the room. Frank Dawson was leaning back in his chair, wiping his eyes. Was he laughing?

"Uh-uh." Petra wagged a finger at Zoe. "I want you to tell me what you've got first. Don't tell me about any suspects, just gi' me what you can about the crimes."

"We don't have any suspects," Zoe told her.

"Well that makes it easier then."

Hardly, thought Zoe. She turned to her team. Connie was staring at the doctor, her mouth wide. Rhodri was chewing his lip, his eyes dancing. Ian leaned against a wall, looking skeptical.

Zoe took a deep breath and returned to the board. "Right, then. So we have what we believe is two attacks, on two men each time."

"What makes you think that?"

Zoe turned back to Petra. "I spoke to Adam Hart. He was with Mitch, the second victim, when he was attacked. The second pair of victims were dumped together. It seems reasonable to assume—"

That finger was wagging again. "Makes an ass of you an' me. Assumin'. Let's not do it, huh?"

Zoe looked to Lesley as if her boss might pull her out of

the fiasco this briefing was turning into. Surely *assuming* was the woman's stock-in-trade.

Lesley gave Zoe a shrug and nodded for her to continue. She leaned back in her chair and stretched her legs ahead of her, ankles crossed.

"In that case," said Zoe. "Let's focus on what we *do* know. Adam Hart talked to me about what happened in his kitchen. The attacker was waiting when he arrived home with Mitch. The man talked to them first, then when they wouldn't co-operate with him, he threatened Mitch and forced Adam to lie on his kitchen table and be subjected to castration surgery."

"It fits with what Adana said," said Adi. "About the knife. The surgical skills."

"You haven't found this knife, I assume?" said Lesley.

"Sorry."

"So he's a homophobe?" said Connie. "That's his motive."

Petra held her hand up but Zoe ignored it. "Adam told me that the man tried to convince him to convert."

"Convert to what?" asked Ian.

"To being heterosexual."

Dawson spluttered at the back of the room. "I've never heard such crap."

"DI Dawson, don't you think you should be working on your own cases?" said Lesley.

Dawson pushed off the wall. He gave Zoe a resentful look then brought a hanky out of his suit pocket and blew his nose loudly. "The Super asked me to sit in."

Lesley's face twisted. "I was with him in the press conference. He knows that Zoe's in charge on this one."

"He also knows that DI Finch is inexperienced. He wants me to keep an eye on things."

Zoe watched Lesley's reaction. Her boss was torn between ripping one off Dawson, and doing as Randle instructed. But she clearly didn't know what to believe. "I'll talk with him later, Frank. In the meantime, you and your team have a full caseload. If you don't mind..."

"Fair enough." Dawson left the room, throwing Zoe a flash of the eyes as he did so.

There was shuffling as the team settled back down.

"Carry on," said Lesley. She sat upright.

Zoe looked back at the board. "Adam told me the attacker had a knife. He threatened him and Mitch with it, and made them sit across Adam's table from him. He then filmed them having a kind of interview. When they wouldn't go along with his idea that they stop being gay, he threatened Mitch with his knife and tied him to a chair. He made Adam lie on the table. Adam couldn't remember much about what happened after that but he described pain to his genital region that would be consistent with his injuries."

Rhodri winced. "Ouch."

"Let's not think about it too hard," said Ian. Lesley flashed him a look.

"What kind of knife?" asked Adi.

"A hunting knife. Long, serrated. Not the knife that was used for the surgery. I don't suppose you've found anything useful at the Lizard Bar, have you?"

"It's a busy bar. Covered in the prints of hundreds of people, so that's a non-starter. We've examined the lock that was broken. A sharp implement was used, some kind of pin. It's a neat job. And then there's the hair we found."

"What hair?" asked Lesley.

"We found a clump of hair a short distance from where the victims had been dumped. It's gone to the lab for DNA analysis, but I think it's likely the blood type will match one of the victims." Adi pointed to the slimmer of the two unnamed men on the board.

"He was careful," said Petra. "Knew what he was doing."

"What does that tell us?" said Lesley.

"Organised offender. He managed to get into Adam Hart's house without being detected so far as I've been told. He had the means to transport his victims from where he attacked them to where he dumped them. And he took the time to clean up. He knew he wouldn't be disturbed while he held them, questioned them, castrated them and cleaned up afterwards. This guy did his research."

"I still think he's gay," said Ian. "The conversion thing's just a cover."

"Why on earth would you think that?" said Zoe.

"Look. I worked the Karlson case, right? It's the kind of thing men like that do when they're rejected. Frustrated. Sexual mutilation. Humiliate his victims, punish them for saying no. Maybe there's something Adam isn't telling us."

Petra stood up. She'd been waggling her foot while they'd talked, twirling her pen in her hand. Standing, she was a good six inches shorter than Zoe, even with the heels.

She walked to the board, heels tapping on the floor. She turned to Ian.

"No," she said.

Ian looked back at her. "Like I say, I—"

"No. Your experience is with heterosexual male offenders. They like to degrade women. They hate women, despite wanting to have sex with them."

Rhodri was leaning forward in his chair. He nodded, his eyes trained on the doctor.

"This man does not hate women," she continued. "Not as far as we know, and that's not relevant anyway. He does not hate men. He very specifically hates *gay* men." Petra stared Ian down. "He seems to believe that he can turn gay men straight, but when he discovers that he can't, he attempts to desexualise them."

"Like Alan Turing," said Connie.

"What, the Enigma guy?" said Adi.

Petra pointed at Connie, who shrank back. "Yes. Alan Turing was subjected to chemical castration to 'cure' his homosexuality in 1952. This man thinks he can do the same by performing a surgical castration." She walked past Zoe to the board and placed her finger on the e-fit. "And I wouldn't be surprised if he's tried to do it chemically in the past."

"How?" asked Zoe.

Petra shrugged. "You'd have to research the required chemicals. But you can buy anything over the internet these days. If he did that, his victims might not have come forward."

"So how does this help us catch him?"

Petra twisted her finger into the e-fit. "You have this likeness. Lesley tells me you're working on another one with the victim, yes?"

"Yes," said Zoe. She was planning to send Ian and Rhodri to City Hospital to talk to Adam this morning while she and Connie tried to track down Mitch and the other two victims.

"We all know you'll get a lot of responses," Petra said. "This man looks kind of... generic."

"Unfortunately, yes."

"So understanding the kind of person he is will help us narrow it down."

Rhodri leaned in towards Connie. "A profile. I knew it."

Petra gave Rhodri a dirty look. She turned back to Zoe. "I'll need to talk to Adam."

"I'm not sure that's—"

"Of course." Lesley stood up. "You go with DS Osman to the hospital while Zoe and the rest of the team track down the other victims."

"Good," said Petra. "Understanding the victims can help us understand their attacker."

"And knowing who they are can help us find out who their attacker was," added Ian.

If Zoe was going to be SIO she needed to direct this herself, not have Lesley give orders. But Petra entering into the equation had thrown her.

"Alright," she said. "DS Osman will take you to interview Adam. Tell me what you've got afterwards."

CHAPTER THIRTY-SIX

Zoe took Ian to one side while Lesley spoke with Petra. Adi gave her a nod as he led his team out, heading back to the crime scene.

"I want a full report afterwards, OK?" Zoe said to the sergeant. "Tell me what she says, what she asks him."

"Of course."

"Good. I hope she doesn't freak Adam out."

Ian looked at the doctor. "She is kind of... odd."

"Maybe it comes with the territory. Her insights could be useful, but I'm more interested in evidence. Let me know if Adam's able to remember anything more. And see if he can recall Mitch's surname."

"No problem, boss."

"Good."

"Talking about me?" The doctor was behind her. She'd approached very quietly considering the shoes she was wearing, and her diminutive size made her difficult to spot.

"Of course not," she replied. "DS Osman and I were discussing what we need from Adam."

"That's all very formal, isn't it? DS Osman. DI Finch. Blah, blah." Petra eyed Ian. "I'm calling you Ian."

He shrugged. "No reason why not."

"Good. Come on then Ian, let's go see our fella."

Zoe winced as Petra led the DS out of the room. She shook herself out then made for Connie's desk. Connie had one of the feeds from the CCTV at the Lizard on her screen.

"Spot anything useful?" Zoe asked.

"Sorry, boss. Nothing, even when I zoom in as much as I can. We don't see his face at all."

"Fair enough. I need you and Rhodri to get on the phone to the hotline. See if anyone's been in touch with a possible ID for our remaining three victims."

"Yes boss." Connie picked up her phone.

Zoe felt a hand on her shoulder. "A word?" She turned to see Lesley looking at her.

Shit. She'd handled that briefing badly. "Yes, ma'am."

"Let's go into your office."

Zoe followed DCI Clarke to her office at the side of the team room. She closed the door and stood against it as Lesley sat on her desk.

"I'm sorry, ma'am. I could have handled that better. I was taken by—"

"That's not what this is about. You did fine. Not brilliant, but fine."

"Thank you."

"It's the press crap about your son. Are you worried about him?"

Zoe blew out a breath. "He's eighteen, and he goes to the gay village at weekends. But he's sensible. I've told him I'd rather he and Zaf spend time at each other's houses for the time being."

"Zaf his boyfriend?"

Zoe glanced out at the team. "Yes. He's Connie's little brother."

Lesley smiled. "That's nice. Is *she* worried?"

"I imagine her mum is."

"Well let's catch this bastard soon, before any other mothers have to worry. But I don't think you need be too concerned."

"No?"

"Look," said Lesley. "I'm not a university psychologist like some people, but I can see a pattern."

"The victims," Zoe said.

"Yes. They're all in their thirties. Adam's an A&E doctor."

"You think our guy preys on middle class gay men?"

"He hasn't targeted younger men."

"I don't think we're ready to assume anything yet, boss."

"That's the profiler's job, I guess."

"Do you think she can help?"

Lesley chewed on a fingernail then surveyed it. "David Randle thinks so."

"He's been watching the same TV shows as Rhodri."

Lesley straightened and raised an eyebrow. "I know you don't like the man, but..."

"He's our boss."

"He certainly is. And he's brought this profiler in, so we get what we can from her."

Zoe eyed Lesley. She was about to suggest that neither of them thought that would be much, but decided against it.

"Work with her, Zoe." Lesley pushed herself off the desk. "Play nice. Whatever you or I think of the politics, we want to catch this bastard, and you never know what might help."

"She might throw us off the scent."

"She might. I'm relying on you to keep your nostrils wide open, make sure she doesn't. And everything she does give us, I want it backed up with evidence. Forensics, witnesses, whatever. You know the score."

"Will do, ma'am."

"Good."

CHAPTER THIRTY-SEVEN

Ian led the profiler to his car, indicating for her to get in the passenger seat. She slid in, removing her heels as she did so and placing them on the floor next to her feet.

"My wife says she hates wearing heels," he said as he turned the ignition.

"Does she?" replied Petra. He waited for her to say more but she didn't.

They drove to the hospital in silence, Ian feeling more uncomfortable the longer it went on. In the briefing he'd made no secret of his skepticism about what this woman did, and she didn't need to pretend to be friendly now. That was fine by him. He'd focus on the evidence, find out what else Adam had to say about the attack. See if he was any closer to remembering who Mitch was. Who took someone home without knowing their surname?

He had, he remembered. A couple of times, before he'd married Alison. That was women, though. Different.

At the hospital they followed the directions to the trauma ward. Adam's bed had curtains drawn around it.

"You can't go in just yet," a nurse told them. "He's got the sister with him."

"Has his condition changed?" asked Ian.

The nurse, a pretty young woman in her twenties, shook her head. "Just having his dressings replaced. You wait over there." She pointed to a couple of chairs near the nurses' station. "I'll get you a cuppa."

"Thanks." He gave her a smile. Petra was watching the curtains, her eyes narrow. What was she looking for?

They took the two seats, Ian surreptitiously drawing his away from the doctor's as he sat down. The nurse returned with two cups of tea.

"Ah, no thanks," said Petra.

"Oh," said the nurse.

Ian leaned forward. "It's OK. I'll take them both."

The nurse smiled at him and placed one of the cups at his feet. He sipped at the other, his eyes roaming the ward.

Ian liked to people-watch. He reckoned it made him a good copper. Always alert, always knowing what was going on around him. What might happen next. The woman at his side was like a weight pulling on him, an unwelcome presence. She still hadn't spoken to him since the conversation about heels.

At last the curtains were drawn aside. Ian stood up, downing the last of the second cup. He took both empty cups back to the nurse's station.

"Thanks," he said to the nurse. "Just what I needed." He gave her a warm smile which she returned, her eyes sparkling.

"We just need you to wait a minute, and then I'm sure you can go right in," she said. "Sorry."

"It's fine." He stood by the desk, watching Adam. He was tall and slim, with short mousy hair and high cheekbones. He wore a pair of blue pyjamas that looked like they came from the 1950s: collared, flannel. Petra was still in her chair, also watching the man in bed. He leaned his head back against his pillows, his forehead creased. He looked as if he was in pain.

"Does it hurt, having his dressings changed?" Ian asked the nurse.

"It can do, yes. Sometimes it... tugs."

Ian shuddered. He could barely imagine what it would be like to go through what Adam Hart had. There were some sick fucks out there.

He swallowed the bile that had risen to his throat and took a deep breath.

"You can go in there now," the nurse said. "Be gentle with him, yes?"

"We will." Ian motioned for Petra to follow as he walked to Adam's bedside, his ID held aloft.

"I'm Detective Sergeant Osman," he said. "This is Doctor McBride. We work with DI Finch."

Adam nodded. He had dark circles under his eyes and his cheeks were blotchy. "More questions."

"Sorry." Ian gestured to the chair next to the bed. "Mind if we sit?"

Petra cleared her throat. Ian looked at her then stood back for her to sit down. The nurse pulled a chair over from another bed and he took that, irritated to be further from Adam than the profiler was.

"Call me Petra," she said to Adam.

"Are you from the hospital?" he asked.

"No. I'm a psychologist. It's my job to understand the

kind of person that would do this to you." She held Adam's gaze, her hands clasped together on her lap.

"OK."

"Good. Now I need you to tell me what he was doing when you first saw him. Where was he?"

"He was in my kitchen. Sitting at the table."

"How was he sitting? Did he look calm, impatient, agitated?"

"Calm. He was waiting for us. Me."

"Both of you?"

"I don't think he was expecting Mitch to be there. To be honest, I wasn't expecting Mitch to be there." Adam closed his eyes for a moment then opened them, looking away.

Ian shifted his chair closer. "Have you been able to remember anything else that might help us identify Mitch?"

"Sorry." Adam looked up at the ceiling. "He told me his name. That's all." He turned to Ian. "You think I'm easy."

"Why would I think that?"

"Picking up some guy when I didn't even know his full name." Adam swallowed. "I've never done that before." He grimaced. "I certainly won't be doing it again."

Petra put a hand on Adam's wrist. He tensed but didn't pull away. "Let's go back to your attacker, Adam. Tell me how he behaved towards you."

"He cut my balls off and killed my friend. That's how he *behaved* towards me."

"I need you to be more specific. You told the Inspector that he asked you questions. That he tried to convert you."

Adam looked at her. "He did. Thought he could convince the two of us to turn straight." He grunted.

"What kind of questions did he ask? What kind of arguments did he make?"

"I can't remember the detail. It felt unreal, like I wasn't there at all. Like I was going to walk into my house again and he wouldn't be there. But I can tell you this. He was articulate, he was coherent. He'd thought about what he was going to say to us. It was bullshit, all of it, but it kind of made sense in its own sick way."

"And when he cut you, how was he? Did he seem angry, or calm? Did you provoke him, or did it come out of the blue?"

"Provoke him?"

"I don't mean it was your fault. I just..."

"I provoked him by being a gay man. I provoked him by bringing another man back to my house. I provoked him by refusing to stop being who I am. So yes, I guess you could say I provoked him."

"I'm sorry, Adam. This is all to help us—"

Adam shook her hand off his and folded his arms. "I want you to leave."

"I'm sorry, Adam," said Ian. "We just need to know more about what happened."

Adam eyed him, his expression hard. "Go." He looked past them toward the nurses. "Nurse!"

The pretty young nurse looked up. She frowned and rounded the desk.

"Tell these people to leave, please. I don't want to talk to them again."

The nurse cocked her head at Ian. "You heard him."

Petra stared at Adam, saying nothing. Ian stood up, wishing he hadn't brought her here.

"Come on," he muttered at her. She gazed at Adam for a moment more then turned to follow him.

He stomped through the corridors, listening to the sound

of her heels clipping along behind him. At last they got to the car and he threw himself into the driver's seat. She opened the passenger door, her movements smooth.

"Well that was a fuck-up," he snapped.

CHAPTER THIRTY-EIGHT

Zoe pulled on her coat. At this time of year she replaced her customary leather jacket with a secondhand sheepskin coat she'd bought in the rag market. It wasn't the most stylish of items, and it smelt when it got wet, but it was warm.

"I'm going to see Amelia Dowd," she said. "Keep me posted if there's any developments."

Rhodri nodded, his eyes on his screen. Connie was on the phone. She raised her hand. Zoe resisted a laugh: this wasn't school.

She waited for Connie to finish. "What's up?"

"We've got a name for Mitch, boss."

Zoe stepped towards the constable's desk. "At bloody last. Who is he?"

"Mitch Ibsen. Twenty-nine years old, lives in the gay village."

"Where?"

Connie checked her notepad. "Pershore Street."

"That's only a couple of streets away from where he was dumped."

"Maybe there's a connection," said Rhodri.

"I doubt it," Zoe said. "The target was Adam. He wasn't even supposed to have Mitch with him."

"Maybe the killer was after Mitch. Followed them back, like," said Rhodri.

"He knocked on Amelia's door," said Connie. "He was asking for Adam."

"You're right," said Zoe. "Mitch was just unlucky. Even so, we need to find out what we can about him. Who called in the ID?"

"His former partner," said Connie. "Jason Hinchcliffe."

"An ex?" Zoe asked.

"That's what they told me."

"Hmm. I should go talk to him."

"You think his ex attacked him?" said Rhodri.

"No. The attacker tried to convert them, remember. His ex wouldn't have done that."

"Unless it was a cover."

"Adam would have told us if Mitch had known the attacker."

"So why d'you want to talk to him, boss?" asked Connie.

"Just in case. He might know if anyone's got it in for Mitch. It has to be followed up."

"You want me to go, boss?" asked Rhodri.

"No, I'll do it. Find Hinchcliffe's address for me, Connie."

"Already got it. Sherlock Street."

"Right round the corner from Mitch. While I'm doing that, you two go and see Amelia for me. Petra reckons the killer had the means to get them from Adam's house to the dump site, and she's right. He'll have to have a car. Amelia might have seen it."

"Neighbourhood watch, boss," said Rhodri. "Busybodies."

"Amelia Dowd didn't strike me as the busybody type," said Zoe. "But she might have seen something."

"We got the reports back from Uniform," Connie said. "They talked to all the neighbours, no one saw anything unusual."

Zoe tapped her chin. "He must have moved them when it was dark. Amelia's his friend. It's worth another conversation with her." She looked at Connie. "She liked you Connie, and I think she'll take to Rhodri. Get her chatting. See what you can find out about what was going on round that street on Saturday. Not just after the attack, but before. He might have been hanging around."

"Right, boss." Rhodri jumped up from his chair.

"What about the other two victims?" Connie asked. "I thought you wanted us to prioritise that."

"You don't need to be at your desks for that. Give the hotline manager your mobile number. Make sure she calls if they get anything concrete. Concrete, though. I know how these phone-ins can get."

"I'll do my best, boss," said Connie.

"I'm sure you will. I'll see you back here later."

CHAPTER THIRTY-NINE

Zoe left the police station car park and drove her Mini towards the city centre. Her route would take her near the Lizard. She could drop in and find out if there was any news from Forensics.

As she reached the inner ring road her phone rang. She hit the hands-free button.

"DI Finch."

"Zo."

"Mo. What can I do for you?"

'That's very formal."

"Sorry. It's turning into one of those days. What's up?"

"Just thought I'd check in after what happened in the press conference."

She waved a hand, pulling away from traffic lights. "I've got thicker skin than that."

"Still. Are you worried about Nicholas?"

"Lesley's been on at me about this too."

"Lesley wasn't there when he was born."

"True." Nicholas's father, Inspector Jim McManus, had wanted nothing to do with her or their son at the time. Mo had been at the birth instead, confusing the midwives when Nicholas had turned out to have pale skin and blond hair. "Don't worry, Mo," she said. "He's a sensible kid."

"Not a kid anymore."

"No." She didn't like to remind herself that her son was growing up and would be leaving home soon.

She indicated to turn off the Bristol Road and made for the gay village. "Anyway. Is there anything more specific?"

"You remember that kid who went missing? Amit Hussain?"

"Yes."

"He's come home."

"Oh, that is good news."

"I'm on my way there now."

"Good. What happened?"

"That's just it. I'm not sure."

"Surely he buggered off to a mate's house for a few nights?"

"I spoke to a few of his mates. None of them knew where he was. Nor the guy who was the closest thing he had to a boyfriend."

"Have you spoken to him? To Amit?"

"Not yet. I'm on my way there now. Hopefully it'll all become clear."

"Good. Glad he's home safe and sound, at least."

"Where are you?"

"I'm on my way to see Mitch Ibsen's ex," she said.

"You got a surname mow?"

"We have. His ex rang in to the hotline."

"You think he might have something to do with it?"

"Not really. But I want to get any background I can. We've got no leads in this case, Mo. Barely any forensics. This bastard is clever, and I have a feeling he's laughing at us."

"You know he's a homophobe."

"That would include a fair chunk of the population."

"Not to this extent."

"No," she said. "But it doesn't help." She pulled up outside the bar and turned the car off. "Did Dawson tell you we've had a profiler brought in?"

"A profiler?"

"That's not what she calls herself," Zoe said. She stopped behind a van that was unloading, tapping her fingers on the steering wheel. "A psychologist, with expertise in... I can't remember what she's got expertise in. Randle's idea, apparently. I've been told to play nice."

"That'll be fun."

"You bet. Look, I'm at the Lizard. Gotta go. Thanks for the call."

"Sure."

She slid out of the car and walked into the bar. Hal Bigham was behind the bar, scrubbing its surface. He looked up.

"Bloody fingerprint dust," he said. "It stains aluminium."

"Sorry," she said. "You getting the place back to yourself now?"

Adi appeared through a door behind him. "Zoe!"

Zoe smiled. "Hey, Adi."

"To what do we owe the pleasure?"

"Thought I'd come and see if you'd found anything else useful."

"You could have called." Adi held his fingers to his ear in a phone gesture and waggled it.

"I'm on my way to do an interview. You're on the way."

"Ah. Nothing special then."

Zoe glanced at Hal. She didn't like Adi flirting with her in front of witnesses. She jerked her head in the direction of the tables and left Hal to his cleaning.

They sat at a table in the window. The plastic sheeting had been removed and a low sun shone in, picking out the fingerprint dust on the shiny surfaces.

"He cleaned up well," said Adi. "There's nothing else."

"So why did he leave behind that hair?"

"Maybe that happened after he cleaned up." Adi shrugged.

"Any sign of cleaning materials on it?"

"Nothing. But we got the DNA analysis back."

"Go on."

"It matches the second victim."

"Damn."

"My hypothesis is that the attacker grabbed him by the hair when he was pulling him out of that sack."

"Have you found any remnants of the sack itself?"

"Sorry."

"Shit. Who is this guy, a professional cleaner?"

"It fits with what Adana said about the surgical skills, though. If you were a surgeon, you'd have pretty stringent standards."

"A surgeon."

"He knew what he was doing with a knife," said Adi.

"I know." She leaned back and shook her head. "OK. I'll talk to HR at the local hospitals. Show them the e-fit. Maybe..."

"Worth a shot," he said.

"And with Adam being a consultant, that might fit with our guy having a grudge against him. Yes, it makes sense."

She stood up. "Thanks, Adi."

He beamed at her. "My pleasure, as ever."

CHAPTER FORTY

"Hello, dear." Amelia Dowd gave Connie a smile and stood back to let her pass. Rhodri slunk behind, muttering a hello.

"Do come in," Amelia said. "I've just made jam tarts."

"Sounds fab," said Rhodri. Connie gave him a hard look. He shrugged. "She offered," he whispered.

Amelia followed them into the living room, patting Rhodri on the back. "Strapping young man like you needs his calories. I'll be right back."

"We can't stay long," Connie called out as Amelia left them alone. She scowled at Rhodri who stuck his tongue out at her and dropped into an armchair.

Connie took the high-backed chair opposite him, her feet tucked beneath her. Rhodri shuffled in his seat, making himself comfortable, and she scowled at him again.

The room was bright and homely. Family photographs lined the walls along with a few prints. A bookcase held library books, Danielle Steele mainly, and a few DVDs. Connie fidgeted as she waited.

Amelia came back with a tray of tea and jam tarts. She gestured towards a nest of tables beside Rhodri and he stood to pull the two smaller tables out.

"Thank you, dear," Amelia said. She set the tray down on the larger of the two tables and put the plates on the other.

She turned to Connie. "Tea?"

"Yes, please." It didn't hurt to be polite. Connie had learned from how Mo fell in with the behaviour of witnesses, putting them at their ease by accepting hospitality.

Rhodri sat forward to take his cup and Connie smiled her thanks at Amelia as she put hers on a side table. Amelia held out the plate and Rhodri took a tart. Connie shook her head.

"Got to watch my weight," she said.

"Surely not, lovely young thing like you."

Connie felt herself blushing. Rhodri was grinning into his tea. *Shut up*, she thought.

"Thank you for letting us come and see you again," she said as Amelia finally sat down with her own cup, which rattled against the saucer.

"Only too happy to be of help," Amelia said. "How is Adam today?"

"I haven't seen him myself," Connie replied. "But our colleague Sergeant Osman has gone to interview him."

Amelia frowned. "Poor Adam. Just when his life was getting back to normal."

Rhodri sat up. "Back to normal?"

Amelia turned to him. "He had a horrible break-up. And there was that business at the hospital."

"What kind of business?" Connie asked.

"I'm not sure. Adam was moved to A&E, that's all he told me. But they argued about it. Bob – that was his boyfriend until two months ago, lovely man but not all that patient – he got annoyed with Adam. Said he was being a doormat. I heard them through the wall." She glanced at the wall between this room and the hallway. Her brow furrowed. "So many arguments."

Connie eyed Rhodri. "They fell out?"

Amelia nodded. "Bob left, in the end. Adam was heart-broken. But it certainly got quieter around here."

"Did the arguments ever get violent?" asked Rhodri.

"Not that I know of. Loud, but not violent. Neither of them was that kind of man."

Connie gulped down the rest of her tea. "We'd like to ask you about what happened on Saturday."

"Of course."

"You've already told us about the man who came looking for Adam. We've got the e-fit."

"I know, I saw it on the television. You did a very good job."

"Did you see if he had a vehicle?" Rhodri asked.

Amelia frowned for a moment, thinking. "I don't remember."

"Do you remember seeing any unusual vehicles coming or going that day? Anyone loading or unloading?"

"I was in my back garden after Adam got home, dear. I always put Christmas lights around my shed. I'm sorry, I wouldn't have seen anything. Have you asked the other neighbours?"

"We have," said Connie. "They didn't see anything either. You sure you didn't hear anything in the night, perhaps?"

Amelia gazed towards the window. "Sorry, no. I sleep at the back. And I take my hearing aids out." She blinked, her eyes wet. "It'd take a hurricane to get through to me."

Connie looked at Rhodri. He shrugged.

Rhodri pointed to the plate. "Can I...?"

"Of course, help yourself."

Rhodri took another tart. He reminded Connie of her brother Zaf, always eating.

"Well, if you do remember anything..." Connie said.

Amelia become more alert. "Hang on a moment. There was something."

Rhodri gulped down a mouthful of pastry. "What?"

"I went to the bathroom in the night. My bladder, it wakes me up."

"And?" Connie asked.

"I heard someone driving away. Doors slamming." She looked at Connie for reassurance. "It must have been quite loud, if I heard it without my hearing aids in, mustn't it?"

Connie nodded. If the attacker had left in the night, and not been quiet about it, then someone would have seen him, even at one in the morning.

"Can you remember what time that was?" Connie asked.

"It was ten past one. I'm like clockwork. I checked the clock, and got a little bit annoyed with myself. I wish I could sleep through, but when you get to my age..."

"Thanks, that's helpful." Connie stood and jerked her head at Rhodri.

He brushed crumbs off his shirt and stood up. "Thanks, Mrs Dowd."

"Do call me Amelia, please."

He muttered something unintelligible through his mouthful of jam tart. Sometimes Connie wished he'd think about the impression he made.

"You've been very helpful," said Connie. "If you think of anything else, please get in touch."

"Oh yes." Amelia looked toward the bookcase. "I have your Inspector's card. I'll let you know if anything else comes to mind."

"Thanks."

Connie stood up and eyed Rhodri, who was still brushing himself down. She resisted the urge to grab him by the arm and drag him out of the house.

As they reached the door, Connie remembered something. She turned back to Amelia.

"You said Adam was moved between departments."

"Yes. I think they had a restructure, or something like that."

"Do you know where he was working before?"

"On– something. What do they call it? Cancer care?"

"Oncology."

"Was he a consultant there?"

"I think so. I don't know all the details."

Connie had no idea if it was common for consultants to move between departments, but she doubted it. Had he moved, or was he pushed out?

"Thanks, Amelia. You've been very helpful."

"Can I tell Adam you were here? I'm visiting him later."

"Of course you can." Connie knew that the boss would want to talk to him again.

CHAPTER FORTY-ONE

Jason Hinchcliffe's flat was a two minute drive from the Lizard, in a squat block on Sherlock Street. She struggled to find a parking spot and had to leave her car on double yellows.

He blinked at her as he opened the door. "Yeah?"

"Jason Hinchcliffe?"

"Yeah." He was in his late twenties with cropped blond hair and a ruddy face. He wore a dressing gown with a faded stain down the front and his feet were bare. He yawned.

"Hope I didn't wake you. DI Finch, West Midlands Police. You called us about Mitch."

"Oh. Yeah." Jason coughed and turned to walk into the flat. She followed. A dim hallway led into a combined living room and kitchen, takeaway boxes piled up on the counters and a few empty beer cans on a low table next to the TV. It reminded Zoe of her own house.

He sat on a threadbare sofa and scratched his leg, tugging his dressing gown closed just before Zoe got an eyeful of something she'd rather not.

"'S a fucking shame," he said.

"You could say that." She pulled out her phone and found the photos of Mitch and of the tattoo. "Can you confirm that this is definitely the man you know?"

He leaned forward, squinting. "That's him, alright." He sat back, the dressing gown pulling open again. Zoe kept her eyes on his face.

"When did you last see him?"

"Properly?"

"What do you mean by *properly*?"

"Well, I run into him all the time. We hang out in the same bars. Bloody awkward it was after we broke up, but you get used to it."

"So when did you last run into him?"

Jason scratched his nose. "Last Wednesday, I reckon. Early hours. I was leaving the Jackal and he was walking past with a group."

"A group of people?"

"No, a pop group." He ignored the look she gave him, picking his nose. "Friends I guess. I'd seen him with them a few times."

"What did Mitch do?"

"Do?"

"For a living."

"Oh, that. He worked at the job centre."

"Which one?"

A shrug. "Beats me."

"Do you know if Mitch had fallen out with anyone? If there was anyone who might want to hurt him?"

"Surely it's the Ripper that killed him? He's just a random homophobe."

Zoe wondered if there was such a thing as a random

homophobe. “We don’t know who killed Mitch yet, but we have to consider all possibilities.”

“They said he was with some other guy, on the TV. A doctor.”

“Adam Hart. Did you know him?”

“Nah. Too fancy for me. Too fancy for Mitch, too.”

“Adam told us he’d just met Mitch, on the day of the attack.”

“Figures. Surely you should be talking to this Adam guy, not me?”

“We are.”

“Cool.”

Zoe eyed him. He didn’t seem too bothered about the fact his ex-boyfriend had been brutally murdered.

“How long ago did you and Mitch split up?”

“About six months.” He looked up, calculating. “Yeah. May, so what, seven months? Doesn’t feel that long. Feels longer too, if you know what I mean.”

“Can I ask why you broke up?”

“We were never really a thing. Not serious, like. We just... drifted apart, I guess. No big drama. I didn’t kill him for some kind of revenge, if that’s what you’re getting at.”

“I’m not getting at anything.”

“Good.” He shifted in his seat and dragged the dressing gown closed again.

“I’d like to show you the e-fit of the attacker,” she said. “You live locally, you might have seen him.”

“OK.”

She flicked through the photos.

“Stop.”

Her finger hovered over the screen. “Sorry?”

“Go back one.”

She went back to the photo of the slimmer of the two victims from the Lizard.

"Shit. That's Yanis." Hinchcliffe had paled.

"You know him?"

"Yeah. I—"

She watched his face. "Go on."

"I had a thing with him. Nothing serious. He broke it off, said he was getting married."

"Do you know his full name? Where he lives?"

He shook his head. "He kept 'imself to 'imself. Sorry."

Zoe sighed. "You never found out his surname?"

"Nah. Sorry."

"OK." She let out a long breath. Hinchcliffe was leaning towards her, peering at her phone. She flicked to the photo of the other man from the same scene.

"Do you know this man?"

"Never seen him."

"But you're sure this other man is Yanis?'

"Yeah. I'm sure." He straightened. "You're going to be thinking it was me, aren't you? What with me knowing them both an' all."

"I'm not thinking anything right now. Where did you meet him?"

"Jackal. He used to drink there."

"How long ago was this?"

"Two years, bit more. Haven't seen him since."

"D'you have a phone number for him?"

"Deleted it."

"I'd be grateful if you'd let me have your phone, for evidence."

"Why? I bloody need it."

"We can extract Yanis's number from it."

"But I told you I deleted it."

"That doesn't matter." Yala might be able to extract a deleted number.

His eyes bulged. "You can do that?" He sniffed and dragged a hand across his nose. "I haven't got that phone anymore."

Shit.

"You sure about that? We'd only need to borrow it."

"Yeah. Contract expired earlier this year. Got meself a newer model."

"You sure you don't remember anything else about him? We need to identify him, so we can tell his family."

"Yeah. Poor bastard." Mitch frowned. "That could've been me."

Zoe curled her lip. Until five minutes ago, she'd thought the four men were just unfortunate victims of a hate criminal. But now she wasn't so sure.

CHAPTER FORTY-TWO

ZOE'S PHONE rang as she walked back to her car: Ian.

"Ian," she said. "How did you get on with Adam?"

"Not good. He took against Petra."

Shit. "What did she do?"

"She was a bit too direct with him, let's say. Are all Scots like that?"

"I doubt it. Did you get any information about the attacker out of him?"

"No. Nor about Mitch."

"Don't worry about that. Mitch's ex-boyfriend phoned the hotline. I've just been talking to him."

"And?"

"He recognised one of the other victims too. Said his name was Yanis."

"Figures. I thought he was Arabic, but Greek works."

"I don't think we should jump to conclusions," Zoe said.

"If it looks like a duck and quacks like a duck," Ian replied.

Zoe held the phone out ahead of her and stared at it. Had he really just said that?

Now wasn't the time. "Are you still at the hospital?" she asked him.

"I'm back at the station. But you need to know there's a public meeting planned in the gay village."

"When? Where?"

"The Jackal. In about half an hour."

She checked her watch. It was 3.30pm. "Already?"

"People are worried. They've set this up themselves, I think the landlord was involved. But you might want to be there," Ian said.

"Lesley too."

"She's at Lloyd House. Meeting with the Super."

"OK. Leave a message there. Randle's assistant, I guess. And get yourself over to the Jackal. I'm not doing this on my own."

"Fine. You want me to bring the good doctor with me?"

Zoe was about to say no but then reconsidered. *Play nice,* Lesley had said. "Go on then."

"*Great.*" He hung up.

She sat in her car for a few moments, thinking. Then she picked up her phone.

"Boss?"

"Rhodri," she said. "How did you get on with Amelia?"

"She bakes lovely jam tarts, boss."

Zoe heard Connie shouting at Rhodri in the background. She allowed herself a chuckle.

"Did she spot anything unusual on the night of the murder, was what I really wanted to know. But I'm glad you've been looking after your stomach."

"Sorry."

"Just tell me what she said."

"She said she heard something. Ten past one in the morning." Connie had grabbed the phone. Her voice was shrill.

"Who's driving?'

"Rhod pulled over."

"Good." Rhodri's car didn't have hands-free. "What did she hear?"

"Slamming doors."

"Did she see anything?"

"No. She went back to bed."

"OK. Get Rhodri to check statements from neighbours again. Go back to them, find out if anyone saw anything."

"No problem. There was something at the hospital, too."

"Go on."

"Where Adam works. He got moved, from Oncology to A&E. Didn't Dr Adebayo say something about Oncology departments sometimes doing castrations?"

"You think a former colleague did it?"

"The surgical skills, boss. She said it was a neat job. Professional."

"OK. You go back to the office, get onto HR at the QE. Find out what you can about Adam's old job, why he left. It'll be a dead end I'm sure, but it doesn't hurt to ask."

"No problem."

"That everything, boss?" Rhodri was back on the line.

"Call City Hospital again. See if they've got an ID for the last two victims. One of them is called Yanis."

"Yanis?"

"Yes."

"Which one?"

She sighed. "The one who looks Greek. According to Sergeant Osman."

"Ah, right," said Rhodri. "I know the one you mean."

"I'll be in a meeting," she said. "Text me if you get any news."

"Righto, boss."

CHAPTER FORTY-THREE

THE MEETING HAD ALREADY STARTED when Zoe slid into the pub. The place was clearly trading again: most of the people attending had a drink in their hand.

The landlord stood at the front, next to a short blonde woman Zoe didn't recognise.

"The police say they're working on finding the attacker, but they don't even know who the victims are. That's why we need to help ourselves. If there's someone killing LGBT people out there, we have to stop him."

Muttering and nods came from the audience. Zoe shifted to get a better view.

"We need to mount patrols!" someone called out.

"More bouncers!" added another.

"No," said a purple-haired woman at the front. "We don't want to make the village a scary place to be. We need to use the buddy system."

"What's that?" the blonde woman asked.

"It's what they tell kids to do in the US, when there's a

paedophile around. Don't go anywhere alone. Stick together."

"But the victims were found in pairs," someone said.

The purple-haired woman shrugged. "Doesn't do any harm."

The pub landlord, Hal, raised his hand. "I've increased CCTV coverage around the pub. Inside, too. I suggest other businesses do the same."

"That won't help," said the blonde woman. "By the time we're looking at CCTV, it's too late."

"Aren't you the detective?" The woman stared at Zoe. Zoe lifted her chin and walked through the crowd, feeling dozens of eyes on her. She joined the two at the front.

The blonde woman put out a hand. "Izzy Gray, I run the Sappho Lounge."

"DI Zoe Finch."

"I know."

Zoe turned to face the crowd. People were shifting to get a better view, talking between themselves. She raised a hand.

"I'm glad you're all here," she said. "Some of you have probably spoken to my colleagues in Uniform."

"Fat lot of good that did," someone muttered.

"We need to talk to anyone who might have seen something out of the ordinary around here on Friday or Sunday nights. It doesn't matter what it is, if it wasn't right, tell us. And we still need to identify two of the victims." She raised her phone. "This man's name is Yanis. We don't know any more than that. If anyone recognises him, please tell me."

Heads were shaking, shoulders being shrugged. If Yanis had spent time in the gay village, it hadn't been recently.

She thumbed through to the e-fit. They had two of them now, Adam had helped with a second one. Both showed a man with a round face. In Amelia's, he wore a dark hat. In Adam's, he had cropped dark hair. She lifted that one up.

"Does anyone recognise this man?"

"Can't see it, love," came a voice from the back. Zoe handed her phone to Hal, and watched him pass it around.

She scanned the crowd. Could he be here?

The door to the street opened and Ian came through, Dr McBride behind him. They nodded at Zoe and shuffled into position near the door, disappearing into the crowd.

A few people turned to look at the newcomers, then went back to Zoe. She raised her voice as her phone came back to her.

"The Force CID Twitter account has got these photos on it, and the website. Please, check it and show it to your friends. If anyone recognises this man, there's a hotline."

"He wouldn't come in places like this, love," said a man standing in front of her.

"No?"

"Man like that wouldn't be seen dead in a gay bar."

"He has to find his victims somewhere," she said. "And he brought them here, after attacking them. He didn't have to come inside for that."

"No, and we bloody won't let him," someone called.

The blonde woman, Izzy, held up a hand and repeated what Zoe had said about the photos. The people in the pub started to break into groups. The meeting, it seemed, was over.

Petra was pushing through the crowd, struggling to make herself noticed. Zoe heard her mutter a few choice insults at people as she passed.

Eventually she was in front of Zoe. She squared her

shoulders. Her hair had loosened since the morning and she no longer wore the bright red lipstick.

"I've been scanning the crowd," she said. "Perps often come to things like this. They want to watch the investigation, to see what's going on."

They had an e-fit. Zoe very much doubted the man would let himself be seen at a public meeting.

"He's not here," she said.

"No. He's not that stupid."

"No."

"We're looking for a married man, or someone in a relationship," Petra said.

"Sorry?" replied Zoe.

"He's the organised type. Planned his crimes, chose his victims."

"We've got nothing to indicate they weren't random."

"Adam Hart lived way out of town. His attacker went looking for him. I wouldn't be surprised if he'd been watching him. The other victims too."

"OK." Zoe pulled her to one side. "Can we have this conversation later?"

"OK. But ask for the tapes." Petra put a hand on the landlord's arm. "Hello, I'm Dr McBride. We need your help."

Hal looked bemused. "Yes?"

"You've installed extra CCTV, you say."

"We have."

"Can you share it with us, daily?"

A shrug. "Guess so."

"Good."

"Why?" Zoe asked.

Petra scratched her eye. "He'll come back to where he left his victims. It's an important place to him. He'll want to relive what happened here. He'll go back to Adam's house, too. Have you got someone watching it?"

"There doesn't seem much point, with him in the hospital."

"Watch that too."

"He's not going to attack Adam again, surely?"

"Not for the reasons you think. He doesn't care about Adam identifying him. He knows how goddamn average he looks. But he'll want to follow the aftermath of his crimes, see what he's put in motion. You stick a couple of bobbies on the house and the hospital ward, just in case."

"Fair enough." Zoe was prepared to request one constable for each location, just to be sure. Anything to *play nice*. "Anything else you need me to do?"

Petra leaned back, looking Zoe up and down. Zoe was aware of the conversations going on around them, in particular that of Ian with Izzy. She wanted to be free of the profiler.

"You think I'm full of shit, don't you?" Petra said.

"I never said anything of the—"

A snort. "You don't deny it." Petra sighed. "I get a lot of this. You think it's mumbo-jumbo. Trying to get inside the head of these bastards. But it's not." She leaned in. "It's psychology, DI Finch. Science. It'll help you find him."

"Good." Anything to get out of this conversation.

"Hmm. We can talk later, back at the station. I know you're busy."

Zoe turned away from her, resenting the way this woman could take control of a situation. Maybe she could be useful, maybe not. But Zoe had more relevant things to focus on.

CHAPTER FORTY-FOUR

Mo sat opposite Mr and Mrs Hussain for the second time, a cup of tea warming his palms.

"We're sorry to have wasted your time," Mr Hussain said.

"It's not a problem. I'm just glad Amit is home safe and sound."

Mrs Hussain stared ahead, avoiding his gaze. Her eyes were red-rimmed and her cheeks pale.

"Can I speak to him?" Mo asked.

Mr Hussain pushed his glasses up his nose. "He's not up to talking to anyone."

"I'd like to find out what happened to him," Mo said. "Has he told you anything?"

"He went to a friend's house for a few nights. Rebellious boys. You know the kind of thing. I can assure you he'll be suitably punished."

"I'm not sure that's necessary..."

Mr Hussain raised an eyebrow. Mo held his stare. It wasn't his business to interfere in the workings of this family.

But Amit was a grown man. And there was a chance a crime had been committed, despite what his parents said.

"I'd really prefer to talk to him."

"No," said Mr Hussain. He stood up.

Mo stared at him for a moment. "Which friend did he stay with?"

Mr Hussain looked at his wife. "Who did you say it was?"

She widened her eyes. "I don't remember."

"Has he definitely told you he was with a friend?" Mo asked.

"I'm not lying to you, Sergeant," replied Mr Hussain.

Mo sighed. Amit was back home. No crime had been committed, or at least nothing was being alleged. He could close the case.

He stood and shook the man's hand. "Well, I'm very pleased that Amit is home. If you do need to get in touch, here's my card."

Mr Hussain pocketed Mo's card without looking at it. He gestured towards the door. "Thank you, Sergeant."

Mo made for the front door, the Hussains following behind. As he passed the stairs he glanced up, wondering if Amit was listening in.

Outside, he looked upwards. A curtain moved in an upstairs window. Mo waited, just in case.

"Thank you, Sergeant." Mr Hussain's voice had lost its friendliness. Mo turned and made for his car.

As he started the ignition, there was hammering on the passenger window. He leaned across. A young man stood outside, his eyes darting between Mo and the door to the Hussain house.

Mo opened the passenger door. "Amit?"

"I'm his brother. Ruhaan."

"Ruhaan. What can I do for you?"

Ruhaan slammed himself into the passenger seat and closed the door. He hunched down as if afraid of being seen. From the photos Mo had seen of Amit, this young man looked shorter than his brother, squatter. But he had the same eyes. He swallowed and turned to Mo.

"They're lying to you."

"About what?" Mo held a breath. "Hang on, is Amit really home? He's not still missing?"

"Oh, no. He's home. He came back this morning. But he didn't stay with a friend."

"I thought not." Mo had spoken to all the friends he could find and not one of them had a clue where Amit was. "Where was he?"

"He won't tell me. But he's been hurt."

"In what way?"

"He's got bruises on his arm. He limps when he thinks no one's looking. And there's an expression on his face..."

"I'll need to talk to him, Ruhaan. Can you maybe persuade your parents—"

"No way. They won't let him out of his room. And they don't know."

"Don't know what?"

"Amit's gay."

"I knew that."

Ruhaan shrank back. "You did?"

"I spoke to his boyfriend. Kai. You think Kai might have hurt him?"

"I think it's worse than that," Ruhaan said.

"How?"

"The Ripper. The Digbeth Ripper had him. I'm sure of it."

CHAPTER FORTY-FIVE

Zoe left the pub, glad to be out in the sharp December air. As she walked to her Mini, a dark car pulled up next to her and a man got out.

"Sir," she said, almost tripping over in surprise.

"Zoe. Hope I haven't missed it?" Detective Superintendent David Randle closed the car door and it drove off.

"The meeting, sir?"

"Nothing else going on around here, is there?'

"It didn't last long. I'm not sure..."

"Let me be the judge of that, shall we?"

She followed him, not sure how the occupants of the Jackal would react to Randle. He pushed the door open and strode in, ignoring the stares.

"Sir," she said as she tried to catch up with him. "Let me introduce you to Izzy from the Sappho Lounge."

Izzy Gray turned to face them. She gave Randle an apprising glance then cocked her head.

"You're too late," she said.

Randle held out a hand. "David Randle, West Midlands

Police. We want to do everything we can to reassure the community that we're going to find the man who—"

"Your DI has already talked to us."

"This is important to us. I wanted to make sure that people understood." People had stopped talking and were staring at Randle. Ian was working through the crowd handing out flyers. Petra stood off to one side, surveying the scene with those narrow eyes of hers.

Randle smiled and stroked his tie. "Good evening, everyone. Thanks for coming along."

"It's not your bloody meeting," Izzy said. "And you missed it."

Randle gave Zoe an accusatory look. She shrugged. He composed himself and turned to Izzy. "As I see. Well, I won't take up any more of your time. My colleague here will give you the number of Lloyd House. If you need help with all this," he waved a hand around, "please do call."

"Sure." Izzy looked at Zoe, who clamped down on her bottom lip. The last time she'd seen Randle flustered was when his former lover had been accused of killing her husband, the Assistant Chief Constable.

"Right," he said. "Zoe, with me."

She walked with him out of the pub, doing her best to match his stride. His car was across the street, waiting. "We've been working with the profiler, sir," she said.

"Good. Psychologist, you mean."

"Of course." Zoe noted that he hadn't spoken to Petra in the pub. "If you wait a moment, I can introduce you."

He waved a hand. "No need." He brushed her arm. She stiffened. "Best be getting off. Back to Lloyd House. Keep me updated, will you?"

"Via DCI Clarke," she said.

"Via Lesley, of course."

She grimaced as he slid into the car and sped off. As she turned back towards her own car, a man came running up.

"Are you the detective?" he asked.

"DI Finch. Yes."

He was panting and his face was red. He had a face full of stubble and short blond hair.

"Good," he said. "You're looking for witnesses."

"On Friday or Sunday nights. Did you see something?"

"I might have."

"Good." She looked up and down the street. "Tell me what you saw."

"Aren't you going to take me to the station?"

"No need. We can do this here."

"Can we go into the pub, at least?"

She eyed him. "Fair enough." They walked back to the pub and she opened the door for him to go inside. He entered, his eyes darting around the space. No one acknowledged them.

She slid behind a group of people and into a chair. "Tell me what you saw."

He took the chair next to her, his eyes shifting between her and the people surrounding them. "I saw a man, Sunday night. Monday morning, really."

"A man."

"He was carrying something."

"What kind of something?"

"Dragging something heavy, I reckon. In a suitcase." He held his arms wide to indicate the size of the case. "Could have been a body."

"OK. Where was this?" She reached into her coat pocket for a pen.

He pointed towards the doors to the pub. "Out there." He scanned the room, his eyes bright. "He was coming from the car park in Pershore Street. He went to the Lizard. Where you found those men."

Zoe cocked her head. "You saw him leave the car park?"

He nodded vigorously.

"What time was this?"

"About half five, I reckon."

"What were you doing here at that time in the morning?"

"I was on my way home. I'd been out clubbing."

"Were there any other people around?"

"Just me. And the man. There was a couple of people over by the markets, setting up I s'pose. But I don't think they saw."

"Right. I'm going to need your name and contact details."

"Jackson Potter." He gave her an address in Stechford, to the east of the city centre.

"Thanks," she said. "Did you see the man's face?"

He shifted in his chair. "He was wearing a hat. Like in that picture you put out."

"Describe the hat. What else was he wearing?"

"Dark. All of it, the hat, his clothes."

"Boss." Ian was behind her, staring at the man.

"Ian. Give me five minutes and I'll be right with you." She hesitated. "On second thoughts, pull up a chair. Mr Potter, this is DS Osman."

Potter nodded at Ian and looked back at Zoe. He tugged on his thumb.

"So," she said. "You said you saw him dragging something heavy from the car park to the pub. Did you see him leave the object?"

"Sorry. He disappeared round the side of the pub."

"Was it just the one time you saw him, or did he come back again?"

A shrug. "No idea. It was cold, I wanted to get home."

"And it was definitely the Pershore Street car park you saw him come from?"

"Yeah. He came out the exit at the side."

"Thank you," she said. "You've been very helpful."

CHAPTER FORTY-SIX

Zoe slammed the door shut, feeling the tension finally drain from her body. If it wasn't enough managing a serial killer investigation, the added complication of having Ian Osman and Petra McBride to contend with made it no easier.

"I'm home!" she called. No reply.

She walked through to the kitchen and put her espresso pot on the stove. She needed to sleep, but she also had case files to go over. She'd received an email from Connie an hour earlier, with Jason Hinchcliffe's police file. He'd been arrested for drugs possession a few times, and charged twice. It had never got to court. In the morning there'd be CCTV from the Pershore Street car park to check. And she was still waiting on Rhodri and the witness statements.

The pot whistled and she poured herself a mug. It wasn't often she took the trouble to make proper espresso, and every time she wished she did it regularly. The liquid slid down her throat, heavy and hot.

She leaned against the counter, weighing up whether to eat now or after she'd gone through the file. There was a tin of baked beans in the cupboard, she could have it on toast. The fridge held no sign of Nicholas having cooked.

She went back to the hall and stood at the bottom of the stairs. He was normally in the living room by now, watching crappy American crime shows. Maybe he had homework.

"Nicholas!"

"What?" The front door opened behind her and Nicholas entered, bringing a rush of cold air in with him.

"I thought you were in your room," she said.

"I went out with Zaf."

"Where to?"

"Just the Anchor."

The Anchor was in Digbeth. Not in the gay village, but not far off. "I told you to stick to each other's houses for now."

He pushed past her. "We wanted a pint. We weren't in the gay village. It's fine."

She trailed him into the living room. He slung his coat on a chair and sank into the sofa. "It's not fine," she said.

Not meeting her eye, he picked up the remote and thumbed through shows on Netflix. "I'm here, aren't I?"

She sat down next to him. Her breathing was fast. "I worry."

He glanced at her. "Don't."

"I'm your mum. I can't help it."

"I'm an adult now. Eighteen. I can look after myself."

She grabbed the remote from his hand, ignoring his cry. "Have you seen the photos of Mitch Ibsen?"

"Who's Mitch Ibsen?"

"The man who died. He was well-built, Nicholas. He clearly worked out. You think you can stand up to someone who can overpower a man like that?"

Nicholas was tall like her, but slim. Skinny, even. Despite all the good food, or maybe because of it.

"I just want you to be careful, is all," she said.

"Mum. There's an entire city full of guys out there. He could go for anyone. You can't let bastards like that stop you living your life."

She leaned forwards. "There isn't an entire city full of *gay* men. And there certainly isn't an entire city full of gay men whose mums are leading the investigation."

"You lead investigations all the time. Why would they target me?"

"Because you're gay." She wanted to shake him. "Can't you see this?"

Nicholas grabbed the remote off her, stared at it a moment, then threw it onto the coffee table. A old coffee mug crashed to the floor.

"Stop it, Mum."

"Stop what?"

He stood up. "Don't treat me like I'm a baby. You're just overcompensating."

She stood up to bring herself to his level. He was four inches taller than her, but her karate had taught her to hold herself like she was bigger. "Overcompensating for what?"

"For everything." He waved an arm to take in their surroundings. "Being a single mum. Working too much when I was a kid. Not being able to bloody feed me properly."

"Nicholas!" She stared at him, her chest heaving. Where had all this come from?

She sat down, deflated. "You know I've done the best for you that I could."

"You wouldn't let Dad near me, when I was a kid."

She squeezed her eyes shut. She'd never told him the

truth about how Jim had reacted to her pregnancy. "Sit down."

"I've got work to do." He turned to face the door but didn't move.

"I didn't stop your dad seeing you," she whispered. "It was the other way around."

He shrugged, his back to her. "Whatever. Just leave me alone." He slammed the door and ran up the stairs, his footsteps reverberating through the house.

CHAPTER FORTY-SEVEN

TUESDAY

ZOE WAS the first into the office the next day. She went to the kitchen to make a cup of coffee then drifted towards her office, taking in the board on the way through the team room. More names had been added to the board: Charlie Hessel and Yanis Liakos. She frowned: they'd identified the other two victims, and no one had told her?

She was eyeing the two photographs when Connie opened the door.

"Morning, boss."

"Morning, Connie. What's this?" Zoe waved her mug in the direction of the board.

"What's what?" Connie yawned and joined her at the board. "We've got names?"

"Yanis and Charlie. When did those get there?"

Zoe had returned to the office after the public meeting the previous afternoon. She'd spent a couple of hours working through statements they'd received via the hotline, none of it useful. She'd requested CCTV from the Pershore

Street car park. When she'd left, the question marks had still been on the board.

The door opened. "You've seen the names."

Zoe and Connie turned in unison. "Did you put them there?"

Ian smiled. "We got a call from the hospital, after you left."

"I thought you left at the same time as me."

"I remembered something. Came back. They'd left a message."

"Why didn't you tell me?"

"I figured it could wait till morning."

Zoe put down her coffee. It took all her strength not to slam it onto the desk. "You figured wrong."

He blanched. "Sorry."

She sat down, her senses ablaze. "What else do we have apart from names?"

Ian went to his desk and grabbed a sheet of paper. "Yanis Liakos and Charlie Hessel. Married for two years, live in Moseley. Charlie woke up yesterday afternoon, Yanis not long after."

"Yanis." So Jason Hinchcliffe had been right. "Right," Zoe said. "I'm getting round there."

Petra walked in, Rhodri trailing behind her. "What's going on?" she said. "You all look like you've seen a ghost."

Zoe eyed Ian. "We've got the full names of the other two victims."

"Good." Petra held out her hand and Zoe passed her the sheet of paper. It held the names and addresses of the men, plus more recent photos.

"Connie," Zoe said. "Get online. Find out what you can

about these two. Who they associated with, what links to Adam and Mitch they might have – apart from Hinchcliffe."

"Hinchcliffe?"

"Yanis went out with him for a while. Before Mitch did."

"So you think the attacker knew them both?" Rhodri said.

"Yes, Rhodri. There's a good chance of it."

"Not a random homophobe then after all."

"Not so fast." Petra held up a hand as Zoe gritted her teeth. "That doesn't fit."

"It fits with the evidence," Zoe said. "We have two victims who share an ex. It's a connection, Dr McBride. The sort of concrete fact that's useful in an investigation like this."

"He didn't know them," Petra said, her eyes on the board.

"How d'you know that?" Zoe asked.

Petra stared at her. "Because if he had, Adam would have identified him, no?"

"Adam only just met Mitch, he wouldn't have known who the guy dated before him. The attacker could have known Mitch and Yanis. They've got Hinchcliffe in common, they could have both known this guy."

"No," said Petra.

"You can't just dismiss a lead out of hand."

The team watched the two women, the room silent apart from Zoe and Petra's voices. Zoe clenched a fist. "Just let us focus on the facts. If they fit your profile, then fine. We can add that to the mix. But we need evidence. Not guesses."

She turned to Rhodri. "Did you get anywhere with Adam's neighbours?"

"I checked all the statements. They were all asked if they heard or saw anything unusual between when Adam said they were attacked and him and Mitch being found. Nothing, boss."

"We need to ask again. Get Uniform knocking on doors. Ten past one on Sunday morning. We have a specific time."

"I did it, boss." Rhodri shifted between his feet.

"Sorry?"

"I went there yesterday evening. Figured people would be in."

"Well done, Rhod. And?"

"Sorry. One guy remembered hearing some car doors slamming but no one saw anything."

"Damn. OK, come with me."

Rhodri looked puzzled. "Boss?"

"You heard what I said. We've got victims to interview." She looked across the room at Ian. "I want you to find out why Adam Hart was moved from Oncology. And who he worked with. Was there a falling out, does anyone have it in for him?"

"They're doctors, boss. You really think—?"

"Just do it, Ian."

"Our man wasn't a practising surgeon," said Petra. Zoe held up a hand.

"Connie," she said. "Carry on looking through social media. Find connections between the victims. And chase the CCTV from Pershore Street car park, early Monday morning."

"Right, boss."

Good." Zoe gave Petra one last look before walking out of the office, Rhodri at her heels.

CHAPTER FORTY-EIGHT

IAN WITHDREW TO HIS DESK, wishing he could go back to his old job at Kings Norton. He called the HR department at the hospital where Adam worked.

"Ffion Jones, can I help you?"

"Ms Jones, my name's Detective Sergeant Ian Osman. I'm investigating Adam Hart's attacker."

"Poor Adam. A really nice man, too. How is he?"

"You know him?"

"Yes. How can I help you?"

"He moved from Oncology to A&E. We have reason to believe he was forced out."

"I can't comment on that."

He dragged his fingernails across the desk. Why would someone be forced to move departments, but not be fired or demoted?

"Was a complaint raised against Adam? Misconduct? Carelessness?"

"No, Sergeant. Dr Hart has a clean record."

"Was he being bullied?"

"If you think someone here attacked him..."

"I'm not saying that at all." He took a breath. "Did *he* make a complaint?"

"Not Adam," she said. "A colleague."

"So it wasn't him being harassed, but a colleague?" This was what happened when you listened to elderly neighbours, Ian thought.

"The colleague made the complaint on Adam's behalf. He didn't want to take it any further, but we had to investigate under the hospital's diversity policy."

"It was homophobic harassment?"

"Look. Sergeant Osman. I need Adam's consent before I can give you any more information about this."

"But it wasn't Adam who made the complaint."

"He was the victim. The alleged victim."

"So it wasn't upheld?"

"You're not going to get round me like that."

He sighed. "Adam is in hospital right now."

"So I suggest you visit him."

"It's not as easy as that."

Silence. He pictured this woman on the other end of the phone, wielding her power like it actually meant something.

"Look," he said. "Just tell me which team Adam was working in at the time. His neighbour says Oncology."

"You want to know the members of the team, so you can approach them."

"Well, yes. Ffion, can I call you Ffion?"

"Ms Jones is fine."

"Ms Jones. Adam was with another man at the time of the attack. The other man died. So this means you're obstructing a murder enquiry."

No response. He heard muffled voices. She had her hand over the receiver and was talking to someone.

"I read that Adam was unconscious when they found him," she said.

"Yes."

"If he's unconscious, he can't consent to us sharing the information," she continued.

"You'd have to make that call yourself. To help with a murder enquiry." He didn't tell her that Adam was awake and sitting up in his hospital bed now.

Another pause, more muffled conversation. "I'm not giving you all the details, but I will tell you whose team he was in. You can draw your own conclusions."

"Thank you."

More silence.

"And...?" Ian said.

"Mr Duncan Carmichael," she said. "Senior Consultant Oncologist. He leads the gynaecological team."

And he's the bully, thought Ian. "Thank you," he said. "You're not going to tell me who Adam's colleagues were?"

"You can find a list on the hospital website."

"That doesn't tell me who made the complaint."

"It was anonymous."

"Really?" He didn't believe her.

"Good luck, Sergeant. I hope you find the killer. It's *not* one of our staff."

"You can't be sure of that."

"We would know."

He wanted to laugh. The idea of an HR department knowing a member of hospital staff was a brutal killer...

Still, he had a name. And Connie could do the website trawl.

"Thanks," he snapped, and hung up.

Petra was watching him. "I'll come with you."

Ian grunted at her. After what had happened yesterday, that was not happening.

"Not for this interview. It's not relevant to your work."

She folded her arms. "You think this consultant might be the killer. You're wrong, but I shall enjoy seeing you learn that."

"In that case, your time's would be better spent here following up leads you believe are useful. I'm going alone."

He stared at her, then wrinkled his nose and turned to Connie.

"Connie, I've got a job for you."

"Sarge?"

"Get me the address of a Duncan Carmichael. Senior Oncology doctor at the QE. And check the hospital website, find out who his team are and where they live."

"I'm still working on CCTV for the boss."

"It won't take you a minute to do this."

She pursed her lips, her eyes on her screen. She swallowed. "Five minutes. Then I go back to what the boss asked me to do."

Ian raised an eyebrow. This was the first time he'd seen DC Williams assert herself. It was refreshing, if annoying.

"Good," he said. His phone rang: Carl Whaley.

He stared at it then back at Connie. "I'll take this in the office." He dived into Zoe's office and shut the door behind him.

"DS Osman."

"Ian, it's DI Whaley."

"I know. What d'you want?"

"Have you spoken to any of your contacts yet?"

"Which contacts?"

"You know what I'm talking about, Ian."

Whaley had accused Ian of being in league with organised crime. Trevor Hamm, Stuart Reynolds, and the rest of them. In return for letting him keep his job, he was expected to feed him information about their activities.

"I've been busy on the Ripper case," he said.

"You heard about Hamm being arrested for supplying drugs to Winson Green Prison?"

"I did."

"They haven't pressed charges. I want to know why."

"Maybe there wasn't enough evidence."

"You and I both know it won't be as simple as that. Someone's helping him. I want you to find out who."

"It was Handsworth nick that arrested him. How am I supposed to worm my way into there?"

"You'll find a way."

Ian sighed. "I need forty-eight hours. DI Finch has given me a shitload of work to do."

"Glad to hear she's keeping you busy."

He looked through the glass. Connie was looking at him, pointing at her computer screen.

"Got to go," he said.

"Don't forget."

"No." Ian hung up and mouthed *fuck off* at his phone. He pulled himself upright and pushed the door open, trying to smile at the constable.

"You've found him," he said.

"Lives in Solihull," Connie replied.

"Of course." Solihull was a wealthy suburban town just outside the city.

"And there are just three consultants in his team. Simon Kleber, Vihaan Agarwal and Penelope Jenkins."

"Get their details too. Is Carmichael in the hospital today?"

"Private practice. The Priory, in Edgbaston."

"Right." Ian pulled on his jacket. "Call me with details for the other three, OK?"

"OK." She gave him a disgruntled look. "After I've finished with the CCTV."

Ian was about to say something about insubordination but then decided better of it. He had no plans to stay in this team for long, so what did it matter how they behaved towards him?

Petra was eyeing him, waiting for him to change his mind. He cast her a derogatory look then backed out of the door.

CHAPTER FORTY-NINE

Yanis Liakos was in a private room not far from Adam Hart. Zoe knocked on the door and went inside, Rhodri behind her.

"Hello, Yanis," she said. "My name's Detective Inspector Zoe Finch. I'm leading the investigation into your attack."

"Inspector."

"Call me Zoe, please." She gestured to Rhodri, who was pulling up a chair. "This is DC Rhodri Hughes."

Yanis nodded at Rhodri, who flashed him a grin. "Alright, mate."

"Mind if we sit?" Zoe asked. Yanis shrugged and she pulled the second chair closer to the bed, aware of Rhodri's awkward expression.

"The nurses have told me not to give you a hard time," she said. "And I've got no intention of doing that. I just need to find out what you can remember about what happened to you."

Yanis blinked, his eyes filling with tears.

"Is that OK?" Zoe asked. He nodded. "Good. Start at the beginning. Where were you and your husband attacked?"

"How is he?"

"I haven't seen him yet," she told him.

"I'm so sorry," Yanis replied.

"Sorry?"

"I should have called out. I should have stopped him. If I'd been stronger, Charlie wouldn't have..." He wiped his eyes. "Sorry."

"You don't need to apologise. Just tell me what happened."

"Want a tissue, mate?" Rhodri said, holding out a box.

"Cheers." Yanis blew his nose and turned back to Zoe. He was propped up in bed, wearing dark blue pyjamas. Like Adam, his legs were covered in a protective shield that raised the sheets above his injuries.

"Go on." Zoe gave him an encouraging smile.

"I was in bed. Reading. Charlie was downstairs, locking up. He always takes ages. He grew up on a rough estate, gets a bit paranoid." Yanis's eyes crinkled. "One of the things I love about him."

"So Charlie was downstairs, and...?"

"I didn't see anything. Too engrossed in my book. *80/20 Marketing*. I run a business, from my garden. You don't need to know that. I didn't see him till his hand was on my mouth."

"Did he come at you from behind?"

"He must have been in the room before I went to bed. The bed faces the door. He could have been under it, I guess." Charlie seemed to shrink at the memory.

"What did he do after he grabbed you?"

"He had a knife."

Rhodri perked up. "What kind of knife?"

"I don't know. Big. Not something you'd want to mess with."

"Was it straight, or curved?" Zoe asked.

"Curved, I think. He was very close to me, it wasn't easy..."

"It's OK," said Zoe. "You're doing great. Could you see how long it was?"

"I don't see what it has to do with—"

"We've already had a report of a knife. We want to know if it matches."

"Oh. It was about this big." He held out his hands to indicate a knife about a foot long.

"Did he threaten you with it?" Rhodri asked.

"He held it to my throat. Told me he'd use it. Made me call out for Charlie." His face crumpled, and they waited for him to regain his composure.

"How long did he have it to your throat for?" Zoe asked.

"Ten minutes maybe. Till Charlie came in."

Zoe nodded, waiting for him to continue.

"He told us that if we did as he said, no one would get hurt. Then he took us downstairs." Yanis looked at her. "He left us in separate rooms for hours. Kept coming back, threatening us. I tried the landline but he'd disconnected it."

Zoe thought back to what Petra had said: an organised type. She was correct on one thing: he'd planned his crimes.

"Did you recognise him?" she asked.

"No. Not at all."

"Was he wearing a hat?"

"No. He had short hair, dark. Round face, ordinary looking."

Zoe pulled out her phone. "Does this look like him?" She showed him the e-fit.

"Yes." Yanis had a pained expression.

"Are you sure you hadn't seen him before? He didn't go to any of the bars in the gay village?"

Yanis frowned. "No way."

"Why d'you say that?'

"Because of what he did. The way he talked. This guy wasn't gay. He hated us. He wanted to *convert* us."

Zoe felt her stomach dip. Rhodri cleared his throat.

Just like Adam and Mitch.

"How did he try to convert you?"

"He had a camera. He filmed us. It was like an interrogation. Both of us together, he brought us into the kitchen for it."

"What sort of things did he say?"

"He tried to convince us we would be happier if we weren't gay. That we'd be able to live normal lives, free of prejudice. Have kids. Then he started going on about God, saying if we converted we could be forgiven."

"Did he say anything more specific about religion? Was he part of a cult, anything like that?'

"Just God. General stuff. To be honest, some of it wasn't that far from what I got from my grandfather when I came out."

"How did you respond to his questions."

"I just said nothing. Charlie started off arguing with him, saying he was full of shit. That we were married, we were happy. It was no use. There's no talking to people like that. I just kept quiet. Charlie stopped talking after a while."

"And then...?"

"He got the knife out. He held it to Charlie's throat this time. I thought he was going to kill him." A breath caught in

Yanis's throat. "He didn't. He told me to lie on the floor. I thought he was going to rape me."

"But he didn't."

"No. Much worse than that."

"He castrated you."

Yanis blinked. "Yes. Me and Charlie, we were going to have kids. We'd found a surrogate." His chest heaved. "I guess that's fucked up."

"That's rough, mate," said Rhodri. Yanis looked at him, his mouth tight.

"Were you conscious when he castrated you?" Zoe asked.

"Yes. The whole thing. He told me to hold still, or he'd kill Charlie. He had him tied to the table by then."

"And then he did the same thing to your husband."

"I was too weak to do anything. I lay there, my head right next to his. I was in so much pain. You can't imagine..."

Yanis closed his eyes. He turned away for a few moments, then looked at Zoe. "Please find him. Get him before he does it again."

"We're working on that." She sighed. "I'm sorry to make you relive this, but I have to know. Did you see the knife he used? Was it the same one he threatened you with?"

"No. It was a craft knife. My sister uses them, for making jewellery. I watched him get it out of a bag. He boiled the kettle, sterilised it I guess."

"And after he mutilated the two of you, what did he do then?"

"He injected me with something. I tried to fight him off, tried to push it out of his hand. But I couldn't. Next thing I knew, I was here."

Zoe looked at Rhodri. They would speak to the doctors, find out what drugs had been in the men's systems.

"Thanks, Yanis. I know this hasn't been easy for you."

He sniffed.

"I do need to ask you one more question."

"Yes."

"Do you know a man called Jason Hinchcliffe?"

Yanis stiffened. "Who?'

"Jason Hinchcliffe. He lives in Sherlock Street."

Yanis swallowed. "Don't tell Charlie."

"Don't tell Charlie what?"

"It was nothing. Just a fling. Before we got married. My last... I don't know. It's got nothing to do with all this."

"You had a relationship with Jason?"

He closed his eyes. "I wouldn't call it a relationship." He grabbed a tissue from a box at the side of the bed and blew his nose, then winced. "I shouldn't have done it."

"I'm not judging you, Yanis," Zoe said. "It's none of my business. But I do need to know if you think Jason might want to hurt you."

Yanis stared at her. "You think Jason did this?"

Her shoulders slumped. "No. You'd have recognised him. But it's a connection. Could Jason have put someone else up to it?"

"Jason isn't clever enough to do that."

"You'd be surprised."

"Jason's a gay man, Detective. He'd never get someone to try to convert us."

It would make a good cover, she thought. But the idea was far-fetched.

"Did you ever meet Mitch Ibsen?"

"I saw him around. It was pretty clear he fancied Jason. I let them get on with it."

"But the two of you never met?"

"Never."

"Have you ever met Adam Hart?"

"Who's he?"

"He and Mitch were also attacked."

Yanis winced. "Poor bastards."

"Mitch died."

"Oh, fuck." His face drained of colour. He looked up at her. "I don't know him, Detective. I promise you."

CHAPTER FIFTY

Detective Superintendent Randle picked up his phone.

"David Randle speaking."

"It's Dr McBride."

He sat up straight. "Hello, Doctor. How can I help you?"

"You brought me in on this case. Just tell your minions to work with me, will you?"

"I'm not sure what you're talking about."

"DI Finch. She thinks I'm wasting her time. I'm sat in the office twiddling my thumbs when I should be out with them talking to witnesses."

"I'm sure DI Finch doesn't think you're—"

"Look, Mr Randle."

"Detective Superintendent."

"Yeah, yeah. It's a mouthful, and you know it. I don't care what your team think of me. But I do care about finding this fucker before he kills again. You either want me working this case, or you don't."

"We do. Your reputation in Scotland is impressive. Especially after the Fife strangling case..."

"Yeah, yeah. Don't flatter me. Just get your bods working with me, or stop wasting my time." She hung up.

Randle blew out a breath. He didn't need this. He picked up the phone to Lesley Clarke. This was her problem, not his.

CHAPTER FIFTY-ONE

THE PRIORY WAS a swish private hospital near the Bristol Road. Ian pulled into the car park and checked himself in the mirror. In his brown jacket and grey trousers he would stand out as a detective here, but that was no bad thing.

He'd spent the journey thinking about that call from Carl Whaley. Whaley had a way about him, an air of smug calm that made Ian want to punch him in the face. But he had power of life and death over Ian. If Alison ever found out what he'd done, and how it might have put the kids at risk...

He rubbed his eyes and yawned, then took a mint from the glove locker and put it in his mouth. He left the car and walked to the reception.

The foyer was spacious and quiet, nothing like the local NHS hospitals. Nondescript music played at low volume and a young woman in a pristine white coat sat behind a shiny glass and chrome desk. He doubted she wore that coat for medical reasons.

He held up his warrant card. "DS Ian Osman, West

Midlands Police. I'd like to speak to Duncan Carmichael please."

"He's got clinic today."

"It's in connection with a murder enquiry."

Her eyes widened and she picked up a phone from the desk.

"Mr Carmichael, I'm sorry to disturb you. It's Julie in reception.... Yes, I am sorry... There's a man here, a police officer. He says it's in connection with a murder enquiry... Yes. Of course."

She hung up.

"You'll have to wait."

"Wait?"

"He's got a patient with him. Regular check-up. It could take a while."

"Check-up? He's an Oncology specialist."

"Patients in remission need monitoring."

Ian pushed down irritation. "Where can I wait?"

She pointed towards a set of plush sofas. "Over there. There's a coffee machine. Help yourself."

He surveyed her. "Julie, can I ask you something?"

She leaned forward. "Of course."

"How many days a week does Mr Carmichael hold his clinic here?"

"Mondays and Wednesdays. Just afternoons, on a Monday."

"And the rest of the time he's at the QE?"

"Yes."

"Does he get along well with people here?"

"I'm just a receptionist, Sergeant. That's not something I'd..."

"Do you like him?"

"Of course I do."

"Of course?"

She nodded.

"You're expected to like all the doctors, I imagine."

"It's not like that."

"No." He drummed his fingertips on the desk between them. "Have there been any complaints about him, by other members of staff? Any unease?"

"Sergeant Osman, I'm afraid I can't answer these kinds of questions." The phone rang and her face relaxed into relief. She pointed at the sofas as she picked it up.

Ian wandered over to the sofas, taking in the room. Photographs of senior managers and doctors filled the wall over the largest sofa. Carmichael was on the second row, smiling, wearing a white coat and a stethoscope. Ian rolled his eyes and stepped in to get a better look. He had sharp eyes and thin, white-blonde hair.

"Sergeant?"

Ian turned to see the same sharp eyes and white-blonde hair right behind him. He held out a hand, hiding his surprise.

"Doctor Carmichael. Thank you for seeing me."

"Mr Carmichael. I'm a surgeon. Surely you coppers should know that kind of thing?"

"Mr Carmichael. Can we go to your office?"

The doctor brushed an invisible piece of fluff off his jacket. He wasn't wearing the white coat today, but a pale grey suit that looked tailored, with a neatly tied maroon tie that made Ian think of David Randle.

"I'm giving you five minutes. I've got patients to see." His voice was sharp.

"Of course." Ian would have to get to the point.

He followed the doctor along silent, thickly carpeted corridors until they reached an open door. Carmichael went inside, not waiting for Ian. He sat behind the large mahogany desk and clenched his hands together on its surface.

"Close the door, if you don't mind."

Ian turned back to the door to close it. Two chairs faced the doctor. He took one.

"So? What's all this about?"

"Are you aware that one of your colleagues at the QE was attacked recently?"

"Adam Hart. Yes, of course I'm aware, you can't bloody well get away from it. What's it got to do with me?"

"Are you aware that Dr Hart is gay?"

A flicker of disgust crossed Carmichael's face. "That's why he was attacked, wasn't it? This Ripper nonsense."

"You think it's nonsense?'

"Of course it's nonsense."

"You think it was someone else? Someone that knew him, maybe?"

"How should I know? That's your job."

"It is," replied Ian. "Which is why I wanted to find out about an incident that took place between you and Adam Hart last March, at the QE. An incident that preceded him being moved to the A&E team."

"He asked for that move. No one forced him."

"That's not what I want to know about." Ian licked his lips. "Did you and Adam get along, Mr Carmichael?"

"We were colleagues. We're not expected to be friends."

"On a professional level, did you get along?"

"As well as you might expect, I suppose."

"As well as you might expect, given Adam's sexuality."

"Dr Hart's preferences have nothing to do with this."

"Is it true that a complaint was made, alleging homophobic harassment?"

"That was never upheld. And it wasn't Adam who made the complaint. Bloody woman, always sticking her nose in..."

So now Ian knew who'd made the complaint: Penelope Jenkins.

"How did you feel, about Adam being moved to A&E?"

"What does it matter what I *feel*?" The doctor stood up. "Since when were the police interested in touchy feely bollocks like this?"

Ian looked up at him. "Mr Carmichael. Can you tell me where you were on Saturday night?"

Carmichael spluttered out a laugh. "Don't be so fucking absurd!"

"Do you remember where you were?"

"Yes, of course I bloody do. I was at home with my wife, like I always am." He raised a hand. "That good enough for you?"

"Can you remember what you did that evening?"

"I had paperwork to catch up on. It's relentless, you know. Especially in the NHS. At least here they have competent people to look after that stuff. I was in my study most of the night. Then we had a nightcap, then bed."

"You can't recall anything more specific."

"My wife will back me up. Ask her."

Ian smiled. "I'm sure she would."

Carmichael shook his arm out to look at his watch. It looked expensive. "Five minutes are up."

"You still haven't told me—"

The doctor loomed over Ian. "I have patients to see. And this is private property."

Ian stood up. "It's a hospital."

"A *private* one. Good bloody job, too. Now bugger off and stop throwing your slanderous allegations around before I call security. Better than that, I'll call my lawyer."

CHAPTER FIFTY-TWO

Zoe pocketed her phone as she stepped into the office. She'd been trying to call Nicholas all morning, but he wasn't picking up, or replying to her texts. She felt bad for shouting at him last night.

Ian was right behind her. "We going to do the briefing then?"

She sighed. Connie and Rhodri were at their desks. Ian took a seat towards the back with Petra in the opposite corner, occasionally shooting him dirty looks.

"OK folks, let's review." Zoe stood in front of the board.

"I checked the CCTV at the car park, boss," said Connie. "There's nothing."

"Nothing at all?"

"Well, not nothing. Sorry. But no one matching the description. Definitely no one carrying a couple of bodies."

"Did you widen the time frame?"

"By two hours each way."

"Hmm. Looks like we'll need to get back to our Mr Potter, then. Find out if he's lying, or just forgot."

"Sorry, boss."

"Not your fault, Connie." She turned to Ian. "How did you get on with Adam's old boss?"

"His alibi is thin and he's an unpleasant sod, but I don't think he did it. Even with him being a surgeon."

"He bullied Adam," said Rhodri. "And he'd know how to do that op."

"He's a gynaecological oncologist," said Petra. "Works with women."

"Still..." said Rhodri.

Petra sighed. "I said you were barking up the wrong tree. This is a serial killer. Not someone looking for revenge on one of the victims."

"I still want to keep that in mind," said Zoe. "Someone put Carmichael's photo on the board, eh?"

Connie turned to her computer.

"Not right now," said Zoe. Connie looked down and turned back to the room.

"We'll talk to Adam," she said. "He'll know more about Carmichael, given that he made a complaint about him."

"He didn't," said Ian. "That was a colleague. Dr Penelope Jenkins."

"She complained on his behalf?"

"And it wasn't upheld."

"But he was moved, nonetheless."

"Dr Carmichael says he asked for the transfer."

"He would say that. Find out what really happened, will you Ian? Speak to the hospital. Tell them this is a murder enquiry."

"I already did."

"Good. Speak to Adam, then."

"He didn't exactly react well last time." Ian glanced at Petra who was tapping her foot on the floor.

"I don't care," said Zoe. "You've got a job to do."

Connie was looking at Ian like she wanted him to burst into flames. Zoe noted it but said nothing.

"OK," Zoe said. "There's also the connection between Yanis and Mitch, via Jason Hinchcliffe."

"Pish," said Petra.

"I beg your pardon?"

"You heard me. It's not a revenge killing."

"Why not?"

Petra clipped to the front in her heels. She wore a tight skirt over thick black tights today, which clashed with her peach-coloured shoes. She grabbed the marker pen and wrote on the whiteboard: *Motive.*

She turned to the room. "We know why this guy attacks. He wants to humiliate gay men. He says he wants to convert them, but I'm not so sure. He wants to hobble them."

"Hobble?" said Zoe.

"Lessen them, remove a part of them. Literally."

Rhodri raised a hand. "He tries to brainwash them?"

"He doesn't have long enough for that. Brainwashing takes time. Days, weeks, months. It's repeated and relentless, wearing a person down. This is different. He's trying to use logic."

"He's a bloody idiot," huffed Connie.

"That's as may be," replied Petra. "But it is what it is. He tries to persuade them to convert, then when they refuse, he removes the body organ that he thinks produces their sexual behaviour."

"Like Alan Turing," said Rhodri.

"Yes, son. You've said that before. Watch the record doesn't get stuck."

"Actually, that was me," said Connie.

"Was it? Oh well." Petra put the lid back on the pen with a flourish and pointed at the photos of Adam's injuries. "This is not a frenzied crime. It's not what you people would call a crime of passion."

"Actually, we don't say that," said Zoe.

Petra waved a hand to dismiss her. "This is planned. It's calm. It takes skill, and a steady hand. Oh I know you're thinking your Doctor Carmichael has a—"

"Mr Carmichael," interrupted Ian. Petra blinked at him.

"He has the skills, aye," she continued. "But he doesn't have the psychology." She jabbed the side of her head with the marker pen. "Ian, you said he was rude and dismissive."

"Yes."

"Would you describe him as calm, when you spoke to him?"

"Not really."

"And all you were doing was asking a few questions." She looked at Zoe. "A man like that does not get all the way through an attack like this and hold his nerve."

"But what if he got someone else to do it?" asked Rhodri. "He doesn't look like the description we've been given, anyway."

"Indeed." Petra pointed the pen at him. "But if he did get someone to do it, then his surgical skills are irrelevant. You're going to suggest he has access to people with surgical skills, being in his line of work an' all." She slammed the pen down on a desk. "But what kind of risk would you be taking as a consultant with a long career and a tidy income, asking one of your colleagues to help you attack gay men? You'd never risk it."

"So where does that leave us?" said Connie.

"Nowhere," replied Ian.

"We don't have to be so negative," said Connie. Zoe raised an eyebrow. Connie looked at her, her brow furrowed. "It's true though, Sergeant Osman wants to give up. But we can't give up." She swallowed. "I'm scared, boss. For Zaf, and for your Nicholas."

Rhodri opened his mouth to speak but Zoe stopped him with a hand on his shoulder. "Let's not let this get personal, folks." She surveyed the board. "We still have the knife, and the injections. Yanis said the attacker injected him and Charlie with something. We need to find out what."

"I'll call the hospital, boss," said Connie.

"Good. Rhodri, I want you on the knife. Find out where you can buy those things."

"You'll be able to get them online," he said. "We'll never—"

"It's not easy to sell hunting knives anonymously. Find the suppliers, get a photo of a knife like the one that's been described to us. Find out where he got it, if you can."

Rhodri shrugged. "I'll try."

"Good. Jason feels like a dead end to me, and so does Carmichael. Ian, talk to the woman who dobbed him in, just in case. Then we need to find Jackson Potter."

"Who's he?" asked Petra.

"He's the man who lied to me about the car park. Connie, can you work your magic with names and addresses?"

"Where did he say he lived?'

"Stechford."

Connie swivelled her chair and leaned into her monitor. “No Jackson Potter anywhere in the city.”

“You sure?” said Ian.

“It’s true.” Connie scowled at him.

“Try variations on his name. Different spellings. Turn it backwards,” Zoe said.

“Already did,” said Connie. “He doesn’t live in Brum.”

“Shit.” Zoe grabbed a hand through her hair. Now she really needed to track this man down.

CHAPTER FIFTY-THREE

The team turned away from Zoe and started to work on their assignments. Connie stared into her screen. Rhodri picked up his phone, and Petra made notes in a pad. Ian rose from his chair and slung his jacket over his shoulders. As he left the room, Connie looked up at his retreating figure, her face twisted.

"Connie?" said Zoe.

The constable looked up. "Boss?"

"Could you come into my office for a moment?"

Connie looked at Rhodri, who shrugged. Zoe walked into her office, waited for the constable to join her, and closed the door.

"You need me to work on something else, boss?'

"No, Connie. Nothing like that."

"OK."

Zoe perched on the desk. Connie stood by the door, tugging at her sleeves.

"You seem to have a problem with DS Osman," Zoe said.

"No problem." Connie looked ahead, not meeting Zoe's eye.

"Don't lie to me, Connie. You clearly don't appreciate working with him. Mind telling me what's happened?'

"Nothing." Connie switched her gaze to Zoe, her eyes steady. "It's fine."

"I saw the way you were looking at him in there. The way you talked to him. He's your senior officer. Would you have talked to Mo like that?"

"Of course not."

"In which case, don't do it with Ian. He deserves your respect."

"Can I be honest with you, boss?"

"I've got a feeling I'm going to regret this."

Connie stared at her, nostrils flaring.

"OK then," Zoe sighed. "Get it out. Maybe then you can go back to doing your job."

"He's not pulling his weight."

"He went to interview Carmichael, didn't he?"

"Yes. But he has a habit of disappearing."

Zoe let herself relax. "You don't have to worry about that."

"But we need all hands—"

Zoe gave Connie a look. "I know what Ian's doing. It's not your concern."

"What's he doing, boss?"

"Like I say. Not your concern." Zoe strode to the desk and sat down. "Now, you've got work to do. Just play nice, alright? We can't solve the case if we're at each other's throats."

"Sorry."

"Apology accepted. Now let's—"

The door flew open. Rhodri stood in the doorway, panting. His cheeks were red and his forehead beaded with sweat.

Zoe turned to him. "Rhod, we're in the middle of—"

Rhodri stared back at her. "You're going to want to see this, boss."

CHAPTER FIFTY-FOUR

Mo SAT at the back of the team meeting, wishing he could be anywhere else. Dawson was tearing a strip off DC Fran Kowalczyk, and it was excruciating to watch.

"Next time you want to lose a vital piece of evidence, warn me, huh?"

"Sorry sir."

"Huh. Right. Where are we?"

Mo's pocket buzzed as his phone came alive. He resisted pulling it out, knowing what the reaction would be.

"Sergeant Uddin? You got something more urgent to do?"

"No, sir."

"Somebody must think so. Just bloody answer it will you?"

Mo took his phone out, trying to ignore the eyes that had turned to him. Fran looked relieved to be out of the spotlight.

Number withheld. He hit the answer icon.

"DS Uddin."

"My brother says he'll talk to you." The voice was young, male. Agitated.

"Who is this?"

Dawson cocked his head and flashed his eyes at Mo, his expression mocking. Mo mouthed a *sorry* and cupped his hand over the phone.

"Ruhaan Hussain. You said I could call."

"Ruhaan." Mo looked up. Dawson's face had turned to stone. He didn't approve of Mo working this case, and had been pleased when Mo had dropped it.

"What can I do for you?" Mo asked.

"I was right."

Mo frowned. "What were you right about, Ruhaan?"

"The Ripper. He got Amit. He was holding him in his house all that time."

Mo stood up. "Amit told you that?"

"Sort of."

"What do you mean, sort of?"

"He's... reluctant. To give me the details. But he weren't at no friend's house. He was taken, by this guy. And he got away."

Dawson took a step forward. Mo held out a hand to stop him. He nodded at his boss, hoping to convey his own excitement.

"Where are you, Ruhaan?"

"At home. Our parents are out."

"I'll be right there, Ruhaan."

CHAPTER FIFTY-FIVE

"WHAT, Rhodri? What do I need to see?"

Rhodri bounded into the room and circled Zoe's desk. As he reached out to turn on her computer she stared at him, perplexed.

"Er, Rhod..."

He blinked at her. "Alright if I use your computer?"

"You already are. What's all the panic?"

"You'll see."

Petra was in the doorway, her normal shrewd expression replaced by one of urgency.

"What is it?" Zoe asked her.

"The victims told you he had a camera."

"Yes."

Petra nodded towards the computer. "He's uploaded it."

"Shit." Zoe pulled in her chair, willing Rhodri to hurry up. "Where?"

"YouTube," said Rhodri. He jabbed at the keyboard.

"Let me," Connie said. She turned the laptop towards

her and clicked the trackpad a few times. A voice rang out: Adam's.

Zoe pulled back to let the team gather around her desk, all eyes on the screen. Adam was sitting in his kitchen, looking into the camera, his eyes dull.

"My name is Adam Hart," he said.

"When did this go up?" Zoe asked.

"Just now," Rhodri said. "We got an email, in the team inbox. The one we gave out for the appeal."

Zoe's breath felt ragged. "We need to get it taken down."

"Don't you want to watch it first?" Petra asked.

Zoe eyed her across the desk. She was the only person in the room on the wrong side of the screen.

"Yes. But I also want to make sure other people can't. Those men have families."

Petra rounded the desk to stand behind Zoe's chair. She put a hand on its back, her fingertips brushing the back of Zoe's neck. Zoe bristled.

"Why is this man in your house?" came a voice from off-camera. The camera panned to Mitch, who was in a chair at right angles to Adam. His wrists were tied to the chair and his mouth was covered in tape.

"Adam didn't tell us about that," Connie said.

"Shush," said Zoe.

"I invited him home," Adam said.

"Don't be shy," said the voice. "You invited him here for sex, didn't you?"

The camera switched back to Adam. "Yes," he said, unblinking.

"Do you understand how perverted and sick that is?"

"No." Adam squared his shoulders.

"You pick up men you've never met and bring them home to sodomise them."

Adam's expression flickered. "It's not like that."

"Tell me what it is like, then."

"I'm not telling you anything."

There was a groan from off-camera. Was the killer hurting Mitch?

"Tell me."

"It's no different from if you brought a woman home. I assume you're into women."

A sharp sound off-camera followed by a cry. The image panned to Mitch. Next to him on the table, a knife quivered, its tip stuck in the wood.

"Don't you presume to know anything about me," came the voice. "Have you heard of the story of Sodom and Gomorrah?"

"I have. It's not actually about—"

"Shut up. The Bible clearly states that people like you are sinners. What do you think to that?"

"No comment." Adam, back in the line of sight, swallowed.

"OK," said the voice. "Seeing as you won't listen, let me try this."

Zoe turned to Connie. "Can you get this taken down?"

Connie shrugged. "It's YouTube, boss."

"We might be about to witness a murder. I don't care if it's bloody *Candid Camera*."

"What's that?" asked Rhodri, just as the door was yanked open and Lesley walked in.

"What the fuck is going on?" asked the DCI.

"We're going to get it shut down," said Zoe.

"Bit late for that. Have you watched to the end?"

"No." Zoe nodded at Connie who leaned over to click the trackpad. The picture sped up. The film was forty minutes long.

"Shit," Zoe breathed. She looked up at her boss. "It only just went up."

"Yes, and I want it bloody well coming back down again. I've already had Randle on the phone."

"He got the email?"

"I have no idea, Zoe. But this has to come down."

"Two minutes off the end, boss," said Connie. The picture came to a halt, Mitch's face in close-up. A bright light illuminated his face.

Mitch let out a strangled cry. Off-camera there was whimpering: Adam? Another sound made Zoe's stomach turn: squelching sounds.

"Sounds like cutting," she said. She felt sick.

Connie put her hand over her mouth. "Oh God."

Zoe wanted to turn it off, to rip her eyes away. But she had to watch. This was evidence.

The camera stayed on Mitch's face, his shoulders and part of his torso in shot. He wore a denim shirt, done up to the neck. His mouth was still taped up and his eyes stared widely ahead of him, not focused on the camera.

"Oh my God," whispered Zoe.

Mitch screamed through the tape. His head shot from side to side and his eyes widened.

"He's..." said Connie.

"Yes," said Zoe.

Mitch's eyes squeezed shut. A spot of blood appeared on his shirt. Where was Adam?

He'd told Zoe that he'd been cut first, that he'd lost consciousness. She'd have to rewind, to find the moment the killer switched between the two men. He might have included footage of himself, even if only his hands.

A strangled cry came from the computer's speakers.

"Turn it to mute," said Lesley.

"It's evidence," Zoe replied.

"Does everyone in this room need to hear it?'

Zoe sniffed and hit the mute button on the keyboard. Mitch stared at them in silence, his eyes on a point beyond the camera. His cheeks were moving, his chin too. He was trying to speak.

Zoe leaned forward and turned the volume up. It was muffled, but there was something.

"Help."

Connie moaned. Rhodri put a hand on her back. Ice ran across Zoe's skin.

She looked up at Petra.

"Does this tell you anything more about him?"

Petra nodded, her eyes steady on Zoe. "It does, detective. It does."

CHAPTER FIFTY-SIX

Mo knocked gently on the Hussains' front door. Ruhaan opened it within seconds, his eyes wild.

"Detective. Come in." He leaned out and looked up and down the street.

Mo stepped into the hallway. "Where are your parents?"

"They went to the mosque."

"How long will they be?"

"Another hour or so."

"Have you told them anything? Has Amit?"

Ruhaan shook his head. His breathing was heavy, filling the narrow space.

"It's bad, isn't it?"

"I need to talk to Amit."

Ruhaan nodded and gestured towards a door.

In the living room, Amit sat on a low chair, staring into a marble fireplace. He looked up at Mo's entrance then glared at Ruhaan.

"I don't want to talk about it."

"You have to, mate. What if he killed someone else?"

Amit frowned but said nothing.

Mo took a seat on the sofa next to Amit's chair.

"Hi, Amit."

Amit shrugged.

"My name's Mo Uddin. I'm a detective working on your case. I'd like to ask you a few questions."

Another shrug.

"How long have you been home?"

Amit looked up at his brother as if unsure of the answer.

"Since yesterday morning," said Ruhaan. "I found him in the back garden."

"Had you been in the garden for long?"

Amit nodded.

"How long, Amit?"

"Dunno. Hours."

It was December. The kid might have frozen to death.

"Did you escape, or did he let you go?"

Amit shook his head.

"Can you remember?"

Amit's eyes narrowed. "No."

"Why not?"

Amit turned to stare at him. "He drugged me." He balled his fists in his lap.

"Who did?"

"The man who grabbed me at the bus stop."

Ruhaan let out a sigh. Mo nodded. "When did he grab you?"

"Thursday night. Ten thirty. Same bus I always get."

"Was it just the one man?"

Amit glanced at Ruhaan. "Yes."

"Did he hurt you, when he grabbed you?"

Amit placed his finger on his forehead. "Yes. I blacked out."

"He hit you on the head?"

"Mmm."

"You're doing really well, Amit. How much do you remember about where he kept you?"

"A room. Dingy. I thought it was a shed, or an outbuilding. But there was another room. He watched me."

"He had a camera?"

"Yes. But that's not how he watched me. Through the door."

"Tell me if I've got this right. The man attacked you, he put you out cold, and you woke up in this room?"

"Yeah."

"Did you see his face?"

Amit nodded. "He didn't hide. I thought he was going to kill me."

Ruhaan edged around Mo and stood next to his brother. He put a hand on his shoulder. Amit shuddered.

"What did he look like?" asked Mo.

"White. Dark hair, very short. He wore all black."

"What about his face?'

"Average looking. Sort of roundish, I guess. Sorry."

Mo pulled his phone from his pocket and brought up the Force CID Twitter account. "Is this him?"

Amit looked at the e-fit, his eyes glazed. "Could be."

"OK. How did you get away?"

"He drugged me. Injected me with something he said would... Then I woke up in Highbury Park."

"When did that happen?"

"Late. Night before last."

"Did he talk to you? Did you hear his voice?"

A nod.

"What did he sound like?"

"Local. Brummie."

"Anything else? Rough, smooth, high-pitched, low-pitched?"

"Smooth, I guess."

"What did he talk to you about?"

Amit tensed.

"This is confidential, Amit. I won't tell anyone." Mo licked his lips. "Including your parents."

Amit drew a breath. "He told me I was sick."

Mo waited.

"He said he would cure me."

"How?"

"The drugs."

"The drugs he injected you with?"

A nod. A tear fell from Amit's nose into his lap. Ruhaan tightened his grip and Amit shook him off.

"OK, Amit. We'll need to find out what drugs he gave you. They could still be in your system. I'd like you to come with me to the station, so we can run tests."

"No."

"If we don't do it now, the drug will leave your system." It already might have, Mo thought, but didn't say.

"My dad."

"We don't need to tell your dad."

"He thinks I was with friends." Amit looked into Mo's face. His eyes were dull, not focusing properly. "He can't know."

"Amit." Mo gave him a tight smile. "I won't tell your

parents about your sexuality. No one is judging you. But this man preys on gay men. You can help us stop him."

"I can't come to the station. Not now."

"OK." Mo considered. "Have you got a container? A jam jar or something? It has to be clean."

"Why?" asked Ruhaan. He lowered himself to the arm of Amit's chair and Amit shifted away from him.

"I need a urine sample," Mo said. "It's not perfect this way, but it'll have to do."

"Amit," said Ruhaan, bending towards his brother. "All you have to do is pee into a jar. It can't be that bad, can it?"

"I can't see the point."

"It's evidence, Amit," Mo said. "It might help us track down your attacker."

Amit looked into the fire. It was unlit, making Mo feel cold. A family picture hung above it in an ornate frame.

"OK," the young man finally said. He pushed himself up from his chair.

"I'll find a jar," said Ruhaan.

"Thanks," said Mo.

He waited while the two brothers disappeared. There was movement in the kitchen, Ruhaan looking for an empty jar no doubt. Then he heard footsteps going upstairs. After a few moments, Ruhaan returned and stood next to the fire, not meeting Mo's eye.

"Thanks for calling me," Mo said.

"He's terrified," Ruhaan replied.

"I know. We're going to find his attacker, and—"

Ruhaan's head went up. "Not of him. Of Dad."

Mo thought of his own parents. His dad was traditional, like this family. His marriage to Catriona had caused a rift between them that had only cooled with his daughter Fiona's birth.

"I'm sorry," he said.

"You understand."

"Yes."

"He'll help you, I think. But he won't do anything public."

"That's OK. He's an adult, we don't need to involve your parents."

"We need you to go soon, they'll be back."

"Not a problem."

The door opened and Amit entered. He held out a jar that had once held cannellini beans. Now it contained urine. Mo pulled a pair of evidence gloves and a bag from his pocket and took it. As evidence this wasn't perfect – who knew how the remains of the beans might compromise it? But it was all he could get.

"Thanks, Amit."

Amit nodded in response, his eyes on the jar.

"I have to warn you, it will become public that we have another victim. But we won't reveal your identity. We won't give the press anything that makes it possible for them to identify you."

"Will you say I'm gay?"

"We will say that the fifth victim is gay. Not you."

Amit looked pained.

"We have to find him, Amit. The public can help us with that."

"OK." Amit looked towards the door.

"I'll leave you now. I'm grateful for your help. If I need to contact you, what's the best way?"

"My mobile," said Ruhaan. "Just say your name, if Mum picks it up. Miss out the police part."

"Will do."

"Just in case, you know."

"I know."

Mo heaved himself up, taking one last glance at Amit as Ruhaan led him out of the room. The young man looked broken. And he couldn't even tell his parents about it.

CHAPTER FIFTY-SEVEN

Zoe's phone rang: Mo. She'd have to call him back.

"Ian, Rhodri, you've still got jobs to do," she said. "Connie, I want you to do everything in your power to get this taken down. And check out the account that posted it."

"I'll do what I can."

"Good."

Zoe looked up at Lesley. "Can you help with this, ma'am?"

"How?"

"We might need someone in authority to contact YouTube. Get the video taken down."

"OK. Connie, you focus on tracking the user down. I'll talk to the Superintendent in charge of the Digital Crime Unit. We'll get this sorted." Lesley eyed Zoe. "Keep an eye on it, in the meantime. He might put another one up."

"Charlie and Yanis."

"Did either of them say anything about a video?"

"Yanis did. He filmed the two of them, before he cut them."

"He'll be putting that up next."

"He probably won't use the same account, ma'am," Connie said. She was still at Zoe's desk, huddled over her laptop. "He'll know we're onto him."

Zoe sighed. "It's going to be impossible to keep this under wraps, isn't it?"

"We have to try." Lesley patted Zoe on the shoulder and left the office, her footsteps hurried.

"It'll already have been copied and downloaded, boss," Connie said.

"Still. Like the DCI says, we have to try. And someone has to warn Adam. Charlie and Yanis too." She looked into the outer office. Ian had gone and Rhodri was on the phone.

She grabbed her phone. "Ian. Forget Carmichael for now. Get to the hospital. Warn the three victims about this."

"He's put a video of the other two up?"

"Not yet. But it's a matter of time."

Connie sat back. "It's impossible, boss."

"What is?"

"I've trawled the Internet for the username for this account."

"Which is?"

"'Heteropride', boss."

"Jeez. You can't find anything?"

"Nothing. No social media, no videos apart from this one. I've put an alert on YouTube for this kind of content though."

"How d'you do that? No, on second thoughts, I don't need to know."

"I've bookmarked Digbeth Ripper and all permutations of that. Castration. Homophobic attacks. Gay conversion. It'll ping my phone if there's anything else."

"Is the video in breach of the platform's terms of service?" Zoe asked.

"Definitely. They'll take it down, as long as they know about it. Eventually."

"Eventually."

"Yeah."

"Is that it?" Ian was still on the line. "D'you need anything else from me?'

"Get a witness statement from Charlie, I haven't been able to speak to him yet. But make sure the three of them are warned. Don't let them watch it."

"That's not going to be easy."

"Yeah."

Connie stood up. She tugged down her jacket sleeves. "I'll be at my desk."

Zoe shook her head.

"Ian, how far have you got?" she said into the phone.

"Just leaving the car park."

"Good. Wait a minute, pick Connie up."

Connie's features hardened. "I'd rather..."

Zoe shook her head. "She'll be out front. The two of you can do this together."

"Right." Ian hung up.

Zoe pushed back her chair. "I know you're not happy about this, Connie. But you two have to find a way to work together."

"If you say, boss."

"I do say. He's an experienced detective sergeant, and you're still learning. You could do worse."

Connie muttered something Zoe couldn't make out.

"Go on then," she said, irritated. "Get to the front of the station, or you'll miss him."

CHAPTER FIFTY-EIGHT

Connie pulled open the door to Ian's car as if it was on fire.

"Connie," he said as she closed it behind her.

"Sarge."

He pulled away before she'd had a chance to buckle herself in. "Any ideas on the best way to break this to them? I was thinking 'you're on YouTube having your balls cut off' wasn't the best."

She winced. "We haven't watched it, Sarge. We don't know if Adam is on the video."

"OK, you watch it then, while I drive."

Connie swallowed the lump in her throat. It had been bad enough watching it the first time, with everyone else in the room. But she had a job to do. She pulled out her phone.

The video was still up, the only one in the Heteropride account. She hit play and skipped the opening moments, which she'd already seen.

"Are you prepared to convert?" The attacker's voice.

Adam sneered. "I don't know what you're talking about."

A pause.

"I'm not sure what crap you've been reading online," Adam continued. "But it doesn't work like that. I'm gay. I've always been gay, and I always will be. I can't just *change my mind* about it."

"You might."

Adam looked to one side, his expression shifting from defiance to horror. "Don't do that to him. Please."

Connie pushed the phone further from her face, her skin prickling. Adam looked back towards the camera. He was focused on a point just to its left. His interrogator's face, no doubt.

They were leaving Harborne now, heading for the city centre. "Anything useful?" said Ian.

"He's trying to convince them to convert to being straight."

"OK."

She felt cold. "Zaf told me about a Facebook group he found," she said. "Before he came out. The guy running it claimed he could do this."

"Who's Zaf?"

"My brother. He even considered it. He was being bullied at school."

"How did that go?"

"He only considered it for five minutes."

"Still. Can't be easy."

"Easy or not, Adam's right. You can't just change your sexuality."

"Surely there are some people who decide they're going to be gay," Ian said. "It is kind of cool, in some circles."

Connie slammed her phone into her lap. "Cool?"

Ian shrugged. "Lipstick lesbians, and all that."

"My brother was beaten by three guys in a pub. He's been called names you haven't even heard of. That is not *cool.*"

"Sorry."

"No." She stared at him. How was she supposed to work with this arsehole? How could they trust him to track down a homophobic killer, when he talked like that?

She clenched her phone, willing herself to breathe.

"Sounds like those religious groups, in the US," Ian said. "Gay conversion therapy."

"It's bollocks," she told him. "All of it."

He raised an eyebrow. "Bollocks, Constable? Apt choice of word."

She opened her mouth but no words came out. She turned to the window and stared out at the traffic, her body hot with frustration and anger.

At last they arrived at the hospital. Connie opened her door before the car had come to a complete stop and jumped out. She needed air.

"Trauma ward," she said, not looking at her boss.

"Yup." Ian looked up at the building. "Lead on."

She wanted to tell him she had no idea where to go, but she also didn't want him to think she was incompetent. She eyed a map as she passed it, scanning for the ward she needed. Luckily, it was marked.

"This way," she said.

"After you."

She led him along a wide corridor until they reached the ward. She pushed through the doors, not holding them open for the sergeant.

Inside, a nurse looked up. "Visiting's over, sorry. You can come back at—"

Connie held up her warrant card. "DC Williams, DS Osman. We're here to see Adam Hart. It's urgent."

"Oh. OK."

"And then we'll need to talk to Charlie Hessel and Yanis Liakos."

"We can take one each," said Ian.

"No," replied Connie.

He put a hand on her shoulder to stop her. She span round and he let go.

"No?" he said. "You giving the orders now?"

"I think we should do it together. That's what the boss wanted."

"She said no such thing."

"She sent us both. Maybe she wanted you to ask the questions, and me to do the touchy-feely stuff."

"You don't strike me as the touchy-feely type."

"No."

"Well, then," he said. "You talk to Adam, I'll take Charlie and Yanis. I need to get a statement from Charlie."

"We should do that together."

"You don't give up, do you? OK, as long as you're done with Adam by the time I've finished with Yanis, we can do it together. Happy?"

"Yes."

"Good." He span on his heel and followed the nurse who was waiting to take him to Yanis. Connie headed in the direction of Adam's bed, realising she hadn't watched the rest of the video and had no idea what she was going to tell him.

CHAPTER FIFTY-NINE

Zoe turned to Petra after Connie left the office. "So?"

Petra leaned against the wall. "So, what?"

"You said it tells you more about him. The video."

"Ah. Yes, it does." Petra pulled a chair over to the desk and sat down. She slipped off one of her shoes and rubbed her foot. Zoe waited. At last Petra stopped rubbing the foot. "Have you got a tissue?"

Zoe rummaged in a drawer and found a pack. "Here." She threw it to the other woman.

Petra grabbed it and took out a tissue. She blew her nose. "I'm convinced I'm allergic to something in your office."

"Any chance you might tell me about the killer?"

"I'm coming to it. You think I haven't been busy thinking, while you lot have been fannying around?"

"I wouldn't call it that."

"Hmm. So. We heard his voice. From an evidentiary standpoint that's not much use. He could be disguising it, it doesn't sound out of the ordinary. Witnesses are notoriously bad at remembering voices."

"I agree." Zoe eyed her laptop. It was still open on the video, paused almost at its end. Comments were mounting up. She tightened her jaw. How long before it was taken down?

"Good," said Petra. "From what I've seen so far, I can tell you that it confirms my suspicions that he prepared for his crimes."

"This only relates to one of them."

"It's the same with the other two men. He knew how to get into their house. He waited. This is all planned. Maybe for some time. He's confident, articulate. He says it's about God, but I wouldn't be so sure."

"You don't think he's a religious nut."

"Your witnesses have told you he didn't say anything about a cult, anything like that?"

"He talked about God. About divine punishment."

"But nothing about a cult."

"No. You think that means he isn't religiously motivated."

"You're catching on. There's more to him than that."

"You sound as if you admire him."

Petra looked back at her, not denying the accusation. "He isn't religiously motivated."

"I don't see how..."

Petra raised a finger. "Let me speak."

Zoe felt her teeth grinding together.

"He picks his victims," Petra continued. "Not high-risk."

"What does that mean?"

"Some victims are high-risk, others are low. High-risk types include prostitutes, drug addicts, petty criminals. The kind of people whose lifestyle puts them at a good chance of coming up against someone who'll hurt them. They know that. Some of them take precautions, others don't. But these men were low-risk. Mitch less so, but he wasn't the target. The targets were Adam, Charlie and Yanis. All professional middle-class types. Homeowners. Not closeted. The perp knows these men are harder to get to than the high-risk ones, but he does it anyway. Which is why he needs to plan."

"So why doesn't he find softer targets?"

"It's a challenge. And it would mean more to him, if he could convert someone with more than just jelly in his head."

"He wants to argue with intelligent men, and convince them they're wrong for being gay?" Zoe said.

"Nail on the head, Inspector."

"Sounds like he's religiously motivated to me."

"There'd be symbolism if it was. He'd leave us clues, evidence of his faith. He'd be proud of it, would make damn sure everyone knew he was doing this for God."

"But he already said he is."

Petra shook her head. "Uh-uh. I listened to your interview with Adam. He said God saw Adam as a sinner. He didn't say God had decreed that he convert."

"What's his motive, then?"

"Something personal. Something buried."

"You're saying that if we find that, we'll find him."

"Perhaps. It's more likely to give you confirmation once you do find him."

Zoe huffed out a sigh. "That's not much use to us then, is it?"

"Look. I can help you narrow it down. You've got your e-fit. We know he's strong, he can haul those men around, even with the help of a trolley. But he's not young. He's considered, intelligent. Degree-level education. He drives an estate car, or more likely a van. But a small one, not a stonking great thing that people would spot."

"That's how he transported them."

"It is. He has some surgical skills, but I don't believe he's a surgeon. He doesn't talk like a surgeon."

"How the hell are surgeons supposed to talk?"

"Och, I don't know. They've got that way about them. Haven't you noticed? He doesn't sound like that."

"OK. So we've got a middle-aged—"

"I didn't say middle-aged. He's in his early thirties, most likely."

"A man in his early thirties, drives a small van, knows how to use a knife. Educated. Single?"

"Uh-uh."

"Married?"

"Or with a partner. A woman, of course."

"Of course. Surely she'd know."

"No. She thinks he's perfectly normal. He's clever, remember." Petra reached down to scratch her foot. "Does that help?"

"That depends," Zoe replied.

"On whether you believe me. Or whether you think I'm full of shit."

Zoe shrugged.

"I'm not." Petra's gaze was cool on her. "Your superintendent wouldn't have hired me if I was."

David Randle, Zoe thought. She had no idea if his judgement could be trusted. She had a thought.

"The surgical skills," she said.

"Yes. Your pathologist said those cuts were fuckin' neat."

"How much do you know about gangland punishment methods?"

Petra's mouth opened and closed again. "A little."

"There are men – and it's always men – whose job it is to administer the punishments. They're not as unsubtle as you might think. I saw one case where a man had his eye cut out for co-operating with us. It was a neat job, stitched up like a professional. You'd have thought it was done in hospital."

"You're thinking he works in organised crime."

"He might do." Zoe stood up. "Or might have. I need to talk to someone."

"Be my guest. But be careful." Petra leaned back in her chair, clamping her hands over her chest.

"Careful, why?"

"He's not going to stop of his own accord, you know. They never do. He'll be watching the investigation. Has probably worked his way into it somehow, been to a public meeting or something."

"We were watching that meeting. He would never have got into that pub."

"He's rung the hotline, or something. He'll be keeping tabs on you."

"I'll keep my eyes open."

"Not just for interference, inspector. He thinks he can outsmart you."

"The bars in the gay village are being vigilant. They've installed extra CCTV. We've told people to stick together, to keep off the streets in the small hours. I don't see how much more we can do."

"I'm not talking about the gay village, Zoe." Petra stood up and looked into her eyes. "I'm talking about you. You need to take precautions. Avoid being alone at night. Check your locks. He'll target you next."

CHAPTER SIXTY

Zoe stared back at Petra. She'd spent the last ten minutes deciding the woman might be talking sense after all. But then, she'd blown it.

"He targets gay men," she said. "Middle-class, low-risk men. You said so yourself." She thought of Nicholas. He didn't fit the victim profile. He was young, lived at home. At school. "And he certainly doesn't target police officers," she added.

"I'm just saying. Be careful."

Zoe shook her head. She opened the door to her office. She wanted to shake herself out, to wash off the intensity of Petra's presence. The woman had a way of looking at you that made it feel like she was getting inside your skull.

She collected her thoughts. She needed to speak to Lesley, get a progress update on the video being taken down. And she needed to track down Jackson Potter.

She stopped walking. She turned back toward her office. Petra was still inside, massaging her toes.

Zoe pushed the door open. "I've met him."

"You have?"

"He approached me, outside the public meeting. You saw him too. He was—"

Petra put up a hand. "Don't tell me. I don't want to be influenced. Does he fit what I just said to you?"

"I talked to him for five minutes. I've got no idea."

"Then find him. Watch him, and see if it fits."

"Yes." Zoe imagined what Lesley would say. Her suspicions were flimsy at most, and would never constitute evidence. She had to gather that evidence. Had to find out who Jackson Potter really was, and link him to the weapons and the YouTube account.

She let the office door shut behind her. "Rhodri, I've got a job for you."

"Boss."

"Prioritise tracking down that knife. Use the images from the video. And call the manager at the Jackal, we need to check CCTV from that meeting yesterday."

She walked to the board and wrote his name: Jackson Potter.

"Who's he, boss?" Rhodri asked.

"He's the one who got us chasing our tails watching CCTV from Pershore Street car park. It was all crap. Designed to throw us off the scent."

"And to involve himself in the investigation." Petra stood outside the door to Zoe's office.

"I thought you couldn't know the details?"

"Bit late for that now."

Zoe paced the office. Rhodri gave her a wary look but said nothing.

"Go on then," she snapped at him. "Get onto it."

Zoe went to the desk Petra had been using. Petra's bright

orange coat was slung over the back of the chair. Zoe stared at it, then pulled out her phone. She dialled Nicholas.

It rang out. She checked her watch. He would be in lessons.

"This is Nicholas. Leave me a message if you know what's good for you."

She hesitated, then hung up. He wouldn't want her clucking around him when he was at school.

The door opened. Zoe turned to see Mo running in. He was panting.

"Mo, you alright?"

He nodded, leaning over to catch his breath. "Why aren't you picking up your bloody phone?"

She reached for it inside her pocket. "What's going on?"

He shook his head. "We've got another one."

"Another what?"

"Another victim, Zo."

CHAPTER SIXTY-ONE

"Where?" Zoe said.

"He's back home," said Mo. "We can't go there."

Zoe frowned. "Back home?"

"He escaped. Or he was allowed to leave, I'm not clear yet. He isn't either."

"This your kid? The one who disappeared?"

"Not a kid. A young man. And yes. Your guy attacked him at his bus stop, knocked him cold and held him prisoner for four days. He got away late Monday night."

"We need to interview him. If Potter held him somewhere..."

"Potter?"

"He's my suspect, as of five minutes ago."

"Who's Potter?"

She perched on a desk. "Jackson Potter. At least that's the name he gave us. He approached me outside the Jackal yesterday, gave me some information which turned out to be wrong."

"So maybe he's just an unreliable witness."

"It's what they do," said Petra. "Killers like this, they inveigle their way into the investigation. There was a case in the USA where they held job interviews for the police, and the killer applied."

"But all he did was give you some duff information," Mo said to Zoe.

"I have to go to the Jackal," Zoe said. "I need to see if anyone recognised him.,"

"I'm getting Amit's urine analysed. He said he was drugged. Injected."

"Like Yanis," said Zoe.

"Yanis?"

Zoe pointed to Yanis's picture on the board. Mo would need to be brought up to speed on the case; they'd hardly spoken the last few days. "One of the Moseley victims. He said the man injected him."

"That's what Amit said too."

Zoe felt her heart pick up pace. She stared at Mo, his eyes reflecting the adrenaline back at her. Behind her, the room had gone quiet.

"It's the same guy," he said. "Got to be."

She nodded. "How is Amit? Was he castrated too?"

"His brother says not. Just the drugs."

"That makes no sense."

"Maybe he got away before the killer had a chance."

"Maybe."

"I need to talk to DI Dawson. Let him know what I've found."

Zoe pulled a face. "He'll have to release you to work this case with us."

"Not necessarily."

"You want me to have a word with him?"

"I can do it myself."

"Good luck."

Zoe hurried into the inner office and grabbed her coat from the back of the door. "Rhod, if you get anything on that knife, call me. And keep me up to date on the video."

"No problem, boss."

The door opened: Connie. She strode to her desk, her face hard.

"Connie? How did it go with Adam?" Zoe asked.

Connie looked up. "He was scared. Humiliated."

"Poor man."

Connie hunched over her computer screen. "It's still online. Nothing else yet, thank God. But it's still up."

"I'm sure the DCI is—"

"It makes no difference anyway." Connie looked up at her. "It's been copied. It's on multiple platforms. The mainstream news sites are even playing the opening seconds."

"Shit." Zoe dumped her coat back on her chair. "What about Charlie and Yanis?"

"Ian spoke to Yanis, took Charlie's statement."

"And you're sure there's no video of them online?"

"Not yet." Connie drummed her fingers on the desk. She seemed angry. What had happened between her and Ian?

"What have I missed?" Ian closed the door behind him. He looked from Zoe to Connie and back again. Connie pointedly ignored him.

Damn, thought Zoe. *This is all I need.*

"What did Charlie say, Ian?" she asked.

"Pretty much the same as Yanis told you. It was almost identical to Adam's video. Trying to brainwash them, threatening them, then when he didn't get his way, forcing them onto the table and cutting them."

"*Not* brainwashing," Petra muttered.

Ian jerked his head up. "I don't think the terminology really matters, do you?"

Zoe stepped forward. "Look. I know it's been stressful for everyone, seeing the video. Having to tell the other victims. But we need to focus on the case. Let's not attack each other."

"I'm not attacking anyone," muttered Connie, her eyes on Ian.

Zoe gave her an exasperated look. She didn't have time for this.

"Just be nice, both of you," she said. She turned to Petra, tempted to say *you too*. Rhodri was staring at his screen. He'd been like that for the whole conversation, staring into the screen but not once moving his mouse or touching his keyboard.

"Right," Zoe said. "We've got new leads to work on. I need all hands on deck."

She went to the board and stared at Jackson Potter's name. She drew a line between him and the victims. Then she wrote Amit's name and joined that too.

"This man gave us misleading information." She jabbed the pen into Potter's name. "He looked similar to the e-fit, except he had blonde hair. My theory is that he dyed it. Grew some stubble." She turned. "I know, I should have spotted it. But I didn't."

"I told you he was intelligent," said Petra.

Zoe pointed at Petra with the marker pen. "You were right. He knew enough to get himself involved in the enquiry, to throw us off the scent, and not to arouse my suspicion while doing it."

She was going to have to admit what she'd done to Lesley. She wasn't looking forward to that.

"We also have a fifth victim." She pointed at Amit's name. "Amit Hussain. Twenty years old, lives on the Alcester Road. He was attacked and abducted on Thursday night, ten thirty pm, at the bus stop near his house. He spent four days being held by our man, but got away the night before last."

"That's the sarge's case," said Connie.

"DS Uddin has been working that case, yes," said Zoe. Ian looked irritated. "He's got physical evidence that he's taken to the lab. I'm hoping he'll be back soon to share with us what he knows."

"What kind of evidence?" asked Ian.

"A urine sample, from the victim. He says he was injected with a drug that made him woozy and disoriented."

"Whoah." Rhodri scraped his hand through his hair.

"Whoah indeed," said Zoe. "So. We have to find Potter. We have to speak to Amit, if he'll let us."

"If he'll let us?" Ian folded his arms across his chest.

"He's not told his parents about his sexuality. Wants to stay anonymous."

Ian snorted. Zoe gave him a warning look.

"We still need to find out where the killer got that knife," she said. "And once we know what drugs he used on his victims, we'll need to find out where you can get those from, trace any transactions if we can."

"You want me to work on that?" asked Connie.

"Yes. Work with Rhodri, he's already on the knife."

"There's two dealers in Birmingham that sell that kind of knife, boss," Rhodri said. He opened his pad and read out two names.

"Have you contacted them?"

"They're both shut for the day. Left one of them a

message, and used the contact form on the other one's website."

"That's not quick enough, Rhod. Visit them in the morning."

"Sorry, boss."

"Just talk to them, alright? They'll have traced transactions."

"If it is one of those," he said. "He might have had it imported."

"Not easy," said Ian. "You'd never get a hunting knife through customs."

"People manage it," said Rhodri.

"Well, let's hope DS Osman's right," said Zoe. "Let me know how you get on. You can head home after we're done, it's late."

"I want to stay," said Connie. "Until the video's taken down."

"Can't you monitor it all from your phone?"

"I'd rather stay."

"Up to you." Zoe turned to the board. Crime scene photos stared back at her. The incisions.

"I've got a theory about organised crime," she said. "If he's not a surgeon, he could have picked up his skills carrying out punishment cuttings."

"That skillfully?" asked Ian.

"Yes. I'll talk to Sheila Griffin." DS Sheila Griffin was Zoe's contact in the Organised Crime unit. She'd helped her on the Bryn Jackson case.

Ian pursed his lips but said nothing. He stared at the board.

"And Ian, I want you at the Jackal. Connie's got the CCTV from outside the pub around the time of the meeting.

Find an image of Potter. Show it around. Find out if anyone recognises him. He went in there with me after the meeting, so they might remember him from that. But push for anything else. If he was hanging around, talking to anyone."

"Right," said Ian.

"OK." Zoe looked at Petra, who gave her an amused smile in return.

"What?" she said.

"I like watching you like this."

"I'm not going to ask *like what*."

"Efficient. Focused. You think you're close to solving the case."

Zoe didn't like the *think* in that sentence. It was condescending. But it was correct.

"Well, I'll take that as a compliment." She slung her coat over the hook on the back of the main office door, knowing she'd be in the building for a while, then left the room.

CHAPTER SIXTY-TWO

Ten minutes later, Zoe had a printout in her hand and was walking towards Lesley's office, putting a confidence into her stride that she didn't feel.

"Come in." Lesley had her feet up on the desk and was slurping soup from a red mug with *World's Most Average Mum* written on it in bold yellow letters. Her phone was ringing but she was ignoring it.

"Press office," she said. "They've gone mental since that video went up."

"Yes ma'am," Zoe said. The phone stopped ringing and then started again. "I've got an update."

Lesley swung her legs around and put down the mug. She lifted the handset and returned it to its cradle. "Good news, I hope?"

"Not entirely."

"OK."

Zoe took a seat. "After the public meeting, a man approached me. He said his name was Jackson Potter. He told me he'd seen someone dragging something heavy out of the Pershore Street car park on the Friday night."

"So you checked CCTV?"

"We did, ma'am."

"And there was nothing."

"You knew," Zoe said.

The phone rang again. Lesley swivelled in her chair and rooted around on the floor behind her chair. She turned back, the phone jack in her hand. She stuffed the phone in a drawer and slammed it shut.

"You wouldn't be sitting here telling me this story if you'd found something, would you?" she said. "You'd have started with the CCTV. So why is it a problem?"

"Dr McBride reckons the killer would try to involve himself in the investigation. He would try to throw us off the scent."

"And this is how you think he did it?"

"Yes."

Lesley scratched below her eye. "I do hope you took his contact details."

"Of course, but they don't match."

"Of course not. Anything else to trace him?"

Zoe put the printout on the table. "This is him, ma'am."

"Not the best angle"

"Best we could get."

"Hmm. False name and address?"

"The address is real, but he doesn't live there. The name is fake. No one by that name in the whole city."

"You tried further afield?"

"Yes, ma'am."

Lesley grabbed the printout and squinted at it. "You need to release this."

Zoe had another sheet of paper on her lap. She brought that one out and put it next to the first. Lesley turned it round so they were both facing her.

"That's the e-fit Adam Hart gave us," Zoe said.

"Shit."

Zoe stood up. "I understand if you feel the need to reprimand me, ma'am."

Lesley pushed the two sheets of paper across the table. She tugged on her fingers, making them crack. "I'm not going to reprimand you, DI Finch."

"I am truly sorry for not seeing the resemblance at the time."

"Sit down, Zoe."

Zoe sat, waiting.

Lesley picked up the two sheets, one in each hand. She put one of them in front of her face, then the other. "There's a resemblance, yes. But he isn't exactly, well, memorable, is he?"

"That's what all the victims said."

"Well then." Lesley folded the sheets together and pushed them across the table. "Stop beating yourself up about it."

"Thank you, ma'am."

"That all?"

"Has DI Dawson spoken to you?" Zoe asked.

"Dawson? No."

"DS Uddin has found a link between this case and one he's working on. A disappearance. It seems that the same man took his victim."

"Another body?" Lesley grimaced.

"No. He's back at home, with his parents."

"Thank fuck for that." Lesley sat up, shuffling in her

chair. She grabbed the mug. “You liaise with Frank then. You’ll be working on this together.”

“Together?”

“We have five victims now, Zoe. We need more manpower.”

Zoe swallowed. “Of course. So who’ll be SIO?”

“I’m SIO on this, if you remember right.”

“Unofficial SIO.”

“You will, Zoe. It’s your case.”

CHAPTER SIXTY-THREE

Connie sat at her desk, clicking refresh on her browser every two seconds. She wished she had the ability to get this thing taken down. Or the power. Even if it had been copied all over the internet, she hated the fact that the killer was beating them.

She refreshed for the hundred and twentieth time and the screen changed. She leaned in.

"Oh, God."

Petra, the only other person in the office, looked up from the pad she was writing in. "What's up?"

"There's another one. Video."

"That's not good."

"No." Connie stuck her tongue between her lips and pressed play. She sped the video up to one and a half speed.

"It's longer. Over an hour."

Petra was behind her desk now, her perfume filling the air between them. She breathed heavily. "Just the victim."

Connie nodded. The camera was trained on a young

Asian man, dark circles under his eyes and hair plastered to his head. His face was blotchy and his eyes looked like he hadn't slept for days.

"DS Uddin's guy," Petra said.

"Yeah." Connie stood up. "I have to tell the boss. Can you carry on watching?"

"Aye aye."

Connie sped outside. The corridor was quiet, most people having left for the day. Where would the DI be?

She ran to the front desk. Sergeant Jenner was on duty.

"Has DI Finch been past here?"

"Not since a couple of hours ago, far as I know. You want me to check the logs?"

"No. I'll keep looking."

Connie ran back towards the DCI's office. At the door she skidded to a halt. She drew a deep breath then knocked.

"Come in."

Connie pushed the door open, aware she was sweating through her blouse.

Lesley put down a mug and looked at her. "DC Williams."

"I'm looking for DI Finch."

"She just left."

"Oh. Sorry."

"What is it that's got you worked up like a herd of wasps?"

Connie swallowed. "Another video, ma'am. Of Amit Hussain."

"Who?"

"The case that Mo's – that DS Uddin's been working on."

Lesley threw her pen to the desk. "Fuck. YouTube again?" She opened up a laptop.

"Yes, ma'am."

Lesley waved a hand to dismiss her. "Go, then. Find Zoe. And make sure DI Dawson knows too."

"Yes, ma'am." Connie looked along the corridor. She ran to Dawson's office.

Zoe was inside, standing with her back to the door. DS Uddin stood to one side, his eyes on Zoe. Connie watched through the glass for a moment then knocked. Zoe turned.

"What is it?" Dawson snapped as she opened the door.

"Everything OK?" Zoe asked her.

"Another video," Connie said, her eyes on her boss. "Amit Hussain."

"Shit," Dawson breathed. "Give us a minute. We'll be right with you."

Connie looked at Zoe, who nodded. Mo looked pained.

"Go on then," Dawson said.

Connie shut the door and ran back to her desk.

In the office, Petra was staring at the screen, her cheek twitching from time to time. Her mouth was held in a firm line and she looked like she wanted to punch someone.

"Is it bad?" Connie asked.

"Not like the others. It's just talk, this one. But more of it." She looked at the ceiling. "We have to find out when this happened. He's escalating."

"Amit escaped just two days ago. After the other attacks."

"That's what doesn't make sense. If he started with the

castrations, why just talk to this lad?" She clutched at her hair and tugged, working the bun on top of her head loose.

Connie shrugged. If the psychologist didn't know, she certainly wouldn't.

Petra blew out a heavy breath. "I need to talk to Zoe."

"She's on her way. Mo too."

"Mo?"

"DS Uddin."

"Good."

Zoe walked in, Dawson and Mo behind her. "Show us," she said.

Petra turned her screen round. Zoe bent down to watch, her fingers gripping either side of the desk. Connie watched the boss's reaction pass over her face as she watched: intrigue, confusion, disgust.

"This is all psychological," Zoe said as the video finished. "He wants to prove that he can convert his victims. When they don't cooperate, only then does he get nasty." She looked up. "Mo, when will we get the results on the urine test?"

"Mid-morning tomorrow."

"That's too slow."

"It's the best I could get."

Dawson stepped forward. "OK. Let's just stop panicking and look at what we've got. This video doesn't tell us anything. Mo, you have to go back and interview this lad. His family, too. I want to know why he was targeted."

"He was targeted because he's gay," Petra said.

"There's more to it than that. Maybe he had a relationship with his attacker, pissed him off somehow. Surely you lot have found some link between the victims?"

"Mitch Ibsen and Yanis Liakos share an ex-boyfriend,"

said Zoe. "But it's a coincidence. And Mitch wasn't a target. He never should have been there."

"Besides," said Dr McBride. "I've been telling you buggers till I'm blue in the face. This is *not* a revenge attack. Our man is *not* gay, he's *not* an associate of any of his victims. He picked them, sure. He watches them. He prepares. But he *does not* know them." She pulled herself up, seeming taller than her five feet nothing. "If I have to say this one more time, I'm out of here."

Dawson snorted. Connie bit her lip as Zoe gave him a sharp look then turned to the doctor. "You don't. Ignore him."

"I beg your—" Dawson began, but Zoe raised a hand to stop him.

Connie felt cold. A thought had been blossoming in her head, along with a chill that ran down her spine.

"He's going to do it again," she said.

"He is," said Dr McBride. "Men like this only stop when they're caught. Or they die. Sometimes."

"No." Connie stared at her, her vision blurring. "He's going to attack tonight."

"What makes you think that?" Zoe asked.

"There's a pattern. Amit was taken on Thursday. Mitch and Adam on Friday. Charlie and Yanis on Sunday. A gap of one day, then two days. Today's three days after the last attack. Wednesday."

"It doesn't necessarily—" began Zoe.

"She's right," said the psychologist. "He's taunting us. He wants to convert these men. He wants to humiliate them. There is a pattern. And I think the videos are his way of warming up to the next one."

"Why?" asked Mo.

"It doesn't *look* like he's escalating 'cos of the way we've discovered the crimes. But it is." The doctor grabbed a marker pen and walked to the board, jabbing it into Amit's photo. "He started with Amit. Young, slim, not difficult to take down. He used drugs on him but didn't cut him. He probably wasn't expecting him to escape, we need to ask Amit more about that." She paused, her lips moving wordlessly. "Or maybe he *did* want him to escape. Maybe he's teasing us."

She shook her head, as if shaking off bugs. Connie stepped towards her, wanting to speak, but the doctor gave her a look that shut her up.

"Then he attacked Adam." Dr McBride pointed the pen at Adam's photo. "He never expected to have to deal with Mitch too. He knew nothing about Mitch's blood clotting problems, didn't know he'd react the way he did. But he was after just one victim again. A more high-risk victim, for him. Older, stronger, with people around who might spot something unusual. No one else in the house, though. Or that's what he expected. He must have got a shock when Mitch showed up."

She shifted the pen to the photo of Charlie. "Then this couple. Escalating. Married. He knew that. He knew their routines, how to get into the house. He was feeling confident by now, kept them waiting for their interrogation. Then he cut both of them. Which he planned, this time."

She turned to the room. "He's going to attack two more victims, either tonight, or early tomorrow morning. Maybe three." She chewed the pen for a moment. "No, not three. They'll be low-risk individuals, but higher-risk to him. High-profile maybe, or stronger. Harder to get at."

She sat down.

"This is bullshit," said Dawson. "If I wanted this sort of stuff, I'd have called in one of the psychics."

The doctor narrowed her eyes at him. Connie could feel the disdain radiating off her. "*Never* lump me in with those charlatans, sonny." She stood and tossed the pen down on a desk. "You need to find one of them. The killer, or his next victims. And you need to do it fast."

CHAPTER SIXTY-FOUR

Zoe sat in her office, anxious to retreat from the tension of the team room. Mo was still out there, with Dawson. Dawson stood toe to toe with Petra, talking into her face.

Zoe had a headache brewing. She had no idea if Petra's hunch could be trusted. And even if it could, what difference did it make? They were no closer to finding the killer. And there was no way of knowing who the next victim might be. He'd attacked near or in his victims' homes. They could hardly tell every gay man in the city to padlock his doors and watch out for a mysterious man in a hat.

She had to follow the threads she already had. She picked up the phone and dialled Sheila Griffin's mobile.

"Zoe, what's up?"

"No small talk?"

"You wouldn't be calling me at this time if it wasn't something urgent. What's Hamm done this time?"

"It's not Trevor Hamm."

"Good. What then?"

Zoe liked Sheila. They'd worked together on the Canary

case, uncovering a high-profile paedophile ring. Two of the three suspects had walked free, but that didn't mean they hadn't done good work.

"You've heard about the so-called Digbeth Ripper."

The sound of Sheila sucking air through her teeth came down the line. "Nasty. Not my line of work, though."

"There's a chance it might be."

"How so?"

"Four of the victims were castrated. Dr Adebayo said it was neat work, professional. We've got a profiler on the team who swears blind our guy isn't a surgeon. So I'm thinking he might have picked up his skills in an organised crime gang."

"That's pretty specialised."

"We know they do it sometimes. Send guys out to India or Saudi Arabia. Teach them surgical skills. Which they then use on gang members who step out of line."

"Oh, I know alright. I've never seen anything that looks like a surgeon would have done it, though."

"What sort of cuttings have you seen, Sheila?"

"Plenty of fingernail removals. A few eyes. You remember the Lordson case. Neat stitchwork, that one. Then there was the Central gang. They went through a phase of drugging young men with Rohypnol and removing their kidneys."

"What was the surgical work like on those?"

"Pretty good, I guess. You think your guy's part of organised crime?"

"Not any more. He's working alone. But he might have been."

"You don't just stop working for those gangs. Not unless you're in a wooden box."

"He might have pissed them off, got himself kicked out."

"Like I say: wooden box."

"So you don't think he could have learned his skills on the street?" Zoe asked.

"It's unlikely. Maybe there are cutters out there who can do this sort of work. But no one who'd now be operating independently, as it were."

Zoe rubbed her eyes. "Fair enough. Thanks Sheila."

"No problem."

Zoe hung up and looked out at the team room. Petra was at her desk and Dawson was talking to Mo, a lock of hair wagging in front of his face. She opened the door to her office just as Dawson left.

"Where are we?" she asked.

Mo turned to her. "I don't see how we can identify a potential victim."

"Victims," Petra said.

"Or victims." Mo gave Petra an irritated look, then turned back to Zoe. "So we have to work on identifying the attacker."

"We've been working on that for four days now," Zoe said. "I don't see how we can suddenly know who he is."

"We've got the photo."

"Which isn't exactly high definition."

"Still, it might help. Dawson's gone to speak to the press office."

"We can do better than that," said Connie. "Can someone email me the image?'

"I can," said Zoe. "Why?"

"I'll send it to the social media team."

"You're pals with them?" Petra said.

"I did a stint with them, before I passed my police exams."

"Good," said Zoe. "Send it to them, tell them they need to release it now."

"Don't we need to run it past the DCI?" asked Mo.

"I've bothered her enough today. It's fine."

"Dawson's going to be pissed off."

"Dawson can live with it."

Mo's face split into a smile. Neither of them had been able to predict how it would be with Dawson coming back. He'd been an obstructive and petty boss to Zoe, holding back her promotion and insisting she take the *girl's* work. She enjoyed standing up to him.

"Dawson shouldn't have gone to the press office without speaking to me," she said. "I'm in charge of the case."

"Go, boss." Connie punched the air.

"Thanks, Connie. Now just get on with your job, will you?"

CHAPTER SIXTY-FIVE

Zoe parked her car in a side street and got out, looking up and down the road before walking to the Lizard. A uniformed officer stood outside.

"Evening, ma'am."

"Evening. Everything alright here?"

"Quiet."

"Good." The fewer people were in these pubs, the fewer people the killer could potentially target.

Or perhaps not. Maybe they were safer here, in public. Not at home, where they could be picked off alone or in pairs.

She pushed through the door, relishing the blast of warm air that hit her. The bar smelled of beer and spicy food again, not of the detergents they'd used to clean up Charlie and Yanis's blood.

Ian sat at a corner table, staring at his hands. A half pint of lager sat on the table.

"Ian." She took a seat opposite him. The manager, Hal, came to their table and raised an eyebrow.

"Diet Coke, please," she said.

"I thought you might be here on business, not for a drink," he said.

"Surely both are allowed?"

He grunted and went back to the bar.

"Any joy?" she asked Ian. "I've been trying your phone."

"I had to switch it off. Low on juice." Ian's phone was on the table between them.

"I needed an update."

"Sorry."

"If your phone's out of juice, which it doesn't look like to me, you speak to someone from Uniform. You use the pub's phone. You can't just disappear."

He shrugged. "I was busy."

"Talking to people around the village."

"Yeah."

"Did anyone recognise him?"

"Nope."

"Don't sound so—"

"I don't sound anything." He downed the last of his lager. "I don't like being put on grunt work."

"Tracking down the attacker isn't grunt work."

"Uniform could have done it, and you know it. That guy standing on the door. He's putting off the punters."

"Maybe he'd put them off more if he was grilling them about Potter," she said.

"Even so. You should have got Rhodri to do it."

"Rhodri's working on the knife."

"And getting nowhere."

Hal returned with her drink and she fumbled in her jeans pocket for cash. She sipped it gratefully, her lips dry.

"You're his sergeant, Ian. If you think he needs better management, then that's your responsibility."

He eyed her. "You know that's not how it works."

"Jesus, Ian. Will you just quit with this? We've got a killer out there who we reckon's going to attack again and you're too busy being pissed off with me to help find him."

"What d'you mean, attack again?"

"You got my text about the second video."

"Yes."

"Dr McBride thinks he's warming up to a fourth attack. There's been a pattern. We didn't see it because Amit's dates were off."

"You think he's going to attack tonight." Ian looked around the pub. "Shouldn't we be warning people?"

"If we warn them now, they'll rush home. Which is where they're most vulnerable."

"Still." He looked at his watch. "It's only 8pm. They're safer going home now than they will be in a couple of hours."

She surveyed the space. It was half empty. A group of men stood at the bar, five more tables occupied by couples and groups. The music was muted.

Behind the bar, the landlord was tidying up, keeping himself busy. He looked worried.

"I can't go panicking people on the hunch of a psychologist," she said.

"No indeed. Why are you listening to her anyway?"

"Because she seems to understand what makes this guy tick."

"Bollocks she does. She's gathering up information after the fact and piecing it together to make it fit with her own theories."

"She's a qualified psychologist."

"Yeah, yeah," he said. "Still makes it mumbo jumbo, in my book."

Zoe picked up her Coke. A few days ago she'd have agreed with him. But Petra had won her trust.

"I'm worried," she told him.

"Not worried enough to go public, though."

"No."

Her phone rang. She grabbed it, relieved to be interrupted.

"DI Finch."

"Hey, Zoe," said Carl.

She went to cup her hand over the receiver, then stopped herself. "Hello."

Ian drank the rest of his lager and stood up. He scanned the room for the toilets then walked towards them. Zoe let herself breathe.

"I'm with Ian Osman," she said.

"How's he holding up?"

"He's a liability. The sooner you take him off my hands, the better."

"I need to speak to him. I gather he had a meeting this evening."

"I don't want to know. And besides, he's supposed to be focused on this case."

"A man can't do two things at once, you know. We're not like you superwomen."

"Don't."

A pause. She could hear Carl breathing into the phone.

"Sorry," he said. "That came out wrong. You OK?"

"This case." She lowered her voice. "The profiler reckons there's going to be another attack."

"On what basis?"

She downed her Coke, glanced towards the toilets, and walked out of the bar. She passed the officer on the door and stopped partway down the street, where she could see him. "We've had attacks on Thursday, Friday, Sunday. One day's gap, then two. She thinks there's a pattern. Three days is today."

"OK. You need Ian, then."

"I don't give a fuck about Ian."

"He's not that bad."

"It's not easy having a DS who keeps going AWOL in the middle of a case like this. I need his full attention."

"You know I need him too."

"Yeah. But..."

"I can't move him, Zoe. Not yet. If he can link Hamm and Randle..."

Zoe thought of Randle, turning up here two days ago. Smarmy as ever. "OK. I don't think I'm going to be able to see you for that drink tonight."

"It's OK. I know what it's like."

She smiled. It was good to date another detective, someone who understood what it was like doing this job. "Thanks."

"Look after yourself, huh?"

"I will."

"I love you."

She blinked. "You do?"

"Should I not have said that?"

"No. Yes. It's fine. Thanks."

He laughed. "I shouldn't have."

"It's nice."

"It's OK. You don't have to say it back."

"It's only been a few weeks, Carl. And I'm worried. This case. Nicholas."

"It's OK, Zoe. I understand. You get back to the case."

He hung up. She held the phone in front of her, staring at it like it had walloped her. That had come out of the blue. It was years since she'd allowed herself to fall in love: Nicholas's dad, in fact. And he'd been lying to her the whole time.

She'd get there. Eventually. But for now, she had a killer to find.

CHAPTER SIXTY-SIX

"AMIT!"

Amit raised his head from the game he'd been playing on his phone. He tensed.

"Amit! Come down here!"

He hauled himself off the bed. His legs still felt sore, and his arm ached where the man had injected him. He still couldn't remember anything between that and waking up in the park.

He opened his door. It was dark on the landing, the only light coming up the stairs from the living room. He shivered.

"Amit! Your father wants to talk to you." His mum stood at the bottom of the stairs. She held her cardigan tightly around herself. Amit's parents never heated this house properly. He was sure they could afford it, but his dad was just too mean.

He rattled down the stairs, searching his mum's face for a clue as to what they wanted to talk to him about. She looked down towards the bottom step, not meeting his eye.

"Everything OK, Mum?"

A door opened above him: Ruhaan, coming out of his room. Amit heard his footsteps move across the landing. He would be listening. Not getting involved unless he had to.

"Come into the dining room." She turned away from him, still not looking at him. She shuffled into the dining room and he followed, his skin prickling.

He stepped into the room, just as cold as the rest of the house. The curtains were drawn and the room felt oppressive. His dad sat at the table, his hands clasped together on its surface. His cheek twitched. Amit's sister sat two seats away from him.

"Saf? I didn't know you were here."

Safiya lived in Hall Green, about three miles away. She had a husband and a six-month-old baby. The baby wasn't with her.

"Where's Kameela?" Amit asked.

Safiya had her head bowed. "At home. With her dad."

"Shame, I haven't seen her in a bit."

Safiya shrugged. She glanced at their dad, still not meeting Amit's eye.

In front of Dad, on the dining table, was a laptop. Safiya's husband's laptop. Amit felt his heart skip.

He lowered himself into a chair. His mum stood behind him, by the door. She fidgeted with her cardigan buttons.

His dad stared into the computer screen. His brow was creased in a deep frown and his lips pursed. The computer was silent. Amit looked at it, his chest tight. He wanted to ask what was going on.

At last his father pushed the laptop away and looked up. He blinked at Amit.

"Why didn't you tell us?"

Amit straightened. "Tell you what?"

"This." His dad gestured at the screen. Amit glanced at it, wanting to know what was there.

"I don't understand," he said.

"You. On the internet." Dad looked at Safiya.

"YouTube," she said.

Amit looked between his dad and sister. "I don't know what you're talking about." He looked at his sister. "What's up?"

She shook her head and looked at their dad. He looked uneasy.

"Please," Amit said. "Tell me." His mouth was dry.

His dad turned the laptop with a flourish, leaning back and folding his arms as he did so. "This."

Amit took in what was on the screen. It was him, sitting in an old wooden chair in a dingy room.

He felt his breath catch.

He struggled to push out a breath. "When did that go online?" he croaked.

His dad stood up. "When did it go online? That's all you have to say for yourself?"

Amit shrank back. "Sorry." He itched to watch the video. He had to see how much of it was there. The man had recorded hours of footage. He glanced at the counter: this was an hour and a half long. The video had been stopped thirty minutes in.

He swallowed. His chest felt it might explode. "Can I watch it?"

"I don't think you need to watch it, do you?" his dad said. "Seeing as you're *in* it."

He shoved the laptop across the table. It span and landed in Amit's lap. He jumped and it slid to the floor. Safiya huddled in her chair, her cheeks ablaze.

"You are grounded. You disgust me." His dad gave him a look of contempt. He rounded the table, pausing next to Amit's chair. Amit drew into himself, trying to pull away but at the same time not wanting his dad to see him pulling away. Behind him, his mum let out a sob.

"I'm sorry," he said.

"Sorry." His father raised a hand, flat, ready to strike. It hovered in mid air, visible from the corner of Amit's eye. He squeezed his eyes shut, waiting for the blow.

The door slammed behind him. He heard feet thundering up the stairs, followed by another lighter pair.

He opened his eyes and looked at his sister.

"Why?" he asked her.

"Sorry, Am." She shrugged. "He stopped me before I could get to you."

CHAPTER SIXTY-SEVEN

Zoe slammed the door, her phone tucked under her chin.

"That's good news, Connie. You get some rest, and we can continue with this in the morning."

Connie had rung to tell her that the videos had at last been taken off YouTube, the account closed down. The high-ups were trying to negotiate access to the account details, but not getting far.

"I don't like going home when there could be another attack," Connie said. "And those videos are everywhere."

"I know. But we've done everything we can. I'll be in early, Rhodri's going to the knife shops. Ian... I'm not sure what Ian's doing."

"What time d'you want me in?"

"Seven."

"I'll be in at six."

"You don't have to."

"I want to."

Zoe tossed her coat at the hook and ignored it as it missed

and slid to the floor. She needed food, followed by a hot bath and her bed.

"Give my love to your family, Connie. Have a rest. I'll see you in the morning."

She tossed her phone onto the sofa and stretched her arms towards the ceiling, yawning. The adrenaline that had kicked in when Petra had made her prediction was gone, replaced with fatigue and anxiety. She picked her phone up again and put it in her back pocket. She needed to keep it with her, just in case.

In the kitchen, the fridge was emptier than usual. She hadn't gone shopping in over a week, and Nicholas had been out with Zaf most nights. She tensed, remembering their argument.

She found some instant noodles and boiled a kettle. While she waited, she dragged herself upstairs and knocked on her son's door.

"Nicholas?"

No answer. She knocked again. "It's Mum. Wondering if you were hungry."

Silence. She pushed the door open.

The room was empty. Nicholas's chair was tucked in under his desk, the surface of the desk tidy. The bed had been made.

She went downstairs and poured water over the noodles. She took out her phone.

"Boss? Everything alright?"

"Fine, Connie. I was just wondering if Nicholas was at yours, with Zaf."

"Hang on a minute."

She heard the phone being put down, followed by Connie walking away. After a moment, she returned.

"He was here earlier, Mum said. They went out."

"Where did they go?"

"Not sure. Sorry."

"OK. Thanks, Connie. See you in the morning."

She dialled Nicholas's mobile, drilling her fingernail into her palm. Now was not the time to give him a lecture, but...

"It's Nicholas. Leave me a message if you know what's good for you."

She opened her mouth to speak, then thought better of it. He never answered voicemail. Instead, she composed a text.

Hi, just wondering with time you'll be home. See you later. Mum xxx.

She deleted two of the kisses and hit send. She watched the screen, waiting for a reply. None came.

It's fine, she told herself. *He's with Zaf.* Annabelle, Zaf's mum, would be just as protective as Zoe. She should stop worrying.

Still, he'd promised to stay at home while the case was ongoing.

She pushed down her frustration at his lack of concern, and slopped the noodles onto a plate. Even she had to admit they didn't look appetising. She opened a cupboard and poured some soy sauce on top.

She slumped down into the sofa and forked the noodles into her mouth, yawning.

When she woke up, there were noodles in her lap and her neck was at a painful angle. She cursed herself and did her best to brush the noodles back onto the plate. Her jeans were stained and smelt of soya sauce.

She picked up her phone.

Be home around 10:30. Don't wait up. N.

She allowed herself a sigh of relief. It was eleven now. He'd already got home and crept upstairs, thinking she was in bed. She hauled herself up, took the noodles into the kitchen and poured it all in the bin. She was too tired for that bath.

She glanced at her son's door as she passed it. He hated being disturbed after he'd gone to bed. She placed her palm on it for a moment then walked to her own room, falling asleep as soon as she hit the pillow.

CHAPTER SIXTY-EIGHT

NICHOLAS THREW his arm around Zaf's shoulder as they left the pub. Zaf was a couple of inches shorter than him, which made him a perfect leaning post when Nicholas had had a couple of beers.

Tonight he'd had more than a couple.

"Come on, you're heavy," Zaf said. He pushed Nicholas off him and Nicholas paused to regain his balance.

"You're gorgeous, you know," he told Zaf.

Zaf laid a kiss on his cheek. "I know. And you're pissed."

"Not pissed. Just happy."

"You've got school in the morning. Me too."

Nicholas rolled his eyes. "Don't remind me." He checked his watch: 11:30. "Mum's going to skin me alive."

Zaf snorted. "You think your mum's protective, try mine."

"At least she isn't a cop."

"Your mum's alright."

Zaf tugged on his arm and the two of them made for the railway station. They were in Selly Oak, not far from

Nicholas's house. Zaf needed to get home, to Gravelly Hill. It was on the other side of the city but conveniently linked by the local train line.

"Come back to mine," Nicholas said.

"I can't get to school, from yours."

"Yes you can. You'll just have to get up early."

"I don't want to get up early."

"Spoilsport."

They paused at a bus stop and Nicholas leaned against the metal, throwing his neck back to lean his head on it. It felt cold. Solid.

"I love you," he said.

Zaf smiled. "I know." He pulled Nicholas close and kissed him. Nicholas leaned into Zaf, letting the kiss wash over him. Zaf's mouth was warm and soft. His body was roasting, compared to the chilly air. Nicholas wished he would come home with him.

"Come on. I've got a train to catch."

"Forget your train," he said as Zaf pulled away. "Come back to mine." He tugged on the lapels of Zaf's coat.

Zaf pushed him off. "I told you. I gotta get up in the morning. And my mum..."

Nicholas blew out scorn. Breath gusted in front of his face. "We're grown ups, man. Our mums can't tell us what to do."

Zaf shrugged but said nothing. He started walking towards the station, then paused as he realised Nicholas wasn't following.

Nicholas sighed and gazed at his boyfriend. He was less blurred now, the beer was starting to wear off. His mum never drank, she hadn't told him why but he knew it was because of his gran. She, on the other hand, drank a lot.

"Come on," Zaf said, looking away from Nicholas towards the railway bridge. "My phone's out of juice. Borrow yours? I'll text my mum."

Nicholas brought his phone out of his pocket and handed it to Zaf. Zaf bent over it, his fingers moving across the screen.

Zaf looked up. "I'll see you on Saturday." He leaned in for a kiss.

Nicholas tried to hold onto Zaf with his lips, to persuade him to stay with the force of the embrace.

"Stop it," Zaf said. "I've got to get my train." He peered down at Nicholas's phone, waiting for a response. He hunched his shoulders against the cold.

Nicholas felt a rush of air as a bus approached. Zaf was looking over Nicholas's shoulder, watching the railway bridge, checking for a train. Nicholas turned to follow his gaze, then turned back to find Zaf gone.

He frowned. "Zaf?"

He heard a shout. The bus flew past, oblivious to them.

"Zaf?"

"Nick." Zaf's voice sounded distant, muffled. "Nick!"

Nicholas scanned the street. With the bus gone, the area around the bus stop was dark. There was movement to his left, shapes shifting in the dark. "Zaf?"

He felt something large and soft hit him. "Run!" Zaf's hand grappled with his then held on.

"What?" Nicholas let himself be dragged along. His feet skittered on the icy pavement and his brain struggled to keep up.

"Didn't you see?" Zaf hissed as he ran.

"See what?"

"That guy." He panted as they rounded a corner. "He decked me. I think we lost him."

Nicholas widened his eyes. The street seemed to have come to life, adrenaline making everything clearer than it had been. He could hear footsteps behind them.

"He's behind us," he whispered.

Zaf tightened his grip on Nicholas's hand and ran. Nicholas pushed focus into his movements and ran with him. He was no longer being dragged along, but was side by side with his boyfriend, the two of them speeding along the street, passing in and out of the light of streetlamps.

Where were they? He cast around, hoping they were near his own road. The houses were dark, curtains pulled against the winter evening. His mouth hung open, his mind racing.

"We have to get to mine," he panted. The footsteps behind were getting closer.

"Just run," Zaf replied. He loosened his grip.

Nicholas let go of Zaf's hand. They could run faster if they weren't connected. He pumped his arms, picking up speed. Zaf fell behind a little.

Nicholas threw his arm out behind to grab his boyfriend, to pull him along. Instead, he struck Zaf, who yelped.

He turned. "Zaf!"

Zaf's eyes were wild. A shadow was gaining on them, his footsteps heavy. Nicholas froze.

"Run!" he yelled at Zaf. Zaf blinked at him, his mouth wide, and righted himself. Nicholas looked into his eyes then turned to run.

He came to a corner and sped round it, not waiting to check Zaf was with him. He pushed all his strength into his legs, picking up speed. Nicholas had been on the school football team before joining the sixth form. He'd been fast, nimble.

He reached another corner. Footsteps were behind him still, but fainter now. He looked over his shoulder as he ran.

"Zaf!"

He heard running behind him, and panting.

"Zaf!"

He heard a shout, and a thud. He skidded to a halt.

"Zaf!"

He peered into the darkness. A streetlight was directly overhead, making the rest of the road dark. He could see little more than shapes.

A figure came out of the darkness. He let himself breathe.

"Zaf?"

The figure grew clearer. It wasn't Zaf. He looked past it, his senses ablaze, his mind full of panic.

Where was Zaf?

The figure was holding something. A wrench, or a stick. He raised it as he ran towards Nicholas.

Nicholas stared for a moment. Where was Zaf? Had he hidden? Taken another turn?

It was dark behind him. He could hear footsteps.

He ran. He turned another corner, confused now. Disorientated. He'd lost track of which way he'd run. Of where home was. Of where Zaf was.

He glanced behind him once more. The man wasn't there. Nicholas allowed himself a quick exhalation, a moment of relief.

He couldn't stop now. He turned back to face ahead, just as something came at him. He cried out but he was running too fast to stop.

His head hit something hard. He screeched as pain ran down his neck, his feet sliding from under him on the frosty pavement. He put out an arm to stop himself, vision blurring, and felt something soft against his skin, followed by something rough. A moment later he hit the ground and everything went black.

CHAPTER SIXTY-NINE

WEDNESDAY

Mo REACHED for his buzzing phone on the bedside table, checking the time before he answered: 5:45 am.

"Hello?" He put a hand over his mouth to stifle a yawn. Behind him, Catriona turned over in her sleep. He slid out of bed, careful not to disturb her, and padded to the door.

"DS Uddin, it's Javed Hussain. Amit's father."

Mo slid down the stairs, wishing he'd thought to grab his dressing gown from the bedroom door. "Mr Hussain."

"He's disappeared again."

Mo put a hand on the kitchen door. "Sorry?"

"My wife went into his room this morning and he was gone."

Mo went to the thermostat and turned the heating on. He flicked the kettle on. "Are you sure he hasn't gone to work?"

"His bus doesn't leave until 8:13 am. My son has routines, detective. We all do. He never leaves this early."

Mo switched on the overhead light and leaned on the kitchen island. He blinked, not fully awake.

"When did you last see him?"

"Last night. We had to reprimand him."

Mo's shoulders sagged. "Maybe he wanted to be alone for a while."

"Sergeant, my son was abducted less than a week ago. And now he's gone again. Does it not occur to you that the two events could be related?"

Mo sniffed. "Abducted."

"Yes, Sergeant. I had to find out on the Internet."

Mo's stomach clenched. He could imagine Javed Hussain's reaction to what had happened to his son. "Mr Hussain, I don't mean to be rude. But a twenty-year-old man not being at home for a few hours isn't a police matter. I suggest you contact his friends. He'll be with one of them, perhaps. Or maybe he just left the house early, to be alone." He considered giving the man Kai Whitaker's name but then decided against it.

"Are you aware that my son was attacked because he is a homosexual?"

Mo slumped forwards. Last time he'd spoken to the man, he and his wife had been convinced that their son had been with friends for a few days, that there was nothing to worry about.

He pulled away from the kitchen island, staring into the blackness of the back garden.

"Did he tell you this, Mr Hussain?"

"We had to learn it online. Fine way to find out that your son is a deviant."

Mo swallowed. "Mr Hussain, I'm very sorry. But right now, this isn't a police matter. If your son hasn't returned in twenty-four hours, please call me. But in the meantime, I think it's reasonable to assume he just wanted some time alone." *Away from his homophobic father*, he thought.

"I expect better from the police. I shall be raising a complaint with your superiors."

"That's your prerogative." Mo mulled over his handling of the case. He had nothing to be reprimanded for, he was sure of it.

"Hmm." The man hung up.

Mo dialled Zoe.

"What time is it?" she groaned.

"Just after six. Sorry."

"Shit. It's OK. I should be in the office already."

"Good job I woke you then."

He could hear her moving about, getting dressed no doubt.

"What's up?" she said after a minute or so. She was out of breath and sounded as tired as he was.

"I've just had a call from Amit Hussain's family. He's disappeared."

"You think he's been taken again?"

"No. His dad read him the riot act about that video, by the sounds of it. He told me his son was *a deviant*."

"Poor kid."

"Yeah. But maybe we need to try and track him down, just in case."

"OK. You got contact details for his friends? Workplace? He's probably just gone in early."

"Let's hope so. I'll check his boyfriend's house first. Before Amit's work starts."

"OK. Are you joining the case team?"

"Yup. Dawson and the others too. We're all one big happy family."

She laughed. "Don't." He heard a door bang. "I'm on my way in. I just hope Connie isn't already there."

"See you later, Zo."

"Yeah."

CHAPTER SEVENTY

Nicholas's head hurt. His bed was cold, he must have kicked the duvet off again in the night. He'd fetch Yoda, her warmth would help him wake up.

He sat up and blinked, prodding his forehead with his fingertips. He'd had a couple of pints last night, but shouldn't be feeling like this.

He rubbed his eyes. He was wearing his jeans and coat, and he could feel damp in the clothes. He opened his eyes, realisation and adrenaline hitting him at the same time.

He was lying on a patch of wet grass. There was a tree above him, its branches bare. Then he remembered: he'd been knocked out cold by something, he didn't know what. Or how long ago.

He pushed himself up and groaned, his heart racing. He just wanted to sleep.

He peered around, his mind foggy. He was in someone's front garden. He looked towards the house, his heart racing.

A light was on in an upstairs window. The downstairs windows were dark.

He stumbled around the tree trunk and onto the pavement. The ground was icy and he almost slipped.

He looked up and down the street, squinting. It was dark, but there was a tinge of light beyond the roofs of the houses. There was a grassy area opposite him, and flats. He was on Raddlebarn Road, a few minutes from home.

He turned and headed for home. The railway line passed under a bridge up ahead. He heard a train approach.

He stopped walking. *Zaf.*

He span around, scanning the street.

"Zaf?"

He plunged a hand into his pocket, fumbling for his phone. It wasn't there. He tried the other pocket. Nothing. He ripped his coat open and delved into the inside pockets.

He'd given it to Zaf, so he could text his mum.

"Zaf!"

A curtain moved in a window opposite. A face appeared. A child. He stared at her for a moment then started to run.

He crashed into his front door and managed to drag his key from his jeans pocket with trembling fingers. He fell inside.

"Mum!"

The house was quiet.

"Mum!"

He thundered up the stairs and hammered on her door. Nothing.

He pushed the door open. Her bed was empty, the duvet neat.

She'd gone to work.

He checked his watch: just gone six.

What had happened to them last night? Had Zaf simply got the train? Had he managed to run away, to hide?

Nicholas clattered back downstairs. He stared at the front door, torn between going out to search for Zaf, and trying to track down his mum.

He had her mobile number in his phone, and the office number. He couldn't remember either of them.

He grabbed the landline in the living room. He dialled 999.

"Emergency, please state which service you require."

"I need to speak to Detective Inspector Finch, in Force CID."

"This is 999. You'll have to call her station."

"I don't have the number."

"Is this an emergency?"

He didn't know. Was it? Zaf could have just gone home. But he wouldn't have left Nicholas lying there on the ground, surely?

He'd been in that front garden. He'd been hidden by bushes. Zaf might have looked for him then given up. His mum would have been waiting for him.

"No," he said. "It isn't an emergency."

He took the stairs two at a time and grabbed the mouse to turn his computer on. He found the West Midlands Police website, the number for Force CID.

"I need to speak to Detective Inspector Zoe Finch. It's her son. It's urgent."

"Please hold the line."

He waited while the on-hold music kicked in, aware that his clothes smelt. He'd have to get a shower, go to school.

How could he go to school, when he didn't know where Zaf was?

"Sorry, but she's in a meeting. I can pass on a message when she's available."

"Can you give me her direct number please."

"We don't give those out over the phone, sorry."

"It's Nicholas, her son. I was attacked last night. My boyfriend, Zaf... Can I speak to DC Connie Williams please?"

"She your mum too?"

"No. She's Zaf's sister. My boyfriend's. Please."

The woman on the other end of the phone sighed and the music clicked in again. After a moment, the music stopped.

"She's not here yet. Sorry. It is very early, you know. But if you were assaulted, you need to report it."

"OK. I'm reporting it to you."

"Not to me. Are you injured?"

"My head." There was a lump.

"Do you need an ambulance?"

"No. I just need to find Zaf."

"Go to your local station. Tell them what happened. They'll want to examine you."

He stared at his computer screen. His temples throbbed. He could go to the nearest station in Bournville. But his mum's office wasn't much further away.

He had his bike, in the shed. He could make it there in fifteen minutes. But he'd been hit on the head. Was it a good idea to cycle?

He had to do something. By the time he got there, she'd be out of her meeting. And Connie would be there.

"OK," he said, and hung up.

CHAPTER SEVENTY-ONE

Zoe and Mo stood in front of Lesley's desk. A bowl of porridge sat on it, steaming away. Zoe eyed it, her stomach growling.

Lesley pushed her chair back and sniffed. She rubbed her nose. "So you think Amit Hussain might have been taken again?"

"I've tried all his friends," said Mo. "Including Kai Whitaker, closest thing he has to a boyfriend."

"Seven o'clock in the morning," said Lesley. "Bet you were popular."

"It wasn't easy to rouse some of them."

"Amit's a grown man. Maybe he's just gone to ground. He's probably sitting in a greasy spoon somewhere, having his breakfast."

"With respect, ma'am," said Mo. "He's Muslim. There won't be many greasy spoons that serve Halal."

"He argued with his parents, you said. If I was him, I'd be hiding out somewhere. Getting away from them. We've got no reason to think it's suspicious."

"He was abducted a week ago," Zoe said. "He managed to escape. Maybe the killer came back for him."

"How did he say he got away?"

"He couldn't remember," said Mo. "I didn't manage to get much time with him. He was sketchy on the details."

Lesley pulled the porridge bowl towards her and started stirring. "Maybe he's hiding out 'cos of that video."

"We hope it's as simple as that," said Zoe. "But I don't think we can afford to..."

Lesley swallowed a mouthful of porridge and grimaced. She pushed it away. "Needs sugar." She brushed off her hands and looked between the two of them. "OK. Say I give you the go ahead to start charging around, hunting him down like a pack of dingoes. Where would you start? You've tried his friends."

"The gay village," said Zoe. "We'll put surveillance on the pubs."

"If we get to that point, it's too late."

"It's better than nothing, ma'am. While we're doing that, we'll put out the e-fit again, the CCTV still. We've got his attacker's voice on tape now, from the videos. That might jog someone's memory."

Lesley wrinkled her nose. "Alright. I'll give you one Uniform on each of the two pubs."

"It won't be those pubs," said Mo.

"There are eight gay pubs and bars in the village," Zoe added. "We need to watch all of them."

"Uniform aren't going to be happy if I ask for eight guys because someone's had a row with his parents and run away."

"They'll be even more unhappy if he turns up dead."

Lesley blew out a long breath. "Alright, then. But keep

digging for other angles. I want to find him before it gets that bad."

CHAPTER SEVENTY-TWO

Zoe and Mo left Lesley's office.

"I'm going to go and see his parents again," Mo said. "And see if I can talk to his brother."

"Let me know how you get on," Zoe said as she pushed open the door to her team room. Ian was waiting. He stood up.

"I need to talk to you," he said.

"It had better be to tell me you've found Amit Hussain."

"What?"

"He's gone AWOL. Chances are he's hiding out after having a ding-dong with his folks, but it could be more sinister. The DCI's given us the all-clear to watch the pubs in the gay village."

She pushed open the door to her office and he followed. The phone was ringing.

"DI Finch."

It was Amanda on the switchboard. "Ma'am. I've got a message for you."

"Go on."

"Your son called about ten minutes ago. He said something about him and his boyfriend being attacked."

Zoe stiffened. "What? When?"

She turned towards the team room. Connie had said she'd be in early. Where was she?

"Did he give any more details?"

"He said he'd been hurt. He's on his way to his local police station, to report it."

Zoe swallowed. "Thanks," she muttered, and hung up. She dialled Nicholas's mobile.

Voicemail. She blew out a shaky breath then tried again. Nothing.

"Nicholas, it's Mum. You tried to get hold of me. Call me. I'll keep my mobile turned on."

Why had he called the switchboard? He normally rang her mobile.

The closest nick to home that was open to the public was Bournville. She grabbed her mobile and dialled.

"Bournville Police Station."

"This is DI Zoe Finch, Force CID. I need to know if you've had a walk-in from a Nicholas Finch. Reporting an assault."

"Hang on a moment."

She waited, wishing she could reach down the phone line and drag the woman back. She tapped her foot on the floor.

"Sorry, ma'am. No one by that name this morning or yesterday."

Zoe grunted and hung up. "Shit." She grasped the edge of the desk.

"You OK?" Ian asked.

She eyed him. "My son was attacked. Connie's brother too."

She looked up as the door to the team room opened: Connie. She hurried out of her office and stopped in front of Connie.

"Have you seen Zaf this morning?"

Connie turned from hanging up her coat. "I left before he woke up. Why?"

"Nicholas rang the switchboard not long ago, said the two of them had suffered an assault."

Connie's face greyed. "When?"

"I don't know. He's on his way to Bournville to report it."

Connie took her phone out of her pocket, her gaze on Zoe.

"Mum?... Is Zaf up yet?... Can you check?"

Connie stared into Zoe's face while she waited for Annabelle, her eyes wide. After a moment, she took a step back, looking like she might faint.

"You sure?" she said. "He hasn't gone to school?... No. It's nothing. Don't worry."

She dropped her phone on the desk, sending it tumbling to the floor. She shook her head at Zoe. "He's not home. Mum hasn't seen him."

Zoe dropped into a chair. "Call him."

Connie bent to grab her phone. Zoe's own phone rang and she shoved it to her ear.

"Is that Zoe Finch?"

"Yes. Who is this?"

"It's Ashlands veterinary practice. We were expecting your son to pick up your cat this morning, she's been spayed. He had an early booking but he hasn't arrived."

"Sorry. What do you mean, early booking?"

"He'd arranged to pick the cat up at 7am."

"7am."

"Yes. If he can't come, we'll need you to pick the cat up by ten o'clock please. Otherwise we'll have to charge for an extra day."

"OK. Charge me extra. I don't care." Zoe hung up. The cat was the least of her worries right now, but it wasn't like Nicholas not to turn up when he'd said he would.

"He had an appointment at the vet," she said to no one in particular. "He didn't show up."

"Nicholas?" Ian asked. She nodded.

Connie was still on the phone, silent. The creases in her forehead deepened with each passing second. Eventually she muttered something Zoe couldn't make out into the phone and hung up.

"No answer," she said. "I left him a message."

Zoe looked at her watch. How long ago had Nicholas said he was leaving for the police station? How would he get there? On the bus, it could take half an hour.

"I have to go and find him," she said. She dragged on her coat. As she reached the door, her mobile rang.

"DI Finch."

"Your son's at the front desk. He's asking for you."

CHAPTER SEVENTY-THREE

AMIT LEANED over the edge of the bridge, staring into the grey water below.

He'd crept out of the house at around four am and walked until he'd found himself at Cannon Hill Park. He'd hidden in some shrubs just outside the park until the gates had been opened at seven.

How deep was the water here? If he threw himself over, would he drown, or would he just make a prat of himself?

Again.

The video kept replaying in his head. His own face, staring across the room at his captor. Answering his questions like it was the sensible thing to do. How had he entertained the idea that the man might be worth talking to? Why hadn't he fought his way out of there? That's what Kai would've done.

His phone rang for the hundredth time in the last hour. His brother this time. Ruhaan would be worried. His mum would be wringing her hands. His dad would be yelling at the walls.

Let him. Amit didn't have it in him to worry about his dad anymore.

When his phone stopped ringing, he pulled it out of his pocket and threw it into the water. It landed with a satisfying splash. Maybe if he followed it, he might sink after all.

The phone bobbed up to the surface. He glared at it, frustrated. Nothing went his way. It floated off under the bridge beneath him. He didn't have the energy to cross to the other side, to see it come out. He'd stood here with his dad when he was small, playing Pooh Sticks, chucking twigs in and seeing whose would come out first. His dad had loved him then. He'd been proud of him.

Now, he was a disgrace. He couldn't even stand up to some petty homophobe. He'd sat there in that room, shivering like a coward. Waiting to see what happened to him.

He was pathetic. His dad was right, but not in the way he thought he was.

He took a deep breath.

The voices echoed in his head, his captor's sharp questioning and his own muttered responses. He'd watched that other video. Adam. He'd stood up to the man, he'd argued back. Amit wondered what had happened to Adam. Was he the one that Ruhaan said had died?

It didn't matter. Amit might as well be dead. His dad would make sure he suffered a social death. Vilified by his family: not one of them. But he didn't fit in with people like Kai, either. They were too brash for him. Too confident.

He looked from left to right. The park was quiet, a distant dog walker chasing a Jack Russell across the grass.

He climbed onto the parapet and stood there, his arms out to his sides. He looked down, then ahead again. It wasn't easy to balance.

But then, he didn't need to balance. He just needed to let go.

CHAPTER SEVENTY-FOUR

Zoe ran along the corridors, Connie close behind. She skidded around a corner into the reception area to find Nicholas sitting on a bench. He turned as he heard her, his face filling with hope.

"Nicholas!" She ran and pulled him up, folding him in her arms. For once, he didn't resist. She held him at arm's length to inspect him. "Have you been hurt?"

He shrugged out of her grasp and touched his head, his fingertips light. "I had a knock on the head." He looked down. "I was out cold for five hours I think. In Raddlebarn Road. Someone's front garden."

A small part of her died at the words.

"Raddlebarn Road?" she said. He'd been minutes away from her as she slept. And she'd thought he'd come home while she slept on the sofa. "I'm so sorry. I should have checked you were home."

He shrugged. "Have you heard from Zaf?"

Connie approached. "He's not at home," she whispered. "What happened to him?"

Nicholas looked at Connie, his eyes filling. Zoe grabbed his hand. She turned to the duty sergeant. "Can we have the interview room?"

"Of course."

Zoe nodded for Connie to follow and led Nicholas into the room off the reception area. He sat in one of the plastic chairs and Zoe took the seat next to him. Connie sat at right angles to him, her eyes not leaving his face.

"What happened?" Zoe asked.

"We were on our way home from the pub." He hesitated. "I know you didn't want us to..."

"Don't worry about that. Just tell me." She clutched his hand, knowing her grip was hard. His hand was limp in hers.

"We were on the Bristol Road, on the way up to the train station." He looked at her. "Not far from home. We didn't go to the gay village."

"You're not in trouble."

He chewed his bottom lip. "There was a bus going past, we were kissing, I didn't notice."

"Didn't notice what?" Connie asked. She leaned towards him, her hands on the table.

He looked at her. "A man. He came at us. It was just movement, in the darkness. One minute Zaf was right next to me, the next he was gone."

Connie let out a moan.

"Did you see the man?" Zoe asked. "What happened to Zaf?"

"Zaf managed to get away from him. He grabbed me. We ran. I can't... I'm not sure which way we ran. We were together. Running." He clenched his fists in his lap. "I let go of his hand. And then..."

"Then what?" Connie urged.

"Then he was gone. I heard... I'm not sure... I might have heard him call out. I can't remember. I was running. Then something hit my head."

"The same man?" Zoe asked.

"No." He blushed. "I think I ran into a tree. I fell, and then when I came round it was early morning."

Zoe put her arms around him for a hug. "We'll need to get you looked at. Your head."

"I don't care about my head." Nicholas pulled out of her grip. He looked at Connie, then back at Zoe. "I just want to find Zaf."

Zoe pulled her shoulders back. She had to forget that this was personal. She had to be detached, professional. She looked him in the eye, her gaze steady.

"We will find him, Nicholas. We'll get him back."

CHAPTER SEVENTY-FIVE

RHODRI BLEW ON HIS HANDS, waiting for the knife dealer to open. This was one of only two in the city, and the closest to where the crimes had taken place. Kelman and Son.

At last a man appeared in the doorway. He flipped the *Closed* sign to *Open* and unlocked the door. When he saw Rhodri, he flinched. Rhodri gave him the most reassuring smile he could, still shuffling from foot to foot. He wished he'd worn a coat over his thin suit.

"Can I help you?"

"Mr Kelman?"

'That's me."

"Can I come in?"

"Of course." The man looked him up and down. Rhodri didn't imagine he looked much like the average knife shopper. In fact, he probably looked like exactly what he was.

"I'm up to date with my paperwork," the dealer said. "I was inspected last week." The door closed with a ping and he rounded the counter and pulled out a thick file from beneath it. He slapped it on the surface, disdain on his face.

Rhodri approached the counter. It was glass-topped, with an array of knives beneath the glass that made him think of the knife amnesties he'd been involved in when he was in Uniform.

"It's not a check," he said.

Kelman closed the file. "Oh."

"We're looking for the person who bought this knife." Rhodri showed the man a photo on his phone.

"I can't tell anything from that," the man said.

"Hang on a minute." Rhodri fished in his suit pocket. He'd made a printout before leaving the station yesterday, the image of the knife blown up. "Does this help?"

Kelman grabbed the photo off Rhodri, his breathing shallow. Rhodri watched him. If this knife had been sold under the table...

"Give me a moment." The man fished under the counter and brought out a metal box. He opened it and took out a fisheye lens, the kind Rhodri had seen jewellers using on TV. He popped it into his eye socket and smoothed the photo out on the counter.

Rhodri watched as the man bent over the photo, his eye roaming over it. At last he straightened.

"Serial number's been partially eroded."

"Filed off, we reckon."

"No. This was done with another blade. It's messy work. Give me a moment and I can try to piece it together."

"Thanks."

The man disappeared through a door with the photo. Rhodri scanned the shop. It was a small, dark room, with no window except the one in the front door. Cabinets lined the walls, knives displayed inside like they were museum pieces.

Kelman reappeared. "I've got some of it." He grabbed another file. "I can cross-check it."

"Can you give me what you've got?"

"Why?"

"Because we need it for our enquiries."

The man shrugged. He scribbled a series of digits on a scrap of paper and handed it to Rhodri. "That's not a lot of use to you without the sales record though."

Rhodri shrugged. There were seven spaces, five of which were filled in. The other two were blank, indicated by dashes.

"Here." The dealer pointed to an entry and turned the file to face Rhodri.

"James Lovetree." He read out the address. It was in Acocks Green, about two miles away.

Rhodri could barely breathe. He stared at the scribbled writing, biting down on his lower lip.

"That help you?" Kelman asked.

"Yes." Rhodri drew out his phone and snapped a photo of the entry. "I'll need to take that from you."

"I need this, for my records."

"We'll return it."

The man pursed his lips. "I don't suppose I have much choice." He pushed the file across the counter.

"Thanks." Rhodri shoved it under his arm and headed outside, resisting an urge to punch the air.

CHAPTER SEVENTY-SIX

Zoe spoke to the duty sergeant, making arrangements for Nicholas to be seen by a doctor. He protested but she was having none of it.

"I have to do my job, Nicholas. I can't stay with you."

He nodded. "What about school?"

"I'll phone in." She kissed his forehead. "I love you."

His cheek twitched but he didn't argue. Instead, he slumped into a chair in the reception area. Zoe gestured for Connie to follow her.

Petra had arrived. She was in the team room with Ian, standing by the board. Photos of Nicholas and Zaf had been added to it.

"Where did you get those?" Connie asked as she entered with Zoe.

"Facebook," Ian replied. He gave Zoe a look.

Connie said nothing, but walked to her desk and sat down. Zoe eyed her. Could she cope with this? Should she be part of the investigation, or should she be sent home?

Mo entered, DC Fran Kowalczyk following him. "Dawson's assigned us to you," he said. "I heard what happened." His eyes searched Zoe's face. "You OK?"

"I'm fine. Dawson not coming himself?"

"Not yet."

"Hmm." She looked at Connie. "Never mind that. We have to find Zaf."

Mo gave Connie a pained look and approached the board. Connie sat in her chair, back straight, eyes staring ahead. She'd have to go home. But Zoe wouldn't send her away here, not with everyone watching.

"Connie," she said. "There are a couple of Forensics files in my office. Can you fetch them please?"

Connie blinked a few times then looked at Zoe as if her boss had just woken her up. Ian cleared his throat and gave Connie a nervous smile. Mo watched her, his face full of concern.

"OK," Connie said, her voice flat. She stood up and trudged to the inner office.

When the door was closed, Zoe walked to the board.

"Right," she said. "This attack wasn't in the victim's home. It was on the street, in Selly Oak. The attacker is getting bolder." She looked at Petra. "Is that normal?"

"Uh-huh. This is his fourth attack in six days. He can see that we're running around like blue-arsed flies and it's making him confident. Cocky. That could be his downfall."

"OK. We need to send Uniform and Forensics to the bus stop where Zaf was taken. Search the road between that and the spot where Nicholas woke up." She swallowed. They'd need a formal statement from Nicholas.

"I'll sort that," Ian said. He picked up his phone.

"We've still got Amit missing," Zoe said. "Mo, any joy with his family?"

"They as good as kicked me out. They accused me of keeping things from them."

"Like what?"

"Their son's sexuality."

"Give me strength." She thumped the desk. "I still think Amit's probably hiding out somewhere. Have you got any leads on where he might have gone? Did you talk to the brother?"

"He'd gone to work already."

"Can you call his workplace, have a word? If Amit has buggered off, he might know where he's gone."

"I'll go round there," Mo said.

"No. I want you to take Nicholas's witness statement."

He raised an eyebrow. "You aren't doing it?"

"He'll be more open with you. We... we argued about whether he should be going out. He might not want to tell me everything."

"Right." Mo nodded. Nicholas had known him since he was a baby, he'd open up to him.

"That leaves us with any leads we've got on the attacker." Zoe had stopped using the word *killer*. She couldn't bring herself to, now that Zaf had been taken. She scanned the board. "There's the fake name, Jackson Potter. The knife. Both knives." She put her hand to her forehead. "Has anyone heard from Rhodri?"

"Not yet, boss," said Ian. He'd put his phone down and was at the back of the room, his arms folded.

"Call him," she said. "Find out if he's got anywhere."

"OK."

She turned to Petra. "I need your help. Anything you can give me that'll help us identify this guy."

Petra's face was grave. "Just what I've already given you.

He's heterosexual. Probably in a relationship. Thirties. He has some reason to hate gay men, but it's more than regular homophobia."

"How so?"

"It's not *them* he despises. It's their sexuality. He thinks he can cure them. It's like..." her face lit up. "Someone he loves was gay. They died because of it. AIDS, or something."

Zoe raised an eyebrow. "AIDS? Bit of a stereotype."

Petra shrugged. "Or a homophobic attack. I don't know. But it's personal."

"That doesn't exactly narrow it down."

"Sorry."

"And there's those surgical skills..." Zoe said. She tapped her teeth with a biro. "Hang on."

"Uh-huh?"

Zoe jabbed the biro into the surface of Rhodri's desk, which she was leaning on. "We've been looking in the wrong direction."

"Have we?" Mo said. Petra stiffened, sensing her professional integrity was about to be questioned.

"Yes. It's not a surgeon. It's definitely not the arsehole Adam Hart used to work for. And it's not a cutter."

"So...?"

Zoe thought back to the phone call she'd had before talking with Lesley. "Who does more castrations than any other profession? Not oncology doctors, but...?"

Realisation hit Petra's face, making her appear younger. "A vet," she breathed.

Zoe nodded. She span round. "Everyone. We're looking for a vet. Find all the vets on that side of the city. Start at each of the victims' houses, and work out. Check their websites, see if they have photos. You know what you're looking for."

The room exploded into a hive of activity. Ian and Fran plunged into chairs and leaned into computer screens.

"He'll be married, or in a relationship." Petra raised her voice to be heard. "Middle class, early to mid thirties."

"More importantly, he'll look like that." Zoe pointed to the e-fit on the board.

Petra pursed her lips. "Can I help?"

"Yes. Please."

"No problem." Petra sat at her desk and started to search.

Zoe made for her office. She needed to be out there, co-ordinating, checking they weren't all looking in the same place. But she also needed to talk to Connie. And she trusted Ian with this.

Connie stood at the open door to the office. "Don't check their websites, boss. At least, not just the websites."

"Connie, you should go home. Your mum needs you..."

Connie stepped forwards, her eyes boring into Zoe's face. "The Royal College of Veterinary Surgeons. The professional body for vets. I'll call them."

"Connie, please..."

Connie put up a hand to silence her. She walked to her desk, her body stiff and her stride purposeful. She sat down and picked up the phone.

CHAPTER SEVENTY-SEVEN

Rhodri ran to his car. He checked the maps app on his phone and memorised the route to the address he'd been given.

As he landed in the driver's seat, he hesitated. He should call this in. But the traffic was getting heavier and the longer he waited, the denser it would get. He'd call when he got there.

He revved the engine and reversed out of his space, his heart racing. He had the killer's name. His address. He was about to solve the case. The boss would be proud.

He sped along the knife dealer's road, slamming on the brakes as he hit a jam at the far end.

"Shit." He banged the steering wheel, wishing he was in a police car. His Saab didn't have anything as fancy as blue lights. It didn't even have hands-free. Hell, it didn't even have electric windows in the back.

The traffic budged a little, then picked up speed. He put his foot down, knowing he was too close to the car in front. *Relax*, he told himself.

But what if the dealer rang Lovetree before he got there? He wouldn't want to be the person who'd sold a knife to a killer. He might warn him off, make sure they didn't catch him.

No. That was a dumb idea. Kelman had helped him. He'd handed over his log book, reluctantly but he'd done it anyway. He knew he'd never wriggle out of this. And besides, he'd done nothing illegal.

Rhodri knew a short cut around the back of where the greyhound stadium used to be, avoiding the outer circle. He pulled off and took it, nipping between parked cars and tightening his grip on the steering wheel. His phone rang in his pocket but he ignored it. He had to focus on getting there.

He pulled up along the street from the address, not wanting to draw attention to himself. He grabbed his phone and checked the display: a mobile number he didn't recognise. He clicked onto voicemail.

"Rhodri, it's Sergeant Osman. How are you getting on with tracking down that knife?"

That was it. No *please* or *thank you*. No *Ian*. He missed Mo.

But he had to call it in.

He dialled the number, making a note to save it for future use.

"DS Osman."

"Sarge, it's Rhodri. I've got the name and address of the man who bought the knife."

There was a hush on the other end of the line. Rhodri could imagine Ian raising his hand, getting the attention of everyone in the office.

The audio quality changed.

"Rhodri, it's Zoe." She was on speaker. "Where are you?"

"I'm in Acocks Green. Shaftmoor Lane. I'm at the other end of the road, didn't want him spotting me,"

"You're in a five-year-old Saab, Rhodri, not a panda car. You can go closer."

"You sure?"

"I want you watching the place. While you wait for Uniform."

"Boss, I think I should—"

"I know what you're thinking, Rhod. The man in that address is highly dangerous. You do not go in until you have backup."

"He might not even be at home."

Connie's voice came on the line. "Rhod, he's got Zaf."

He heard whispering, hissed remonstrations. The boss was telling Connie off.

"What?" he said.

Zoe sounded angry. "Connie's right. We believe he abducted her brother last night."

"Which means he could be in there."

"We have no evidence—"

"I've got to go in there, boss. What if he..." The word hung unsaid on his lips.

"No, Rhod. Just get yourself a bit closer and tell me what you see."

"I'll have to put my phone down."

"Put it on the passenger seat," she said. "Uniform are on their way. Armed response too. There'll be no sirens, we don't want to alert him."

"OK." Rhodri placed his phone on the passenger seat and pulled out of his parking space. The road was busy, traffic slow. He tried to count the house numbers as he made his way along. Eventually he came to it. He found a spot and parked haphazardly.

"I can see it, boss."

"What do you see?"

"It's not a house, boss."

"It's not residential?"

"No. It's a vet's."

CHAPTER SEVENTY-EIGHT

"Get online, someone," Zoe said. "Vets in Shaftmore Lane, Acocks Green."

"Got it." Connie's eyes were wide and she looked like she was running on pure adrenaline. "Petcare Veterinary Practice." She frowned, peering into her screen. "No sign of him, though."

"What? Let me see."

Zoe hurried to Connie's desk and swivelled the screen towards her. Rhodri was still on the line, her phone in her palm.

Onscreen were mugshots of eight people wearing scrubs. Four vets and four veterinary nurses. None of them looked anything like their man.

"Shit."

"What now?" Connie asked. Her voice was thin.

"First, you're going home. It's not appropriate for you to be in the middle of this."

"With respect, ma'am. I'm the best tech on your team. If there's evidence online, I can find it. You need me."

"I *need* you to look after yourself. You can't possibly think straight, with your brother missing."

Connie stood and turned to face Zoe. Her face was inches away, her eyes unblinking. "Working keeps me from thinking about it, boss. If I walk out of here now, if I have to get on a bus, I'll go to pieces."

"What about your mum?"

"She's got my sister."

"I don't know you had a sister."

"I do."

Zoe surveyed Connie's face. There were goosebumps on her skin and her breathing was elevated. She was in fight or flight mode.

"Alright, then." She dreaded what would happen when she had to explain this to Lesley. But for now, she had a man to track down.

She jabbed at the screen. "Where are the names?"

"Hang on." Connie eased herself into her seat, her shoulders heaving. She flicked through screens. "Here. Partners. James Lovetree and Jennifer Taylor."

"James Lovetree. Is there a photo of him?"

"The two first vets on the team page, ma'am." Connie returned to that page. The vets included an elderly white man, a middle aged black woman and a younger Asian man.

Connie put her finger on the first man's photo. "He's too old."

Zoe put her phone to her ear. "Rhodri, are you there?"

"Sorry, boss, you're breaking up."

"Rhodri, don't..."

"That's better. Sorry, lost signal for a moment there."

"Are you still in your car?"

"There's a greasy spoon opposite the vet. Gives me a better view."

"Any sign of backup yet?"

"Not yet."

"Right. James Lovetree is the manager of the vet's. But he's in his sixties."

"Maybe someone else here used his name," Rhodri replied.

"Or maybe it's unrelated." Zoe felt like her head was full of fudge.

"It can't be," Connie muttered. "The surgery, it has to be a vet."

Zoe nodded. "Rhod, see if you can find out about other people who work there. Anyone who looks like our guy."

"Is there a flat above the vet's?" asked Connie.

"Good point," Zoe said. "Residential. Rhodri, is there any sign of a flat in the same building?"

"There's windows, boss. Can't tell if it's a flat."

Zoe drew in a long breath. "Rhodri, can you hang on a moment? Stay on the line, but wait." She brought her phone to her side and turned to Petra. "Did you catch all that?"

"Sure did."

"Any thoughts?"

"I don't think our man lives in a flat above the shop, if that's what you're asking."

"No."

"He's used his employer's address."

Zoe frowned. "But if you're going to use a fake address, why use your work? Why not use a proper fake address?"

"Is the dealer required to check?"

"No. But the council can do spot checks."

"James Lovetree's registered at that address. It'd have been enough."

"But if they spoke to him, they'd know it was a false name."

"Banking on them not checking," said Connie. Zoe nodded.

"Boss?" Zoe could hear Rhodri's voice from the phone in her hand.

"Rhodri."

"Backup are here. What do I tell them?"

"Put the officer in charge on the line."

She waited, scratching an insect bite on the back of her hand, wondering if Yoda had fleas. They needed someone from CID on the scene, someone more senior than a DC.

"Sergeant Ford here."

"Sergeant. This is DI Finch, Force CID. The address you're standing outside is connected with the Digbeth Ripper case."

"Ma'am. What are our instructions?'

She tapped her fingers on Connie's desk. "Accompany DC Hughes to the property, Sergeant Ford. He needs to question the owner. I don't want them knowing there's a squad outside, though."

"No problem, ma'am."

"Be ready to take your guys in if you need to, but hold off just in case."

"Received."

"Thanks."

Rhodri came on the line again. "You want me to go in?"

"I want you to speak to James Lovetree. Talk to him nicely. Show him the e-fit, ask if he has an employee matching the description."

"Right, boss."

"Be careful, Rhodri. Sergeant Ford's got your back if you need it."

"Don't worry about me. I'll be fine."

Zoe pursed her lips, hanging up. Connie was staring into her screen, fingers moving across the keyboard. She took a breath. "Got him."

"What?" Zoe almost fell over the desk to see Connie's screen.

"James Lovetree hasn't got any social media accounts, but he's mentioned in someone else's."

"Whose?"

Connie enlarged a photo. A grey-haired man sat on a bench, a younger man beside him. The younger man had cropped dark hair and a round, nondescript face.

Zoe's chest hollowed out. "That's him. Potter."

"Says here he's called Brandon Lovetree, boss."

"Well done, Connie." Zoe grabbed her phone, knocking her fist against her temple as she waited for Rhodri to answer.

"Rhod?"

"Boss?"

"It's Lovetree's son you're after. Brandon Lovetree."

"Brandon. Right, boss."

"Be careful, yes?"

"Course."

Connie and Petra were watching her, both silent.

"I'm going to Acocks Green," Zoe said. She grabbed her coat.

CHAPTER SEVENTY-NINE

Zoe wove through the traffic on the Stratford Road, cursing the winter weather. Rain beat down on the windscreen and made it almost impossible to see the cars outside. And when it rained like this, the traffic always got twice as bad.

Her phone rang.

"DI Finch."

"Zo, it's Mo."

"How was Nicholas?"

"I'm about to go in to see him. But I just got off the phone to Ruhaan Hussain."

"Please tell me his brother's turned up."

"Sorry. But he did give me some useful information."

"Go on." The traffic started to move and Zoe let out a sigh of relief. She gunned the accelerator, muttering under her breath.

"Apparently Amit said something to him about hearing dogs barking."

"Dogs?"

"He thought they'd sent out a search party, men from the community looking for him. Using dogs."

"Makes sense. We've just found out that the man who took him could work at a vet's."

"What?"

"We've got a name, from the knife dealer. Brandon Lovetree. His dad runs a vets in Acocks Green." She slammed her hand on the steering wheel.

"Zo? You OK?"

"Just struggling with this traffic. I'm on my way there now."

"How did you find the knife dealer?" Mo asked.

"Rhodri, believe it or not."

"You underestimate that lad."

"Seems I do. And he's not a lad." Zoe braked as a car pulled out from a side road. "I need to get off the phone. Thanks for letting me know about Amit. Give Nicholas my love, will you?"

She stopped at a traffic island. There was gridlock, an Uber blocking the route out on the other side. "I don't bloody believe this," she said. She flicked her blue lights on again but couldn't see a way through.

"What's up?"

"I'm trying to get to the vet. I don't want to leave it all on Rhod. But this traffic..."

"Grim?"

"It's the rain. Bloody pissing it down."

"Good luck."

"Yeah. Tell me how you get on with Nicholas, OK? If he can remember anything that can help us find where Zaf is right now..."

"Don't worry, I know what I'm doing."

"I know you do. Sorry." She hung up, her stomach hollow. She could imagine how Anabelle Williams was feeling right now. Stuck at home, watching the phone, unable to help find her son. If it was Nicholas who'd been taken, Zoe would tear down the walls of the police station to get information about what they knew.

Anabelle was more patient than she was, thank God.

She inched forward as cars tried to move out of her way. *Wait for me, Rhodri*, she thought.

CHAPTER EIGHTY

"If you're concerned, use the code word," Sergeant Ford told Rhodri. Rhodri stared back at the man, adrenaline speeding though his veins. He was sure he'd met him before.

"What's the code word?"

"Oranges."

'How the hell am I going to work that into a sentence?"

"You'll find a way. I can't give you a word you might use by accident."

"OK."

"You want a vest?"

"Huh?"

"A stab vest. You can put it under your jacket."

Rhodri looked across the road, at the vet's surgery. They were sitting in his car, watching the street. Sergeant Ford had removed his helmet before approaching, so he didn't look as conspicuous as he might. Still, there was the vest and the POLICE logo on the back of it. Rhodri knew that people were glancing into the car, wondering what was about to kick off.

The armed response vehicle would be around the corner, laying low in a quiet street. Residents would be peering through their windows, pulling curtains aside. The van was unmarked, but still it stood out to Rhodri.

"Let's get this over with," he said. "I don't need a vest."

"You sure?"

"Yeah."

"I'm putting my helmet back on though. Regs."

"You're not bringing a gun?"

"Just a handgun." Ford gave him a lopsided grin. "Wouldn't want him getting excited, would we?"

Rhodri gulped down the bile in his throat. His palms were damp.

"OK. Let's go."

He pushed open the door of his car, turned to lock it and strode across the street in one motion, knowing that if he hesitated, he might stop in his tracks. At the door to the vet's, he paused.

"Front door?" he said.

Ford nodded.

Rhodri pushed open the main door to the vet's and a bell above their head pinged. Three heads turned to look: a nurse behind the counter, an elderly man with a mangy-looking dachshund, and a woman with a cat in a cage and a toddler on her lap. The woman grabbed the toddler by the arm and pulled him close.

Rhodri approached the desk, trying to appear calm. "Can I speak to Doctor Lovetree, please?"

"He's in surgery right now."

"It's in connection with an inquiry. We need to speak to his son."

"Brandon?"

Rhodri felt his shoulders tense. "Yes. Brandon. Does he live here?"

"Not likely." The nurse sniggered, then caught Ford looking at her and stopped abruptly. She was young, younger than Rhodri, with dark hair scraped back in a ponytail and clear skin.

"Does he work here?" Rhodri asked.

"Not that much. He manages the kennels."

"Kennels?" It was all Rhodri could do not to lean over the counter and grasp her lapels shouting *what kennels?*

"We run a kennels and cattery. A kind of animal hotel, you might call it. And we have a few sick animals there too."

Rhodri forced out a smile. "Can you tell me where it is please?" He was aware of Ford scanning the room, his hand inside his vest. On his gun. The people in the waiting room were silent apart from the dachshund, which had started barking wheezily.

"Here, have a leaflet." The nurse leaned towards Rhodri. "It's lovely there, he makes sure they're looked after. I sometimes think Brandon loves those animals more than he does his girlfriend."

Rhodri nodded, mute. The psychologist was right: he was in a relationship. He thought about showing the woman the e-fit, and decided not to. He already had Brandon's name.

"Thank you," he gulped. "You've been very helpful." He eyed Sergeant Ford the way you might look at a dangerous dog, gesturing for them to leave.

CHAPTER EIGHTY-ONE

Mo WALKED into the reception area, pulling a smile on his face for Nicholas's benefit.

The space was empty, no one there apart from Sergeant Jenner behind the desk.

"Tim," he said. "D'you know where Nicholas Finch has gone?"

"He said he needed the loo."

Mo let out a breath. "Fine." He sat on the bench and waited.

After five minutes, he stood up. "I'm just going to check on him."

He walked to the toilets off the corridor running along the front of the station, the ones they let interviewees and witnesses use.

"You OK, Nicholas?" he called. One of the cubicles was closed. He put a hand on it. "Nicholas?"

The door gave way. The cubicle inside was empty.

He checked the other cubicle, the one whose door was open. No one there.

The door from the hallway opened and Mo span round. "Ni—?"

It was a cleaner. She frowned at him. "Sorry, bab. Thought it was unoccupied like."

"Have you seen a young man in here? Light brown hair, tall?"

She shook her head. "Sorry. I wouldn't have come in if there were anyone in here."

"No." Mo sped out and hurried back to the reception area, hoping to find Nicholas there waiting.

The bench was occupied but not by Nicholas. A DC from another team sat on it, next to an elderly woman she spoke to in a low voice.

Mo turned to Jenner. "I don't suppose he's come back while I've been gone?"

"Sorry, mate. You sure he didn't go to find his mum?'

"His mum's... hang on a moment. Did you see her come out?"

"Twenty minutes ago."

"Was he here then?"

"No. She'd have spoken to him, if he was."

"And he's not in the interview room?"

"I just checked it. Empty."

Mo slumped. He needed Nicholas for that statement. He needed to be able to tell Zoe he was safe. And he needed him not to be putting himself at risk.

"Thanks, Tim," he said. He pushed open the door to the inside of the station, hoping Nicholas had somehow found his way to the team room.

CHAPTER EIGHTY-TWO

JENNIFER CROSS TUGGED on her daughter's hand. Lola had woken at five again this morning and Jennifer wanted to go home and lie on the sofa. Maybe if she put *CBeebies* on, the child would slow down, just for half an hour.

"Swans!" Lola cried. Jennifer followed her towards the lake, knowing she should be more alert. She rubbed her eyes and dug her heels in.

"No, Lo."

"But they so big."

"Yes. Dangerous, too. You mustn't go near them."

"Their beaks, Mummy." Lola gigged. "Tha' one's looking at me funny."

Jennifer allowed herself a tired smile. One of the swans was indeed looking at her daughter funny.

"Just a little bit closer," she said. "We can watch the ones that are swimming. But don't go near the ones on the path."

"OK," Lola replied in a singsong voice. Jennifer let her daughter pull her closer to the water. The park was deserted this morning, rain driving everyone away. It didn't seem to bother Lola, though. The child was unstoppable.

"What's that, Mummy?" Lola pointed towards the water.

"Another swan, I guess." Jennifer pulled her hood further over her head, glad she hadn't had the energy to take a shower yet. Lola was in an all-in one waterproof and bright red wellies, her favourite outfit.

"No," Lola said. "It's a man. He swimming?"

Jennifer pulled her daughter in close. "Where?" She squinted through the rain.

"There!" Lola shrieked. She was still pointing into the lake.

There was a shape in the water. A dark shape, bobbing with the slight swell as the rain hit the surface. Jennifer felt nausea hit her.

"Come away," she urged.

"Mummy, it's a man. Bad man. Only swans allowed to swim here!"

Jennifer looked over her daughter's head. The shape was nearing, floating towards them. She buried Lola's face in her own waterproof, determined that the child shouldn't see. For herself, all she could do was stare.

As the shape came closer it hit the metal barriers that stopped boats reaching the shore. The jolt made it spin in the water.

Jennifer let out a shriek. A man's face stared back at her. A young man.

CHAPTER EIGHTY-THREE

Ian watched Zoe run out of the office. He called after her but she was too focused on getting to the vet's. On helping Rhodri.

More interested in dashing around after her precious DCs than in doing her job as SIO.

He turned back to Petra and Connie. They both looked back at him. Petra hesitant, Connie pushing determination into her face.

"You need to go home, Connie," he said. "You heard what the boss said."

She shook her head. "She said I could stay. You need my expertise."

"Everyone's expendable, Constable. I'm your senior officer and I'm telling you to go home."

Connie leaned back and folded her arms across her chest. Ian looked across the room to where Petra watched them, biting her lip. Was she laughing at them?

Ian had had enough. "Connie, can you come with me to the DI's office, please."

She wrinkled her nose at him and stood, giving him a blank look as she passed. She marched into the inner office and held the door open for him. He followed, his body alight with tension.

He closed the door. "Connie, I'm giving you an order. It's in your own interests, and to be quite frank, those of the DI too."

Another shake of the head. "I'm not going anywhere."

"Your brother has been abducted. We're looking for him. You don't need me to tell you all that. And you also don't need me to tell you that an officer so closely involved with an investigation is always reassigned."

"Zoe's son is involved in this and she's still on the case."

"Nicholas is safe and well and here in the station. Your brother is—"

"Go on. Say it. My brother's being held by a homophobe who'll probably cut off his balls. A homophobe that I'm getting the distinct feeling you agree with."

"Connie!"

Her nostrils flared. Connie had been studious and timid when he'd started working with her. Now he saw what she could be like when she was in distress, he wasn't so sure about her fitness to do the job.

He caught movement out of the corner of his eye, the door to the outer office opening. Mo entered. That was all Ian needed, the sainted Mo Uddin. He watched Mo and Petra talking for a moment, their lips moving but their conversation inaudible through the glass.

"Connie, if you don't do as you're told I'm going to have to give you a formal warning. You don't simply decide when you'll obey orders and when you won't."

Connie had seen Mo too. She watched him through the

glass, her brow furrowed. Could she hear him? Could she lip-read?

"I want you to go to your desk, gather up your personal belongings, and leave the station. There won't be formal action taken against you and you will be able to return to duty when your brother has been found."

Her head shot round to face him. He caught his breath. *Dead, or alive.*

"If you say so," she said, her voice hard. She stood up, pushing over the chair she'd been sitting in, and threw the door open. She strode to her desk, grabbed her coat and bag, and continued to the outer door. Mo and Petra watched, mouths open. Fran Kowalczyk sat at a desk, trying not to look up. Ian could see the tension in her face. She'd report back to Dawson on this: Zoe Finch's team unable to keep themselves in line. Collapsing under pressure.

Mo knocked on the door to the inner office.

"Come in." Ian almost fell into the chair behind the desk.

Mo opened the door and leaned in, his feet not crossing the threshold.

"Bad news, Ian."

"What now?"

"Nicholas Finch has gone AWOL."

"Oh, *shit*." That was all he needed.

CHAPTER EIGHTY-FOUR

Zoe had found a route through the congestion at last. Her phone rang as she found herself picking up speed.

"Rhodri. Everything OK?"

"Fine, boss. I spoke to the veterinary nurse."

"Not the vet?"

"Didn't need to." He sounded proud of himself. She could picture him, sitting in his Saab with his chest puffed up. It would be funny in any other circumstance.

"Just get to the point, Rhodri."

"Sorry, boss. They've got a kennels. Kennels and cattery. Brandon runs it. It's south of the city. Headley Heath, out past Stirchley."

Zoe was ten minutes away from the vet's surgery in Shaftmore Lane. The kennels was further from the city centre, but her route from the station had brought her closer to it than Rhodri was. She took a right turn onto the Alcester Road, out of the city.

"I'm on my way there," she said. "Tell Uniform to meet me there."

"No problem."

She overtook a Corsa dithering over a left-hand turn, and glanced at the satnav. She should pull over and programme in the address, but she knew this side of the city, she'd grown up over here. She was confident she could find her way.

She checked the screen again, slamming on the brakes as she looked up to see a woman with a child in a yellow rain coat step into the road.

"Look where you're going!" Zoe cried.

The woman glared at her. Zoe put a hand on her chest. *Calm down. You've got to wait for Uniform anyway.*

She muttered an apology to the woman and pulled over to the kerb, heart slamming into her ribs. She programmed the address into the satnav.

She needed to slow down.

She breathed in through her nose as the woman hurried away, occasionally glancing at Zoe over her shoulder. Her training, both in the force and in karate, had taught her to do this. Breathing in through the nose helped calm a racing mind. It helped her to focus, to think ahead.

She started the engine and pulled away from the kerb, careful to check her mirrors. Ten minutes and half a mile of traffic jams later, she was there. She pulled up on a grassy verge, her front wheel juddering as she hit a pothole.

It was quiet out here, the only sound the distant hum of the M42 and the drumming of the rain on the roof of her Mini. The weather had sent any wildlife into hiding.

Zoe opened the boot and brought out her stab vest, then put her coat on. It was tight over the vest, but she could just about do it up. She brushed at her coat: rain and sheepskin didn't mix.

According to Google Maps, the kennels was beyond a

hedge next to the car. She plunged her hands into it to pull the greenery aside and peer through.

A van sat about fifty metres away in a scruffy-looking yard. Beyond that were a brick-built structure and a row of wooden sheds, presumably where they kept the animals. No sign of movement.

Zaf, are you in there?

She checked her watch. Eleven twenty-two. She'd spoken to Rhodri thirteen minutes ago. Force Response would be on the blue lights, they should be here any minute. They'd turn the sirens off when they got close. And *close* in an area like this could be quite a distance: the sound would travel.

She turned to see Sergeant Ford emerging from an unmarked car that quickly drove away. She'd worked with him before, on the Osman case.

"Sergeant Ford." She shook his hand.

"DI Finch. What have we got?"

She pointed through the hedge. "There's a brick building, probably the HQ. A few sheds for the animals."

"I can't hear them."

He was right, there was no barking. She pulled the hedge further aside. There was no movement, no sign of any animals. Mesh pens ran alongside the sheds, each one divided into enclosures for each animal. No dogs moved inside them. No cats either.

"Maybe they're all inside," she said. "Or they're barking and the rain's drowning them out."

"I used to work with dogs, ma'am. Not all of them are subdued by weather like this. Some, quite the opposite."

"You think he's emptied the place out?"

"He might have. But he might have kept a few of the dogs with him. Protection."

"Hmm." She brought her hand to her mouth, considering. "Do we need to call in the dog team?'

"My team are trained to resist dog attacks. I'll make sure everyone has extra arm and leg shielding. If we bring more dogs in, it'll just be chaos."

She nodded. Her mind worked over the possibilities. Lovetree could be in there, with Zaf. He might have Amit, too. But then, this might be a dead end.

"OK," she said. "We believe there are two members of the public in there, and our target. One of the members of the public is the brother of a CID officer."

"We'll take utmost care, ma'am. We always do. Can you show me photos?"

She grabbed her phone and showed him the e-fit and CCTV still, plus a still of Amit from the YouTube video. Zaf was trickier.

"The other lad's black," she said. "Mid-height. The target will be the only white man in there, and the oldest by at least a decade. His name's Brandon Lovetree. The two civilians are Amit Hussain and Zaf Williams."

She remembered the photo she'd taken of Zaf and Nicholas playing with Yoda the previous week. She brought it up and showed it to Ford, trying not to look at it too hard.

"He's that one?" Ford pointed at Zaf in the photo.

"Yes. Eighteen years old. He might be injured."

"I'll need to brief my team. But first I need authorisation for weapons use."

"Of course."

She opened her car door and sat inside, leaving the door

open so Ford could hear. The rain was thickening, covering the countryside around them in heavy mist.

"DCI Clarke."

"Ma'am, have my team briefed you on the latest developments?"

"Ian's with me now. He looks pretty pissed off."

Zoe let the comment go: Ian always looked pissed off about something. "I'm at a kennels just south of the city," she said. "Brandon Lovetree works here. Based on evidence given to DS Uddin by Amit Hussain's brother, we have reason to believe this is where he brought Amit. And where he might be holding Zachary Williams."

"Ian said he sent Connie home."

Good, Zoe thought. How he'd done it, she didn't like to imagine. "Ma'am. I need your approval for weapons use, if necessary."

"You've got Force Response with you?"

"Sergeant Ford."

"Good. He's one of their best. Alright."

"We have your authorisation, ma'am?"

"You do. Take no risks, Zoe. I know Connie's brother could be in there, but you let Ford's team do their job. No heroics."

"Yes, ma'am."

CHAPTER EIGHTY-FIVE

Connie stumbled out of the station, trying her best not to cry. She ignored Sergeant Jenner speaking to her as she passed the front desk.

Outside, she gulped in air, oblivious to the rain that was already soaking her clothes. Her jacket was slung over her arm, her bag dangling from her fingers. She sniffed and looked across the car park.

Zoe had said she could stay. She'd recognised that Connie had something to contribute, that the team needed her. But Ian... well, Ian clearly hated her. She'd be raising a formal complaint.

But first, there was Zaf. She knew they were looking for the son of a vet, and where the vet was based. Acocks Green. Could she go there? Or should she stick to investigating online, tell the boss if she found something?

She rounded the side of the building towards the bike shelter. She didn't much fancy riding home in this weather, but she had her waterproofs in her pannier and it wasn't as if she hadn't done it before. She didn't want to go home, her mum's fear would cloud her judgement. Maybe she'd go to a café instead, get internet access. She didn't have a laptop with her, but she did have her phone.

A man was huddled over a bike, fiddling with its lock. She approached, pulling her own bike free of another one that was propped against it.

"Connie." The man looked up from his bike lock.

She looked up. "Nicholas?"

"What are you doing out here?"

"They sent me home."

"What?" He let go of his bike and it crashed into the pack, making a noise that set her teeth on end.

"I'm too emotional," she said. "Too close to the case."

"That's bollocks."

"Yeah." She looked him over. "What are you doing out here? I thought you were supposed to be giving a statement."

"I realised I didn't have anything useful to tell them. I'm going back to where Zaf was taken, see if I can find any clues."

"You won't. Forensics are already there."

"Oh." He looked as if she'd punched all the fight out of him. "I guess I'll go to school then."

"Don't. Come with me."

"Where are you going?"

"I'm going to find a café with wifi and do some digging on the man who took Zaf."

"You know his name?"

She nodded. They didn't know for sure yet. And she wasn't supposed to tell Nicholas. But the way Ian had treated her...

"His name's Brandon Lovetree. He's a vet, or he works at a vet's."

"A vet?"

"Explains the surgical skills."

He paled. "Don't."

"Yeah." She tugged at her sleeve. "Come on then. We'll go into Harborne. Leave the bikes."

"OK."

CHAPTER EIGHTY-SIX

Ian's phone rang as he walked back into the team office. He checked the number and carried straight on into the inner office, ignoring Petra's questioning look.

A call from West Midlands Police headquarters could only be trouble.

"DS Osman."

"Sergeant Osman, glad I caught you."

"I'm in the middle of an urgent operation right now..."

"I wouldn't do that, if I were you."

"Sorry?"

"You don't even know who this is and you're telling me to bugger off already. Even though you know this call is from Lloyd House."

Ian said nothing. He looked through the glass. Petra switched her gaze towards the board. He needed to give her something to do. In fact, no. If she damn well couldn't think of anything to do for herself, why should he babysit her?

"This is Detective Superintendent Randle, Sergeant."

"Sir." Ian pushed his shoulders back, almost saluting but then stopping himself. His breathing became shallow.

A chuckle on the other end of the line. "I don't believe we've met."

"No, sir. What can I do for you?"

This was the man that DI Whaley expected Ian to spy on, from this farce of a job in Force CID. It was clear that Whaley himself was in a better position to do that, seeing as he worked in the same building as the man.

"Congratulations on your move into Force CID, Sergeant."

"Thank you, sir."

"Exceptionally fortunate for you."

'Well I wouldn't..."

"...especially given that you were under investigation yourself not a couple of months ago."

Ian clamped his lips shut. He thought Whaley had kept that quiet. He'd been taken in for questioning, sure, but that had been for just a few hours, and it had been for alleged involvement in the kidnapping of his children. Which, as had been proven, he had nothing to do with.

At least, that was the official story. In reality Whaley had held him because of his connections to organised crime.

"I'm sure you're aware, sir, that the allegations against me for involvement in my children's abduction proved to be unfounded."

Another chuckle. "Such formal language, Sergeant. I am aware of that, yes. Amongst other things."

Ian felt ice run down his back.

"I also know the reasons why you were transferred into Force CID."

"Sir." What could he say to that? A transfer form had

been completed, with the usual waffle. Experienced officer, relevant skills, blah blah. A front.

"And I suggest you focus on something else."

Ian opened his mouth to speak, closed it again, then cleared his throat. "I'm sure I don't know what you're talking about, sir."

"Hmm."

Petra was pacing the room now, scratching her head. Something was brewing.

Ian waited for Randle to say something. He reached for words himself, but there was nothing to say.

Seized by sudden emotion – courage or anger, he couldn't be sure – he raised his phone and hit the End call button. Hard.

CHAPTER EIGHTY-SEVEN

Zoe followed DS Ford and his team of three men and one woman, her eyes on their backs. Rhodri was behind her, having arrived a moment after she'd spoken to Lesley. Ford had given him a stab vest to wear and a brief pep talk. She could feel nerves radiating off him and hoped he'd be OK.

Ford gestured towards his team and two of them peeled off, heading along the hedge past the entrance to the kennels. They would be looking for alternative ways in. Ford leaned into the hedge, peering along the rough gravel driveway. Weeds peppered it and wet litter clumped on the grass verges.

After a few moments, Ford stiffened and put a finger to his earpiece.

He turned to Zoe. "There's a gap in the hedge about a hundred metres up. We go in that way."

He sent the remaining armed officer across the gap in the hedge, his movements quick and silent. Zoe darted after him, glancing up the driveway towards the buildings. No movement. Rhodri followed.

They continued with the hedge to their right, arms brushing along it. No cars came along the narrow lane, no one walking in this weather. The officer in front of Zoe stopped at a narrow gap in the hedge. There was barbed wire beyond it, cut open.

"Did we do that?" Zoe asked.

The officer shook his head. "Already like that."

She nodded and squeezed through the gap. A rusting estate car stood about twenty metres away. She ran to crouch behind it, glad of the rain to obscure the view from the building. Two windows faced this way, and a door. One of the windows was boarded up. The sheds for the animals were blank, all the openings to the pens on the far side.

"Stay tight behind me," Ford said. "Both of you." He and his colleague darted out from behind the car to a collection of bins that afforded some shelter closer to the building. Zoe looked back to check Rhodri was with her then ran forward, taking care not to slam into the bins as she reached them.

She leaned against the bins, her breathing heavy. She closed her eyes for a moment, willing the adrenaline out of her system. When she opened them, Rhodri was staring at her.

"You OK, boss?"

She held a finger to her lips. "Fine."

He nodded, then ducked down. Ford was moving off again, making for the side of the brick building this time. She waited a moment for him to give the signal then followed, sliding to the floor beneath a boarded up window.

"What now?" she asked him.

"There's two doors. The one we saw from the road, and one round the back. We're just checking the one round the back. He put a finger to his earpiece and frowned. "No go.

Just the one way in. But there's a van round there. A vet's van."

"Lovetree," she breathed. Ford shrugged.

Zoe knew that Force Response didn't like there being a potential exit that they couldn't use as an entry point. It meant leaving officers watching it, in case the target came out that way while they went in the other. And they wouldn't know he was about to do that until he came out of the door.

"Come," Ford said. He shuffled towards the main door to the building, his feet and bottom on the ground. Zoe's coat scraped against the rough brick. Rhodri let out a low yelp as his hand snagged on a nail sticking out from the wall.

She eyed his hand and shot him a questioning look. He gave her the thumbs-up and she nodded in return.

PC Janek, the one woman in Ford's team, had gone on ahead and was on the other side of the door. She crouched near to the door, her gun raised. Zoe shivered, thinking of Zaf.

"Don't forget," she said to Ford. "Two civilians in there. Both young."

"Don't worry." He gestured towards PC Janek and she raised herself up, poised to grab the door.

"When I give you the signal, you follow us, in," Ford said to Zoe.

"Got it."

Rhodri stared ahead of him, his hands raised in front of him and clasped together. Almost like he was holding a gun. *Not your job, Rhod,* she thought.

Ford shifted his weight so he was almost upright then ran to join his colleague. After a moment's silence, he gave her a curt nod and she kicked the door. At the same moment, he slammed his shoulder into it.

The door gave way, opening inwards and pulling the two armed officers in with it. Zoe craned her neck but they were gone.

She waited. Rhodri's breath was loud in the rural quiet and his breath steamed out in front of his face. She patted her cheeks, they were cold.

Soon her feet were numb from holding herself still.

"What now, boss?" Rhodri whispered.

"We wait. Like he said."

Rhodri huffed out a steamy breath. She knew how he was feeling. But thank God it was him here with her, and not Connie.

She heard a muffled shout. "First room clear!"

Was that the signal?

She shared a glance with Rhodri, then shifted her weight to give her sore feet some relief. She nodded at him then made for the doorway, keeping low.

She crept through it and into the hallway beyond. It was damp and grimy, with cold paint flaking off the walls. A wooden sideboard leaned against a wall, looking like it might fall apart if she so much as breathed in its direction.

She drew in a long breath through her nose, pushing calm into her body. She could hear movements up ahead. Voices. There was a single door, open, leading into another room.

She shuffled to the side of the door, peering around the frame to check for occupants. PC Janek was in there, turning over items, shifting furniture.

"Where's Ford?" Zoe hissed.

Janek pointed up ahead. There was another door, with flaking green paint. It had swung shut.

"You stay there." The officer pointed at Zoe then Rhodri.

She eased the door open and went through. Zoe watched her disappear.

She wished Mo was here. What had Amit and Ruhaan told him about this place? He'd said it had been vague. But being here, looking at the space, might jog his memory.

Janek put her head round the door. "No one in here."

Zoe went through to the second room. A table stood in its centre, flanked by two chairs. Both were wooden, with flaking blue paint. On the table was a video setup. A camera on a stand, attached to a phone. A desk lamp pointed to one of the chairs.

"Where the hell did they go?" Zoe asked.

Ford shook his head. "They might not have been here recently."

She pointed at the phone. "You don't leave a crime scene without your phone."

"Unless he wants us to watch what's on it, boss," Rhodri said.

She felt her stomach dip. *Zaf.*

She snapped on a pair of gloves and reached out for the phone, dreading what she might find.

CHAPTER EIGHTY-EIGHT

Connie put a mug in front of Nicholas and collapsed into her seat. It was a latte, frothy milk threatening to spill over the top. He hadn't asked for coffee, but she seemed to have decided what was best for him.

"That'll warm you up," she said.

"You're not my mum."

"I'm like your big sister," she replied. A cloud passed over her face.

He picked up the coffee and slurped up some of the milk. She shot him a look as if to say *drink nicely*. He grimaced.

"Right," she said. "Let's find this bastard." She bent over her phone, her own cup of weak tea untouched in front of her.

"I'll help," Nicholas said. "Tell me his name."

She leaned in. "Brandon Lovetree."

"He's a vet?" he said, opening up his phone.

"Son of a vet. James Lovetree."

"Right." The first hit in the search results was the Petcare veterinary practice. "Got it. Shaftmoor Lane."

"That's the one."

"No sign of a Brandon though."

"Keep searching. See if they've got a blog, anything like that. He might be mentioned. I'll do social media."

The vet's did have a blog, but it was a half-hearted effort. The most recent post was from over a year ago.

"Doesn't look like they update it very often."

"I've got him on Facebook." Connie waved her phone.

"And?"

"He knows how to adjust his privacy settings. Typical."

"You can't get in."

She looked over the top of her phone. "Who said that?"

He smiled back at her. "Hang on. I've got him. Something about them opening a kennels. A photo. That's him, right?"

He held out his phone. Connie enlarged the photo with her fingertips. "Looks like it. Where's the kennels?"

"Hang on."

He thumbed through the rest of the post. There was nothing about the location of the kennels.

"How do they expect to get any customers, when they don't tell you where it is?" he sighed.

"Try googling kennels."

"Good idea." He switched to the Maps app and typed in kennels. Six listings came up in Birmingham.

"Nothing called Petcare, or Lovetree."

Connie frowned, engrossed in her own screen. Behind her, the door to the cafe opened and two men walked in. Nicholas recognised them: they worked with his mum.

He leaned in. "Don't look round."

Connie's eyes widened. "Huh?"

"Two of your colleagues behind you."

Her face fell. "Shit." She lowered her phone so they couldn't see it over her head. "I've got into his account."

"How the hell did you do that?"

"Don't ask."

"Is it legal?"

"Like I say, don't ask."

He tapped on the fourth of the kennels listed. The websites for the first two he'd checked were sparse affairs, single-page jobs with photos of animals and contact details. A third had been a holding site. This one redirected to the vet's.

"Hang on," he said.

"Hmm?" Connie scrolled down her screen, her finger moving fast. Her frown deepened.

"It's taken me back to the vet's site. Which means this must be it."

"I've got a photo," she said. She turned her phone to show him.

"Headley Heath kennels and cattery. Same one I've got," Nicholas said. It was south of the city.

"And there's this," Connie said. She scrolled down the page and stopped at another photo.

A shiver ran across Nicholas's skin. "Shit."

Connie pursed her lips. She looked up from the photo to his face. Nicholas returned her stare then looked at it again.

The photo was of Brandon Lovetree. Mid-height, cropped brown hair. The man from the e-fit. He crouched on the ground in front of a dilapidated brick building. And either side of him was a large dog. Two Alsatians.

CHAPTER EIGHTY-NINE

Zoe turned the phone over in her hand. It was an iPhone, not a new model. She stared at it, her chest tight.

"Right," she said. She pressed the power button.

Rhodri's breathing was loud in her ear. She wanted to swat him away, but knew he needed to see this as much as she did.

Her own phone rang.

"Fuck off," she muttered. "Not now."

The ringing stopped as the iPhone came to life. No password, no security at all, by the look of it. She thumbed through the menu screens, looking for a video player.

Her phone rang again.

"Shit." She pulled it out of her pocket, the iPhone in the other hand. It could be Lesley.

No: it was Mo.

"Mo," she said, "It's not a good time."

"You need to know this. Amit Hussain has been found."

"Where?"

"They pulled him out of the lake in Cannon Hill Park a few hours ago."

No. "Dead?'

"No. I'm at the QE. He's under observation, but he's going to be OK."

She let herself breathe. "How did he get there?"

"Not sure, but it looks like attempted suicide."

"He wasn't taken there?"

"A woman walking her dog saw him heading towards the bridge about half an hour before he was spotted in the water. He was alone."

"Poor kid," she said.

"Yeah. His parents are here."

"Good. Look, I've got to go."

"There's something else," Mo said.

"What?"

"Nicholas didn't hang around for his statement."

"Sorry?"

"I went to get him, and he'd left the station. I'm sorry, Zo."

Zoe hissed breath through her teeth. "Not your fault." She looked across the room at PS Ford, then cradled her phone closer to her ear. "He might have gone back to where he was attacked. Can you tell Adi?"

"I will."

"Thanks. Tell me when he turns up."

She should call Nicholas, right now. Find him. But she was in the middle of an operation, and he wouldn't answer anyway.

She plunged her phone into the pocket of her jeans and returned her focus to the iPhone. She found a video player app and flicked it on.

Onscreen was Zaf. He sat in the wooden chair right next to her now, a cut on his upper cheek.

She thrust the phone at Ford. "They were here."

"Is there a time stamp, boss?" Rhodri asked.

"I don't know." She tapped on the edges of the screen in search of information, but nothing came up.

"Here." Rhodri held out his hand.

"No," she said. "We have to watch it."

He nodded. She hit Play.

Zaf was looking across the table, past the camera lens. Lovetree would be on the other side, in the second chair. Zoe kicked it, sending it clattering to the floor. It was evidence, but right now she didn't care.

What have you done with him?

Onscreen, Zaf stared back at the man. His face was drawn and he looked scared. But he wasn't talking. She heard Lovetree off-camera, asking him questions. The same ones he'd asked his other victims. Zaf stared back at him, saying nothing.

A hand shot out from the edge of the frame and clipped Zaf on the cheek. He flinched but continued to stare ahead. She watched, mesmerised.

Her phone rang.

Not again, Mo. She grabbed it, her eyes on the iPhone. She hit Answer.

"Mo?"

"Mum."

"Nicholas? Look, I can't talk to you right now. I'm... I can't tell you where I am. Just go home and stay home."

"Mum. I have to tell you something. Me and Connie. We've..."

"Connie? What are you doing with Connie?"

"Long story. Look, Mum."

PS Ford shifted position, alert. His gaze was on the door they'd come through, her back to it. She swallowed and went to end the call.

She turned, slowly, lowering her phone. She didn't have time to put it in her pocket. She clasped Lovetree's iPhone in her other hand.

Brandon Lovetree was in the next room. She couldn't see his face, but she could see the shadow he cast in the outer doorway.

Rhodri drew in a tight breath. He shrank into the wall beyond Ford. He was invisible to Lovetree.

She, on the other hand, was not. He would see Ford, staring back at him, gun raised. He would see Zoe, standing between him and Ford, no weapon.

She lowered her hand. Nicholas's voice was indistinct.

Lovetree stepped forward. She glanced downwards.

"He's got dogs, Mum," Nicholas said. "Big ones."

I know, she thought. Lovetree clasped two dog leads. On the end of each was an Alsatian. Both of them stared at her, their gaze even more steady than his.

She let her phone fall to the floor, her mouth dry.

CHAPTER NINETY

"GET DOWN!" Ford cried. Zoe threw herself sideways and down, into a crouch, just as Lovetree slung his hands out in front, releasing the dogs. Zoe pulled herself up and staggered back. There was another door to this room, the one Ford's colleagues were watching from outside. They'd already checked it: it was locked.

No way out.

She climbed onto one of the chairs and then the table. Ford flew past her, his arm outstretched. He'd holstered his gun and held a taser.

The first dog leaped through the doorway. Zoe yelled out. She bent down to grab Rhodri. The dog hadn't been able to see him from the other room but it could now.

"Rhod!" Zoe cried. Rhodri turned from her to the dog, his face wide with horror.

The dog paused for an instant, then pounced at him.

There was a popping sound and the dog froze in mid-air. It hit the floor, its legs convulsing.

Ford had stopped it with his taser. Rhodri backed off, his eyes glued to the dog.

The other dog wasn't far behind.

"Rhod, get up here!" Zoe shouted. Ford's taser was attached to the first dog, unusable.

She heard scuffling from the outer room. Lovetree?

The second dog came upon the first. It pulled up, whimpering. It bent to lick the other dog's fur.

Zoe held her breath. Had the shock of seeing its mate forced the aggression out of it? Could she restrain it?

"Stand back." PC Janek stepped into the room. She fired her taser and it hit the second dog, which screeched in pain. Rhodri groaned.

Zoe put a hand on his arm. "It's OK, Rhod. They're big dogs." Those tasers were calibrated for ninety-kilo men. She had no idea what they'd do to a dog. But she did know what those dogs could do to her and Rhodri.

She jumped down from the table. PC Janek bent over a dog, checking its pulse. The outer room was empty.

"Where's Lovetree?" Zoe snapped.

"He ran outside, soon as he let the dogs go. My colleagues have gone after him."

Zoe ran for the door. She stopped at the threshold, scanning the driveway. Then she heard shouts from off to her left. The sheds.

She ran towards the first shed. The voices got louder.

"Inspector! Stop!" Ford was behind her. She ignored him.

"Where are you, you fucker?" she shouted across the empty space. Rain lashed at her face, plastering her hair to her head. The voices were muffled now.

She stopped to listen. He was here, somewhere. Had the armed officers confronted him, or the other way around?

And where the hell was Zaf?

Ford was next to her. "You have to stay back, ma'am." He pulled out his handgun and ran towards the sheds.

"Zaf!" she called, the rain muffling her voice. She cast around her, trying to make out sounds. The rain was too heavy.

Zoe ran after Ford, heading for the sheds. Instead of going around the blank side like him, she made for the other side, where the pens were.

"Zaf!" she cried. If he was in one of those sheds, he might hear her through the doorways that had been put there for animals to get between the pens and the shed. "Zaf!"

She caught movement up ahead. Someone heading around the corner of a shed.

"Zoe!"

She ground to a halt. "Zaf?"

"Zoe! Here!"

She squeezed her eyes shut and punched the air. He was alive, at least.

"I'm here!" she called. "Where are you?"

"Dog kennel!"

She turned in the direction of the voice. Rain battered against the metal roof of the shed, making it difficult to hear. She pushed her hair out of her eyes.

PC Janek appeared the way she'd come.

"I heard Zaf," Zoe said. "The civilian."

"Where?"

Zoe gestured with her head. "In there somewhere."

Janek ran to the pen. It was made of thick wire, six feet high.

"Zaf!" Janek called.

"In here!"

The woman rattled the pen, tugging at the thick metal. She turned to Zoe. "It won't budge. You stay here, I'll go round the other way."

"No." Zoe ran past her towards the far end of the shed. There had to be doors on one or other of the ends.

She slipped as she turned the corner, her boots catching in the wet. She threw a hand out for balance and avoided landing in the mud.

There was a door.

"Janek! Ford!" she cried. "Zaf's in here!"

Zoe scanned the space. Where was everyone? One of the officers would be in the brick building, watching the dogs. Janek was around the other side. But Ford, and the fourth officer?

She looked behind her. Rhodri? Where was Rhodri?

She ran into the door, slamming her shoulder into it. It rattled but didn't give. She backed up and ran at it again, this time aiming a high kick just below the lock.

It sprang open, revealing a heavy smell of animal shit. She put her arm up to her nose.

Stop, she told herself. *Lovetree could be in there.*

She took a few deep breaths, trying to focus. She stepped forward into the dark shed. She was in a corridor, mesh doors lined up on her right. On her left was a blank wall. At the far end, another door.

She held herself against the wall next to the first mesh door, then peered around it. It led to a concrete pen, which in turn led through a hole in the wall to the outdoor area. It was empty.

She repeated this five times, each time finding the pen

empty. She could hear Zaf calling up ahead but she couldn't risk responding.

The door she'd come through was banging on its hinges every time the wind changed direction, making her flinch each time. It banged again, heavier this time. She turned to see a man walking in, stooped. Lovetree.

Zoe threw herself against the wall. In the darkness he might not have seen her. She tried not to breathe.

He leaned over and balled his fists on his thighs. He was out of breath. He was tired.

She clenched her fists then loosened them. She jumped out, emerging from her hiding place against the wall. She ran towards him, not stopping as he pulled himself upright and stared back at her.

He wasn't tall, only an inch taller than her. But he was broad. And he'd carried those men to the pubs. She had only one chance.

As she neared him she dropped into the zone she entered in karate tournaments. *Turn to the left – smaller target – shoulders back, balance tight. Leading leg bent at the knee, then push out from the hip. Jab!*

Her foot slammed into his stomach, sending him staggering backwards. She didn't stop to watch his reaction, but instead kept coming at him, her hands raised in front of her face. Not her fists, she knew better than that. Her hands were flat, ready to strike.

He righted himself and roared at her. She gritted her teeth and leaned back, putting all of her strength into a second kick. The floor was wet and she slid as she leaned back. Her foot came up only a foot or so, but she caught him in the shin. He yelped.

She threw her hand down to the floor, knowing she had

to push herself up quickly if she lost her balance. As her fingertips reached the wet concrete, PS Ford crashed through the door behind Lovetree.

Lovetree span round but he was too slow. Ford was on him, bringing the man's arm up in a tight lock behind his back.

Zoe let herself slide to the ground. She'd disabled Lovetree, but without Ford appearing, he might have regained his composure and overpowered her.

She counted to three then pushed up, bringing herself upright. Her foot was on fire and her fingers hurt where she'd hit the floor.

Ford clapped handcuffs onto Lovetree's wrists. Lovetree whimpered, making her want to kick him again.

Zoe stepped forward. She grabbed a clump of hair and shoved it back from her face.

"Brandon Lovetree," she said. "I'm arresting you for false imprisonment, grievous bodily harm with intent, and murder. Now shut the fuck up while I check on Zaf."

CHAPTER NINETY-ONE

As Zoe turned away from Lovetree, PS Ford repeated the caution. He did it properly this time. In spite of everything, she allowed herself a smile.

Zaf was in a pen halfway along the shed. Zoe reached it and tugged on the door. Zaf stared at her from the other side, his face pushed up to the metal grille.

"Are you hurt?" she asked him

"Just a couple of hits to the face." He lifted his fingers to his cheek.

"He left a video," she said.

"He didn't finish it. You interrupted us."

"Good." She turned towards Ford. "Has he got keys?"

Ford rooted in Lovetree's pockets. Lovetree shouted at him, something about his rights.

I'll show you rights, Zoe thought.

"Here." Ford tossed a chain of keys her way. She tried them one by one, aware of Zaf's rising agitation.

"It's OK, Zaf," she said. "He's under arrest. You're safe now."

"What about Nicholas?"

She paused with a key in the lock and smiled at him. "He's fine. I just spoke to him."

Zaf let out a cry of relief. His hand went to his mouth and he bit down on his knuckles. She watched his relief, thinking how lucky her son was.

At last she found the right key. She opened the door and Zaf stumbled into her arms. He smelled of wet dog.

"Let's get you home to your mum, eh?"

CHAPTER NINETY-TWO

"We've got him. Zaf's OK, Lovetree's in custody."

"Well done, boss." Ian lowered the phone and turned to Petra. *They've got him,* he mouthed. She shook her fists in triumph.

"I'm taking Zaf home to his mum," Zoe said, "then I'll come back to the station. I'll tell Connie."

"I sent her home."

"Against my instructions."

"She was a liability, boss."

A pause. Ian felt sweat prickle on his skin.

"I had already made that call. Connie was better off on the job. As it turns out, she carried on investigating even after you kicked her out."

"She did *what*?"

"She found Lovetree online. Got into his Facebook account. We've got him interacting with fundamentalist Christian groups, researching gay conversion therapy."

"So he was a god-botherer, after all?"

"He was using them for information. Tell Petra she was right about his motive."

He glanced at the psychologist. "No need. I put you on speaker two minutes ago."

"What was his motive, Inspector?" Petra asked. "Someone he loved?"

"His brother. He was gay. Died five years ago, not clear why. But from what we can see on Lovetree's Facebook account, he blames it all on his brother's sexuality."

Petra allowed herself a satisfied smile. Ian lowered himself into a chair.

"Where is Connie now, boss?"

"I don't know," Zoe said. "And that's your fault. If you'd let her stay where she was..."

"...she'd have hacked into a private Facebook account from these offices."

"That's her *job*, Ian."

"She didn't have a warrant to do that."

"We had a warrant to search the kennels. To use force. She did what she had to do, Ian." A pause. Petra was watching his face. She was enjoying this. "Are you OK with that, Ian?" Zoe continued.

He pulled his fingers till they clicked. Petra winced.

What would happen if he said no? Would she kick him off the team, relieve him from this godawful job spying on her boss?

He ground his fist into the desk. "Yes, boss."

"Glad to hear it. I'll see you shortly."

She hung up and he went back to the inner office. He'd enjoyed treating it as his own just for a few hours, playing at being a DI. He needed to toe the line, if he was going to advance up the ranks.

But then...

If he was helpful to David Randle, then the wheels might be greased for him.

He picked up his phone and closed the door behind him. He would do this before Zoe or her pathetic constables returned.

CHAPTER NINETY-THREE

Zoe walked into the police station, aware that she looked a mess. Her hair was drying out, sticking to her skin. And her sheepskin coat looked like someone had taken a live sheep and run it through a washing machine. It would go in the bin, soon as she got home.

Nicholas was sitting in the reception area. He looked up as she came in and stood, his expression sheepish.

"Mum."

She took his hand. "You worried me."

"I just wanted to find Zaf."

"I know. But next time, leave that to us, eh?"

He nodded. She brushed his head playfully.

"You did good work, you know. Tracking him down online."

He shrugged. "Wasn't all that hard. Reckon I could do your job."

She hissed. "Cheeky!" They both laughed.

Mo emerged from the interview room. "Shall we do that statement, Nicholas?"

"Do you still need me to?" Nicholas looked at Zoe.

"We certainly do. You can give us information that will help us send Lovetree away for a long time."

"Don't call him that."

"I'm not bloody calling him the Digbeth Ripper."

"Lovetree. It's too nice a name. I don't want to call him anything."

"Well I'm afraid you and Mo are going to have to use something when you describe him in the interview."

"You're not doing it?"

"I thought you'd be happier with Mo," she said.

"I don't mind."

"It's OK, love. I've got to interview *him*."

Nicholas grimaced. "What about Zaf?"

"He's at home. We'll take his statement when his mum's had enough time to cluck over him."

"He's not hurt?"

"Nothing his GP can't patch up."

Nicholas's shoulders slumped. Zoe knew that feeling: the adrenaline was leaving him.

"Go on," she said. "Get it over with. Someone needs to pick Yoda up."

His eyes widened. "Oh my God! I forgot. I'm sorry."

"It's OK. I'm glad you did. It helped me make the connection."

He nodded and followed Mo into the interview room.

Zoe stood outside for a moment. She could go into the next room along, watch the video feed. Check that her son was doing ok, that he was helping. But she didn't need to.

She could trust him to do that all by himself.

CHAPTER NINETY-FOUR

THURSDAY

CARL DUMPED the takeaway bag on the table and sat down. They were at his, the first time Zoe had been here. It was a two-bedroomed flat in a leafy Art Deco estate just off the Bristol Road. Nice, but a bit soulless. He needed more books. More mess.

She leaned forward and started taking out cartons. "I needed this."

"I aim to please." He pulled a carton of rice closer and began to spoon it onto his plate.

She piled chicken jalfrezi onto her plate then took the offered rice and lumped that on top.

"You can't do that," he said.

"Do what?"

"Put the rice on top of the curry. It's just wrong."

"All goes down the same way."

"The rice soaks up the sauce. Can't do it if it's on top."

She shrugged. "As long as it's hot, spicy and filling, I really don't care."

He looked into her eyes for a moment. She blinked under his gaze. Was he about to tell her he loved her again? She wasn't ready for that.

"I heard you were quite the ninja yesterday," he said.

She scoffed. "Who gave you that bollocks?"

"Sarah Janek, Force Response."

"How d'you know her?"

He grinned. "Jealous?"

"Just curious." She'd surprised herself by feeling a tiny prickle of jealousy. "She's not dodgy, is she? One of your targets?"

"No." He forked some curry into his mouth then waved his hand in front of it: hot. "An old friend from training."

"Hmmm." Zoe leaned back, pulling her plate close to her face. At home, she'd be all but shovelling this in, not caring if Nicholas was watching. She could never eat when she was on a tough case, and was always starving afterwards. This case had been tougher than most.

"He'd have overpowered me if it wasn't for Sergeant Ford."

"I very much doubt it." Carl blew on his rice.

They ate in silence for a few moments. Zoe considered asking if he had Netflix but then decided that would be rude.

"Did you know what they did to Alan Turing?" she said.

"Huh?" Carl swallowed a mouthful.

"National hero, pretty much invented the computer and won us the war. And they chemically castrated him, cos he was gay."

"They what?"

"It's what Lovetree did to Amit Hussain. Tried to do. He gave him DES, the same drug, or a version of it. Doctors say it didn't work on Amit, it has to be administered on an ongoing basis. But still. He gave him tranquillisers too, really messed with him."

"Poor kid."

Zoe emptied her plate then spooned more curry onto it. "This is good."

"How's Ian getting on?" Carl asked.

She rolled her eyes. "That's the only reason you want me here."

"No." His gaze was intense. "It really isn't."

She returned his gaze for a while then shook it off. "He's being a bit of an arsehole, to be honest. Sent Connie home. But I guess she did deserve it."

"Connie? Surely not."

"She's taken against him. It's made him jumpy around her. It's not going to be an easy relationship to manage."

"No sign of him making any contact with organised crime?"

"He's hardly going to tell me, is he?" she replied.

"No." He sighed. "I'm not sure if we're wasting our time with him. I stuck my neck out to stop him getting a formal warning for his association with Stuart Reynolds. And now I could very well end up with egg on my face."

"Nah. Just pilau rice." She picked a grain off his cheek, then popped it in her mouth.

He wiped the spot she'd taken it from. "Still."

"Let's not talk about work, huh? I've been given leave for another two days. Apparently I need time for my injuries to heal."

"You didn't tell me you'd been injured."

"Fractured little toe. It's nothing."

He put down his plate and lifted her foot into his lap. She leaned back and let him remove her shoe.

"That's nice," she said.

"It can be even nicer," he replied. He took off her sock, bent over, and kissed her toe.

CHAPTER NINETY-FIVE

Amit sat in the back of the car, watching the rain run down the window. He felt like his lungs were still full of water, his body heavy with it. But the doctors had said he was OK to go home.

Home.

He eyed his dad in the front seat, humming to himself as he drove. His dad did that when he was tense. Amit's heart was racing, his flesh crawling. When he got home, he would be in trouble.

They reached the house and Amit's dad pulled into the driveway. Amit's sister peered between the curtains in the front bedroom. He hoped she had Kameela with her. That might lighten things. Dad wouldn't shout at him with a baby in the house.

Would he?

The car door opened. Amit's dad stood outside, holding it open for him. Amit frowned and got out.

"Thanks."

His dad nodded in acknowledgment.

Amit closed the door and followed his dad up the path. The front door opened as they reached it, his mum framed in the light from the hall. He welled up at the sight of her.

"Amit, darling." She pushed her husband out of the way and threw her arms around her son. He gave in to it, not caring that she was hurting his sore ribs. That she was almost suffocating him. He stood in her arms, limp.

She drew back and kissed him on the forehead. "I made daal. Your favourite."

He smiled. Daal had been his favourite when he was ten. But it was the thought that counted.

Mum took his hand and led him into the house. She exchanged a look with his dad as she turned to the kitchen. Amit caught it, worried.

Safiya was in the kitchen, little Kameela giggling in a high chair.

"Kameela!" Amit cried. He ran to the baby and gave her a tickle under the chin. She laughed and poked a spoon full of rice into his face.

"Good to have you back," his sister said. She rounded the table and gave him a hug. The contact warmed him, pushing away the memory of the cold water in his lungs.

Dad entered. He cleared his throat and the two siblings sprang apart. Safiya frowned at Amit. They both knew what was about to come.

"Sit down," his dad said. Amit did as he was told.

Safiya gathered Kameela up in her arms, making for the door.

"Where are you going?" their dad said.

"Just changing her nappy," she replied.

"You did that five minutes ago, according to your mother."

"Babies poo a lot."

"Don't talk like that with me."

"Sorry."

Ruhaan was in the doorway, his arm around Mum. He gave Amit a tight smile and a nod. Amit returned the nod.

Their dad reached out a hand to pull Safiya back.

"Come here. Sit. Your brother's home. He's safe." He turned his gaze on Amit. He didn't smile, but he didn't look stern either. "We're going to eat a family meal together."

CHAPTER NINETY-SIX

Zoe turned the key in the front door lock, as quietly as she could. It was one in the morning. She'd spent half an hour trying to explain to Carl why she couldn't stay over. Admittedly, it would have taken her two minutes if she hadn't been so reluctant to leave.

She closed the door behind her and removed her shoes. She padded into the living room. A table lamp was lit.

She crept across the room towards the kitchen. A dark shape shifted on the sofa.

"Nicholas?"

Nicholas sprang up, smoothing down his shirt. Zaf sat up next to him, blinking.

"Mum."

She smiled. "I'm home. Didn't want to leave you."

"I'm fine. I've got Zaf."

"And Yoda, I see." The kitten emerged from between the two young men, stretching and yawning.

"The three of you all fell asleep together, didn't you?"

Nicholas blushed. "S'pose so."

"It's cute."

"Mum." Nicholas glanced at Zaf. "Don't talk like that."

"Sorry." She walked to the kitchen and switched the coffee machine on. Coffee was probably a bad idea. But she didn't have to be in work in the morning. She heard muttering behind her in the living room, and rustling. The front door opened and closed.

"He's welcome to stay."

Nicholas sat in the middle of the settee, staring at the blank TV set. "He wanted to be with his family."

"Is he going to get home OK?"

"He called an Uber."

"I'd have given him a lift."

"All the way to Gravelly Hill?"

"Yes, all the way to Gravelly Hill. After what that boy's been through, I'd take him to the ends of the earth."

"Not a boy, mum."

"Not a boy." She sat down and put a hand on Nicholas's knee. He flinched but didn't push it away.

"I'm sorry, love," she said.

"What for?"

"I underestimated you. I treated you like a child."

"I was stupid." He shifted away, letting her hand fall to the settee. "I shouldn't have run off like that."

"Good job you found Connie, eh?"

He flinched. "So you're only OK with me buggering off because I had Connie looking after me."

"I think the two of you were looking after each other. You needed it. You both love him." She gestured towards the front door.

Nicholas blushed. "He's OK."

"He's better than OK," she said. "I saw his face when he found out you were safe."

Nicholas smiled. "I wish you hadn't."

"Not much I could do about it. Unless you wanted me to leave him in that kennel?"

"Don't." His face hardened.

"He wasn't hurt, Nicholas. Not seriously. We interrupted before that could happen."

Nicholas nodded. Silent tears flowed down his cheeks. She reached out her arm, not making contact. Waiting.

He gave her a look that reminded her of when he was small. He leaned against her, letting her stroke his hair as he cried.

READ ZOE'S PREQUEL STORY, DEADLY ORIGINS

It's 2003, and Zoe Finch is a new Detective Constable. When a body is found on her patch, she's grudgingly allowed to take a role on the case.

But when more bodies are found, and Zoe realises the case has links to her own family, the investigation becomes deeply personal.

Can Zoe find the killer before it's too late?

Find out by reading *Deadly Origins* for FREE at rachelmclean.com/origins.

Thanks,

Rachel McLean

READ THE DI ZOE FINCH SERIES

Deadly Wishes, DI Zoe Finch Book 1

Deadly Choices, DI Zoe Finch Book 2

Deadly Desires, DI Zoe Finch Book 3

Deadly Terror, DI Zoe Finch Book 4

Deadly Origins, the FREE Zoe Finch prequel

Made in the USA
Las Vegas, NV
24 November 2020